I0694272

DRAGONS AND BOXERS

An American caught in the martial arts whirlwind of the Boxer Rebellion

Kyle Fiske

Dragons and Boxers

By Kyle Fiske

ISBN-13: 978-988-8552-59-7

© 2019 Kyle Fiske

Cover art by R.P. "Kung Fu Bob" O'Brien

This book has been reset in 10pt Book Antiqua. Spellings and punctuations are left as in the original edition.

FICTION / Historical

EB124

Published by Earnshaw Books Ltd. (Hong Kong)

1

Fenchow, Shensi Province, China.
November, 1899

"WHAT WOULD you like, Mr Wei-lin?"

Old Mr Liu smiled with genuine warmth at Wayland. He didn't understand why foreigners would want to leave their homes to come and live among the Chinese, but the young man was pleasant and polite, and he was a good customer.

"Two buns, please, Mr Liu," Wayland said in fluent northern-tinged Mandarin. The steam rose off the hot pork buns into the chilly air of Fenchow, as Mr Liu passed them to Wayland. Wayland ate one down quickly and wrapped the other in a cloth and packed it in his shoulder bag.

"Getting a bit cold out, isn't it?" he added.

"It is indeed, Mr Wei-lin," Mr Liu said. "Might be some snow coming soon. How is your family doing? Do you have seasons like this in America?"

"We get the cold and the snow in Boston," Wayland said, "but it's more of a wet cold, not dry like Fenchow. We're pretty used to it here, though. We'll be fine."

After five years in China, Wayland Cooper wore the clothes, ate the food, and spoke the language fluently, but he was never going to be Chinese. There was a time when that conclusion, as obvious as it was, had not seemed particularly important to him.

That time had passed.

"Foreign devil," someone nearby muttered.

Wayland couldn't tell where it had come from, but the tone was accusatory. He turned to the people at the butcher's stall to his right but didn't see anyone looking at him. He turned and looked behind, but there were only common folks going about their business, shopping, talking, laughing.

Mr Liu smiled apologetically; he had heard it too. "Always a few bad ones in the crowd, Mr Wei-lin. Don't pay any attention."

Wayland nodded and smiled. Mr Liu was a kind man.

Wayland continued on the through the crowd, carrying his shopping of flour, salt, sugar, potatoes, and greens back to his family's compound up on the north side of the town. He remembered how strange and foreign everything seemed when he and his family first came to Fenchow, almost five years ago. He was only thirteen then. When his parents had called him into the sitting room of their home in the seaside, north-of-Boston town of Beverly on that summer afternoon and told him the family was going to China as part of the Methodist Mission, he had mixed emotions. He would be sad to leave his home and schoolmates, but on the other hand, what an adventure! How many boys his age got to travel to the other side of the world? His parents were enthusiastic, and he loved and trusted them; he was on board.

They took the train across the country to San Francisco, and from there traveled to Honolulu, and then by ship across the Pacific to Yokohama, Japan. From there, they steamed to Shanghai and then finally went inland to the city of Fenchow in the northern province of Shensi.

His mother Dorothy had gotten terribly seasick on the long ocean journey, but Wayland had no trouble being out on the waves. The ship was over four hundred feet long and about forty feet wide, and Wayland was keen to explore every part of it. He often went up on deck and peered over the rail into the fathomless depths of the Pacific. Wayland and his parents were three of the sixty cabin passengers, and in addition, there were some three hundred Chinese travelers on the ship, in the steerage class. Wayland found himself constantly staring at them. Most of the men sported queues, and the women wore their hair pulled back. Their strange clothes and mannerisms fascinated Wayland. Would they seem less odd when he saw them in their own country, a civilization and culture of their own making, or would the bigger picture then be even more strange to him? How would he be perceived? Would he stand out, and be a curiosity to the Chinese just as they were for him now?

Now, five years later, he still didn't have clear answers to those questions. He walked on through the busy, dusty streets. Shensi Province was dry and cold in the winter, and prone to dust storms, but this day was relatively mild. He saw a crowd gathered up ahead, and he could hear the clanging of cymbals and the clamor of active voices. It was probably some manner of street performers; Wayland always enjoyed the displays of jugglers, acrobats, fortune tellers and martial artists that regularly set up shop in town. He walked up to the circle of people, already three rows deep, and saw the performers. One slim, muscular, bare-chested man had two spear points pressed against his throat. The butt-ends of the spears were firmly planted in the ground, and the man slowly pushed forward. Another man, a bit older and not quite as slim, was announcing to the crowd that his colleague had incredible martial skills unmatched in the region. The spear shafts gradually bent as the muscular man slowly stepped forward, straining. Gasps and sighs came from the crowd, and the tension was palpable.

"Who will win, the hero or the spears?" the older man said

with a theatrical flourish. Leaning forward, with his body tensed and the spear shafts bending to their limits, the younger man paused for what seemed like an eternity. The crowd collectively held their breath, and then with a final effort the younger man stepped forward convincingly, and the two spear shafts snapped in the middle. The spear points rebounded harmlessly from the man's throat and fell to the ground as the shaft ends flew into the air and onto the dusty street. The man stepped back and punched his right fist into his left palm, saluting the crowd as he bowed slightly.

"The hero has won!" the older man shouted, and the crowd erupted in cheers and applause. The older man picked up one of the spear points and brought it round to the onlookers, inviting them to test its sharpness. One young woman smiled and touched the point with her index finger, and then snapped her hand back and put her finger in her mouth, wincing in pain. The crowd applauded again, and Wayland smiled and clapped enthusiastically along with them.

The older man passed a bowl around, and the onlookers eagerly dropped coins in and continued their clapping.

"Thank you, thank you all! We are poor travelers from Shantung, and we appreciate the kindness and generosity of you people of Fenchow. But please remember, what you saw here is not some mere trick. These are the martial arts of our group, the Righteous and Harmonious Fists. We can teach these techniques to anyone who wants to learn them. You will learn to make your body impervious not only to spear and sword but also to the firearms of the foreign devils! Are you tired of being second-class citizens in your own country? China is being torn apart by the foreign powers! We Chinese, who are the heirs of a grand civilization, who were scholars and philosophers when men in the West were primitive barbarians, are now seen as easy prey by the foreigners. They preach a new religion and tell us that our ways are worthless. They come with their new inventions and tell us that the ways of our ancestors are inferior. Our country is now seen as a meal to be divided up and devoured. We don't have to accept this! Join us, and we can restore the greatness of China and throw out the foreign devils!"

The crowd cheered again, and Wayland became a bit uneasy. His hair was black, and he wore Chinese clothes and a cap, but he knew that anyone who looked twice at him could see that he was a foreigner.

"I've had just about enough of the foreign devils," someone behind Wayland said.

"They're right, you know," another man said. "Those foreign Christians don't have any respect for our ways. They came from the other side of the world just to tell us we're ignorant, and in the meantime, they rob us blind."

"Just a bunch of stupid tricks," came another, older voice. "You can't trust people from Shantung anyways. I saw that spear-breaking routine fifteen years ago, and it's all a sham to make money. They can break a phony spear, but they can't last five seconds in a real fight. Stand up to foreigners' bullets? I don't believe it. They'll just get a lot of people killed."

"Still, they're right that China should be for the Chinese," Wayland heard from a woman to his right. "I don't know who could disagree with that. And this drought. We haven't had any rain for weeks. What are we going to eat if the crops fail? I've heard that the foreigners have been driving away the rain clouds."

The hair on the back of Wayland's neck stood up. The drought conditions were on everyone's mind, and people were looking for someone to blame. The crowd wasn't exactly hostile, but just in his own limited experience, he knew that could change in the blink of an eye. Wayland decided that this might be a good time to get back home.

He made his way out of the crowd and through some mostly empty back streets, and after another fifteen minutes was at the main gate of his family's compound. It was a little after four in the afternoon, and it was starting to get dark.

He knocked on the wooden gate. "It's me, Wayland," he called.

The gate swung open, and Wayland was met with the smiling face of the gatekeeper, Chin Fai. He was an older man, in his late fifties. Chin Fai was missing one of his front teeth, and that gave him a slight lisp when speaking. He was sharp, though, and had a good sense of humor. Wayland liked him.

"Hello, Mr Wei-lin," Chin Fai said. He smiled as he opened the gate and let Wayland through.

Wayland raised his eyebrows as he remembered what he had. He set down his bags of groceries and rifled through his shoulder bag. He found what he was looking for and pulled out the cloth-wrapped pork bun. "I know you get hungry after your long, difficult day at the gate, Fai. I didn't think you could wait until dinner time."

"Ah, Mr Wei-lin, you're always so good to me," Chin Fai said, taking the bun. "Mmm!" he added, as he brought the still slightly warm bun to his nose. "If only my wife could cook like this." He took a big bite and shook his head in pleasure.

Wayland picked his bags back up and walked through the courtyard as Chin Fai shut and bolted the gate behind him.

"Hi Mom, I'm back," Wayland said, as he came through the door from the courtyard to the inner hall of the compound. For the former Chinese residents of the house, the inner hall was where the family greeted guests or held ceremonies, but for the Wayland and his parents, this was the main work space of their mission and school.

"Did you get everything?" Dorothy Cooper asked.

Wayland's mother Dorothy was a gentle yet strong-minded woman, and she looked ten years younger than her actual forty-five. She had her blonde hair tied up in a bun, and she had that slightly flustered expression on her face of someone who was trying to juggle a few too many things.

"You got the flour and salt?" she asked.

"I got the flour and salt," Wayland said.

"Because I need those if I'm going to make a peach pie this weekend."

"I got them, Mom," Wayland said, with a hint of annoyance.

Dorothy paused for a moment, and then her furrowed brow changed to a smile. "I'm sorry, Wayland. How was your trip into town?"

"It was okay," Wayland said. "I didn't have any problems." He made an effort to sound casual.

Dorothy walked forward and put her hand on her son's shoulder. She looked him in the eye. "Was there trouble?"

Wayland smiled. He could never fool his mother. "Not really trouble. Just some street performers, talking about the foreigners and, well, you know."

"Any worse than we've heard before?" Dorothy asked. There had always been some measure of anti-foreigner sentiment since they arrived, but it had generally been negligible. A few bad apples, and all that.

Wayland shrugged. "I don't know." It *was* worse, but there was no need to let his mother know that.

"Well, it's in God's hands," Dorothy said. "We never know what tomorrow will bring. Now put those groceries away, and get washed up. Dinner will be ready soon."

$$2$$

THE NEXT MORNING, the Coopers—Wayland, his mother Dorothy and his father James—were all up shortly after six. It was a Tuesday, and they were in their normal mid-week routine. Wayland's room was one of the side rooms at the back of the compound next to the main bedroom of his parents. After washing and taking care of their toiletries, Wayland and his parents met in the main hall where they usually took their meals together. The cook, Tang Hu, wouldn't arrive for another hour to make breakfast for the students, and for the family, Dorothy usually just sliced some of the steamed millet loaves and then fried the slices. She served these with bread and butter, coffee and whatever fruits were available—grapes and peaches were common in Shensi in season and not too expensive. James always said grace before the meal, and after their morning prayers, the three would talk about their plans for the coming day.

The mission had eleven Chinese boys and three girls as permanent students. This wasn't as many as they had hoped to have after being in China for several years, but it was something. Patience was a virtue, James always said. The students ranged in age from ten to sixteen years old, and they were all from local families in Fenchow. They lived, ate and slept at the mission, and they paid about thirty-five cents a month in tuition. This didn't cover their actual costs, but the Methodist Society of Boston that sponsored the Coopers and the mission made up the difference.

Also staying at the mission were two adult Chinese women who had converted to Christianity, and Gong Lihao, the Chinese teacher for the students. The gatekeeper Chin Fai, the cook Tang Hu, and the other two servants, Li Bojing and Yu Enlai, worked at the mission during the day, but they went back to their own homes at night. All in all, it was quite a happy, if strangely mixed, conglomeration of people.

"Brother Winslow in Taigu has some twenty-five Chinese students, I hear," James said. He took a bite of his fried millet. "That should give us reason for optimism. He came and started his school just a bit before we did."

"I think we've got a nice beginning here," Dorothy said. "Although it certainly does seem to be slow work."

"We make friends, we distribute our leaflets and pamphlets, we engage in conversation with the people. That's really all we can do. We can't force our beliefs on them. We can only pray that God will open their hearts to our message." James smiled, but it was a smile tinged with frustration. "Why it should be so difficult to spread such good news will always be a mystery to us, I'm sure."

"From what I can see, when I go into town and stuff, we do have a pretty good reputation," Wayland said. "They know they can trust us with the school, and buying and selling, and things like that."

"That counts for something," Dorothy said.

James nodded. "Small gains, but important ones. We have to always remember that we represent the body of Christ here, and we have to be twice as good to be given any credit. Remember that scandal in Shantung, where the two Catholic missionaries took part in a shady land deal, and the local farmers were all thrown off their own land? That's just the type of thing we need to avoid at all costs. Who knows how many Chinese souls rejected the gospel when they heard of that?"

"Yes, but surely that situation was an exception. Every group has its bad apples," Dorothy said.

"*We* know that," James said. "But the average Chinese here might not see it that way. One story like that gets magnified and passed around and around. Man gravitates towards sin, and towards rejection of God. Our Lord didn't make any distinction between the Chinese and the Western man; in our souls, we're all the same. Give any man a reason to turn away from God, and he will grab at it. We have little margin for error here."

"And that's what the Boxers prey on," Dorothy said.

The Boxers. The group's origins were somewhat hazy, but the Boxers were a quasi-religious and revolutionary political movement, drawn mainly from the peasant class. They gave themselves various names, "Society of Righteous and Harmonious Fists," "Militia United in Righteousness," or Yihetuan, but foreigners generally referred to them as Boxers due to their practice and utilization of martial arts. The Boxers also believed in and employed magical spells and incantations native to the traditional folk religions. The Boxers were on the rise in response to the growing influence of foreigners in China, and they were stridently anti-foreigner and anti-Christian. They had no qualms about using violence to achieve their aims, and their numbers were growing rapidly. They had first appeared further east, in Shantung, but the movement was spreading.

"Indeed," James said. "The Boxers themselves may be superstitious, ignorant brutes, but they are not without appeal. They speak of patriotism and love of one's own people. As far as that goes, those are good, healthy things, and one is to pity the people without those virtues. But they've taken it too far, they've lost the proper balance. This wild, frenzied xenophobia. That's never a good thing, either in China or anywhere on God's earth."

A knock came at the door.

"Come in," James said.

The door opened, and it was Lihao. "Mr Cooper, I am sorry to interrupt you, but a man is here to see you."

"What man?" James said.

"A Mr Sun," Lihao said. "He said it is a medical concern."

James nodded and quickly stood up. Sun had come in last week with a bad cut on his leg, and James had put some tincture of iodine on it and bandaged it up.

"I'll see him in a moment, Lihao. Thank you," James said. Lihao smiled and shut the door.

Most of the work of the mission was in the realm of proselytizing and general education, but they also occasionally functioned as a makeshift clinic. James was not really a physician, but he was a bright man, and he had a general understanding of how to administer basic first aid; the mission had also trained him on the use of common Western medicines and drugs. The body was the gateway to the soul, the mission always believed. He remembered a disagreement he had had with another church member back in Boston. The man had argued that there was something slightly immoral about missionaries using material inducements to "lure in" the natives and then springing the doctrines of Christianity on them. James had countered by arguing that if it were immoral to do that, then Christians would have to abandon the idea of feeding the hungry or providing clothes and shelter for the poor. God had created man as a physical being, with physical needs and wants. And as God chose to do this, one mustn't disparage the physical nature of humankind. The other man wasn't entirely convinced, but he couldn't refute James' position.

During his time in China, James had also gained an appreciation for traditional Chinese medicine: it had its place and in certain circumstances could indeed be beneficial. But still, with its emphasis on balancing cold and heat, and regulating the body's energy, James had concluded that it was more effective at preventing illness and maintaining health. When it came to treating an injury or full-blown sickness, the Western medical approach was much more effective. And from the experience James had gained at the mission, it almost seemed that because the Chinese had such little exposure to Western drugs, the treatments seemed to be even more effective on the Chinese than they were on foreigners.

The locals who came in for treatment and medicines had a broad range of ailments; skin diseases, sores and wounds, dysentery, measles, flu, glaucoma, and just about any other sickness or physical problem imaginable. If it were something basic, then James would treat it with the medicine he had or the first aid that he knew. Morphine for pain, iodine and alcohol for wounds, laudanum for diarrhea, quinine for catarrh. If it were something more serious, he would send them to Dr. Westwood, the British missionary up in Taiyuan. He was a trained surgeon and could perform operations and also dispense a much wider variety of medicines. Due to their effectiveness, Western medicines were immediately popular among the Chinese; if only the gospel were so readily accepted, James often lamented.

James stepped out into the courtyard, and he saw Mr Sun. Mr Sun was tall, heavy and sloop-shouldered, and he was one of those fellows with an almost permanent half-smile, as if he was just ready to break out into hearty laughter at any moment. It was hard not to like him.

"Mr Sun," James said, with genuine affection. "What can I do for you today?"

"Well," Mr Sun said, "You did tell me to come back in a week to see how my leg was doing, and so I'm back."

"Yes, that's right," James said. He pointed over to the small table and bench. "Have a seat right there, and I'll go get my medical bag."

Mr Sun sat down on the bench, and James returned with his leather bag. He pulled a small footstool over and propped Mr Sun's leg up. He then rolled Mr Sun's pant leg up and gently undid the wrapping he had put on last week.

"How is it feeling?" James asked.

"Very good," Mr Sun said.

James was a little worried. When Mr Sun came to him last week, he thought the wound might be starting to get infected. He cleaned it out as best he could, and put the iodine tincture on it and hoped for the best. Now, it was time to see. He slowly lifted the bandage off the wound and was relieved to see that it looked excellent, with no sign of infection.

"Well?" Mr Sun asked. He still had the half smile on his face.

James raised his eyebrows and nodded. "I would say it seems to be healing nicely. Stay here for a moment, and I'll put a fresh bandage on the wound. It should be all healed up in a week or so."

"Thank you, Mr Ku-pr," Mr Sun said, with his perpetual smile. "I knew I made a good decision by coming to you."

James re-bandaged the wound and sent Mr Sun on his way. As the big man walked down to the main gate without any limp, James watched him and felt a sense of satisfaction. This wasn't some triumphant religious conversion; he hadn't offered any theologically profound words of advice, and indeed he probably hadn't changed the metaphysical worldview of Mr Sun even a bit. Still, he was able to help a good man in a small way, and Mr Sun had appreciated it. He had made someone's life a little bit better. Maybe that wasn't everything that he and his family had come halfway across the world to do, but it was something.

3

ON THE LAST THURSDAY of the month, Dorothy told the cook Tang Hu that he could have the day off, as she wanted free reign in the kitchen. Food was getting more scarce and expensive, but Wayland was able to fill some of her shopping list, and she spent the morning preparing roast duck, yams, greens and some biscuits and butter for their Thanksgiving celebration. Given the ongoing drought throughout the province, this year they had cut back the scope of their usual American-style festivities. Still, there was enough for all to enjoy and the Coopers, as well as their Chinese students and helpers, ate their fill. James had a bit of trouble explaining to some of the more recent students that American Thanksgiving wasn't exactly a traditional Christian holiday, but when he mentioned that it was similar to the Chinese Mid-Autumn Festival, they got the general idea.

For dessert, Dorothy brought out several squash pies that were the best approximation of pumpkin pies that she could make given the local produce. All agreed that they were delicious, and all thanked Dorothy for the wonderful meal.

The next morning was overcast. Wayland was up early, and it was clear he had plans of some sort.

"Did you finish up your Latin homework?" James Cooper asked his son.

"I finished that, Dad. Even did the essay due next week," Wayland said, smiling. He had one shoe on and was hopping on that foot as he slipped the black canvas shoe over the other.

"What's the rush?' James asked.

"Lihao is going to give a lesson in Chinese boxing in a minute. He asked me if I wanted to learn, and I said I do," Wayland said. He felt he was beyond the age of asking his father's permission, but he was genuinely curious about his father's opinion on the matter.

James Cooper furrowed his brow. "Have you thought about what you're going to do next year?"

Wayland grimaced. He didn't want to discuss that right now.

"You're at an important time in your life, son. Your choices are going to impact the rest of your days. Now, you've talked about going to college in Boston, or maybe England or Europe to study history and become a teacher. The home schooling I've given you here should have you more than prepared. You're a fine student. Are you still thinking of that? You're going to need to apply soon if that's your plan."

"I don't know," Wayland said with some exasperation.

"Or do you want to stay here in China? We can do great things here; I have no doubt of that. There's a place for you with us if that's what you want. I'm not kicking you out."

"I know, Dad," Wayland said. "I do like it here, but... I don't know if I'm cut out to be a missionary. Don't get me wrong, I believe in what we're doing, but for you and Mom it was a... a calling. I don't know if that's how I feel. I'm not sure I have the passion for it that you do. Maybe I'd be better off doing something else."

James put his hand on his son's shoulder. "And that's to be expected. God has different plans for each of us, and the last thing I want to do is pressure you into something that you don't really want. But I am going to pressure you to do *something*. You're not a child anymore, and your mother and I can't tell you what you have to do. But you have to make a decision. Time is precious, and I know at your age it seems like it will stretch out forever, but it doesn't. Whatever path you may choose, you have to get *on* that path."

Wayland nodded. "I know. I'll make a decision soon."

James knew his son understood his position, and there was nothing more to be said on that subject. "So, Lihao likes boxing? I didn't know that." He smiled and shook his head. "He's a man of many layers."

"You don't mind if I study with him?" Wayland asked.

"We're in this country, and we have to learn as much as we can about the people here and their ways if we're going to bring them the true Gospel. Lihao is a good man and understands the Christian message, and if he likes boxing, there's nothing wrong with that," James said. "He's our brother. I've heard several Chinese sayings since we've been here, and one of my favorites is, 'If I meet three men in a day, surely one of them can be my teacher.' Why don't you see what he can teach you."

"You don't worry that he's teaching some Taoism or Buddhism with the practice?" Wayland asked. He was pushing his father a bit, but it was a question that genuinely interested him.

"That will be something for you to judge," James said, smiling. "Never forget that Christianity is a broad-minded religion. The heathen religions may have an imperfect understanding of God, or gods, as it were, but it doesn't mean that we must reject everything they teach. Where their beliefs overlap with the truth of Christ—and in many places they do—we must honor them accordingly. But as Christians we must believe that where pagan teachings contradict Christianity, it is the Christian doctrine which we must affirm. And that's just a matter of logic and reason. Two contradictory viewpoints might both be false, but both cannot be true. And truth is a worthy pursuit. Always remember this. The modern world seems to understand this less and less with each passing year."

"So, it's okay?" Wayland asked.

James rubbed his beard and smiled at his son. "I don't believe Lihao will lead you astray theologically. But whether he's any kind of boxer or not, I have no idea."

Gong Lihao was a Christian convert from Taiyuan, and was now a traveling preacher, bringing the word of Christ throughout Northern China. He had been staying in Fenchow for several months and was one of the first native contacts that the Coopers had made. Since then, he had spent a great deal of time helping the Coopers with their fledgling school. James was initially skeptical of Lihao; there were more than a few "Rice Christians" in China, ones who professed devotion and conversion to Christianity but were, in fact, more interested in the material benefits from having an association with the relatively wealthy and increasingly influential foreign missionaries. Upon meeting Lihao, however, James was quickly convinced of the man's intelligence and sincerity. It wasn't anything he did, and it wasn't anything he said (although he was later to find that Lihao was quite well-versed in orthodox Christian theology). But James had that immediate, inexplicable and conclusive feeling that Gong Lihao was a man that could be trusted.

***

Wayland came out into the courtyard. It was a gray, cloudy day, and it looked and felt like it might snow at any time. The temperature was right around freezing, but there wasn't much wind. Gong Lihao was standing up in front, facing the others who were there to learn. There was the cook, the two older women, one of the young girls and three young boys who were students at the mission.

"And welcome, Wayland," Lihao said. The others turned and

smiled and nodded at him. Wayland was usually the occasional English teacher of the younger ones, and he suspected that they were amused to see him as the student.

"I think this is all of us today, so we can get started," Lihao said. "To begin with, I want to explain what we're going to be learning. It's called *T'ai Chi Fist*. It has its ancient roots as a martial art, but today some in China see it as a more scientific form of exercise, a type of moving meditation. It will help you relax, become more peaceful, and keep your body healthy."

"Excuse me, Lihao," Wayland said. "But it is a form of boxing, isn't it?"

Lihao nodded. "Yes, it is a style of Chinese boxing, and it can be used to fight. But we don't want to focus on that. The self-defense side will come to one naturally from correct practice."

Wayland nodded politely, although he wasn't quite sure he believed that. He remembered from his youthful lessons in Western boxing back in Boston that even when one explicitly trained to fight, the skill didn't come very easily. Still, Wayland thought, best to keep an open mind.

"The history of *T'ai Chi Fist* stretches back to antiquity," Lihao said. "It began centuries ago at Wudang mountain, in Hubei, which is just to the south of us. The Taoist hermit, Zhang Sanfeng, created the art after studying other martial styles and blending them with breathing and meditation techniques. He was a peaceful man who rejected fame and wealth, and he traveled the land in search of truth. His art was created to preserve peace and to harmonize man with the world, and not to inflict violence. His teachings have been passed down among the Chinese for centuries, and I will do my best to pass them down to you."

The other students spread out a bit, giving themselves a bit of space, and Wayland did the same. He wondered if there was some Chinese etiquette involved in classes like this, whether to line up by age or sex or ability, but he couldn't make out any pattern. He decided that he'd just stand in the back row.

Wayland raised his hand, and Lihao nodded. "What does *T'ai Chi Fist* mean, actually?" Wayland asked.

"Good question," Lihao said. "In English, it would translate to 'Grand Ultimate Fist.'"

"So, it's the best, the ultimate Chinese fighting style?" Wayland asked.

Lihao shook his head, smiling. "No, that's not what the name means. It has to do with Taoist philosophy, with that view of the world. First, you need to understand the word *Wu Chi*. That means 'infinite, with no extremities.' Like the universe before creation."

"Like just stretching out for countless miles in every direction? Like the infinity of space?" Wayland asked.

"Not exactly," Lihao said. "To the Chinese, it means more like being on a boat in the middle of a river, in a heavy fog. The fog is so dense that you can't see where the water ends and the shore begins. That is *Wu Chi*. And from *Wu Chi* comes yin and yang, the separation into polarities. The interaction of day and night, warm and cold, aggressive and passive, male and female, where you can clearly see where the water ends and the land begins."

"So *T'ai Chi* is yin and yang?" Wayland asked.

"No," Lihao said. "*T'ai Chi* is the *mother* of yin and yang. It's what causes *Wu Chi* to discriminate into yin and yang. If we're talking about the universe, then we as Christians can say that God is *T'ai Chi*. The universe was void and formless, and God created everything from that void. But if we're talking about this martial art, then our mind is the *T'ai Chi*. When we practice the martial art, the beginning posture is called *Wu Chi*, and when we begin to move, our mind directs us to form postures and execute techniques, from *Wu Chi* to yin and yang."

Wayland nodded. It seemed a bit complex. His boxing instructor in Boston never talked much about any philosophy beyond a stiff left jab and keeping your guard up.

"First of all, let's loosen up and relax," Lihao said. His shoulders dropped, and his arms were loose, and he bounced up and down, his arms flapping at his side. Wayland and the others followed suit.

"Now let's stretch," Lihao said. He lifted his arms as high above his head as he could, held them there for a second, and then slowly turned first to one side, and then the other. The students all did the same.

"For those who have never studied martial arts," Lihao said, and he made eye contact with Wayland, "Chinese styles usually have one or more 'forms'. These are patterns of movements, really just a number of techniques linked together. These forms serve several purposes. Firstly, they teach you how to move in accord with the style, and also they are a catalog of the basic techniques and movements. Learning them in a sequence helps you to remember them all. And finally, doing them all in a sequence is a good bit of exercise, and it strengthens and loosens up the body."

Wayland nodded. He felt energized from stretching out, and he was ready for a good workout.

"One of the unusual things about the *T'ai Chi* style of boxing, at least the Yang style, which is what we're learning," Lihao said, "is that the sequence is performed very slowly at first, and very softly. Indeed, that's the characteristic of the style. Power comes through softness and yielding. You might even say this art is in accord with the example of our Lord Jesus. The soft overcomes the strong, and yielding is more powerful than attacking."

Wayland was intrigued by this, but also a little disappointed. Theology had its place, but he wanted to learn boxing! How could you fight by moving slowly and softly?

Lihao began in the opening stance, with his feet at shoulder width, and his arms at his side. He then lifted both arms to chest height, palms facing each other, and brought both hands down. Wayland and the other students mirrored his movements.

"This next technique is called 'grasp the sparrow's tail,'" Lihao said. He turned his body slowly to the right and brought his right hand up and out. He repeated the technique several times as everyone followed along. "Now you do this, and I'll examine you."

The students all practiced moving from the first stance to 'grasp sparrow's tail,' and Lihao walked around, correcting them.

"Too tense," Lihao said. He put his hand on Wayland's shoulder. "Up here, your shoulders and elbows, too tense. Try to relax all your muscles. Let your *chi* flow."

Wayland was somewhat familiar with the Chinese concept of *chi*. It was supposed to be 'breath' or 'energy,' but he didn't understand how it was supposed to apply to martial arts. And relaxing all his muscles? If he did that, he'd just fall over, wouldn't he? The whole thing didn't seem to make much sense. He did as he was told, however. He went through the motions of 'grasp sparrow's tail,' and he relaxed his shoulder and arm, and did everything slowly.

"Good," Lihao said. "*T'ai Chi Fist* is sometimes called 'moving meditation,' and you should try to think of it like that. Keep your muscles relaxed, and move slowly. Let yourself feel at peace, and your body's energy will flow."

"But this is a kind of *boxing*, isn't it?" Wayland asked again.

"Of course," Lihao said.

"Well then, how do I use this 'grasp sparrow's tail' to fight?" Wayland asked. "Is it a block, or a strike, or what?"

"Go ahead and punch at my head with your right hand," Lihao said.

Wayland did so. He didn't punch as hard or as fast as he could, but he did it at a reasonably normal fighting speed. Lihao wasn't expecting Wayland to strike so quickly; he tried to deflect the punch, but Wayland's strike ended up tapping him on the chin.

"Sorry," Wayland said. He smiled politely.

Lihao was slightly flustered but maintained the tone of the teacher correcting the student. "Remember, in *T'ai Chi Fist*, we do things slowly. Now punch me again."

Wayland did so, punching in slow motion. Lihao was able to use the 'grasp sparrow's tail' to deflect Wayland's punch to the side, and then Lihao came back with a slow palm strike to Wayland's chin.

"Do you see?" Lihao said. "That's an example of how to use the technique. But that's only one application. Always remember that in *T'ai Chi Fist*, numerous applications can be derived from each technique. It just depends on the situation. You have to always be on your guard, and open to what the circumstance dictates. Your opponent's moves will lead you to the best counter. After much practice, these moves will become instinctive, and you will learn to follow your opponent's energy, and use it against him."

Lihao's words were logical, and Wayland nodded politely. He couldn't shake one thought, however: he could have easily punched Lihao. Lihao was thin and of average height. Wayland had learned from his boxing days in Boston not to judge a fighter by his size: his Irish boxing coach was only about 5'2", but he could hit with a wallop. He was quick, too. Wayland didn't see any of these traits in Lihao.

"And this is going to work in a real fight?" Wayland asked.

He was incredulous, but he made a conscious effort to keep his tone sincere and respectful.

"Yang Lu Chan was known as Yang the Invincible," Lihao said. "He was the founder of the Yang school of *T'ai Chi Fist*, and he was famous for his fighting ability. He traveled around the country accepting challenges, he was never defeated. He went on to be a military instructor in Beijing."

The others continued diligently repeating the 'grasp sparrow's tail' technique, and Wayland followed suit.

"Relax, relax," Lihao said, correcting Wayland again. "Soft and yielding. That is the essence of *T'ai Chi Fist*. There are many famous stories about Yang Lu Chan and his abilities. Once, he was practicing in his courtyard, and he was moving so slowly, a sparrow mistook him for a tree and landed on his palm. He could sense the weight of the sparrow, and whenever the sparrow tried to push off with its legs to fly away, Lu Chan would yield with his palm just enough to prevent the sparrow from taking off. The sparrow kept trying to fly away, but it was unable to, as Lu Chan kept yielding each time it attempted to push off."

Wayland thought about this for a moment, and it didn't seem too likely to him. For a moment he thought it better to go along with Lihao, but then his analytical mind got the better of him.

"Hold on a second," Wayland said. He stopped his practice and turned to face Lihao. "That's just a story to get you thinking about the deeper principles, right? I mean, it's not supposed to be taken literally, is it?"

"That's a true story," Lihao said. "My teacher told that to me directly, and he was a man of great integrity."

"Well," Wayland said. "It makes sense if you think of it as a story to get you thinking about yielding, that you have to be so sensitive that you could even feel a sparrow trying to fly away from your hand. But it doesn't mean it really happened."

"It did happen, absolutely," Lihao said.

"But why would the sparrow even land on his hand in the first place?" Wayland asked. "Have you ever had a wild bird land on you for no reason? It doesn't make any sense."

"You foreigners, you don't understand the Chinese ways," the older woman said. "We appreciate the truth of Lord Jesus, but we have our own culture too. China has many great accomplishments and many great men."

Wayland was getting a bit exasperated. He always tried to be respectful to Chinese customs and traditions, but he had also been taught that truth was paramount, even if it hurts people's feelings. "It doesn't matter if you're Chinese or Western or African or from the moon. The story just doesn't hold water."

Lihao smiled and put his hand on Wayland's shoulder. "I appreciate your train of thought, but to get back to the main subject, I think you're looking at *T'ai Chi Fist* the wrong way. It's not about competition, and it's not about always defeating your opponent. That's what Western boxing teaches you, but this art is very different. When you have fully mastered *T'ai Chi Fist*, you will understand that there is no opponent. There is no enemy. You will learn to be at peace and to control your emotions."

Wayland nodded. Lihao was an admirable man, and in many respects the equal of his father. And *T'ai Chi Fist* was certainly a fascinating martial art, and he was intrigued by its theories and the few techniques he had learned. After dinner, Wayland went back to his room and practiced some of the moves that Lihao had taught. They certainly felt much different from the Western boxing he had learned, but there was also a strange, appealing quality to them. Wayland thought he would continue with the lessons, but he still didn't have a lot of faith that Lihao was genuinely able to defend himself. It was something to pass the time, though.

The time. It was always moving. *You've got to make a decision, you've got to choose a path.* His father's words still echoed in his mind, and they had never been far from his thoughts over the last few months. He knew that most young men his age were moving on in their lives, starting a job, getting married, going to university, joining the military. There were a million things he could do. But choosing one thing necessarily meant rejecting others, and that was the tough part. What was right for him might disappoint his family, and what was wrong for him would surely disappoint himself. And how could he even know what was right for him?

4

CHRISTMAS WAS USUALLY Wayland's favorite holiday and season, and he had experienced several wonderful Christmases since they had come to China. But things were different this year. Tension was increasing between the missionaries and the locals, and all were on edge, given the relentless drought.

A week before Christmas, after the students had finished the last class of the day, Wayland was helping his father tidy up the classroom.

"So, what do you want for Christmas, Dad?"

In most years, this was a prelude to some warm banter which always led to James asking Wayland what *he* wanted; but this wasn't most years.

James sighed heavily, and when Wayland looked into his face, he was surprised to see that his father was on the verge of tears. He had never before seen his father anything less than stoic.

"I'm sorry, Wayland. I try to put on a strong face, but I... I don't know. There's no rain, no snow, and the winter wheat is just about dried up. How can we even enjoy a meal when the people around us are so hungry? And what can I do? Just tell them to accept our faith, and everything will be fine? That's why we have the clinic here — because the body is the gateway to the soul. And the body is starving... "

"Things will work out, Dad," Wayland said. He tried to think of something else to say, but he wasn't used to being in the position of comforting and reassuring his father. "There's a verse about that, isn't there, about not worrying?"

James put his hand on his son's shoulder and forced a weak smile. "Yes. Matthew 6:27. 'Can any of you by worrying add a single hour to his life?' It's true. We must trust the Lord's will, and accept whatever his plans for us may be. And it will still be Christmas, the day to celebrate the birth of our savior. We'll carry on as always. It's just... "

"What is it, Dad?" Wayland asked.

"Please don't let your mother know that I'm worried. I want to shield her as much as possible from our dangers. I'd like to shield you too, son, but... you're a man now. I wish with all my heart that I didn't have to put such a burden on you, but I can't do this all alone. I need your help if we're going to get through this. I don't say it often enough, but I love you so much. I'm so proud of the man that you've become."

Tears came to Wayland's eyes, and he and his father embraced.

On Christmas morning, Wayland, Dorothy, and James had a private time alone, and Wayland distributed the presents from under the small pine Christmas tree they had set up and decorated in the living room. Dorothy was particularly pleased with the heavy woolen shawl that James had ordered from a shop in San Francisco, and Wayland was surprised and delighted at the fine leather half-boots that his grandparents had sent him from Boston; they fit perfectly. James was more than happy with the small package of fine pipe tobacco and Swiss chocolate that Dorothy and Wayland had somehow managed to acquire and keep secret from him.

After lunch, James gave a brief sermon to their Chinese students about the meaning and joy of the birth of Christ, and following a final prayer, they all enjoyed a celebratory lunch of roast pork, yams, and greens. Dorothy had made up fourteen cotton bags, one for each student, and every bag was filled with candy, nuts, and popcorn and tied with a bright red ribbon. Those were handed out to the delight of all. And that was how Christmas of 1899 passed at the Cooper mission and school in Fenchow, China.

***

Although the tensions remained high and the drought continued, January and February passed without serious incident.

On the 15th of March, a little after ten in the morning, light snow was falling and there was a knock at the door of the main compound. One of the brightest young students, Deming, hurried to the door and opened it, and he was met with the strange, bearded visage of an unknown foreigner.

"Good day. I am Per-Johan Norling. The Coopers are expecting me," the man said in perfect, unaccented Mandarin.

Deming nodded and bowed, and opened the door, and then he hurried into the kitchen. "Mrs. Cooper, there is a man here to see you," he said. "A Western man."

"Thank you, Deming. Please show him in," Dorothy said. She poked her head into the washroom to quickly look in the mirror, and she adjusted the straight pin holding her blonde hair in a bun. She quickly fixed her collar and pursed her lips, and then she stepped back into the dining room. The place settings of her best silverware and plates were laid out neatly on the table, which was draped with an elegant white linen tablecloth. The décor was a little incongruous with the old, uneven wooden table underneath, but it was the best she could do under the circumstances.

Although Per had been living the austere life of a missionary in the city of Turfan far in the west for several years now, Dorothy always remembered the last (and only) time they had met. A little over five years ago, as the Coopers first made their journey from Boston to Fenchow, they stayed an evening with the China Methodist Society in San Francisco. The Society treated them to a wonderful farewell dinner at the Cliff House restaurant. Dorothy and her husband were not a family of considerable financial means, but the evening had been paid for by a wealthy benefactor of the Society, and it was the first and only time she had ever dined in such an expensive restaurant. They were joined by several members of a Swedish missionary society who, the following month, would be traveling mostly the same route as the Coopers to their own missionary assignments in China. One of them was Per-Johan Norling. James had taken to him quickly, and for Dorothy's part, she thought that he was perhaps the most handsome man she had ever seen. Tall and athletic, blonde and with a close-trimmed, pointed beard, he was dressed impeccably in a gray coat with covered buttons and matching waistcoat, dark trousers, short turnover shirt collar, and a gray ascot tie. He had bowed politely when he was introduced, and from his curious half-smile, Dorothy immediately inferred a warm yet mischievous persona just under the surface of the man's formal attire and proper manners.

Over dinner, both Dorothy and her husband were fascinated by Per-Johan's cosmopolitan adventures and travel stories. He had grown up in Stockholm and Copenhagen, and Berlin, Paris and London were all quite familiar to him, either from his studies as a young man or in his financial business ventures as an adult. Despite his worldliness, his stories were never boastful or self-aggrandizing. Indeed, he seemed to have a sharp sense of self-deprecating humor and a nuanced perspective of the human condition. He clearly had both keen intelligence and a proper understanding of his own spirituality. His account of his motivations for leaving the higher social circles of Europe for the life of a missionary in China emanated quite naturally from his personality and view on life, Dorothy thought. The fact that her husband also gravitated towards this man alleviated some of the subtle guilt she was feeling for her undeniable romantic attraction to the handsome Swede; he was clearly a man of many admirable qualities.

As the evening wore down, dessert and coffee finished the meal, with brandy and cigars for the men. Goodbyes and heartfelt farewells were finally made as the evening grew late, and the Coopers and Per promised to do their best to keep in touch and to visit each other at some point during their stays in China. Dorothy had to laugh when Per-Johan even called Wayland "young sir," and bowed graciously to him when they all had to leave. Per-Johan Norling was not the type of character the Coopers met regularly in their quiet small town north of Boston.

Per-Johan was, it turned out, assigned to a Swedish missionary outpost in Turfan and reached his destination some six weeks after the Coopers had settled in Fenchow. The Coopers had exchanged several letters with Per-Johan during the first year of his stay, and although he said he was having some difficulty adjusting to the jarringly strange culture and setting, his faith remained unshaken, and he was enthusiastic about the potential of his work. After the first year, though, the letters stopped. Dorothy had written several more times but to no response. As the Coopers found it difficult enough to keep up with their own duties and daily affairs, James assured his wife that Per-Johan was probably just too busy to respond and that she shouldn't worry. Dorothy did worry, though, and she finally wrote to the Swedish Missionary Society inquiring about Per-Johan. She received a reply some weeks later, in a somewhat dispassionate letter which merely stated that Per-Johan was indeed well and at work at his mission. Dorothy thought it a bit odd that he would have simply stopped writing, but she figured that James had probably been right, and she gave it little thought. That is until they received the letter from Per-Johan last month. The letter was formal and without intimacy. It just said he would be arriving in Fenchow for a visit, and he told them the date he planned on coming. That date was today.

Deming came around the corner, and Dorothy inhaled and straightened her posture. Behind Deming walked a man, a man that Dorothy did not recognize. He was attired in the common wadded breeches and coat of a Chinese laborer, and he wore his blonde hair long and tied back. His beard was full and unkempt, and his face was dirty. It was only when he spoke that Dorothy realized that this had to be the man she knew as Per-Johan Norling. The difference between the man of her memories and the one that stood before her was astounding.

"Mrs. Cooper, how do you do?" he said. His voice was familiar, but there was little affection in his tone.

"Mr Norling, how good it is to see you!" Dorothy said. She had imagined that she was going to hug him, but instead, she graciously offered him her hand. He took it and nodded without smiling.

"I have left my mission. I came here to see you while there is still time, to see what your plans are," he said.

"Our plans?" Dorothy asked. She smiled. "I suppose we have the same plans as when we came: to bring the gospel to the poor people in this land."

"These poor people, yes," Per-Johan said, half whispering. "Poor people, indeed. But what if they don't *want* the gospel? I don't mean they don't understand it. I mean if they fully understand it and reject it?" he muttered.

Dorothy honestly wasn't sure if he was talking to himself or her. "Now, surely it can't be that bad, can it? We have not found it easy here, but we aren't discouraged. There are many good souls among the Chinese and many sharp minds."

"Sharp minds... yes. Sharp as a blade, Mrs. Cooper. Sharp as a blade." The grin that crept across his face frightened her.

Dorothy forced a smile, and she gestured towards the washroom. "Please, do freshen up, Mr Norling, and have a seat at the table. My husband and son are teaching a class of our boys right now. I'll go fetch them and have them take a break... so that we can enjoy lunch together."

Per-Johan grunted and made his way to the washroom and closed the door. Dorothy looked at the meticulously arranged table and frowned slightly, and then she went to inform her husband and son that lunch was ready.

****

"Turfan?" James Cooper said. "I'm extremely curious as to your experience up there. I don't suppose you had too many evening meals that were comparable to your time in Paris, eh?" He laughed heartily.

Per-Johan flashed a brief smile, but it was an uncomfortable one. His eyes shifted around furtively as if he was half-expecting to find mortal enemies lurking in the Cooper household. "No, by the grace of God I was not tempted by extravagance," he said.

Dorothy wasn't quite sure what to make of that comment, but she was determined to make this a pleasant social engagement. "I wanted to make something special to celebrate your visit, and I came across a recipe in one of my cookbooks for a Swedish pork roast. You know how these cookbooks are. I'm not sure if it's really Swedish or not, but it's as close as I could get." She motioned for the cook, Tang Hu, to bring over the tray of roast pork, and he did so, smiling as he set it down on the table. Deming then brought over some baking powder biscuits and butter, and a large bowl of steamed green beans.

"And your noodles, Tang Hu," Dorothy said. She turned back to Per-Johan. "We haven't completely developed a taste for Chinese food, but Tang Hu had told us that Shensi has the best noodles in China, and we all agree that they're quite good. Made with oats, I believe, and with a dipping sauce of some of the local vinegar that they're quite proud of."

"I guarantee you will enjoy these," Tang Hu said in Chinese as he brought the steaming bowl of hot noodles to the table and set them down with evident pride.

"The sauce is really great," Wayland said enthusiastically.

When the food was all on the table, each bowed their heads, and James said grace for the group.

"Our Heavenly Father, thank you for allowing us to gather together in your name, and for your blessings in allowing us to serve you in this faraway land. We beseech you for guidance and strength in spreading your word to these people, who are no less deserving and in no less need of your grace than we. And Lord, we give special thanks today for granting us the welcome company of your faithful servant, our friend Per-Johan. Amen."

"And may God have mercy on us all," Per-Johan said, barely loud enough to be heard by the rest.

Dorothy raised her head and passed the platter of roast pork to Per-Johan, and he took a small slice and then set the tray down. He picked up the fine silver knife and fork at the sides of his plate and began to aggressively cut the sliced pork as the Cooper family looked on. Per-Johan gulped down one huge bite, and then another. He raised his head, and his eyes met those of the others. He paused for a second and then bowed in acknowledgment of his faux-pas.

"I'm sorry, I've become accustomed to eating alone for a good while now," he said. He picked up the platter of roast pork and passed it on to James, who smiled politely.

"Don't worry about it," James said. He smiled sympathetically. "We've all had to make some adjustments out here."

Per-Johan grunted in agreement, as the other dishes were passed around the table. "Cook," he said curtly. "Bring me some chopsticks, if you would. I can hardly use these things," he said. He looked at his knife and fork as if they were unknown implements and pushed them to the side. The cook brought him his chopsticks; he virtually attacked his food, using the chopsticks as deftly as any of the Cooper's hired helpers.

"Did you say things were going well at your mission?" James said, again trying to engage Per-Johan in conversation.

"I didn't say," Per-Johan replied, through a mouthful of noodles. "But no, I wouldn't say things were going well. These are a heathen people, and I don't think our presence is going to change that."

Dorothy tried to put a good light on things. "We've certainly had our difficulties here, but one cannot lose hope."

"No, I don't lose hope," Per-Johan said. "Peter was crucified upside down, and it was his greatest glory. He maintained his hope. It was more than he could have asked for, to be martyred in that manner."

James was unsure of Per-Johan's intent. "Peter's death... was noble, without doubt, but surely we can aspire to a different end and still be fulfilling God's plan for us?"

"Perhaps," Per-Johan said. "Perhaps not. The storm is building. Can you not feel it?"

"The Boxers, you mean?" James asked. Wayland's eyes perked up at the mention.

"The Boxers," Per-Johan said. He gulped a swallow of tea, and some dribbled down his chin. "They're not to be taken lightly."

"This country seems to have a non-stop parade of rebellions

and uprisings, war and rumors of war," James said. "I'm not sure this current talk is of any different sort. The people here have some hostility towards foreigners, no doubt, but it's not excessive. I daresay we receive better treatment here than a Chinaman would in a good many parts of the United States."

Out of the corner of her eye, Dorothy caught a glimpse of movement on the white tablecloth next to her guest. To her horror, she saw a small centipede scurry up onto Per-Johan's plate, and Per-Johan noticed it at just about the same time.

"Oh, my word! I'm so sorry," Dorothy said.

Per-Johan grunted, and casually picked the centipede off his plate and tossed it back onto the floor behind him.

"Give me your plate, and I'll get you a new one," Dorothy said. She called to Tang Hu, but Per-Johan shook his head.

"Nonsense. It would be wicked indeed to throw away God's blessings over nothing." He picked up a piece of pork with his chopsticks and leaned his head down close to the plate. It was a large piece, and he ate it in one bite.

Dorothy and James made eye contact for a second, and then Dorothy slowly sat back down, smiling politely.

"Do you know more about the Boxers?" Dorothy asked. "We've had such a jumble of news and rumors here, and the official reports we get from Western sources are sometimes so different from what we hear from the locals and our Chinese friends. And the Chinese are so superstitious; it's hard to separate truth from fairy tales."

"The Boxers are not from a storybook," Per-Johan said. "And no, Mr Cooper, this is not some common peasant rebellion that will be quickly put down by the local magistrate. They mean to kill us; to kill all foreigners. To slaughter us like animals." He took a bite from a biscuit, chewing loudly. He washed it down with another gulp of hot tea.

"I don't think the locals here would go along with that," Wayland said. "We have a lot of friends here, and we help people, with medicine and the clinic and the school."

Per-Johan looked to Wayland and stared at him a moment. Wayland felt as if the man was judging whether his words were even worthy of a response.

"No, most people here don't want to kill you," Per-Johan said. "But that's not the question, is it, boy? The question is whether most people here will do anything to *stop* you from being killed by the Boxers. And I'll tell you the answer: they won't."

Dorothy could see a trace of fear in her son's eyes. "Now, I'm sure it won't come to that," she said, but she knew she didn't sound as confident as she intended.

"What are those devils all about, after all?" James asked. Wayland and his mother both looked to Per-Johan expectantly.

Per-Johan looked up from his plate as he was still chewing. The right side of his mouth curled up a bit, but it wasn't exactly a smile. "The Boxer movement, the current Boxer movement at least, started in Shantung, and they've been spreading west. One of my assistants, the best Christian I've ever known, he was a native of Shantung. He taught me a great deal about the Boxers... about many things." He looked down at his plate and seemed to lose his train of thought.

"They formed in Shantung, then?" James asked.

Per-Johan kept staring down for a moment, and then raised his head. "Shantung is a unique region. Confucius and Mencius were both born there, two of many great minds. And for every noble, contemplative thinker that arose, there also came leaders of cults and many strange sects. Martial arts of many types were practiced. You've heard of the *Water Margin*? The Chinese novel?"

"Yes," Wayland said. "A band of outlaws, like Robin Hood,

weren't they? A hundred and eight of them?"

"A band of outlaws," Per-Johan repeated. "Or heroes, as the Chinese see them. Their base was near Liangshan in southwestern Shantung. Then there was the White Lotus sect, which rose and fell many times during both the Ming and Manchu eras. It was a Buddhist cult, believing in the Eternal Venerable Mother as the creator of mankind, and the provider of salvation at the end times. They often fomented rebellion against the empire."

"These were violent groups?" James asked.

"Sometimes, but not always," Per-Johan continued. He grimaced and scratched his neck as if it was difficult for him to pull the swirling facts and details from his mind and articulate them to others. "Some of the White Lotus sects were peaceful, even vegetarian and pacifist, although they ran afoul of government religious orthodoxy. But they were not to be admired, at any rate. Heathen cults, who could not help but go astray without the guidance of the true gospel."

"So the Boxers are a religious cult?" Wayland asked.

"Partly," Per-Johan continued. "Shantung also has a long tradition of martial arts groups. The 'Cudgel and Whip Society,' the 'Armor of the Golden Bell,' the 'Big Sword Society.' These were primarily groups practicing martial arts for the defense of their villages—banditry was widespread. But over the last hundred years they have all blended and merged and exchanged ideas and beliefs. Some groups grew, others shrank, they all had different motives and goals. It's very difficult to trace with any accuracy. The ones known as the Boxers today are essentially several groups, including 'Boxers United in Righteousness,' 'Plum Flower Boxers,' 'Red Lantern Shining,' and 'Big Swords,' and possibly others that I don't remember. They are mainly illiterate peasants, but the one thing they are all clear on is that foreigners in general, and Christians in particular, are the enemies of China and must be wiped out or driven from the country."

"But why do they hate Christians so much? We're only here to do good. Lord knows this isn't an easy life for us, and we see few earthly rewards," Dorothy said.

Per-Johan looked up at her with that slightly unhinged smile. "Because, my dear, you sneak out at night and poison their wells."

Dorothy frowned. "What? Why would we do something like that? It's ridiculous."

"And the drought, the failing crops? That's because you fan the air with all your might to drive the rain clouds away. And recently there was a British ship boarded by the Chinese just as it was setting sail from Tientsin back to London. Do you know what the Chinese authorities found in its hold? A cargo of Chinese eyeballs, as well as women's' nipples, all to be shipped back to Britain."

"That's preposterous," James said. He was indignant. "Ignorant fantasy. It doesn't even make sense."

"Don't you understand?" Per-Johan said, looking James in the eye. "It doesn't matter if any of it is true. Preposterous to us, yes. But countless thousands of Chinese *believe* it to be true. That's what matters."

"So their hatred is all based on lies?" Dorothy said.

Per-Johan smiled. "We foreigners, even missionaries, have more wealth than most Chinese. You may think you've taken a vow of poverty coming to this country," he said, holding up the fine silver fork next to his plate. "But surely you know you have much more than the average Chinese?"

"Well yes, but..." James started to respond.

"And money means power, and with the fallen nature of man, power will always be used unjustly. In many areas, Christian groups collude with the government, and Chinese Christians are given special privileges not granted to ordinary Chinese. And this power is often used to settle old scores, to punish enemies and reward friends. And of course, our old enemy is always present in everything. Satan does not want the Gospel to be preached here, and he fights us at every turn."

"Now I've heard claims that the Boxers say they're invulnerable to weapons, even to bullets," James said. "How do these people believe that? Many of the Chinese we've met here are extremely intelligent. How do they fall for such nonsense?"

"Oh, but it's not all nonsense," Per-Johan said. "I have seen Boxers resist a blow from a sharp sword. Some of the female Boxers, those of the Red Lanterns... " Per-Johan leaned in close and lowered his voice to not much more than a whisper. "It is said that they can fly."

"Now you're just teasing us," Dorothy said, trying to lighten the mood. She could see that Per-Johan wasn't laughing, however.

"Do not underestimate what can be done by those who ally themselves with Satan!" he said and pounded his fist on the table. Per-Johan stared back at the shocked faces of those at the table for a moment, and then gathered himself.

"Forgive me," he said. "I forget my place. I am merely a lowly servant of Christ, and I am your guest."

Dorothy smiled nervously and nodded. She paused for a moment, and then made another effort to turn this into a normal, friendly meal. "How about some dessert? I was able to make a chocolate cake this afternoon," she said. She motioned to Tang Hu, and he brought over the cake plate with a tall, round, chocolate-frosted chocolate cake on top. Dorothy cut it and went to serve a piece to Per-Johan, but he stopped her.

"No, it is too rich for me," he said. "But you enjoy it." He called to the cook in Chinese. "Can you bring me some millet congee?" The cook nodded and returned to the kitchen to prepare it.

Dorothy had used up a good deal of their cocoa to make the

cake for their guest, and she was disappointed that he refused it. She smiled as if nothing were wrong, however, and served the cake to James and Wayland. The cook brought Per-Johan his bowl of congee, and he grunted his approval.

The four ate in silence for a moment, and then Per-Johan abruptly put his hand on Dorothy's and looked at her with a searing intensity.

"I have fond memories of our first meeting, and I felt I owed it to you to see you once more." He looked around to James and Wayland. "I know... I must seem a strange figure to you now, but I implore you to listen to me. Leave this country. Leave it now. While you still can. Today if possible."

Dorothy looked at her husband nervously, and James stood up.

"Mr Norling," James said, "we sincerely appreciate your visit and your concern, but we are not strangers in this country, and we will keep our own counsel on whether we should stay or leave. I don't see the situation the way you do. We didn't expect things to be easy here, and we can't pack up and leave every time there's some trouble."

Per-Johan sighed and nodded solemnly. "You must do as you see fit, of course."

"And you, " Dorothy asked. "Are you heading for the coast? Leaving China, then?"

Per-Johan shook his head and took another spoonful of his congee. "I am heading to the mountains west of here. I will continue to preach for as long as I am able."

"Will it be any safer there?" James asked.

"Perhaps. My earthly fate is of little concern to me, Mr Cooper. And I have no family."

Per-Johan finished his meal, and within a half hour he was gone.

5

Over the next few weeks, the Cooper's routine in Fenchow was reasonably normal, but the somber warnings of Per-Johan were still echoing in each of their minds. Conflicting accounts came in of Boxer activity and movement. At one moment a large force was said to be heading west out of Shantung. At another, the local authorities were supposedly cracking down on the Boxers, and the brutes were on the verge of being permanently dispersed. Besides the news reports often contradicting each other, James was aware of his own bias. He was an optimist by nature, and sometimes to a flaw. It was often easier to deny that danger was imminent than to deal with the fear and uncertainty of believing otherwise.

And there were also the Chinese Christians to consider. They were a community living with perhaps more fear than even the Western missionaries. Foreigners still had some degree of protection from the local Chinese authorities, who would at least have to answer to their imperial superiors should foreigners suffer under their rule. Although the Western powers did make some effort to ensure the protection of native Christians, they were often an afterthought rather than a major concern. To the Boxers, however, the Chinese Christians were a primary, despised target; they were seen as traitors and enemies, and often they were slaughtered without mercy. James wondered if he, in good conscience, could take his family and flee Fenchow, in essence running out and leaving the poor Chinese Christians to the wolves. Was that the model of Christian courage and faith that he wanted to present to the Chinese?

James thought again of Per-Johan slamming his fist on the table, and the wild look in his eyes. His countenance had conveyed fear, yes. But not just fear for his own personal safety. The look in his eyes was one of apocalypse. Certainly, Per-Johan had not been entirely mentally stable. His dire warnings were perhaps not the ramblings of a raving madman, but neither were they a sober, measured analysis of the situation. Still, might it not be better to err on the side of caution? A miscalculation on his part could lead to not only the complete failure of their mission but quite possibly to the brutal deaths of his family and himself.

Compounding all this was the ongoing local drought and worsening food shortages. The first half of 1900 had seen the least rainfall of any year in recent memory, and the whole province was facing vastly reduced crop production. The dry winds seemed to blow hard every single day, without letup. Dark clouds would occasionally gather with the tantalizing promise of rain, but after a few sprinkles — or more often nothing at all — they would dissipate without dropping any significant moisture on the parched landscape below. The Coopers had cut out any luxuries or second servings with their own meals, but they still felt guilty eating as well as they did, knowing there were so many people in the city and surrounding region going hungry.

Dorothy had written several letters to the Boston newspapers, describing the situation and urging both charitable organizations and private citizens to send aid, but even if the calls were heeded (and that was by no means certain), it would probably be at least several months before any of that aid actually made its way to Fenchow. And any relief sent from abroad would amount to no more than a token measure when compared to the scope of the need.

***

It was a little after noon on Sunday. Having finished the morning services, James was in his study, already preparing the following Sunday's sermon. He liked writing his next one while the last sermon was fresh in his mind; ideas always came to him while he was preaching, but there was never enough time to follow every tangent that he would have liked. And he had to force himself to keep restating the most basic Christian precepts and teachings rather than venture off into more complex theological concepts. It was always tricky to gauge both the sincerity and the understanding of many of the Chinese Christians. The younger Chinese students seemed to be able to grasp the lessons without much difficulty, but it wasn't always that easy with the adult converts. Just last week James had had a heated debate with one of the older women; she had been a Christian for over six months, and she was still insisting that Jesus was the biological son of Adam. Sometimes it was difficult for him to mask his frustration, but he always reminded himself of the difficulty anyone would have in grasping profound religious concepts from a completely foreign culture.

James had written about two-thirds of next week's sermon, which would focus on the Book of Job, when there was a knock on the door.

"It's me," Wayland said.

Wayland came into the study. He had just come back from another trip into town, partly to pick up some supplies, but more to pick up news and get a sense of what was going on outside the walls of their compound.

James took off his reading glasses and looked up at his son. "Well, what do you see out there?"

Wayland shook his head. "There are more Boxers in town. No doubt about it. There was a big gathering by the main market. A bunch of young fighters and a couple of their leaders. They were whipping up the crowd again pretty good."

James slowly brought his hand up and rubbed his forehead. "What were they saying?"

"Same things. Saying that the foreigners were trying to lead them away from their own gods and that their ancestors were angry with them. And that's why we were having the winds and the drought. They said China should be for the Chinese, and not enslaved by the foreigners."

"Enslaved," James said. He shook his head. "We leave our homes, our comfort, our safety, and we travel halfway around the world to bring them the only thing that can truly free them, and they call it 'enslavement.'"

"And they said we were poisoning the wells too, just like Mr Norling said."

"Of course. We helped two women and a man break free from opium last week, we treated a case of glaucoma, and we're teaching a half-dozen young girls to read. And after that, of course, we went out and poisoned the wells. Makes perfect sense, doesn't it?"

Wayland frowned and nodded. He hesitated for a moment, not wanting to say what he had to say, the news that none of them wanted to know. "I... I think that story we heard is true."

"What?" James said, looking intently at his son. "What did you hear?"

Wayland sighed. "It's like everything, lots of rumors, and you don't know what to believe. But they said that foreigners had been killed at Taiyuan. By the Boxers."

"Did they give any names?" James asked.

"They said... all of them."

"Was this just street talk?" James asked.

"I don't think so," Wayland said, shaking his head. "They said the word came from the magistrate."

James leaned back in his chair. "Dr. Westwood... and his daughters." He sighed wearily.

Dr. Westwood was the British surgeon and missionary who had become both a professional colleague and a good friend to James. If James's Chinese patients had severe medical problems that were beyond the scope of his knowledge, James would refer them to Dr Westwood. The good doctor was based in Taiyuan, some seventy-five miles to the northeast, but several times a year he made his rounds to the other Western missionaries in the area, and he had visited the Coopers a number of times in the last couple years. His wife had suffered a nervous breakdown three years ago from the stresses of the missionary life, and she had gone back to England to recover. His twin daughters, Eva and Martha, had elected to stay in China with their father. They were the same age as Wayland, turning eighteen this year.

"Son," James said, trying to find the right words. "We're in quite a spot here. You're a man now, and more is expected of you. I won't lie to you, this is more than you should have to deal with, more than I ever had to deal with at your age. But we're in for a rough ride."

"Sure, Dad," Wayland said.

"But I don't want you to get discouraged, either. Don't be alarmed by every rumor or tidbit of news. We're only getting a partial picture here, and in the long run, things might not turn out as bad as they seem. Don't ever give in to despair, and don't borrow trouble from tomorrow; we'll do the best we can each day. The Lord's ways may be incomprehensible to us, but we have to trust in his plan, whatever it may be."

6

IT WAS LATE in the afternoon of the next day, and James, Dorothy, and Wayland stood in the central courtyard. They had all come out when they heard the commotion, and now they knew it was from a crowd on the street outside their compound. It was hard to judge exactly how many people were out there just from the noise, but given the situation, it was a concern. Their gatekeeper, Chin Fai, had not shown up for work this morning, and James made sure the main gate was securely bolted. It sounded like there were dozens, if not hundreds, just outside their walls.

"Nothing to get excited about," James said. "We can't worry about things that we can't control. What are we having for dinner tonight, dear?" James asked. His tone was calm and measured.

Dorothy looked at Wayland and then back to her husband, and forced a smile. "I'm not sure, but I'll... I'll see what I can come up with." She turned and went back inside.

"Son," James said quietly to Wayland. "Do you think you can get up there and take a look without being seen?" He nodded towards the small buckthorn tree to the right. It was the largest of the trees inside their compound, and its leaves had just begun to come in.

Wayland looked over to the tree, and then back to his father. He smiled and nodded. He had climbed the tree countless times, and he knew he could go up just far enough to be able to peer over their compound's walls without being spotted from the outside.

He walked over and put one boot onto the trunk as he hopped up and grabbed the lowest large branch. He quickly pulled himself up and then slowly climbed until he was just about level with the outer wall of the compound. Wayland was quite sure that he was not visible through the leaves, but he was cautious as he carefully lifted his head to peer over the wall. What he saw was not comforting. The crowd was several rows deep; there had to be a few hundred people lining the street. Some were there just for the spectacle, but many were visibly angry; they were waving their fists and shouting epithets. Wayland's heart began pounding. He had never been in a situation like this.

"What can you see?" James asked, and his son's fearful expression said more than any words.

Wayland lifted his head back up to look over the wall. One man in the crowd was particularly vexed; he picked up a stone and with an angry effort threw it up over the wall. Wayland ducked, but the rock flew well past him, and it was clear that the man didn't see him and hadn't been aiming at anything in particular.

Wayland looked back down to his father, and he spoke in a hushed tone. "Just a big crowd... some are angry... not sure about the rest. Just here for the show, maybe. Wait a minute; something's happening."

He adjusted himself in the tree branch to get a little more comfortable, and then he peered back over the wall. A chant was coming from the crowd, and as Wayland listened, it turned into a song. They kept repeating the same lines over a simple melody, and after the third or so repetition, Wayland could start to make out the words:

"The red lantern shines
Lighting the path for the people
Woosh, with a wave of their fan

Up they fly to heaven."

The crowd continued to sing, and each repetition seemed a bit louder than the one before. Then Wayland saw some motion in the crowd. Someone was making their way through the throng, moving forward, and the people were parting to give them room. The crowd cheered and applauded, and as the individuals came to the front, Wayland could now see who it was. They were three young women, probably in their late teens or early twenties. They were each dressed in identical red trousers and coats, red shoes and red hats, and each carried a red lantern. The taller girl in the middle also held a red fan. Wayland had heard of the Red Lantern brigades before, but this was the first time he had actually seen any of them.

The main Boxer movement was for men only, and indeed any contact with women was forbidden to the Boxers, as it was thought that the female 'yin' energy would have an adverse effect on their martial arts skills and magic. Nonetheless, auxiliary Boxer movements of women formed, and the primary female group was the Red Lanterns. There were many legends about the capabilities of these young girls. Like their male counterparts in the Boxers, they were also said to have supernatural abilities and experience spirit possession; their powers, however, were usually different than those of the men. They were variously attributed with the ability to fly, to throw swords through the air at enemies from a great distance, and to have magical powers to heal men injured in battle.

Wayland looked at the young girls, and although they were quite striking in their matching red outfits, he was a bit dubious about these fantastical claims. He did notice that their feet were not bound, and they didn't wear their hair in the traditional manner. And they certainly looked confident. They stood together, side by side at the front of the crowd, just a few yards from the outer wall of the compound. The girls took their positions, and each got into what appeared to be some sort of martial arts stance as a hush came over the crowd. All three closed their eyes and tilted their heads back. The tall girl in the middle began shaking, subtly at first, but then more noticeably. The other two followed suit, and gasps came here and there from the onlookers. The girl in the middle suddenly shrieked, and then all three fell to the ground, convulsing and twisting in the dusty street. This went on for several moments, and then all three stopped abruptly. They slowly got to their feet, and as if in a trance, joined hands.

They began to chant in unison, and Wayland understood most of it:

"We are the Mother Sky Faeries
Sent down from Heaven
To teach the way to men
To men who have lost the way
Who have let the foreign devils
Usurp their beliefs and insult the gods
The earth is dry and arid
And no rain has fallen
Because the gods are angry
But if you rise up, and expel
The foreign devils, and kill
A dragon, a tiger and three hundred rams
There will be peace in the land ."

Their voices had a strange affectation; Wayland wasn't sure if it was just some theatrical flourish, or if they had actually put themselves in some kind of trance. When they finished, the onlookers cheered; the three girls started again, repeating their chant. Wayland then saw movement from the back of the throng: someone else was making their way to the front. The crowd was parting again, but this time there was no cheering. It was the officer of the local magistrate, and he had a half-dozen purple-uniformed government soldiers with him. They pushed their way through, knocking several people aside as they made their way to the three Red Lanterns.

"What is this all about?" the officer asked. He spoke calmly but appeared to be in no mood for nonsense. He was a short man, but stocky and powerful, and he moved with measured confidence. It was clear that he not only commanded men but that he was, in fact, in command.

"We are the Mother Sky Faeries, and we serve Hanba, the Goddess of Drought," the tall girl said, and her voice still had the same theatrical quality. She rolled her eyes back, and so did the other two girls, nearly swooning.

"You're really Mother Sky Faeries, and not just putting on a show to stir up the crowd and cause trouble?" the officer said. He struck the tall girl in the face.

She turned back defiantly. "We are the Mother Sky Faeries, and we speak to the people!"

The officer grabbed her by the back of the collar and threw her face down into the street. He motioned to his men, and they threw the other two girls down in the same manner; all three of the Red Lantern women were prostrate in the dust. There was some grumbling from the crowd, but none dared to intervene against the soldiers.

"You're the Sky Faeries?" the officer said. He took out his wooden truncheon and swung with both hands, striking the tall girl on the back of the upper thigh once, twice, and a third time. The impact was so hard Wayland could hear the "smacks" all the way up in his perch. The tall girl was silent, and the officer moved over and hit each of the other girls in the same place, and just as hard. The girl on the right let out a horrible cry of pain, and Wayland winced.

"You're still the Sky Faeries, you're sure of that?" asked the officer.

The tall girl was steadfast. "Yes."

"Give them one hundred strokes each," the officer said, "or until they confess."

The soldiers took their positions over the girls, and each had their truncheon. They began beating the girls in steady, measured strokes. It only took about five before the two shorter girls begged for mercy.

"No, stop! Please! We were just pretending!" one cried.

"We aren't Sky Faeries! Don't beat us!" the other said through her tears.

The tall girl gritted her teeth and wouldn't relent. Neither would the officer. It was a test of wills, and the crowd would see who could hold out longer.

"Keep beating them all until they all confess," the officer said. He sniffed angrily and looked down on the girls with contempt. The soldiers obeyed.

Wayland could barely watch the horrible scene. He had received a few spankings in his life, but he had never been hit as hard as these girls were being struck. He imagined that they'd barely be able to walk tomorrow. The two girls were shrieking and crying with every blow now, and even the tall girl was groaning at each stroke.

"Let them go!" came a voice from the crowd.

"It's shameful!" said another.

"They've had enough, show mercy!" came another voice. With this one, though, the officer saw (or thought he saw) who said it. He grabbed a man from the crowd and smashed him on the shoulder with the wooden truncheon. The man fell to the ground, and the officer kicked him in the ribs, hard. The man struggled up and scurried away. The officer pointed at the crowd and yelled something at them that Wayland couldn't exactly make out. The crowd cautiously stepped back a few feet, giving the officer and soldiers a wide berth. The soldiers kept beating the girls until, at last, the tall girl could take no more.

"Enough! I'll tell the truth! We aren't Faeries!" she finally said, sobbing fiercely.

The officer raised his hand, and the soldiers stayed their hands. They stood motionless, with their batons in the air, as they awaited their next order.

"Pick them up. We'll take them to the magistrate's office," the officer said. The battle of wills won, he turned to the crowd. "Take heed as to what you've seen here. Anyone who stirs up the people or causes trouble, this is what you'll get! We won't have lawlessness here! Do you all understand that?"

The crowd murmured and parted. The three Red Lantern girls could barely stand, and the soldiers half carried, half dragged them away. The officer followed, warily eyeing the crowd as he passed through. Wayland thought he heard a few yells in support of the Red Lanterns, but he wasn't sure. As soon as they were gone, the buzzing of the crowd picked back up again; the tension that was there earlier did not seem to have dissipated much at all.

"Wayland," James said.

Wayland stared at the scene for a few moments and wasn't sure what to make of everything that had just transpired.

"Wayland, what did you see?" James asked, with a bit of exasperation.

Wayland snapped back to focus and looked down at his father. He worked his way out of his perch and dropped back down to the ground. He told his father everything that had happened, as best as he could make out from his vantage point.

James rubbed his beard thoughtfully, but his expression was

stern. "If Red Lanterns are in town, we can be sure the Boxers are here in even greater numbers."

"At least the government troops aren't supporting them," Wayland said. "It seems like we can still count on them for protection."

"Yes, it seems that way. For now at least," James said. "Still, if popular opinion turns too much against us, then the government won't be able to protect us around the clock. And if that's the way the people really feel, you can bet the magistrate isn't going to go out of his way to antagonize them. The officials might be getting pressure from above to protect us, but they're not going to risk inciting rebellion."

"I still don't think that the people here have turned against us," Wayland said. "Most don't mind us at all, and they're just going about their own lives. It's just the Boxers stirring things up."

James nodded. "That's how it's been as long as we've been here. But things can change. Maybe it's true that the new governor does have sympathy for the Boxers."

"I don't know," Wayland said. "It's a confusing country."

"It's a confusing world," James said. "You'll understand that more when you're older. The foundations of this world rest on sand, and any security we build by our own efforts is always fleeting. That's why we put our ultimate faith in the Kingdom of Jesus. Where treasure doesn't rust."

Wayland smiled and nodded as James ruffled his son's hair. His father wasn't one of those preachers who trotted out trite scriptural quotes from habit, but instead was one who saw his faith ultimately as an explanation of reality, and of the truth of the human condition. Wayland thought that even if James Cooper was not his father, he would still be a man more than deserving of deep respect and warm admiration.

The two went inside to see just what Dorothy was preparing for supper, and the buzzing of the crowd faded.

7

OVER THE NEXT few days, the crowds gradually disappeared from outside the Cooper's compound, and that provided some immediate relief. But in the bigger picture, things were getting worse, not only in Fenchow but in all the neighboring towns and provinces. The Boxers were operating with impunity, and Western missionaries and their Chinese converts were facing constant threats up and down the countryside. No mail was getting through; Boxers were stopping any Chinese travelers in the area, and if they were found with any foreign correspondence, they were summarily killed. James Cooper was increasingly worried, and he felt like a noose was slowly tightening around his neck. No, not just around his neck—that he could have handled. Around all of their necks.

James came into the kitchen, as Dorothy had just put a kettle on the stove for coffee. "Lihao just brought word. The Eldridges will be here later today," he said.

Dorothy nodded. "Well, they were planning on a visit this summer anyways. It's just a little earlier."

James nodded. He appreciated his wife's desire to see the situation as just a minor variation of normality, but he had trouble masking his growing worry. "Miss Cameron will be coming with them."

Dorothy's face brightened. "Oh, that will be wonderful," she said. "I do so like Grace, and she's very fond of the children. And they adore her."

Lihao came into the room and bowed politely. "Excuse me, Mr Cooper, but Mr Chen is here to see you. He's the father of Deming. He would like to speak to you."

"Oh, certainly," James said. "I'll be right there." Deming was one of his brightest students, but like the others, he hadn't been to the school in over a week.

"I'll tell him," Lihao said, and left the room.

"I'll get the rooms ready for the Eldridges and Miss Cameron," Dorothy said. "I've got bedding all washed for them." She smiled as she looked at her husband, but she rubbed her hands together nervously.

"Don't worry," James said. He took Dorothy by the shoulders and kissed her gently on the forehead. She nodded and wiped her eye.

James walked out to the courtyard and saw Lihao talking with a bespectacled young man of about thirty-five. James could see that the man looked troubled.

"This is Mr Cooper," Lihao said in Chinese as James approached. James smiled and bowed slightly. "And this is Mr Chen," Lihao said. Mr Chen bowed as well and offered his hand to shake, which James did.

"Mister Cooper," Mr Chen said. "I am the father of Deming. We met once before when my son started school."

"Yes, Mr Chen, I remember you. Deming is a fine boy, one of my brightest students," James said.

"Yes, his mother and I are very proud of him. I cannot thank you enough for all that you have done. I am something of a scholar myself, and I am amazed at some of your lessons that he has conveyed to me. Mr Cooper, I have come here to apologize for his absence this last week. I feel that…"

"You do not need to apologize to me, Mr Chen. I understand

the situation as well as you do."

"I... must think of my family. As much as I would like to have my son continue his studies with you, the risks are too great."

"I would do the same in your situation, I'm sure," James said. "If anything, the Boxers reserve their greatest hatred for you Chinese that associate with us. I would not want to see any harm befall you or your family."

"We are in difficult times in my country, Mr Cooper," Mr Chen said. "Dark times. But I would hope that you don't judge all of China on the example of the Boxers. They are not China. They are not the future."

"I don't judge China on the Boxers." James put his hand on Mr Chen's shoulder. "I have met with many wonderful people in this country, and I have a much more positive view of the Chinese people now than I did when I arrived here. All nations struggle through their turbulent times. I fought in my own country's Civil War. Terrible destruction and bloodshed. This is our lot as human beings, I fear. Still, we must have hope for a better future."

"I have studied your religion," Mr Chen said, nodding. "I am not sure I understand all of it or agree with it, but I admire many of its teachings. I know that it is not the hateful creed that the Boxers say it is."

"Thank you, Mr Chen. Please, I know you're risking danger even to come here. You must leave. I can show you out the back gate if you'd like. You won't be seen."

"No, I will leave the way I came, through the front."

James patted Mr Chen on the shoulder. "Thank you again for coming. It means a great deal to me. And keep Deming at his studies. He has great potential if he can discipline himself."

"Please, it's not much, but I hope this may help you," Mr Chen said. He pressed a British five-pound note into James's hand.

James looked at the bill and was going to refuse it. But then he looked at the expression on Mr Chen's face and knew it would be nothing short of an insult if he didn't accept it.

"This *will* help us," James said. "I accept it, and I thank you. My wife and my son thank you, too."

Mr Chen bowed, turned and left through the front gate.

James sighed heavily and looked at the five-pound note. He put it in his pocket and shook his head as he watched Mr Chen close the gate behind him. Life was full of surprises, he thought, but perhaps the hearts of average, ordinary people were the greatest mystery.

Still, his Chinese students, friends, and converts were now gone, all except for Lihao. He couldn't blame them for thinking of their own safety, but he wondered how deep their Christian convictions really were. If they left his school as a vanguard of a secret, spiritual army, passing on the Good News to their countrymen, James thought, that would be more than he could ever hope for. If, however, they merely drifted away from the words of Jesus and fell back to their old ways, then all his work would have been for naught. Perhaps he shouldn't be so pessimistic. Even Peter himself denied his Lord three times before the cock crowed that day.

James sauntered back through the courtyard. It was a bright morning, and the temperature was comfortable, although the dry breeze still carried its seemingly endless supply of gritty dust. His gaze happened to fall upon the trees he had planted around the edges of the courtyard last summer. There were eight in all, five pines and three flat-leafed arborvitaes. He had tended to them faithfully, watering and fertilizing them with manure on a regular basis. And his efforts had paid off; each of the trees had grown significantly and was thriving. Would they continue to do so after the departure of him and his family? So many of one's efforts come to nothing. The work, the time, all based on a faith in the future. A blind faith, perhaps.

James was almost back to the main hall when he heard the rapping on the outside gate of their compound. His heart beat a bit faster. With all the confusion in the city, there was no telling who might be seeking entry to their compound. He turned and walked back to the gate and peered through the viewing slot, and saw the familiar faces of Victor and Ginny Eldridge, and their children Tommy and Ellie. Grace Cameron was with them, as well.

"Oh, I'm so glad it's you," James said as he slid the bolt back and opened the gate.

"Thank you, James," Victor said. He held the gate open for his wife and children and Miss Cameron to enter. Each smiled as they passed James.

"Did you have any trouble getting here?" James asked, as he firmly shook Victor's hand, and bid welcome to Ginny, Grace and the children.

"Not really," Victor said. Victor was a big, barrel-chested man, and his voice was booming and full. His mutton-chop sideburns lent an almost comical air to him, although through their acquaintance James had come to greatly appreciate Victor's intellect as well as his wit.

"We're going in to see Dorothy, dear," Ginny said. She gave James a quick hug and kiss on the cheek.

When she and the children and Miss Cameron were out of earshot, Victor turned back to James. "Not as comfortable a trip as I would have liked, I must say."

"No?"

"It's bad out there, James, it's all changed. Not like it was even a few months ago. Something is in the air... tension, anger, violence. I didn't let on to the women, of course, but I was scared. Damned scared. Don't know who you can trust, or if someone's going to be swinging a sword at your head around the next corner."

James shook his head. This wasn't the news he wanted to hear. "I don't know how it all went so bad. We've done nothing but good here, as far as I can see. Caused no trouble, lived simply, made no demands. We help people, Victor. Education, medicine, the Word of God."

"That's true enough for the likes of you and me," Victor said. "but many people are in China for a lot of reasons. We both know that Joe Chinaman hasn't always been treated fairly. Lots of issues at play, with trade and business, and government and politics. We're all flawed creatures, as you well know. It's easy for us to see China as backward and pagan, but the greed and arrogance on our side can't be denied. Pride, James. Pride was Satan's greatest flaw, and it may well be ours, too."

James nodded. "True enough, but still, why would we even come here if we didn't think we had something better to offer them?"

"Perhaps," Victor said, and he sighed heavily. "I feel it may be too late in the day for us to debate that. At any rate, old man, I can't tell you how much I appreciate your kind invitation to us."

"And is everyone well?" James asked.

Victor raised his eyebrows and inhaled. "As well as can be expected, I suppose. Oh, Ginny and I are fine. We knew what we were getting into and what the risks might be." He paused for a moment and smiled glumly. "It's the little ones. They didn't sign up for this, if you know what I mean. And Miss Cameron, as well. She's a brave one, but she hasn't tasted much of life. Very sensitive, and with the kindest heart. To be honest, James, I'd give all the world if she could be lighted back to her home in Dublin right now. She's an innocent soul in the wrong place at the wrong time, I do believe."

"Well, we're happy to have you come here, and to be honest, I think the company helps Dorothy more than she would let on. You know women. It will do her good to have some of her own sex around her. Better than just us men, and the constant threats and fear." James put his hand on Victor's shoulder. "Come in and have a cup of coffee."

***

Lihao and Miss Cameron were in the back courtyard playing with the children while James and Wayland sat down at the kitchen table with Victor and Ginny. Dorothy brought the coffee pot over to the table and filled each of their cups before sitting down herself.

"What was the real turning point, do you think, Mr Eldridge?" Wayland asked.

"Oh, I don't know if there's ever one specific moment you could point to. History paints with a broad brush, my boy, and we mortals usually can't see the big picture. Still, I reckon that our fate may have been sealed when the new governor Yu Hsien was assigned here this past spring."

"He was the governor of Shantung, wasn't he?" Wayland asked.

"He was, and the Manchu court dismissed him because he supported the Boxers and stirred up their violence," James said.

"That's right," Victor said. "But rather than remove him from power, they just reassigned him here. And as soon as he got here, he picked up where he had left off. He has a deep and profound hatred of all foreigners, and he's inflamed the worst passions of the natives. Now, to be fair, it's not completely irrational to be suspicious of folks. It's a big world out there, and not every group of people out there mean you well. It's understandable that China might want to place restrictions on foreigners operating in their country and to control their own borders. Every nation has a right—indeed a duty—to do that. But a blind hatred of all foreigners... It's always wrong."

"And once things get stirred up, emotion and sentiment of the mob often take over. And then the time for reasoning is passed," James said. His tone was grim.

"But our situation isn't hopeless, is it?" Ginny said. "We still have many Chinese friends... and... I mean, it's not chaos out there. The government still has some control over law and order, don't they?"

"They have control, dear, but it depends on exactly who they want to rein in: the Boxers... or us," Victor said.

"And that's what seems so unclear at this point," Dorothy said.

James nodded. "The government is doing a bit of a balancing act. They're getting pressure from the foreign powers to protect Western property and people in China, and then they've got the Boxers to deal with. And the Boxers have a lot of popular support among the common folk. If they go too far one way, the Manchu court could face open rebellion from their own people, and if they go too far the other, they could face war with the Western nations, which they wouldn't win."

"But that's all a bit out of our hands," Victor said. "I think the question now is what are we going to do? I don't know how much longer we can stay here... the crowds are gone for now, but..."

"I think our route east to Peking and Tientsin port is now probably cut off for us, with all the Boxer activity," James said.

"Lihao said that maybe we could go west, and hide out in the mountains like Per-Johan was planning," Wayland said. "It's an option, anyway." Wayland had always been used to quietly deferring to his parents' view on serious matters like this, but things had changed. He knew that he was old enough to shoulder some of the responsibility for difficult decisions at this dangerous time and that his parents would make better use of the help of another adult, rather than the dependence of a child.

"Yes, Lihao mentioned that to me as well," James said. "It might be our only option."

"We've packed with a trip like that in mind," Victor said. "And Miss Cameron has as well. We're essentially ready to go at a moment's notice if you give the word, James."

James looked at his wife and his son Wayland. "We'd better be prepared, at least. Let's get everything in order and packed. And let's only take what we absolutely need. It would be best for all of us to travel light."

***

"I can't reach it," Ellie Eldridge said, standing on her tiptoes and stretching her hand up as far as she could. There was a big black crow's feather that had settled way up in the needles of one of the pine trees that grew around the edge of the courtyard. "Mr Lihao, could you get it for me?" Ellie had just turned ten. She was a little small for her age, but a bit of a tomboy. Her blonde hair was cut short, and she wore the breeches and cotton shirt that most Chinese youngsters wore.

Lihao walked over and took Ellie by the waist, and he lifted her up so she could just reach the feather. "There you go, Ellie."

"Ah, thank you," Ellie said. She smiled as Lihao set her back down and she proudly held the feather up to show him.

Grace Cameron was a couple of yards away in the courtyard. She was down on one knee talking to Ellie's brother Tommy, who was two years younger than his sister. "Look at what your sister has," she said, pointing to the feather.

"Hey, look at that!" Tommy said and ran over to get a closer look. Tommy's hair was blonde like his sister's, and he was dressed almost identically to her.

Ellie put the feather in the back of her hair so that it stuck straight up. Tommy looked at her wide-eyed. "I'm an Indian princess, and you're my brave," she said to her brother. "Now go and get your bow and arrow, because we're going to hunt buffalo."

Tommy smiled eagerly and ran off to find something to stand in for a bow and arrow.

"They're quite a pair, aren't they?" Miss Cameron said to Lihao, as she walked up to him. She smiled warmly. "You have an easy way with the children. They like you."

"That is very kind of you to say, Miss Cameron," Lihao said.

"You can just call me 'Grace,'" she said.

"Grace, then," Lihao said, smiling. Ellie and Tommy were flitting about the courtyard, hunting their buffalo, while Lihao and Miss Cameron strolled next to each other.

"I have always been fond of children," Lihao said. "I had a happy childhood myself, with very loving parents. I liked being a child, if that makes sense."

Grace smiled. "I know exactly what you mean. It was the same for me. Being an adult is so much more difficult, wouldn't you say?"

Lihao nodded. "When a child plays games and imagine things, like Ellie with her feather, it is all so serious and important. But at the same time, it is very light and free from worry and anxiety."

"It is indeed," Grace said. She sighed. They walked on for a bit in silence. "Your English is quite good. Much better than my Chinese, I must say."

"Thank you," Lihao said. "It has improved greatly since I began studying and teaching here with the Coopers. To learn a language, one must speak it every day, I think. It is very difficult to learn only from a book."

"And I think that's why I haven't advanced too quickly,"

Grace said.

"It does take time, and it is more than just learning words, too. One must learn to think differently. Our cultures are so different. Although, after becoming a Christian, I think I understand the Western way of seeing the world better."

"It's funny how many things we just take for granted, and don't even imagine that in another country they might see the same things very differently," Grace said.

Lihao nodded, and the two were silent for a moment.

"You said that you liked children. Do you have any of your own?" Grace asked. She wasn't sure if this was too personal a question to ask, but she felt very comfortable with Lihao, and she didn't think he would be the type to take offense easily.

Lihao shook his head. "I am not married, although I plan to be someday. And I do hope to have children." He sighed and scratched behind his ear. "I am afraid that becoming a Christian has... alienated me from my countrymen to some degree. I am something of an outcast, and finding a wife will be more difficult for me."

Grace Cameron felt a natural twinge of sympathy. She put her hand on Lihao's arm. "That's funny that you should say that. Although our circumstances are different, it's very much the same for me."

"You are not married, Grace?" Lihao asked, turning to her.

"No," she said. "I still hope to be, but I felt a stronger calling to devote my life to my faith. Perhaps God will put me in the position to be married someday, and perhaps not. Many things in this world are out of our control."

Lihao looked at her warmly. "I do not mean to speak inappropriately, but I think a man would be very fortunate indeed to find a wife such as you."

"Why, thank you, Lihao. That's very kind of you." She tried

to sound nonchalant, but she felt herself blushing and her heart beating just a bit faster. "You've... decided to stay with the Coopers and us?"

"I have."

"But you, more than anyone, understand what we're facing. Wouldn't you want to save yourself?"

"Of course I want to save myself. But as a Christian... and as a Chinese, I would not be much of a man if I ran out on my friends, on people who had treated me so kindly, and who were in their moment of need."

"Mr Lihao," Ellie said, as she came running up to him. "We got five buffalo!"

Lihao picked her up and lifted her into the air. "You killed five of those giant beasts? Just the two of you?"

"I got three of them," Tommy said, running up. Grace put her hand on his shoulder.

"An Indian princess and her brave, hunting the wild buffalo! You two are quite impressive!" Grace ruffled Tommy's hair.

"What's that noise?" Ellie said.

"What noise?" Grace asked.

Lihao was holding Ellie in his arms, and he cocked his head to one side. She was right. There was a commotion of some sort outside the compound.

"What is it?" Grace asked.

Lihao set Ellie down and hurried over to the main gate that led to the street. He opened the door slightly and peeked out. The crowd had returned. There were probably three dozen people outside the compound. Out of the corner of his eye, Lihao saw something coming towards him, and he pulled his head back just in time to avoid being hit by a baseball-sized rock that had been thrown. It bounced off the wooden gate, and Lihao slammed the gate shut and bolted it.

"Let's get the children inside," Lihao said.

"Come on, let's go hunt for buffalo inside," Grace said. She guided Ellie and Tommy back towards the main living quarters, and she and Lihao followed close behind.

8

It was a tense night for everyone. James locked the gate, but it wouldn't be a great challenge for someone to get over the walls. James, Victor, and Lihao took turns on watch, in two-hour shifts. James had his old 1873 model .44 Winchester and a good deal of ammunition, and each handed off the rifle to the other when the shift changed. Around three in the morning, James relieved Lihao from his shift.

"Did you have any trouble?" James asked.

"No, it was quiet," Lihao said. He handed the Winchester back to James. "I don't think it is likely that anyone would come over the walls at night, but it is wise of us to stand guard."

"Why don't you try to get a little sleep, Lihao," James said.

Lihao nodded gratefully. "It sounds like a good idea, but I'm not sure I would even be able to fall asleep now..."

"Yes, I know. I just lay in my bed with my eyes wide open. Still, you should give it a try. We may need our rest."

James started his patrol around the outskirts of the compound. He wasn't a man of violence, either by nature or by ideology, but neither was he a stranger to conflict, having served in the 2nd Massachusetts Cavalry during the Civil War. The heft of the Winchester's wood and steel felt good in his hands. It was at least some degree of power that he was able to wield, in a country and a situation where he seemed to have an ever-dwindling amount of control.

Other than a couple of false scares here and there, it was a quiet night. As the dawn turned into morning, though, the activity outside the compound increased. James walked up to the main gate and quietly slid back the heavy wooden bolt. He opened the gate an inch or so, just enough to get a view of the situation. What he saw wasn't encouraging. The crowds had grown. Probably a few score at this point. There were about an even number of men and women, and more than a few children as well. Some were in groups talking. Some were singing songs and others engaged in heated political arguments. But most were just milling about, waiting to see what was going to happen for the entertainment of the day. James shut the gate and slid the bolt back into place.

By noon, the crowds had grown even more. There were chants of "foreign devils," and the odd rotten peach or cabbage would occasionally sail over the walls and into their compound. James called Victor, Wayland, and Lihao into his private study to discuss their options.

"Not looking good out there, I gather," Victor said. He sat down at the small table, and Wayland and Lihao took their chairs on the opposite side. James remained standing.

"We have the Winchester and a twelve-gauge shotgun, with a good deal of ammunition," James said.

"And I have my Colt Navy revolver, with about fifty rounds," Victor said. "But clearly, we're not going to be able to hold off a sizable force of Boxers, should they finally decide to come over the walls."

"And should we even fight at all?" James said. "We're all men of God... our Lord did not resist the evil of his foes with violence. Many of our brothers and sisters have been martyred in China in the last few weeks. They did not return hate for hate or violence with violence. Is that not something we should consider? If our situation is indeed hopeless, should we not die as Christians?"

"I think we have to try to defend ourselves," Wayland said. He was trying to come up with a religious justification for that, but he knew it was probably futile to try to debate theology with his father. Still, in his deepest heart, he felt that it would be wrong to just submit to the violence of the mob.

James rubbed his chin and then turned to Lihao. "What do you think?"

Lihao looked sternly at the other men, and a weary smile came over his face. "We are in a challenging situation, and there is no doubt about that. If it was only myself, I should advocate that we do not engage in violence against our enemies. I suspect it would be the same for each of you. However, I am unmarried, and my family is far away. That is not the situation you find yourselves in. Gentlemen, I must be very blunt about the nature of the Boxers. They are brutes. They often engage in violence for its own sake, and through it, they express their most hateful passions. Death would not come easy for us, and things worse than death may precede our end. Torture, mutilation... rape of the women. I must be honest and tell you that these are very real possibilities, perhaps even likelihoods."

Victor ran his palm over his forehead and down his cheek. "We can't allow the women to befall that fate, whatever we do."

"But even if we try to fight back, how are we going to stop that from happening if we're overrun?" Wayland asked.

James and Victor exchanged somber glances, and it then dawned on Wayland what the other option was.

James shook his head. "No, there must be another way. I'll try to talk to them."

"They'll tear you apart, man!" Victor said.

"Lihao? Do you think there's a chance they'd listen to me?" James asked.

"I honestly do not know," Lihao said.

***

James walked across the compound to the front gate, but Dorothy took his arm and stopped him. "Please don't go out there, dear. It's just not worth it. You're not going to be able to reason with a mob," she said. Her lips trembled in genuine fear.

"I have to try," James said. He stopped, and took his wife firmly by the shoulders and looked her in the eyes. "It's important that I try, dear. You have to trust me on this. Don't worry, many of these people are our neighbors. They know us." He brushed a tear from his wife's eye and turned back towards the gate.

He pulled the bolt of the gate, and then looked back at his wife. He paused for a second and then pulled the gate open and walked outside. A murmur and several gasps swept through the crowd as James walked out. He didn't know what to expect as he looked out at all the people gathered. He recognized a few faces here and there.

"Go back across the sea, foreign devil!" one voice yelled, and there was a cheer from the crowd.

James raised his hand. "Hold on now," he called. "Many of you know me. We have lived here for several years, and all we did was open a school and a clinic. You know that we have never caused you any harm or trouble. I recognize some of you that are here now. I have given you medicine, helped you and your families."

"You tell us our religion is no good, that our Chinese ways are no good!" someone yelled.

"No, no... we have never said that," James said, trying to speak loudly while still conveying a tone of humility. "We are just trying to make your lives better, to share with you the gift that we have been given."

"Why do you poison the wells, then?" another shouted, and

the crowd murmured its agreement.

"We have poisoned no wells," James said. He sighed and shook his head. "Why would we do that? It makes no sense." Someone threw a rotten peach, and James was just able to get his hand up in front of his face. It disintegrated and splattered all over him. The crowd cheered.

"The Boxers will teach you a lesson, just you wait!" a man up front said. He was an older man, and his face was twisted in anger.

The crowd surged forward, and an angry woman grabbed his sleeve. James pulled his arm away, but her grip was strong, and it ripped his shirt. A man ran up and threw a weak punch that landed on James's shoulder, and then the man hurried back into the crowd, still holding his fists up in defiance.

"Please, friends!" James said, his voice heavy with emotion. "We're not your enemies."

Another man stepped forward to grab his wrist, and James wrenched himself free and stepped backward. It was no use.

"Get back in here!" Victor yelled from behind the gate. James did just that, and Victor quickly slammed the gate shut and bolted it. The thumps of several more projectiles hit the wooden gate, and a cabbage and several bricks flew in over the walls. Victor pointed the Winchester up in the air and fired a shot. The report cracked through the air, and the crowd gasped and retreated a couple of yards en masse.

"That should give them second thoughts about coming over the top," Victor said.

The next hours were nerve-wracking for all inside of the compound. Grace Cameron and Lihao tried to keep the children amused, and Dorothy made coffee for everyone. James and Victor smoked their pipes, and Wayland held the Winchester, keeping his eyes peeled on the grounds of the compound to spot any intruders.

"What's our plan, dear?" Ginny said as she massaged her husband's shoulders.

"I think we'll have to try it tonight," Victor said, looking over at James.

James nodded. "We'll make a break right around midnight. We can go out the back gate, the one we never use. It's been blocked off since we got here, so I doubt anyone will be watching for us there."

"And to the mountains, then?" Dorothy asked.

"It will be a difficult journey at best, but I think it will be our best option," Lihao said, as he walked in from the kitchen. "I know the way. If we can get out of the city, I can take us through back roads that should almost certainly be deserted."

"It's our best shot," James said, although his expression conveyed glum resignation more than any optimism. "So everyone be prepared to travel, and to travel lightly."

A loud banging came from the courtyard, and a voice called from the other side.

"Open up. Open up in the name of the Governor of Shensi Province!" Whoever it was was pounding on the outer gate with some force. Everyone exchanged nervous glances.

"I'll go see about it," James said, and he went out to the gate.

"Open now!" came the voice. James slid the bolt back and opened the gate a crack. He saw the uniform of an officer of the Magistrate. The man was holding a piece of paper, an envelope of some sort. James opened the door the rest of the way. He was a young man, and his expression was serious and bereft of either sympathy or malice. He thrust the envelope in James's face.

"The orders of the Governor of Shensi Province, Yu-Hsien," the man yelled in a formal, official tone. "Tomorrow, you will leave Fenchow, and you will be escorted to Tientsin. Follow these instructions."

James took the envelope from the officer and nodded politely. There were some twenty soldiers with the officer, and they were standing in formation just across the street. The crowd had backed off, giving the soldiers a wide berth. The officer turned curtly and strode back to his troops.

James bolted the gate again and walked back across the courtyard to the living quarters. Dorothy and Wayland were at the door waiting for him, and James raised his eyebrows as he walked past them. "A note from the governor, apparently." Wayland and his mother exchanged nervous glances, and then followed James back inside.

"Lihao, I don't read Chinese too well. If you would be so kind," James said, as he handed the envelope to Lihao.

Lihao opened the envelope and took out the written proclamation. He scanned it, his lips moving as he mouthed the words to himself, and then he turned to the group. "It says that we are to leave Fenchow tomorrow. The Empress Dowager has decreed that, pursuant to the hostilities with the foreign powers, all foreigners are to leave China. In line with that, Yu Hsien, the Governor of Shensi Province, has sent troops to escort the foreign missionaries from Fenchow to Tientsin, where they will be able to embark by ship out of China."

Ginny sighed and smiled brightly, and Dorothy walked over and hugged her. "Thank God," Ginny said.

James raised his hand, and he wasn't smiling. "Let's hear the rest of it."

Lihao continued. "Prior to the evacuation, the foreigners will surrender all weapons of any type. Furthermore, ownership of all property held by the foreigners will henceforth be transferred to the government of China and said foreigners will be compensated for the fair value of their property by the government upon the party's arrival in Tientsin. Troops will escort foreigners from Fenchow promptly at noon, on the second day of June. No delays will be considered. This is the official order of Governor Yu Hsien of Shensi Province, and shall be obeyed by all under pain of death."

James looked around the room, meeting the glances of all present. He knew that they were looking to him for leadership, but he honestly didn't know if he was up for the task. Nothing was said for a moment.

Finally, Dorothy broke the tense silence. "What do you think, dear?"

James sighed heavily; he looked at his wife, and then spoke to everyone. "The second of June. That's tomorrow. I don't think we have any choice. I don't know if we can trust the words of Yu Hsien, but I do know that it's a chance for us, and a better chance than waiting here for the Boxers and the mob to storm the walls. I think we should make our preparations and be ready to leave tomorrow. What do you all think?"

James genuinely wanted to hear any other opinions, but none were forthcoming. They all trusted his judgment, and they nodded silently.

"It's in God's hands now," Victor said. He walked over and put his hand on James' shoulder.

James looked at Lihao for some confirmation. He respected both Lihao's character and intellect.

Lihao walked to James, and his expression was placid. "I agree. We have no other choice."

James turned and put his hand on Lihao's shoulder, and he spoke quietly to his friend so that no one else could hear. "What do you really think our chances are? Is this a genuine offer?"

"These are strange times," Lihao said. "It is hard to say. I give us even chances that the orders will be followed. I do not see what other choices we have. The soldiers will be watching the front and back entrances now."

James showed no expression, but inwardly he felt a small sense of relief. "Thank you, Lihao."

9

THE NEXT DAY was overcast again; another one of those June days that seemed to promise much-needed rain, but which would probably once more fail to deliver. Everyone had been up until after midnight the previous evening, making preparations for the journey. Even after taking to their beds, nobody had been able to get much sleep.

When dawn broke, the twenty soldiers sent by the Magistrate were still standing guard outside the mission, and now there were some more men with them, men not wearing uniforms.

Lihao was busy packing a bundle of clothes and other things when Dorothy approached him.

"Lihao," Dorothy said. She smiled gently, and despite the sadness in her eyes, her voice was cheerful. "You've been as good a friend and as strong a Christian man as I've ever known. But... " She looked deeply into Lihao's eyes. "James and I have been talking. We... we want you to escape, to get away while you can. We don't know what this journey will bring, but as you know better than anyone, our safe passage is not guaranteed. You can do *good* in this country, probably more good than we've been able to do, because these are your people. You've more than fulfilled any obligation to us. There's no need for you to stay any longer."

Lihao's expression conveyed a peaceful resignation that Dorothy slightly envied; he genuinely did not seem to share the same gnawing fear and dread that she felt.

"I cannot simply leave you, just to save myself," Lihao said. His voice was calm and steady. "Is that what our Lord did? Did he put his own earthly safety first, and abandon his principles and his duty? I have no immediate family, and I have no other responsibilities. My fate will be the same as yours, Mrs. Cooper."

Dorothy tried to speak, but the words wouldn't come. Her throat tightened, and all she could think to do was to hug Lihao. The two held each other tightly for several seconds. Lihao released his grip, but Dorothy was reluctant to let him go and held on for another moment. Finally, sighing, she relaxed her arms and stepped back. Lihao smiled his enigmatic smile, and Dorothy wiped a tear from her cheek.

"I am indeed blessed by the Lord to have met a man like you," she said.

James came walking into the room, his face drawn and haggard. He forced a smile at Lihao and Dorothy. "I think we're just about ready to head out," he said.

"Lihao is going with us," Dorothy said, glancing affectionately at Lihao. "I tried to talk him into leaving, but he wouldn't have it."

James turned to Lihao, and their eyes met. James's face softened for a moment, and he nodded at Lihao. The two understood each other. James clapped his hand on Lihao's shoulder, and he turned back to his wife.

"Do you have everything packed?" he asked.

"I have what we need, and what we can take," Dorothy said.

Wayland came into the room, followed by the Eldridges and Grace Cameron. Victor quietly cracked a joke of some sort, although only his wife and Miss Cameron heard it. They both shook their heads in mock offense, but couldn't suppress a grin despite the gravity of their circumstance.

"What was that, Victor?" James asked.

"Oh, not worth repeating," Victor said. "A bit of gallows humor, I suppose. Still, you have to laugh, don't you?"

"What time is it, dear?" Dorothy asked.

James looked at his watch. "Nearly eight."

A loud rapping came from the front gate.

"It is time," yelled a muffled voice. "By order of governor Yu Hsien, you will now be escorted to Tientsin. Prepare to depart."

"Right on time, I suppose," James said. "Are we all ready?"

"Yep," Wayland said. Dorothy nodded, as did Lihao.

Victor looked back at his wife, and she managed a smile. She had Ellie under one arm and Tommy under the other, and she squeezed them both to her side.

"Now don't you two worry," Miss Cameron said. She knelt in front of Ellie and Tommy. "Your auntie Grace will be right here for you the whole way." She tickled Ellie under the chin and got a giggle out of the little blonde-haired girl.

James motioned for them to start. Dorothy led the way, carrying only her pocketbook and one small suitcase. Mrs. Eldridge, Grace and the children followed. "Go ahead, son," James said, and Wayland and Victor came behind the women. Lihao started to follow, but James put his hand on his shoulder, stopping him.

"What do you think?" James' voice was barely above a whisper, and in it was a fear that Lihao had not heard before.

Lihao wanted to be optimistic and provide inspiration for his friend, but he respected James Cooper too much not to be honest with him. Lihao smiled weakly and shook his head. "I do not think we are in a very good spot."

"That's my impression, too. I don't think they plan on getting us to Tientsin. But in God's name, I don't see what we can do but go with them. We've got no choice."

Lihao shook his head in somber agreement. "Still, the ways of the Lord are mysterious. Who can say what the future will hold?"

James sighed heavily. "Lihao, there's something else I wanted to talk to you about. These last few nights, we've taken our turns patrolling with the Winchester and the shotgun. I know I told you that I had decided to go along with the proclamation of the governor, and give up all our weapons. I struggled with this, but I went back to scripture, and I remembered Jesus telling his companion to put down his sword, and not to resist the Roman authorities. Jesus was ready to accept his fate, and this seemed reasonable to me. But then I thought of my wife, and Mrs. Eldridge, and Miss Cameron. Perhaps a worse fate awaits them than death at the hands of the Boxers? Isn't that what you said?"

Lihao nodded gravely. "The Boxers are not civilized men; many are certainly guided by their base instincts. Your fears are not unfounded. But the governor has demanded that you give up your weapons. If you don't comply, will you not be further incurring the wrath of the authorities?"

"I'll turn in most of the weapons to them," James said. "I don't see that I have a choice. But I have to think of the women, as well." He opened up his coat to reveal the handle of Victor's Colt Navy revolver protruding from his inside breast pocket.

"I understand," Lihao said.

"And one other thing, Lihao. Last night, right over there," James said, as he pointed over to the far corner of the courtyard, "I buried 80 taels of silver and two boxes of our jewelry and valuables. About a yard to the left of the tree. If by some chance you're able to make it back here, please take that money and do with it as you feel best. I trust your judgment."

"Yes, James," Lihao said, fighting back the tears.

They set out a little after nine in the morning. Nearly two thousand people were gathered around the mission compound, eager to see the foreign devils' departure. There was an ominous silence throughout the crowd as the foreigners, led by James, came out of the front gate. The troops led them to the mule-drawn carts which had been prepared for them. The officer of the guard gestured, and James paused to let the others go ahead of him; he gently motioned them to board, and they all loaded their gear and climbed into the two carts. In one went James and Dorothy Cooper in the front, and Wayland in the rear seat. In the second, bigger cart was Mr and Mrs. Eldridge in the front, and in the back were Ms. Cameron, Lihao, and the children. The twenty soldiers on foot were spread out in front of and behind the cart, and on both sides. Leading the whole procession was the officer of the soldiers, riding his white horse. The party started off; the crowd murmured, and a few children ran alongside the cart for the first hundred yards or so, until finally, even they lost their enthusiasm. They soon passed the city gates, and before long were out in the countryside.

Despite the trying circumstances, after being holed up in the compound for the last few weeks, it was a bit of a relief for all to be out in the open country, in the fresh air and under the wide sky.

"It is a fine day, wouldn't you say?" Grace asked Lihao.

Lihao looked up at the sky, and the sun was beginning to break through the cotton-white clouds. He looked down to the innocent faces of Ellie and Tommy, and then to the sublime beauty of Grace, and he sighed inaudibly. "It is indeed beautiful, Miss Cameron."

"Now Lihao," Grace said. "I've told you several times just to call me 'Grace'," she said, feigning annoyance.

Lihao chuckled warmly. "It is a beautiful day, Grace."

"I'm inclined to agree with you," Grace said, as she cast a wry smile back at him.

In the cart ahead of them, Dorothy was not feeling so optimistic. "Dear," she said to her husband. "We could meet anyone out here, out on the road. From Boxers to common bandits. Can these soldiers really protect us?" She squeezed her husband's hand.

"They could protect us... if they're so inclined."

"You think they're not?" Dorothy asked.

"I don't know, dear," James said, and he forced a smile. "It's really in the Lord's hands now."

Dorothy smiled back, but her husband's comments did not encourage her. She sensed that he harbored darker suspicions. He was trying to keep her from worrying, but Dorothy could tell that her husband was fighting back his own despair. "I... I love you, James. And I wouldn't have changed anything. Not for the world."

James leaned in and gently kissed his wife on the forehead. "I've made many mistakes in this life, but marrying you wasn't one of them." Dorothy's smile forced its way past her tears.

"Hey, I'm here too, you know," Wayland said, making an effort to lighten the tone.

Dorothy smiled as she wiped her eyes, and she turned and reached back to caress her son's cheek. "Wayland... " was all that she was able to say, but her eyes conveyed much more.

They continued through the countryside for a few hours and passed through several small villages, where seemingly every man, woman, and child came out to witness the strange spectacle of the foreigners in their caravan, escorted by government troops. A little after noon they arrived at a larger village. As they came to a halt on the main street, the leader of the troops dismounted his horse. He took his hat off and looked back at the foreigners for a moment. He then looked up at the sun, and he wiped the sweat from his brow and put his hat back on. A few local men came out carrying buckets of water for the horse and for the mules that were pulling the carts. A wizened old man walked up to the group of travelers, smiling pleasantly. He lifted his basket to show the wares that he was selling: small, sweet melons.

"Would you like one?" Dorothy asked her husband.

James was packing tobacco into his pipe, and he smiled at his wife. "No, but get a few if you want."

Dorothy found some coins in her purse and gave them to the man. "And give a couple to the people in the other cart, too."

"Thank you, Miss," the old man said, grinning. "May good fortune come to you." He handed several melons to Dorothy and gave a few to Lihao and Miss Cameron in the cart behind.

"Thank you, Mrs. Cooper," Lihao called, and Dorothy nodded back. Lihao brought out his pocket knife and cut pieces of the melons for little Tommy and Ellie Eldridge, who ate the sweet fruits with great delight.

James took a draw on his pipe and leaned back in his seat, trying to look relaxed. The soldiers paced about nervously, their eyes downcast and furtive. Their faces were grim, and they were mostly silent, not even talking to each other.

After fifteen minutes, the commander climbed back on his horse and motioned for the caravan to start up again. Soon, they were several miles past the village and out in the country, with no houses or people anywhere in sight. They were driving on a narrow road through a large field of sorghum when the commander of the troops raised his hand for the party to halt.

"We'll rest here for a moment," the commander proclaimed for all to hear, and he dismounted his horse. He motioned for his second-in-command to approach, and the two conversed, their voices lowered. The rest of the troops stood still; they didn't look around, and they were silent.

"What is it?" Dorothy asked her husband.

"I don't know," James said. He felt his heart racing as he looked at the commander and his second, trying to guess the nature of their conversation and suspecting the worst.

"Look, someone's coming," Wayland said.

The others turned and saw several men approaching. They weren't government soldiers. Their faces were painted, and they carried various weapons; one had a pair of hook swords, others had common sabers, and one man had an iron ring, about a half meter in diameter. These new men approached the troops, and the commander nodded as they came closer. The man with the iron ring began talking with the commander, and occasionally the two would look over at the foreigners. After a few moments, the commander called over his second in command, and the three continued talking.

"What do you think, Dad?" Wayland asked, leaning forward in the cart.

"Boxers," James said, and Wayland's heart sank.

The second-in-command suddenly turned and walked towards the carts carrying the foreigners. He was a young man, no more than twenty; his face was blank, but his voice conveyed a youthful nervousness. "Everyone out of the carts, please. We need to inspect them for contraband," he said. "Standard procedure."

"Contraband?" Dorothy said quietly to James and Wayland. "But they provided these carts themselves. How could there be any contraband in them?"

"Just do as they say, dear," James said, as he took his wife's elbow and helped her out of the cart. Wayland followed, as did Lihao, the Eldridge family and Miss Cameron in the other cart. The group drew together instinctively, furtively. A gentle breeze blew through the sorghum, making it bend and sway peacefully, hypnotically. The sky was clearing, and was now mostly a bright blue.

"I love you both... so much. God have mercy... " James said, his voice hoarse and trembling as he pulled his wife and his son close to him.

"Now!" The commander yelled. There was no hatred in his voice, just the cold tone of authority. "Carry out your orders!"

The click of numerous rifle bolts sounded almost in unison, and in an instant, the thunderous explosion of large-caliber gunshots rang out.

Wayland heard a bullet whiz by his head, and he sensed some impact; although he himself wasn't hit. It had to have been either his mother or father. The acrid smoke from the rifles wafted through the air, and Wayland's senses reeled. *So this is it, the way we will all die. Our last moments on Earth.* These thoughts ran through his mind, but his body wasn't going to go so easily. He saw figures running towards him, soldiers, and they were brandishing their weapons. A woman screamed behind him—it was Mrs. Eldridge, it registered in the back of Wayland's mind, and the children were both shrieking. It was difficult to make things out clearly through the haze of smoke from the rifles, and Wayland turned towards the source of the scream in time to see both Victor and Ginny Eldridge fall to the ground, fatally wounded by the gunfire.

"Grace!" Lihao yelled, and Wayland saw a man without a uniform—certainly a Boxer—raise his saber to strike Miss Cameron. At the last moment, Lihao was able to pull her out of the way and took the full impact of the saber cut meant for her. Lihao tried to put his arm up, but the blade came down hard between his neck and shoulder. Wayland half fell and scrambled toward his friend, but blood was already spurting from Lihao's wound, and Wayland saw that the saber had cut so deeply into Lihao's shoulder that it took the Boxer a moment to pull his blade free.

"Bastard!" Wayland yelled, and was finally able to get to his feet, but just as he did Lihao fell to the ground clutching his neck, desperately trying to stop the profuse bleeding. Wayland ran to Lihao and kneeled; his adrenaline was pumping, and tears filled his eyes, and all he could think to do was to try to put Lihao's collar against the wound. The blood continued to pump out with each beat of Lihao's heart, and Wayland knew that he wasn't going to be able to stop it. Lihao looked up at Wayland, his eyes glassy, and then he died.

"Foreign devil!"

Wayland turned and saw one of the uniformed soldiers, with his face contorted in anger. The man raised his saber to strike. Wayland stumbled backward and raised his arm from instinct, although his intellect told him it would be no defense. The soldier was just about to bring the steel blade down on Wayland when a shot rang out. The soldier winced as a crimson dot appeared in the center of his chest. He dropped his saber and fell to the ground, dead. Wayland looked to see where the shot had come from and saw his father holding his smoking Colt Navy revolver. He still had his pistol!

"Run, Wayland!" James Cooper said to his son. "Get away!"

Wayland's mother Dorothy was a few feet away from her husband when one of the Boxers grabbed her by the arm. The Boxer raised his saber to strike her when James Cooper stepped in and shot the man in the head, from no more than a yard away. The man crumpled to the ground, and James pulled his wife to his side.

"Mom!" Wayland cried. She looked weak, and Wayland wasn't sure if the blood on her dress was her own or from one of her assailants. More gunshots rang out, and Wayland heard Grace Cameron cry out. He turned around to see her, and the sight would forever be imprinted in his memory. Grace was down on one knee holding Ellie and Tommy Eldridge in her arms, desperately trying to protect them. The hail of gunfire struck all three of them, and they fell together. Grace and Tommy Eldridge were still, but Wayland could see little Ellie still trying to crawl away. Finally, she too stopped moving. One of the soldiers put his boot under Tommy's body and flipped him over before bayonetting him. Wayland thought he saw the smallest hint of pity in the soldier's expression, but he couldn't be sure.

Everything was a blur for Wayland; in one sense it was happening too quickly for him to even react with any effect, and yet it also seemed to be happening in slow motion, as if each shot and scream and groan were stretched out for eternity. The cries and reports, the moans and acrid smoke from the gunpowder, people running in all directions, and the senseless fear; it was terror such as Wayland had never known.

One of the soldiers ran towards him, and Wayland thrust both hands out with a power that he had never before exhibited. The impact of Wayland's strike knocked the soldier's rifle out of his hands, and the man himself was beaten backward and down to the ground.

"No! Get back from her, you..." James Cooper shouted and raised his pistol as one of the soldiers came again at his wife.

"Dad, look out!" Wayland screamed, but it was too late. Before his father could turn, the Boxer with the iron ring stepped in from the side and struck James Cooper in the head with his weapon. The dull, sickening sound of the deadly ring impacting on James Cooper's temple reverberated through the din, and as he fell to the ground, Wayland knew that his father was dead.

"God damn you!" Wayland cried as he rushed at the Boxer.

It took a fraction of a second for the Boxer to turn, and before he could bring his ring up, Wayland was on him. Wayland landed a clean punch on the Boxer's jaw, but it seemed to have little effect.

"Son of a bitch!" Wayland shouted as he swung wildly, again and again. But his foe had recovered and was easily countering each of Wayland's blows. The Boxer showed no emotion as he engaged with Wayland, and it was with little effort that he struck Wayland's chest with his palm, sending Wayland flying backward.

The blue sky and white clouds spun as Wayland tried to get up. He was able to raise himself on one elbow just in time to see his mother fall to her knees over the body of his father. The Boxer with the iron ring stood over his mother and raised his weapon to strike the final blow.

"Mom!" Wayland screamed, his voice cracking and desperate. He tried to rise, but he couldn't feel his legs anymore. Out of the corner of his eye, he saw something rushing towards his head, and then all was dark.

10

"No mud this time of year. We can take the shortcut," Old Wu said.

He tugged on the reins, and the horse turned left; it continued its easy trot and pulled the small two-wheeled, covered cart off the main road and onto the lower path. Old Wu's white beard blew in the dry wind, and he squinted to keep out the dust from the dirt trail. Dust seemed to be in the air everywhere at this time of year, indoors and outdoors, at nighttime and during the day. It got in houses, in clothes, in noses and mouths.

"All right, I'll leave the driving to you," Master Gao said.

Master Gao truly considered Old Wu to be a friend, despite their twenty-six year age difference. Old Wu had been a companion of his father, and ever since Master Gao was a boy he had had a great affection for the older man; now, there was no one he trusted more, and he had no greater respect for any man's judgment. The two men had made the trip from Tientsin to Fenchow and back again at least once a year for more than twenty years, and they both knew the route like the back of their hand. Master Gao's own martial arts master, Han Tao, lived in Fenchow, and Master Gao always visited him for his annual birthday celebration, and sometimes for other occasions.

"How did your tea go?" Old Wu asked. Traditionally, Han Tao always called Master Gao in for a private meeting and a cup of tea just before his favorite pupil headed back to Tientsin. Old Wu didn't like to pry too much as to the nature of their confidential conversations, but if Master Gao wanted to talk, he would listen.

Master Gao shook his head. "I don't think we'll be making this trip too many more times," he said. "Master Han told me that he's been quite ill this past year. He says it doesn't show much, but he can feel it deep in his bones. He doesn't think he has too much time left."

"Aiya," Old Wu said. "And I thought he looked quite well. Still, it will come to all of us. You worry about it less as you get older, though. All of our days are numbered."

Master Gao reached back into the satchel on the wooden seat next to him and found his pipe and tobacco pouch. He packed and lit the pipe, drew in until the tobacco glowed, and then exhaled. The smoke dissipated quickly in the wind as their small cart bumped and jostled along the well-worn path.

Master Gao paused a moment before speaking again. "He left me with a task."

"Oh," Old Wu replied. He had an idea of what this might be.

"Yes. A task I do not relish."

"Your brother?" Old Wu asked. He kept his eyes on the road.

"My brother."

"A damned mess," Old Wu said. "How you two came from the same parents, I don't know."

The path sloped down and curved past a small grove of trees. As their cart rounded the corner, Old Wu and Master Gao could see something up ahead. There were several men out in the field just to the side of the road. Two were standing, and the other two were crouching down as if looking for something on the ground. As Old Wu drove the cart closer, they could see that the men were looking over some kind of trench or pit. The two men standing looked up at the approaching wagon.

"Aiya, look at that," Old Wu said, and pointed up ahead.

Several patches of dark-red blood dotted the road and surrounding fields. Some of it had mixed with the dust, and some stood in large, unadulterated pools. The grass and brush were trampled down.

"Stop," Master Gao said quietly, and Old Wu did so. "You stay here."

One of the men who was standing began walking towards them. "Keep going! This is none of your business!" he yelled.

A humorless smile flickered across Master Gao's face. He stepped down from the cart and began walking towards the man. As he got closer, he could see what the others were crouching over — bodies. There had to be six or seven, obscenely dumped in a small trench. Master Gao could just make out the corpses of a Chinese man, what appeared to be a foreign woman, and the lifeless face of a yellow-haired foreign child, a girl that seemed to be no more than nine or ten.

"Did you hear me?" the first man demanded. He was tall and dressed like a farmer, but he talked like a soldier, somebody used to being obeyed. "I said move along! This is none of your business!"

Master Gao stopped and calmly surveyed the situation. One of the crouching men stood and turned to him. He was holding a foreign woman's leather pocketbook.

"What happened here?" Master Gao said. "Robbing the dead? Are you even men?"

"They don't need their possessions anymore. And we don't just rob the dead. We rob the living, too," the tall man said. He kept his eyes on Master Gao as he nodded to his companions. "Go see what they've got in the cart." The one still on his knees stood up; two others were arguing with each other over what appeared to be a silver bracelet.

The tall man sneered at Master Gao. "And we'll start with

you. Hand over what you've got if you don't want to end up in this pile," he said, pointing to the pit. The sickly sweet, coppery smell of blood was in the air.

Master Gao ignored the man and walked by him. The man put his hand on Master Gao's shoulder, and Master Gao instantly turned his waist and brought his arm back up and around the man's forearm, locking it at the elbow. With a slight jerking of his body, Master Gao broke the man's arm with an audible snap, which was followed closely by the man's high-pitched scream. The tall man dropped to the ground, writhing in pain.

"Son of a bitch!" the next man said. He was shorter than the first man, and faster. He drew his knife and lunged at Master Gao in one quick motion. Master Gao softly but swiftly swept his own left palm up, pushing the man's knife thrust away. As the man continued his forward motion, Master Gao jerked an intensely powerful short punch directly into the man's solar plexus. The man froze, gasping for air. His knife dropped to the ground, and he tried to speak, but no words would come out. He fell to his knees.

At this point, the other two had a better idea of Master Gao's skills, and Master Gao understood that his advantage was now lessened. Both of the men had their sabers drawn, and they took up combative postures, slowly circling Master Gao.

"If you need any help, just let me know!" Old Wu hollered from the cart, and Master Gao could hear the old man's laugh.

"He's unarmed," one of the thugs said to the other. "Just attack him!"

"Why don't *you* attack him, if it's so easy then?" the other said.

The first swore and then spat on the ground. He rushed in with a downward slash of his saber, and Master Gao immediately recognized that this man had more courage than skill or good sense. Master Gao turned to one side, and as the slash missed he grabbed the man's sword hand by the wrist, and then with his extended fingertips struck the man's throat. The man gurgled and dropped his weapon, and he fell back, still choking. Master Gao picked up his fallen foe's saber and calmly turned to the remaining man.

"We... we didn't do this!" The man said, pointing back to the bodies. He backed up nervously, and then panicked and raised his saber to slash at Master Gao.

Master Gao lunged in quickly with his blade and in one deft motion cut the man's wrist, causing him to drop his weapon. The man cried in pain and grabbed his hand, which was already spurting blood.

"Be glad I didn't take your arm off," Master Gao said as he advanced, and the beaten man nodded as he whimpered.

"Now speak! What happened here?" Master Gao asked.

"We didn't do it!" the man said. He was almost crying. "These were the Christians from Fenchow, the foreigners. It was the government troops who did it! They were supposed to be escorting them to Tientsin, but they just killed them here. Some Boxers were here, too. We're just from the village back there, and we heard the gunfire." he said as he jerked his head back towards the road. "Don't blame us for just trying to get a few things. We're half starving in this drought! We didn't kill anybody!"

Master Gao looked at the man for a moment. He didn't seem bright enough to be much of a liar. "Get your friends and go back to your village."

The man nodded, and with some difficulty, the four men hobbled away. Master Gao walked over again to the bodies. He could now clearly see the limp, blood-soaked figure of a foreign woman. The yellow dress she was wearing almost matched the color of her hair. From the wounds on the bodies of the victims, some had been killed by gunfire; others with blades — sabers and bayonets most likely. Some of the wounds had been caused by blunt force. Master Gao looked over the awful spectacle for a moment, and he sighed. Women and children. All defenseless. *How do men do this to one another?* He picked up the leather pocketbook that the thief had dropped, and he brought it over and gently placed it on the arm of the dead woman in the yellow dress.

They at least deserved a decent burial, and Master Gao decided he would notify the local authorities in the next town. He turned back towards Old Wu and the cart, but then abruptly stopped; he heard something. He listened. It came more clearly: a moan. It was coming from the pile of bodies. Master Gao rushed over, and he heard it again. It was male, and it was coming from back to the left in the pit. Master Gao saw a young Chinese man laying there. He felt the man's throat, but there was no need to check for a pulse, as he was already cold. He heard the moan again. He saw that there was an arm sticking out from underneath the body of the Chinese man. Master Gao felt the wrist, and it was warm. It was a young man, and he was a foreigner.

Master Gao quickly brought the young man out onto the grass. The young foreigner had slipped back into unconsciousness, but he was alive. He had a cut on his forehead, but the blood was dried — it wasn't that deep. Master Gao felt over the young man's body and assessed the situation. He had a dislocated shoulder, probably a fractured arm, and his left leg was a broken. Quite possibly internal injuries, as well.

"Old Wu!" he yelled. "Come over here!"

Old Wu got down from the cart and hurried over. He looked at the pile of bodies and shook his head. "What happened here?"

"Foreigners, Christians," Master Gao said. "Massacred. But this one's not dead."

"Will he live?" Old Wu asked.

"I think so," Master Gao said. "Let's put him in the cart. Careful, he's very badly injured."

The two men gently brought the young man back to their cart and placed him in the back, with a blanket underneath him and one on top.

"These must have been the foreigners that were to be escorted to Tientsin. That's what all those crowds were gathered for in Fenchow," Old Wu said. He looked back at the figure under the blanket. "I don't know what we're going to do with him."

"Too much hatred of foreigners in the air," Master Gao said. "And one of those men told me that these people were killed by government troops, with help from local Boxers. I suppose that none of them would be too happy to find out that a witness survived. We can't leave this young man around here to be killed."

Old Wu nodded and stroked his beard. "Then I guess we'll just take him to Tientsin with us."

Master Gao paused for a moment. "Not the way he expected to get there, I imagine."

Old Wu grunted to the horse as he flicked the reins, and with their unexpected new passenger aboard they continued their journey home to Tientsin.

The trip from Fenchow to Tientsin by cart typically took from a week to ten days, depending on the weather and the conditions of the road. But that was when Master Gao and Old Wu were traveling by themselves, following their familiar routine. This trip was now quite different.

The sky was overcast the next morning, as the two sat in the front of the cart. Old Wu held the reins.

"Looks like it might sprinkle a bit," Old Wu said.

"It always looks like it might rain, but it never seems to," Master Gao replied.

Old Wu grunted in agreement. The two rode in silence for several minutes.

"Will he live?" Old Wu asked.

"I give him even chances," Master Gao said. "His injuries are severe, but he is young and strong."

Master Gao had a fair degree of skill in bone-setting and traditional medicine, and he was able to set Wayland's broken leg and fashion a rudimentary splint the previous night. He had also bandaged the boy's head and put his injured arm in a sling. He and Old Wu had rearranged some of the dry goods they were bringing back, and they were just able to lay down an old blanket and fit the young man in the back of their small covered cart.

Old Wu grunted. "What will we do at night?" He nodded towards the back of the cart. "We've still got a ways ahead of us before we get home."

"Well," Master Gao said. "When we're between towns, we can just set up our camp like we always do."

"We'll probably have to steer clear of some of the bigger inns, though. Can't stay at the Pleasant Spring or the Golden Lily. Too many people, we couldn't keep him hidden," Old Wu said.

"There are a few smaller ones, maybe where we can get a private room. We'd be able to bring him in after dark."

Old Wu shook his head. "Ah, the Pleasant Spring. You know the two waitresses there are the highlight of my trip. Sisters, I think they are."

Master Gao cast him a disdainful glance. "At your age?"

"Well, I'm not in the ground yet. I'm just trying to lighten the mood," Old Wu said.

"You know what could happen if we get caught on the road with him. The Boxers have killed more Chinese than foreigners—

and many for even carrying a foreign letter, let alone an actual foreigner."

"Oh, what's there to be worried about?" Old Wu said. He turned and spat. "With their stupid magic tricks, how are any Boxers going to stand up to you? Let alone you and me together."

Master Gao smiled. He wasn't precisely sure of Old Wu's age, but if the old man weren't eighty, he soon would be. Old Wu had never lost the courage of his youth; still, both of them knew well enough how dangerous it was to be traveling with the young foreigner.

Wayland slowly returned to consciousness. His eyes were still closed, but he became vaguely aware of the wooden cart rumbling underneath him and the clip-clop of the horse's hooves out in front. For a moment, the rhythm of the trotting blended with some half-focused dream that faded just out of his reach, but then it all came together. Images and sounds flooded over him, gunshots, shouts and screams, it all came flashing back.

"No!" he shouted. He tried to raise himself, but pain shot through his body.

"Quiet!" came a voice from the front of the cart. The man was speaking Chinese, and Wayland didn't recognize the voice.

"Where am I?" Wayland asked in English.

"Quiet, I said! If you want to live!" Master Gao replied in Chinese.

"Listen to Master Gao!" said the older man next to him.

Wayland sensed a deadly urgency from the two men, and he remained silent. He heard other voices, and he felt the cart come to a stop.

"What is your business?" came a gruff voice. The horse whinnied, and Wayland sensed that there were many people now surrounding the cart.

"We are just travelers, going back to our home in Tientsin,"

Master Gao said.

"Are you Christians? Have you had any contact with foreigners?" The voice was angry, intimating violence.

"As I clearly said," Master Gao replied. He spoke in a tone of calm authority. "We are just going to our home in Tientsin. We have been visiting relatives. What is the meaning of all this?

"We are the Righteous and Harmonious Fists! We give the orders here! What is in your cart?"

"There's nothing in our cart, just our blankets and some dry goods we picked up in Fenchow."

"Search it!" The man said.

Wayland's heart began pounding. The small curt lurched to the side as he felt the pressure of someone stepping up onto it.

"How dare you?" Master Gao shouted. There was the sound of a scuffle and then the groan of a man being thrown to the ground.

"I am Gao Jinhai of Tientsin. I will not be accosted by ruffians and bandits on the roadside. I will not submit to be searched like a common criminal."

"You are Gao Jinhai?" one of the men on the road said.

"I am he."

Wayland could hear some heated discussion from the men outside the cart, but he couldn't make out exactly what they were saying.

"Well, move along then. But be on the lookout for foreigners," the gruff man said. "They have no place in China from now on, and neither do their supporters."

Master Gao grunted, and Old Wu snapped the reins, and the horse and cart resumed.

Wayland slowly exhaled, and his muscles relaxed as he sank back onto the blanket. He was still groggy and wracked with pain, but he had a fairly clear conception of what had just happened:

the two men driving the cart had just risked their own lives to save him. And he still didn't know who they were. The two men rode on in silence, and the only sounds were the horses trotting and the rumble of the cart. The danger passed, for now at least, Wayland's eyes became heavy, and he soon lost consciousness.

When he awoke again, all was dark. He had no idea how long he had been out, or if it was even the same day. He was still on the blanket in the back of the cart, that much he knew. They seemed to have stopped out in the country somewhere, as it was mostly quiet, except for crickets chirping and the crackle of a small fire. From close by, voices came through the night air, and Wayland tensed; then he recognized them as the two men who had been driving the cart. There was the tinkle of a spoon on a tin pot, and he could hear one of the men approaching the cart.

The curtain was pulled back, and Wayland found himself staring at the wizened, white-bearded face of Old Wu.

"Who are you?" Wayland asked in English.

Old Wu smiled politely and shook his head. "I don't understand you," he said in Chinese.

The old man turned to his companion. "Master Gao, the boy is awake."

He turned back to Wayland and held out a steaming cup to him. "Here, this is a medicinal tea that Master Gao prepared for you. It will help you."

Wayland leaned forward, and Old Wu brought the cup to his mouth. It smelled odd and unfamiliar to Wayland, but not entirely unpleasant. He took a long drink.

Master Gao came up to the cart and stuck his head in.

"Please, where am I? How did I get here?" Wayland asked.

Old Wu and Master Gao exchanged glances, and Master Gao raised an eyebrow.

"You speak Chinese?" Old Wu said.

"Yes." Wayland tried to sit up, but his whole body felt stiff and weak. His shoulder was quite sore, but when he attempted to move his legs, that's when he noticed something was amiss. His left leg seemed immobilized. He pulled the blanket back and saw that the leg was tied up in some kind of splint that kept it from bending.

"Please, don't try to move too much," Master Gao said. "Just lie back. How are you feeling?"

"I think I'm going to die," Wayland said, with a tone of resignation.

"I don't think you are, and I have some expertise in these matters," Master Gao said.

"What's your name?" Old Wu asked.

"In English, it's Wayland."

"Wei-lin?" Old Wu said, somewhat hesitantly.

"Close enough," Wayland said. "What happened to my parents? We were in a caravan, evacuating to Tientsin when they attacked."

"I will try to tell you as much as I can, Wei-lin," Master Gao said. "Old Wu—this man here—we were on the road from Fenchow back to our home in Tientsin."

"We were coming from Fenchow," Wayland said. "That's where we lived. We are Christian missionaries."

"I thought as much," Master Gao said. "Old Wu and I came upon the scene of your attack. We found you unconscious but alive. I tended to your injuries as best I could. We packed you in our cart, and that's where we are now. We still have several days journey before we reach Tientsin."

"I was with my parents. Did you find anyone else?" Wayland's eyes were pleading, desperate.

Old Wu turned his head away, and Master Gao's face darkened. "It was a terrible scene. There were no other survivors.

It was almost a miracle that we came upon you."

Wayland exhaled weakly, and tears came to his eyes again as he brought his palm down over his face.

"I am sorry for your loss, truly," Master Gao said. He had an urgency to his tone. "But our journey over these next days is fraught with danger. I must ask you to remain silent at all times until we reach Tientsin. Do you understand? It may mean the lives of all of us."

"Why are you doing this?" Wayland asked. "You should have just left me there. Left me to die." He lay back down and turned away from the two men.

Master Gao sighed and looked over to Old Wu.

"Just try to rest, young man," Old Wu said to Wayland. "We'll be back in Tientsin in no time."

11

Wayland Wayland first became aware of voices. Someone was talking, although they sounded like they were in another room. The words faded in and out, but Wayland heard some snippets about what was going to be prepared for dinner that evening. They were speaking Chinese, but Wayland was confused; that wasn't the voice of their cook or any of their Chinese hired help.

He was lying on his back, in bed... but where was he? He opened his eyes. It was daytime, and from the sun coming in the window to the courtyard, it felt like late morning. The ceiling came into focus, and then he turned his head to the side. The wall next to the bed was nondescript, with just a simple vertical Chinese landscape painting hanging on the wall, showing a patch of flowering narcissus plants emanating from a cluster of rocks. Wayland looked at the painting for a moment; the colors were faded as if it had been hanging there and exposed to the sunlight for years. Something clicked for Wayland, and he bolted upright in bed.

"Dad!" he cried in English. Images came flooding back to him. The caravan, the attack. The sound of shots and the smell of gunpowder in the air. He remembered his father shooting one attacker, and then being struck by the man with the iron ring. It was chaos, with shouts and terrible screams, and the sound of swords striking flesh. He remembered that he saw his mother and tried to fight his way over to her, to protect her. The look of terror and confusion on her face, and then... that was all he remembered. He closed his eyes, and the tears came.

"Aiya!" came a voice. Wayland looked up and saw the white-bearded face of Old Wu.

"He's awake?" Master Gao said as he came into the room. A young woman followed Master Gao, and her expression was one of inquisitive concern.

"Suyin," Master Gao said to her, "make him some tea and millet congee."

Suyin nodded and hurried to the kitchen.

"That was almost a week ago, you've been in and out of consciousness since then," Master Gao said to the injured young man. "You were seriously injured. Your head was cut." He walked over to Wayland and examined the top of his head. "Although that seems to have mostly healed. Your right shoulder was dislocated. Your left forearm was cracked, but not broken. Your left leg was broken in two places. It's been set properly and is mending well. You should recover completely, I believe."

"Christians?" Old Wu said.

Wayland sniffed and wiped his nose, and he nodded. He paused for a moment, as he formulated his words in Chinese. "I'm American. My parents and I came to China as missionaries — Methodist. We had a school and a clinic in Fenchow; we've been in China for several years. We had a Chinese man in our group. What happened to him?"

"We came across no other survivors," Master Gao said. "There was a Chinese man among the bodies."

"Lihao," Wayland whispered, casting his eyes down and pausing for a moment before continuing. "From Taiyuan, he taught at our school. He was a good man... he was my friend." Wayland sighed. "Were... were the bodies buried?" he asked.

"We did not have time to bury them, but we told the

authorities in the next village we came upon, and they assured us they would send someone to bury the deceased properly," Master Gao said.

"How did this happen?" Old Wu asked.

Wayland looked Old Wu in the eyes and paused for a moment, as the memories came flooding back to him. "We had been trapped in our house in Fenchow for a few days, because of the Boxers. We thought we were going to be overrun. We were going to flee to the mountains, but then that route got cut off." Wayland groaned and twisted his stiff neck. "Then the order came from the local magistrate that we were to be escorted to Tientsin, to leave China and sail back home. We had an escort of twenty soldiers. They said they'd protect us from Boxers if we were attacked on the way."

"And the Boxers did attack?" Old Wu asked. He already had an idea of what happened, but he wanted to hear Wayland's version. "Were the soldiers over-matched?"

Wayland smiled coldly and shook his head. "The soldiers didn't fight the Boxers at all. They helped them."

"Government troops, killing like that?" Old Wu shook his head. "We are in dark times."

"We used to get along well with everyone in Fenchow. We didn't have any problems at all. It got worse when Yu Hsien came in."

Master Gao nodded slowly. "Yu Hsien was governor of Shantung, and he supported the Boxers. His hatred for foreigners has obviously not abated. But are you sure Boxers were involved in the attack on your group?" Master Gao asked.

Wayland nodded. "They must have been waiting for our caravan. We were a few hours into the trip, going through the countryside, in between villages. I guess they waited until we got out in the middle of nowhere."

"That was indeed a deserted spot," Old Wu said. "Not too close to anything."

Wayland continued. "All of a sudden a bunch of them appeared, eight or ten of them. Some of them had their faces painted. They didn't even say much to the soldiers, as if it was all planned. They just started... killing."

Master Gao looked at Wayland with deadly seriousness. "Could you describe any of the Boxers?"

"I remember one of them. His weapon was an iron ring, about this big." Wayland held his hands a couple of feet apart. "He was the one that killed my father... and my mother, I'm pretty sure."

Master Gao rubbed his chin and turned to Old Wu. "Iron Ring Wang?" Old Wu furrowed his brow and nodded.

"You know him?" Wayland said, leaning forward on his elbow.

"He's... known in those parts," Master Gao said. "A violent man, a criminal. Even before this Boxer movement started."

Wayland sensed that Master Gao knew more than he was saying, but he didn't press the issue. "I don't suppose there's much chance of him being arrested if the government was actually on his side," Wayland said.

"Justice is a rare commodity these days," Old Wu said, stroking his beard.

Wayland turned to Master Gao. "This is all a lot for me to take in, but I must thank you. You saved my life. I remember when we were in the cart, you put yourself at risk to save me." Wayland looked around at the walls. "You brought me to your home and tended to my injuries. I would pay you if I had any money. I can do work for you. Whatever you'd like."

Master Gao shook his head. "You owe me nothing. Really, you should thank Old Wu. He was the one that suggested we bring you back here."

Wayland turned to Wu and smiled meekly. "Thank you, old sir."

Old Wu waved his hand dismissively. "Ah, I would have done the same for anyone, Chinese or foreigner. We're all human beings under heaven," Old Wu said.

"Still," Master Gao said, "it may be better for you to stay here with us for the time being. Your injuries have not fully healed, and Tientsin is not a safe place at the moment."

"Not safe at all," Old Wu said.

"What's happened? The Boxers?" Wayland asked.

"Since you've been here, Tientsin has been... a war zone," Master Gao said. "Shortly after we brought you here, some thousands of Boxers converged on Tientsin. First, they went through the old walled city—that's where we are now—and killed any foreigners they found, and also beat or killed any Chinese they suspected of siding with the Christians. We did not let them enter our house."

"And they looted, too, stole things from their countrymen, not just from the foreigners," Old Wu added. "They were just criminals. Animals."

Master Gao went on. "After they had gone through here, the Boxers then moved on to the foreign concessions on the southeastern side of the city. They mostly carried spears and swords, and they were driven back by the firearms of the foreigners. At that point, the government decided that they would side with the Boxers against the foreigners. General Nieh Shih-cheng was commanding the troops, and he ordered artillery to target the foreigners. From what I understand, Russian and American troops unloaded from offshore to reinforce the foreign settlements, but they were bogged down by the troops."

"And what did the brave Boxers do? They ran away, back to the countryside," Old Wu said. "They let the Chinese soldiers face the foreigners alone."

"Finally, the foreign troops received their reinforcements. German, British, French, Russians, Japanese, American. These soldiers all fought together, and the Chinese troops could not hold their positions. Tientsin fell to the foreigners," Master Gao said.

Wayland was sympathetic to the Chinese, but still, he was glad to hear that the Boxers had been driven out. And if the imperial troops had thrown in their lot with them, maybe they got what they deserved. Still, Wayland wasn't entirely sure of the sympathies of Master Gao And Old Wu, so he decided it was best not to comment.

"Your injuries will need some time to heal, and you may stay here as our guest as long as that may take. But then, what would you have us do with you?" Master Gao asked. "We can bring you to the foreign concessions. You can go back to America."

"I've been in China for five years," Wayland said. "My parents were here, my life was here. Everything my parents dreamed of, for themselves, for me...it's all gone. What would I go back to?"

"You must have some family back in America?" Old Wu said. "Your own people to turn to?"

"I have no one. I have nothing left," Wayland said. He turned over so that he was facing the wall, and he shut his eyes. He was silent.

The young woman Suyin appeared carrying a tray with a bowl of millet congee, a small pot of tea and a cup. The conversation had ceased, and from the looks on the faces of Master Gao and Old Wu, she sensed their concern. Wayland appeared to be asleep. She looked to Master Gao for direction.

"Just leave the the tray on the table," Master Gao said quietly. "He needs to rest." He motioned to Old Wu and the three left the room.

Suyin went back to the kitchen, and when they were out of earshot of Wayland, Old Wu put his hand on Master Gao's shoulder. "Do you think your brother was involved in this?

Master Gao frowned. "It seems likely. Iron Ring Wang is one of the Boxers under his command."

"Damn it," Old Wu said. "That brother of yours…"

"Let's keep this between us, old friend," Master Gao said, just above a whisper. "There's no need to tell the others. The boy won't be here long, and at any rate, I will settle things with my brother very soon."

12

OVER THE NEXT weeks, Wayland's recovery progressed, and he began feeling stronger. With the help of a crutch, he could make his way to the bathroom without assistance. He was given a couple of old sets of clothes by Master Gao, and as the eighth month of the Chinese calendar approached, he was starting to feel a bit more like his old self. He still had some pain when he put all of his weight on his leg, but he could tell that Master Gao had set the bones properly and the leg was mending as it should.

It was a sunny morning when he heard Suyin's familiar knock on his door.

"Good morning, Wei-lin," she said, as she came in and set down his breakfast tray. It was a bowl of hot millet congee with sweet potatoes, a peach, and a steaming cup of tea. "How are you feeling?"

"Pretty good, thanks," Wayland said.

"How is your leg?"

"It's better," Wayland said, rubbing his knee. "It still hurts a little, but not as much as it did."

"Keep your weight off it for a while still," Suyin said, in a perfunctory tone. "Your Chinese is getting better too."

"Thanks. I guess you learn faster when you don't have any choice. You know, Suyin, I still haven't been given the grand tour of this place," Wayland said. He flashed a smile, hoping to elicit a similar response.

"Hmm," Suyin said. "You need to know where something is?"

"No, I pretty much know where everything is. I just haven't been given a tour, told about the house or the history or anything... it's kind of customary in my country."

"Oh, well I'll see if Old Wu might have some time."

Wayland still had trouble reading Suyin; was she just speaking sincerely, or was she teasing him? "Or... maybe you could show me around?" he said.

Suyin shrugged. "It doesn't matter to me. There's not a lot to see, but if you want to go around the house and grounds, I can show you. Finish your breakfast, and I have some things to do. I'll be back in an hour. Be ready." She turned and left without waiting for a response.

Almost exactly an hour later, Suyin came back, and Wayland was up and waiting. Suyin stood at the door and politely motioned for Wayland to proceed. Wayland stood up from the bed and grabbed his crutch that was leaning against the wall; he put it under his shoulder and made his way past Suyin and out the door.

It was a beautiful, crisp autumn day, sunny but clear and with a bracing, cool breeze. Wayland inhaled deeply, and the scent of autumn was in the air.

"So your room—the room you've been staying in—it's normally just used for storage. We didn't really know you or know how long you'd be staying with us, or even if you'd live, to be honest. We just set you up in there. You're not too far from the kitchen, and we thought that would make things easier," Suyin said. "Have you been in a Chinese house before?"

"Yes," Wayland said, as he hobbled out from his room and into the main courtyard. Master Gao's residence was a traditional double-courtyard Chinese house, with the surrounding rooms each under a roof but the inner courtyard open to the sky to let in as much light and solar heat as possible. All the rooms opened to the inner courtyard. "In Fenchow my parents and I lived in a single courtyard home, quite a bit smaller than this one, maybe half the size."

"This one is rather large," Suyin said. "This was Master Gao's uncle's house, and when he passed away, he left it to Master Gao, to keep it in the family. So you know that the main entrance is on the southeast side," she said, pointing to the main gate.

"*Feng Shui*, right?" Wayland asked, and Suyin nodded. Wayland thought she might be impressed with his knowledge of that term; she wasn't.

They continued walking along the single-story residence, and as they did Suyin pointed out the various details.

"This is a small pool that's fed by underground springs," she said, pointing to a square wooden frame in the center of the courtyard that surrounded a glistening pool of water. "It's mostly for decoration, or maybe for putting out a fire. It doesn't fill fast enough for us to use it as a water source."

"Where do you get your water from?" Wayland asked.

"There's a city well just down the street," Suyin said. "We carry the water from there to the kitchen, here," she said, pointing to the next room they passed. There was the familiar wood-burning stove with the hole for the round carbon steel pan that was used for virtually all of the cooking. "We keep these filled with water," she said, pointing to two large ceramic jars on either side of the stove.

"That's similar to what we had in Fenchow," Wayland said.

"And we keep the food there, too," Suyin said. She pointed to some dried pork sausages that were hanging from a hook on the ceiling, and next to them were some bunches of dried chilis and some other vegetables and herbs that Wayland didn't recognize.

They continued walking along the center courtyard.

"This is the library," Suyin said, as they walked by a small room on the left. There was a table with an oil lamp on it, and with several stools pushed underneath. Against the wall was a bookcase crammed with Chinese tomes, both old and new.

"Do... do you read?" Wayland asked. He tried not to sound insulting or condescending, but from his experience in Fenchow, it was not too common for Chinese girls to be literate.

Suyin nodded. "Old Wu taught me when I was quite young, and he still gives me lessons. He said it was important for everyone to be educated, girls as well as boys. You speak Chinese fairly well for a foreigner. Do you read it?"

Wayland shook his head. "I tried to learn, but to be honest, I never made much progress. Speaking and understanding the language is easier than reading. At least it was for me."

"Huh, I can't say. I've never learned another language," Suyin said.

"Maybe I could teach you English, and you could teach me to read Chinese?"

Suyin raised her eyebrows slightly as she looked at Wayland, who was shifting on his crutch. "Maybe you should learn how to walk again, first."

Wayland smiled. She was a tough nut to crack. "All right, let's get on with the tour." They continued walking.

"This is a spare bedroom," Suyin said, pointing to a room on the right. Wayland looked in and saw a big brick *k'ang* at the back of the room. "One of Master Gao's great uncles used to live here. The *k'ang* is heated from the kitchen stove. If... you're going to be staying here through the cold months, you should probably move into this room."

Wayland sensed that Suyin was looking for some clarification of his plans, but he didn't have anything to offer. "That's good to know," he said, "When can I move?"

Suyin shrugged. "Anytime. It will probably get cold soon. Do it tomorrow if you want."

"Okay, I will," Wayland said.

Suyin continued the tour. "This is Old Wu's room," Suyin said, pointing to a room on their left.

It was a cozy looking room with a big brick *k'ang* in the back, several calligraphy-laced landscape paintings on the wall, and books strewn about the place—some on the bedside table, a few stacked on the bench, and a volume of *Outlaws of the Marsh* sitting on the lone chair in the room.

Wayland grinned. "That's pretty much exactly what I'd expect Old Wu's room to look like."

Suyin chuckled and nodded in agreement.

"What is Old Wu's story?" Wayland asked.

"His story? What do you mean?" Suyin said.

"Well, his background. How did he come to live here? And for that matter, I don't know much about any of you, other than what I've guessed. I've been pretty open about my past, but what about you... I mean, all of you? How did you all end up here?"

Suyin looked at the ground for a moment before answering. "Well," she said, looking up to Wayland's eyes. "This place belonged to Master Gao's uncle years ago. He was a merchant, he sold dry goods and some textiles here in Tientsin, and he became quite wealthy, which is how he came to have a house of this size. He never married and had no children of his own, but he was always fond of his nephew, Master Gao, and he left this house to him in his will. That was about twenty years ago, I guess."

"And Old Wu?" Wayland asked.

"Old Wu was a companion of Master Gao's father, back in Fenchow," Suyin said. "Master Gao grew up in Fenchow. Things were not that great for the Gao family there, and there was more opportunity here in Tientsin. Master Gao got married, and his uncle offered him a position with his business here, and Master Gao accepted. He and his wife came to live in this house. After only a year or so, I think, Master Gao's uncle passed away. And not long after, Master Gao's wife became ill, and she also passed. When Master Gao's father died in Fenchow, Old Wu had no other family, and Master Gao invited him to live here.

"And how did you come to be here?" Wayland asked.

Suyin paused for a moment before answering. "I... had no family. Master Gao took pity on me and took me in."

"So what's your family name, then?"

"It's... Gao," Suyin said.

"Oh, so Master Gao adopted you, then?" Wayland asked.

"He's treated me like his daughter," Suyin said.

Wayland nodded respectfully. There might be more to the story, but if Suyin didn't want to tell it now, it was no business of his. Her respect and gratitude for Master Gao were sincere, and Wayland was satisfied with that. "And that young man I've seen around. Lunghui, is that his name? What's his background?"

"He studies under Master Gao." Suyin said, "Oh, maybe this hasn't been explained to you. Master Gao is an expert in martial arts, and he teaches a few students here. Lunghui is his top student."

"I see," Wayland said. A slight thrill passed up Wayland's spine; he had always loved sports and athletics, and he remembered with fondness the rudimentary lessons he had received in Chinese boxing from his friend Lihao.

"He doesn't like to talk about it that much," Suyin said. "He's very skilled, but he doesn't take many students. He doesn't think there are many out there who are worthy of being taught."

"Has he taught you?" Wayland asked.

"I have no skill or natural ability," Suyin said, "but yes, I am one of his students."

"Oh," Wayland said. The fact that Master Gao considered Suyin worthy of his teaching didn't surprise him. Wayland was already aware of Suyin's character and intelligence, and he could tell just by the way she moved that she was naturally graceful and athletic, but he appreciated her humility. He remembered something his father had always said to him: "People who are genuinely accomplished in some field don't boast of their knowledge, because they have some real understanding of how far away they are from their highest potential. People with low skills often boast of the little that they have learned; they are ignorant even of their ignorance."

"And that's pretty much... the story, as you call it," Suyin said.

"And how does Master Gao makes his living?" Wayland asked. The Protestant, economically practical part of Wayland was not to be denied.

"He has some business ventures," Suyin said. "He does some exporting and importing of dry goods and textiles, and he has some contacts in the area. He has a reputation as an honorable businessman. He also came into some money after his uncle died, as well. We all live quite a frugal life here, so there really aren't too many expenses. He and Old Wu often visit friends in town, playing mahjong or just socializing."

"I see," Wayland said.

Suyin paused for a moment, and then offered her observation. "But really, Master Gao loves martial arts more than anything. He spends a good deal of his time practicing and studying the arts on his own. He's very humble, but his skills are of the highest level."

13

JUST BEFORE DAWN the next morning, Wayland was on his platform bed, still asleep. It wasn't a restful sleep, though, as he turned from one side to another in the throes of a disturbing dream. He was back reliving the day of the massacre, but the details were different, jumbled. He and his family were back in Massachusetts, in a seaside park in the town of Beverly on a sunny day in June. The park was on a small hill overlooking the harbor, and his parents were walking ahead of him on a slate stone path that led through the well-manicured grounds. Two young boys were playing catch with baseball gloves and a ball over to the right, and a handsome married couple was laying out the contents of their picnic basket on a light blue blanket spread over the grass. In his dream, Wayland stopped for a moment to look out at the sun shining and sparkling on the dark blue waves. A few sailboats were out on the water, and he could smell the fresh salt air.

Then, something was wrong. From somewhere a woman screamed, and then confusion ensued as a mass of figures approached, rushing and aggressive. They were the purple-uniformed Chinese troops and painted-faced Boxers, with their red sashes around their waists. They were brandishing sabers and rifles, and their faces were twisted with blood lust.

"Wayland, watch your mother!" his father yelled. He drew his pistol, shooting several times into the approaching horde.

"Mom!" Wayland yelled, but as he tried to run to her, the ground beneath his feet turned to mud. It was just like the mud their mule cart had gotten stuck in on their first arrival in China when they first made the journey to Fenchow. His mother was terrified, and she looked to her son, but Wayland could barely move. He would just get one foot out when the other would sink further in. One of the Chinese soldiers grabbed his shoulder, and Wayland shook him off and then threw a punch at the man's face. It glanced off, and the man grabbed at him again. He was close enough that Wayland could smell his sweat, and Wayland swung over and over at the man, but he couldn't land a clean punch. He looked up, and his mother and father were nowhere to be seen; two of the Boxers were arguing over possession of the picnic basket, as the previous owners lay dying on the grass, their faces covered in blood. Several gunshots rang out, and Wayland could smell the gunpowder. Another rifle crack sounded, and then Wayland's body jerked. He opened his eyes.

He lay there for a moment, looking at the ceiling. He simultaneously remembered where he was and realized he had only been having a bad dream. It was another couple of seconds before he remembered that, in essence, it wasn't a dream at all. The familiar melancholy began to settle over him when a crack of wood sounded from across the compound, and then sounded again. It was the door to the storage room, banging in the wind. Someone hadn't shut it tightly.

Wayland leaned up in bed and yawned, stretching his arms up and twisting his waist. The sun was up. He winced from a slight pain in his shoulder. It had mostly healed, but if he put too much stress on it, the pain flared up. He got out of bed and leaned over the basin on his small table, splashing water on his face. He felt a tinge of pain in his leg again, as well. *I'm not even twenty, and I feel more like I'm fifty.* He sighed, and for a moment felt sorry for himself.

He had aches, but he also knew that his leg and shoulder had been set properly by Master Gao. Sure, there was some pain, but nothing felt out of place or fundamentally dysfunctional. *What do you do when you're out of shape and weak? You exercise. You work. You move. You don't give up; you push forward.* His emotions told him to feel sorry for himself, but his logic told him that with some effort, he could get himself back into proper physical condition. He sided with logic.

Wayland dressed and stepped outside his room into the central courtyard. It was now about nine in the morning, and nobody seemed to be around. Suyin was probably running errands, Master Gao said he was going to be meeting a business acquaintance in town this morning, and Old Wu was nowhere to be seen. He had the place to himself, he thought. Might as well make some good use of his time, and it was easier to start exercising when nobody was there to watch him.

He started jogging in place, lightly and slowly at first. He had lost a good deal of weight from his ordeal, and he had only begun to put a few pounds back on in the last couple of weeks. He felt lean, but with so much time in bed, he also had a sensation of weakness that he had never known before. He remembered his mother, and sometimes even his father asking him to lift the heaviest boxes or packages at the mission; he was sure both of them were stronger then than he was now.

Wayland kept jogging in place, and he picked up his pace a bit. His leg was still a bit sore, but not in any one particular spot. He thought this was a good sign. He could feel himself breathing heavily, though. He sure didn't have his wind. After a few minutes, he stopped and put his hands on his knees as he caught his breath.

Strength, work on that. He dropped down to his knees and then extended his hands to try a few push-ups. He gingerly lowered his body down for the first one, testing his shoulder. A slight twinge of discomfort, but not too bad. He tried another one. A small jolt of pain shot through his shoulder. It wasn't bad enough that Wayland thought he had re-injured himself, but it hurt enough that he wasn't going to try any more push-ups today.

He stood and rubbed his shoulder and slowly swung his arm around, wincing slightly. No, he wasn't going to accept this. He had been in bed for weeks, and Suyin had been waiting on him like a child for longer than that. He was going to make himself stronger one way or another. He started jogging in place again, and then remembered another exercise from his boxing days back in America: jumping jacks. He bounced up and down a couple of times, spreading his legs and bringing his hands up over his head. It felt okay. He increased the intensity — three, four, five — and then another shot of pain, this time from his left leg. He sighed heavily and reached down to rub it. *Damn it, it hurt.*

"Aiya, so hard!" Old Wu said.

Wayland jerked his head back and was surprised to see Old Wu standing behind him.

"So hard," Old Wu repeated, shaking his head.

"What's so hard?" Wayland said.

"Everything you're doing. Are you intentionally trying to aggravate your injuries?"

"Of course not," Wayland said. "But I've got to build up my strength somehow. I've hardly done anything physical for a couple of months."

"Yes, you have to build up your strength, but in the right way," Old Wu said. He walked over to Wayland and put both hands on Wayland's shoulders. He frowned. "Everything so stiff and tense."

"Well, I want it to be stiff and tense," Wayland said,

increasingly annoyed at Old Wu's tone. "Not soft and weak."

"What do they teach you in that country of yours?" Old Wu said, shaking his head. "You think soft means weak?"

"I don't know. I'm sure you've got the answer though, so why don't you just tell me?" Wayland said.

"No, if you don't value my knowledge, you don't have to hear it. It makes no difference to me," Old Wu said, and he turned to walk away.

"Okay, okay," Wayland said. "I'm sorry. I'll listen. Tell me what I should do." He knew that Old Wu had tried to make him feel guilty, and it worked.

"Well, if you're really that interested," Old Wu said, and for a second Wayland thought he saw a slight smile cross the old man's face.

"Yes, I'm really, really interested," Wayland said. Despite his efforts to the contrary, Wayland was smiling himself.

"Do this," Old Wu said. He stood straight with his feet apart, and he extended both hands out, with his palms down. He slowly brought both hands down to his waist, and then raised them back up and repeated the movement.

Wayland adopted the same stance and tried to replicate Old Wu's movement.

Old Wu stopped and turned to Wayland. "Keep going," Old Wu said, and Wayland did. "Relax the shoulders. Relax the arms. Relax the waist. No, keep the spine straight, keep the head up and alert. To relax doesn't mean to go limp, it just means don't tense muscles that you aren't using."

"Okay," Wayland said. He kept moving his arms up and down slowly.

"Now get your whole body into it, but gently. The power comes from your feet and legs, push from the ground. The *chi* should go up your body like a wave on the ocean. Feel it move up your spine, up the top of your head, out to your arms. Your whole body should feel connected, like a string of pearls."

Wayland did as he was told, and something started to feel different. His body did feel connected. "It's like... dancing," he said.

"Yes, yes, very much like dancing," Old Wu said. "But the music is in your body, in your head. Now keep going, and breathe slowly and deeply. Feel the *chi* going through your body, going out to your fingertips."

Wayland had heard the term *chi* many times since he was in the country, and the Chinese seemed to apply it to so many things that Wayland could never really get a good grasp of exactly what it was. Was it breath, or energy, or blood circulation? But they also talked about *chi* in regards to houses and weather, food and medicine. He kept moving and tried to keep his body relaxed as Old Wu had instructed him. He didn't know about *chi*, but he could feel his body getting warmer, particularly the palms of his hands and the soles of his feet. "I'm feeling something."

"Yes," Old Wu said, not surprised. "Keep going." He put his hand on Wayland's left hip. "This was the leg you had broken. Shift your body to put just a little more weight on this leg. Gently."

Wayland did so, and he kept up with the gentle movements and deep breathing.

"Learn to feel your body... deeply. Feeling exertion and strain is good; feeling pain is not good. Learn to tell the difference. When you know how to listen, your body will tell you how far you can push it. Practice what I tell you, and you will get stronger without injuring yourself."

Wayland kept moving, and it did feel good. He nodded at Old Wu. Old Wu watched Wayland's exercise for another minute or so, not saying a word. "Am I doing it right?" Wayland asked.

Old Wu grunted in the affirmative. "More or less." The old man turned abruptly and walked away; he was mumbling something to himself, but Wayland couldn't make out what he said.

***

Later that afternoon, Wayland walked by the kitchen when Suyin called out to him.

"Hey, would you like some soup noodles?" she asked.

Wayland raised his eyebrows as he leaned his head into the kitchen. Suyin was working over a steaming pot of chicken stock boiling on the stove, and a stack of fresh noodles was on a plate just to the side.

It had taken Wayland a while to get used to the eating arrangements at the Gao compound. Living with his parents, they generally kept their three meals fairly regular and timely, and attendance was pretty much mandatory, barring some extenuating circumstances. For the first weeks at the Gao's, Wayland was unable to get out of bed, and Suyin or Old Wu had served him all of his meals. As he began to recover, though, he saw that meals were a little more casual for everyone here. Formal, extravagant dinners were generally reserved for special occasions; for most days, everyone in the compound took their meals when it suited them. Sometimes all or some of them ate together, but just as often they didn't, and it was up to each person to get something when they could. As Wayland still wasn't much of a cook, he wasn't about to pass up Suyin's offer.

"That sounds great," he said. Suyin ladled out the hot broth into the bowl and slipped some noodles in.

"Chili oil?" She asked.

"Please," Wayland said, and Suyin poured a small amount of oil on top of the noodles before handing the bowl and a spoon to Wayland.

"You like spicy food now, huh?" Suyin asked, smiling.

"Mmmph," Wayland muttered, trying to talk as he slurped up a spoonful of noodles. He chewed for a second and swallowed. "I'm getting to."

"Mmm... do I smell noodles?" Old Wu poked his head in and smiled.

"I've got some all ready for you, Old Wu. Here you go," Suyin said, handing the bowl of hot noodles she had just prepared for herself to Old Wu.

"You're such a good girl," Old Wu said, and he sat down on the chair over in the corner with his bowl, slurping noodles on the way.

Suyin smiled warmly, and Wayland noticed that it wasn't an affectation; she was genuinely happy to give her bowl to Old Wu. There was no annoyance on her face. She quickly prepared herself another dish and leaned against the wall as she took a sip of the still-steaming broth.

They all turned as Lunghui came walking in. Lunghui was in his mid-twenties, tall and thin, but wiry; probably quite strong, Wayland mused. Lunghui's face was grim.

"Do you want some noodles? I just made them," Suyin asked.

"No," Lunghui said. He paced back and forth as if he didn't know what he wanted. He finally reached to the cupboard for a jar of rice wine, and he poured himself a bowl. He gulped it down.

"A little early in the day for that, isn't it?" Old Wu said calmly, as he sipped a spoonful of broth. It was also quite unusual, as Lunghui wasn't much of a drinker. Lunghui didn't answer.

"What's the matter?" Suyin asked.

"I was just over in a neighborhood by the West Gate, getting some herbs for Master Gao at Cheng Yunxu's shop," Lunghui said, pouring himself another bowlful of wine from the ceramic jar. "He hadn't opened his shop since the fighting, and Master Gao had a long list of herbs for me to get."

"Did something happen to him?" Suyin asked.

"Not him, but to his niece Hualing, and her husband." He paused for a moment, gathering his words. "It seems that when the foreign troops entered the city, some of them started going house to house, breaking in to see what they could steal. They went in Hualing's house and found her there, with her husband and their son, only five years old. Her husband told them that they didn't have anything of value, and begged them to leave. They took Hualing into the back room and several of the troops... they raped her. When her husband tried to stop them, they shot him. Killed him in his own home."

"Aiya," Old Wu said, shaking his head.

"And when they finished with Hualing, she was so crazed with grief and shame that she screamed at them as they left, she begged them to kill her. And they did. They bayoneted her to death."

"Oh no... " Suyin said.

"That's what their little son told the family, and he saw it all," Lunghui said. "They left him alive, for some reason."

"What soldiers were they? German, or Russian? They couldn't have been Americans," Wayland asked, visibly shaken.

Lunghui stared at him coldly. "I don't know. Does it matter?"

"It matters a lot," Wayland said.

"Not to Cheng Yunxu and his family, it doesn't," Lunghui said. "Just foreign troops, that's all I know." He glared at Wayland and slammed his wine bowl down on the table, and then he stormed out.

"I can't believe Americans would do that," Wayland said, mostly to himself. Suyin looked down at the floor.

"Who knows?" Old Wu said as he went back to his noodles.

"Who knows why men do these things to other men, all under the eyes of Heaven?"

At about eight that evening the sun had set, and Wayland bid goodnight to Suyin, who was reading by lamplight in the library room. The incident that Lunghui had related still gnawed at him; Wayland had a pretty good idea of what Lunghui thought of foreigners, himself included. Yet, on that front, he knew much more than Lunghui did. He knew what was in his own heart, and he knew why his parents had come to China. It wasn't because they thought so little of the Chinese people; it was precisely the opposite. They believed that the Chinese were made in God's image, the same as all men, and they were worthy of salvation. Maybe all Westerners weren't like his parents, but he couldn't help that.

He walked into his room and shut the door, and then lit his oil lamp. He would read a while before he went to sleep, he thought. Old Wu would pick up the odd Western books for Wayland here and there when he found them. Some of them were German and French, which Wayland couldn't read, but most of them were English. As Old Wu didn't read English, it was always a mixed bag as to what he would bring back; sometimes it was a novel, sometimes it was nonfiction, and now and then it was some exceedingly dull technical manual. Whatever he brought, Wayland was always very grateful to Old Wu. And Wayland now had two copies of the English version of Jules Verne's *20,000 Leagues Under the Sea*, his all-time favorite story. He had already read it several time times before he even came to China, and it was like a warm, comforting link to his old life, to growing up in America, to his parents. To a happy past. He thought he'd start that book again.

It had been a warm day, typical for Tientsin at this time of the year, but it wasn't humid, and as the sun went down it was quite comfortable. Wayland spread his blankets out over his *k'ang*, and slipped out of his shirt and pants, down to his underwear. He rotated his right shoulder, the one that had been dislocated. It felt good. Really good, actually. He began circling it around, gently, just as Old Wu had shown him. After a few moments, his arm began to feel pleasantly warm. There was definitely something to this. Old Wu had some real insights, Wayland thought. He had to give him that.

Wayland brought his lamp to the side of his bed, got his book and lay down on his back. He opened up to the first chapter and began reading. Almost unconsciously, Wayland brought his left leg up and began circling it gently, as if he was pedaling a bicycle with it. This was the leg had been broken in two places, but it was feeling rather warm and comfortable at the moment. He continued the motions for a while as he lost himself in the mystery of the Nautilus; his eyes soon got heavy, and the book slowly dropped to his chest. The lamp continued to burn gently in the cool evening air as Wayland fell fast asleep.

14

WAYLAND'S RECOVERY progressed. He took to heart Old Wu's advice, and he began to listen to his body. The idea that moving so gently and slowly could actually build up his strength and stamina was somewhat of a revelation. At first, it seemed counter-intuitive, but he couldn't deny the reality of the results; he began to feel increasingly strong and full of energy. Old Wu would occasionally observe Wayland's practice, and now and then he would dole out some more tips.

The next week, he showed Wayland some of his personal exercises, which he called *chigong*, and Wayland saw that the elderly man seemed to be amazingly limber and flexible. When Wayland asked him how he was able to manage that, Old Wu gave a typically cryptic response: "Watch the noodle makers here in town. The way they stretch the noodles out to dry. Have you ever seen them?"

"I guess so, back in Fenchow," Wayland said.

"All right, same thing," Old Wu said. "Making noodles seems simple enough, but it's not that easy. The dough is malleable and must be properly stretched, but when beginners stretch them too far, the noodles break. The secret is stretching them far enough, but not too much; they must spring back, and not snap in two. It's an art that can only be learned from practice. Do you understand?"

"I think so," Wayland said.

"Good," Old Wu replied. "You have many noodles in your body." He bent down and pointed to Wayland's ankles, then his calves, his knees, and his thighs, and up to his waist. He touched his wrists and elbows, his shoulders and his neck. "Stretch them all, just far enough, but not too far." Old Wu brought both hands up above his head, and he slowly twisted his body to the right, and then to the left. Wayland was amazed at how far the old man could rotate, much further than he himself could.

"Thank you, Old Wu," Wayland said.

"And you must do this every day. Once or twice a month is no good. No good at all. Better to give up completely than do that. Do you hear me?"

"Yes," Wayland said.

And he did hear. The more that Old Wu told him, the more Wayland began to see that he was a man to be listened to. Despite his eccentric demeanor, he was keenly intelligent; more than that, he was wise. Wayland's father had explained to him the difference between intelligence and wisdom many times, and it was a lesson that always stuck with him.

"I'm not going to show you every exercise, you can figure it out your own. If you only do what I tell you, how can you ever achieve anything worthwhile? Learn the principles that I've taught you, and ponder them yourself," Old Wu said.

Wayland nodded and then turned as Master Gao approached.

"Old Wu, Wei-lin," Master Gao said, and both nodded.

"Wei-lin, you have made quite a remarkable recovery since you've been here," Master Gao said. "Some of that is due to your own effort, and I think you've had some help from Old Wu, here, as well."

"Yes," Wayland said. "I can't thank you enough for you and Old Wu bringing me here, and giving me time to recover."

Master Gao smiled and shook his head. "No need for thanks.

Our meeting was destined, I feel. Life is strange, and one must accept and appreciate what the heavens deem fit for us. You have been a respectful guest, and your presence here and recovery have been appreciated by all of us. I would like to invite you to a celebratory dinner in your honor, this evening. Would you do us the favor of attending?"

"Well... of course," Wayland said. "I don't think I deserve it, but... sure!"

"Excellent. Then it's set," Master Gao said. "Please wear your finest clothes, and dinner will be served in the main hall at seven o'clock."

"Ah, it will be a fine evening, I'm sure," Old Wu said.

Wayland bowed respectfully, and Master Gao and Old Wu walked away.

Wayland scratched the back of his neck. Surely Suyin and Old Wu already knew about the plans for this dinner? They would have had to plan the menu, and they would have done the shopping for the ingredients. They must have all been in on it and kept it from him. Wayland smiled and felt a warm twinge. They were planning on surprising him.

Wayland wore the best clothes he had, the best clothes that Master Gao had given him actually, and he arrived at the main hall a few minutes before seven. It was a clear day, and the temperature was pleasant. Suyin and Old Wu were already there, and the table was set quite elaborately. Numerous dishes in bright blue, red and yellow earthenware were on the table at the back; they were covered and steaming hot.

"Please, be seated," Suyin said to him, motioning towards one stool. "You sit here, facing East, facing the entrance. That's the seat of honor." Wayland nodded and took his seat. Wonderful aromas wafted through the air; the hot oil from stir-frying, the tang of vinegar, some hints of cinnamon and pork, garlic and chili pepper, and other smells that Wayland couldn't quite recognize, but which made his mouth water.

"Good evening, everyone," Lunghui said, as he came into the room. "Good evening, Wei-lin."

"Good evening," Wayland said. He smiled politely, but Lunghui still made him uncomfortable. Lunghui and Old Wu took their seats.

"Ah, it seems I am a bit late," Master Gao said, smiling as he came into the main hall.

"Not at all," Suyin said, bowing. "Everyone is just arriving."

"Good," Master Gao said. He put his hand on Suyin's shoulder and smiled. He looked at the perfect settings on the table, with all of the best plates, dishes, and bowls arranged in their proper places. "Thank you for all your work, Suyin."

"Please, sit," Suyin said to Master Gao. He did so, and all the guests were seated for the meal to commence.

Tea was served first, and Suyin filled each cup with steaming, freshly brewed tea. She filled her cup and then sat down.

After Suyin was seated, Master Gao stood and raised his cup of tea with both hands.

"Thank you, everyone, for being here tonight. This evening, we are honoring our Western guest, Wei-lin. His arrival here, as you all know, was a strange mixture of fate, circumstance, and coincidence. And even though young Mr Wei-lin has experienced a terrible tragedy in his life, we have been blessed by his presence here, and we hope that we have been able to offer some small degree of hospitality to him."

Master Gao turned directly to Wayland.

"Wei-lin, I can see from your character that your parents must indeed have been exceptional people. I am certain that they would be very proud of the man that you are, and tonight we celebrate your arrival at our home." He bowed slightly to Wayland. "May you enjoy good health and many blessings in your future." he took a sip of his tea, and everyone else did as well.

Wayland stood up and held his teacup in both hands. His gaze panned across the room as he looked fondly at each of the diners. He felt a lump in his throat and tears welling up in his eyes, but he forced them back.

"Master Gao, I can't thank you enough for your kindness. You've brought me, a complete stranger and a foreigner, into your home and you've treated me like family. My parents thought enough of China to travel halfway across the world to serve the people, and I can now see that their goal was even more worthy than they knew. Thank you, all of you."

They all drank their second cup of tea, and then it was time for the meal. Old Wu brought the first plate to the center of the table; it was cooked eggplant cut into bite-sized pieces and slathered with a salty garlic sauce. Each took a couple of pieces and placed them on the small plate in front of them.

Wayland took a couple of bites with his chopsticks and smiled up at Old Wu. "Mmm... excellent," he said.

"My wife showed me how to make that dish many, many years ago. It was her favorite dish," Old Wu said. It was clear from his tone that he genuinely appreciated Wayland's praise.

Suyin brought over the next dish, and she placed that next to the eggplant. "This is called *Lianpi*," she said to Wayland. "It's a dish of noodles with hot chili oil and our local vinegar."

Wayland nodded respectfully. He was familiar with the dish, as he had had it once or twice in Fenchow, but this version was prepared a little differently.

Suyin turned her chopsticks over to use the other ends and served the others; she placed a serving of the oil and vinegar-slathered noodles on each of the diners' plates, and finally on her own.

"Mmm... " Wayland murmured as he inhaled deeply. He was famished, and the aroma of the tangy vinegar sauce was deliciously enticing. Suyin smiled to herself at Wayland's enthusiasm.

"So, you like Chinese food now, Wei-lin?" Old Wu asked as he slurped up a mouthful of the spicy noodles.

"I do," Wayland said, as he deftly used his chopsticks to pick up a small piece of eggplant. "When you're hungry, you eat anything that's served to you."

Master Gao smiled politely and nodded as he ate his noodles.

Wayland immediately realized that what he said didn't come out exactly the way he intended. "Oh, I'm sorry," he said, shaking his head, "that doesn't sound right. I've come to love the food here; it's excellent. But it does take a while for one's tastes to adjust to a whole other style of cooking when you've been used to something else for so long."

"Do you miss Western food?" Suyin asked.

"Not too much," Wayland said. He thought about it for a moment. "Maybe just a couple things. Cheese and bread, I guess."

"I liked the Western bread I've tried," Old Wu said. "But cheese... " he wrinkled his face and shook his head. "Tasted like sour milk to me. And too rich." He chuckled.

Wayland laughed heartily. "Well, some kinds are stronger than others. I guess it's an acquired taste."

"Speaking of new tastes," Old Wu said, "Suyin, let's get the main dishes on."

Suyin nodded, and she and Old Wu went back to the counter next to the stove. They each brought two covered plates back to the table.

"These are dumplings made with lamb and carrots," Suyin said, lifting the lid off the first plate. "It's another of Old Wu's recipes."

Wayland's eyes brightened at the scrumptious-looking, still steaming dumplings.

"Those are my favorite," Lunghui said, grinning.

"Oh, what's this?" Wayland asked as Old Wu approached with another covered plate.

Old Wu lifted the lid off. "This is steamed, fried pork. Pieces of pork are steamed and then dipped in egg and quickly fried, and then a sauce is made of soy, wine, and chili pepper. Very tasty, a favorite dish in Tientsin."

"And for Master Gao, some simple stir-fried spinach," Suyin said, lifting the lid off another plate to reveal a shiny, bright green plate of steaming spinach in a light sauce.

"I need some plain dishes. I can't eat too much rich food," Master Gao said. "Suyin takes care of me. She's an excellent cook."

"I can tell," Wayland said, smiling at her. Suyin bowed slightly and smiled back with just a hint of embarrassment.

"And what about me?" Old Wu said, with mock indignation. "I made those dumplings all by myself, you know."

Master Gao raised his eyebrows and turned to Wayland. He waited to finish his chewing and then said, "Old Wu is quite a good cook too, you know. That's the truth."

"Well, you learn a lot when you've had about a hundred and fifty years of practice," Lunghui said.

"Mind your manners, youngster," Old Wu said, and playfully tapped Lunghui on the top of the head. "You should be so lucky to be as sharp as I am when you reach my age."

"And speaking of manners," Master Gao said. "We can't have a proper meal without some good wine."

"I'll get it," Suyin said, but Master Gao waved his hand.

"You sit down and eat, Suyin," he said. "I'll get it." Master Gao went over to the counter and brought out the tray of freshly washed, blue-patterned wine cups. Each guest took a cup, and then Master Gao brought over a black ceramic jar with a bright red paper seal over the top.

"Do you like Chinese wine?" Suyin asked Wayland.

"To be honest, my parents only drank alcohol on a few holidays, and it was always a European wine. I haven't had much Chinese wine."

"Ah, then you're in for a treat," Old Wu said, rubbing his hands together. "Some of the finest wines in China come out of this region."

Master Gao sat down and broke the paper seal, and Suyin took the jar and poured a drink for Wayland, then filled the other guests' wine cups, and finally her own.

Master Gao raised his cup, and everyone at the table did the same; Wayland followed suit.

"Drain your cup!" Master Gao said, smiling.

Master Gao and each of the guests downed their cupful of wine, but Wayland hesitated a bit. He brought the cup to his nose, inhaling the strong, sweet aroma of the alcohol. The others looked over at Wayland, and their pregnant expressions told him that they expected him to do the same.

Wayland downed his, and even though the wine was at room temperature, it felt warmer than that going down. It was MUCH stronger than the red wine his parents drank at Christmas. "Whooh," Wayland uttered, coughing a bit. He waved his hand back and forth in front of his mouth of few times, and the others laughed. Their laughter wasn't mocking though, it was warm and jovial, and Wayland chuckled too. "What's it called?"

"It's called *fenjiu*. It's a specialty from the area. It's made from sorghum, and then distilled. A little bit like your whiskey," Old Wu said.

"I've never actually had whiskey, so I guess I'll just take your word for it," Wayland said.

"Just remember, when you drink a toast, you have to finish your whole cup in one drink," Lunghui said. "And it's rude to refuse to drink, too." He picked up the wine jar and poured another round for everyone.

Old Wu raised his glass. "To the Eight Immortals of the Wine Cup!"

"To the Eight Immortals of the Wine Cup," they all repeated and downed their cupful.

"Who were they?" Wayland asked. He could feel himself grinning a little more than he meant to; the *fenjiu* was having its effect on him.

"They were a group of Tang Dynasty scholars, known for their love of wine and poetry," Old Wu said. He slowly stroked his beard, and then his face brightened and he raised his finger as he remembered the line he was searching for:

"Li Bai drinks one measure of wine and writes a
hundred poems;
He sleeps in a wine shop in Chang'an market;
Even if the emperor himself should come to invite
him, he would not board
the imperial barque."

Suyin clapped and laughed. Wayland smiled, and his gaze stayed on her. She didn't laugh often, but when she did, her laugh was vibrant, warm and genuine. She brought her wine cup to her mouth and took a sip. Her hands were so feminine and graceful, her smile so gentle, yet with just a hint of sadness. Something about her. She might not be considered beautiful by conventional standards, but after all, wasn't beauty in the eye of the beholder? *And I'm the beholder.* Wayland could feel a gentle warmth moving from his chest and up to his face. Probably just the alcohol. No, not just the alcohol. Wayland realized that he had been staring at Suyin long enough that others might notice, and Suyin looked up and caught his eyes. They held each others' gaze for a split second, and then both turned away. Lunghui looked at Wayland with subtle displeasure; Wayland glanced over to Master Gao, who was observing all with a gentle bemusement.

The *fenjiu* flowed, and all savored the food. Wayland couldn't ever remember enjoying any meal more than this. The group laughed and talked and ate their food quite leisurely. Everyone especially enjoyed Old Wu's stories about his younger days, when he first started learning martial arts and was hopelessly clumsy and slow-witted. They all chuckled at that, because it was quite clear, at least to Wayland, that the old man had probably never been too slow-witted. But like most truly wise and kind-hearted people, Old Wu could laugh at himself and most enjoyed telling stories where he was the fool.

There was a pause in the conversation, and Lunghui saw his chance to address an issue that had been weighing on his mind. "I have to ask, Wei-lin, and I mean no offense, but... why did you and your family come here, to China? I know you're missionaries and you believe in your religion, but still. Why do you have to travel around the world for that? Can't you just practice it in your own country?" His tone was polite, and his expression was benign, but Wayland sensed something of a challenge from Lunghui.

"Well," Wayland said, measuring his words thoughtfully, "my parents believed very strongly in their faith, and they wanted to spread it as much and as far as they could."

"But still, you know that Chinese people have their own religions and beliefs? Our civilization is thousands of years old. Did they not think that was worth anything?" Lunghui said.

Old Wu frowned, and Master Gao raised his index finger slightly to Lunghui. "Lunghui, this is a dinner in Wei-lin's honor; we're not here to interrogate him. Remember your manners."

"I'm sorry," Lunghui said with sincerity, but with a hint of annoyance.

Wayland smiled and shook his head. "That's okay. I don't mind talking about it. It's a legitimate question."

"For Chinese, it's considered impolite to argue about serious matters over dinner," Suyin said quietly to Wayland.

"But if you want to answer, you may do so, Wei-lin," Master Gao said.

Wayland could tell from his expression that perhaps he also wanted to hear what Wayland had to say about this.

"Thank you," Wayland said. If there was anything that still caused him difficulty in this country, it was Chinese social graces. Things that would seem innocuous to Westerners sometimes were considered quite rude by the Chinese, and vice-versa.

Wayland scratched his temple, thinking of how he could possibly sum up his parents' beliefs—their lives—over a few minutes of dinner conversation.

"I guess I would put it like this. My parents believed that Christianity is true; is *the truth*. But they didn't look down on Buddhism, or Taoism or the folk religions here in China. All religions teach many of the same truths, and in all countries. These are truths that all men know in their hearts. We all know it's wrong to steal, to cheat, to murder, to lie, to commit adultery. We know that greed and cruelty are always wrong, and that kindness and compassion are always good."

"That's right, we Chinese believe the same things. So why do you have to bring Christianity here?" Lunghui said. He looked at Master Gao and then back to Wayland. "Again, I mean no disrespect to you or your parents. But other foreigners have come here and have taken advantage of the Chinese, to take from us and give nothing back."

"I can't answer for all foreigners," Wayland said. "I don't understand politics or international relations, or trade agreements. I can only speak for my parents and the other missionaries I knew. You asked why they preached Christianity? I said they appreciated many aspects of Chinese religions, and they did if the different religions were in agreement on something. But if they disagreed, then my parents believed in the Christian view. That's just logic. If the two religions say different things about something, then they can't both be true. Christianity says that all men are made in the image of God and have an eternal soul, and my parents thought that the Chinese souls were just as valuable as the souls of foreigners, and can be saved in the same way. That's why they came."

"Then how do you explain all the other foreigners doing terrible things in China? Don't they believe your Christian religion? Why are they so awful if they were given the so-called truth of Christianity?" Lunghui said.

Wayland nodded. "Do the Chinese believe it's wrong to steal?"

"Of course," Lunghui said.

"And do some Chinese people steal?"

"Well... yes... " Lunghui said.

Wayland took another sip of his *fenjiu*. He had never been drunk before, but he figured that he was pretty close at this point. He shrugged his shoulders. "Of course they do. Christianity says that all men are flawed, fallen creatures, who gravitate towards sin. This is true of all men. I don't know if I believe everything that my parents did, but I certainly believe this. I've never seen anything to make me think this isn't true."

"But there are good men and bad men, surely?" Lunghui said. "There is a difference."

"I sure don't know everything," Wayland said. "I'm not a preacher like my father. I'm just telling you what I've been taught. I guess Christianity teaches that good men might not be as good as you think, and bad men might still be saved."

"I have read some of your Bible," Old Wu said, as he stroked his white beard. "There is much wisdom there, although many of its moral precepts, from what I can understand, have already been taught in China for centuries before your religion arrived on these shores."

Wayland nodded. "My father said as much. Truth is truth, and all men have some understanding of it."

Master Gao smiled benignly, and he scratched the back of his neck. He looked down at the table for a moment, gathering his thoughts before he looked back up to Wayland. "Perhaps there is something from our Chinese traditions that you might ponder, Wei-lin. There is a saying in Taoism. It says 'The great *Tao* is only two or three sentences. Once spoken, it's worth less than two pennies.' Do you understand what that means?"

Wayland's brow furrowed, and he shook his head. "I don't think so."

"It means that understanding is not the same thing as comprehension."

Wayland thought for a moment and then shook his head again.

Master Gao rubbed his chin. "Let me put it this way. Words come easily to men. But words aren't the same as experience. This life that we are given can only be truly understood by living it."

Old Wu brought his wine cup to his lips and downed the rest of his *fenjiu*. He set the cup back down on the table and raised his index finger. "Very true, Master. However… " Old Wu hiccuped twice and then continued. "On this subject, I feel I must quote the renowned poet of antiquity, Bao Juyi, who, in his poem "The Philosopher," said:

> "Those who speak know nothing;
> Those who know are silent."
> These words were spoken by Lao Tzu.
> If we are to believe that Lao Tzu
> Was himself one who knew,
> How comes it that he wrote a book
> Of five thousand words?"

Master Gao burst out with a hearty belly-laugh, as did Suyin and Lunghui. It took Wayland a moment, but then he too began to chuckle. Old Wu had a mischievous smile on his face as he reached for the wine jar to pour another round for all.

15

THE NEXT MORNING Wayland was up early. He had a medium-sized map of Tientsin spread out on his table, and he was tracing a path on it with his index finger. From what Master Gao and the others had told him, the city had calmed down quite a bit from the violence and mayhem of the previous weeks. Suyin had brought him this English map of the city, and Wayland had studied it enough that he felt he had a pretty good grasp of the layout and the sections. He thought that it was time for him to venture beyond Master Gao's walls; he couldn't stay hidden forever. And Wayland had one overriding priority: to wire his grandparents in Boston to let them know that he was still alive. He could hardly imagine the grief they would have experienced after being informed that their daughter and son-in-law had been killed, and in such a brutal, senseless fashion. His grandparents had always doted on him, and he was sure that the news of his survival would at least bring them a glimmer of hope and strength. He wasn't positive exactly what his grandparents had been told about him, since his body was not found with his parents, but he figured that they would have assumed the worst.

Tientsin was home to just over a million people, much larger than Fenchow. Being a port city, it was also much more cosmopolitan. With the foreign concession areas in the southeast part of the city, foreigners were much more commonplace here. Whether that was was helpful or detrimental to Wayland at this point was unclear to him. Despite the violence and conflict of recent weeks In Tientsin, Wayland still thought he would stick out slightly less here than he did in Fenchow. Suyin had offered to go out with him and take him around the city, but Wayland politely refused. He felt that he had been sheltered enough over the last three months, and it was time that he took responsibility for his situation.

Wayland walked out of the gate of the Gao compound at a little after 8:30 in the morning. He felt some slight anxiety going out by himself, as the memories of those last few days in Fenchow were still fresh in his mind. He glanced both ways as he came out onto the street, but there were few people around. Several yards to the left, an old woman was carrying home her morning shopping, and on the other side of the street to his right was a young mother doing her best to keep her two rambunctious boys under control. Wayland wore his usual blue breeches and jacket, and with his hat pulled down he wasn't too conspicious, despite the fact that he wore his black hair short rather than in the queue that was standard for Chinese men. He walked calmly towards the East Gate of the walled section of the city. His walk even looked mostly Chinese. It probably wouldn't make sense to most people back in America, Wayland mused, that Chinese people walked differently. But they did. After a few years in China, Wayland himself was able to quickly pick out a foreigner on the streets just by the way they walked, even if he couldn't see the man or woman's face. It wasn't something you could put your finger on—it wasn't a matter of grace or strength, vigor or propriety. It was just slightly, minutely different.

Wayland had asked Suyin, Master Gao, and Old Wu if there was an American concession in Tientsin, but they couldn't seem to agree. Master Gao thought there was one, but Suyin said that there used to be, but it was now part of the British area, and

Old Wu wasn't sure. There were undoubtedly several telegraph stations in the city, and Wayland finally decided to find one in the British Concession. He had learned to speak Chinese rather quickly, and he was fluent. But he had only cursory familiarity with other European languages, and he wasn't keen to try to conduct business in French or German. And like most Americans, he felt an instinctive affinity for the British. Despite any political or cultural differences between the two nations, they were, in a sense, family.

It was a bright, ideal autumn day as Wayland made his way through the old walled city. He came through the East Gate and out into the surrounding streets. The signs of the battles from earlier in the year were everywhere. Buildings that had been shelled, storefronts boarded up, and piles of rubble and trash were on all sides. He overheard a pair of older men talking and pointing at a damaged section of the wall surrounding the old city, and one man said that there were rumors that the foreigners were going to take down the wall altogether and widen all the streets. Wayland looked around at all the houses and buildings and storefronts crowding into the narrow streets, and he had no idea how anyone would go about widening them.

He continued east and finally came to the Chin-Tang bridge spanning the Peiho river. The river was probably a hundred yards wide at that point, and the bridge was busy with a variety of traffic. There were pedestrians on foot, the odd horse or ox-drawn cart, merchants pushing hand-carts of their wares, and several rickshaws. A small troop of soldiers came marching in formation from the opposite direction, and as they got closer, Wayland recognized them as Japanese. The local Chinese didn't seem to be paying them much attention, and so Wayland didn't either. He kept his head down and kept moving. A dog was barking up ahead, and Wayland smiled. Dogs sound the same the world over. As he walked along, he saw the dog through the crowd. It was small and brown, a mutt of some sort, the kind of dogs you saw all around China. Wayland kneeled and whistled. The dog turned its head at the sound, saw Wayland down at his level, and trotted over, its tail wagging excitedly. Wayland held his hand out, the dog licked it happily, its tail never stopping. Wayland reached into his pack and pulled out one of the pork buns that Suyin had packed for him. The dog caught a scent, and its eyes lit up. Wayland broke off a piece of the bun and tossed it up in the air; the dog grabbed it before it hit the ground and gulped it down. It turned and looked expectantly at Wayland for the next bite.

"Okay, you'll get one more," Wayland said. He tossed another piece of the bun to the dog, and then put the rest in his own mouth. As the dog quickly ate his portion and then gazed up at his human benefactor, Wayland stood and looked over the iron railing of the bridge down to the water a few yards below. The river was a dark gray-green color, and it flowed slowly but steadily under the bridge. Wayland didn't know if large bodies of water had the same mesmerizing effect on others as they did on him, but they always brought out his pensive, reflective side. The water continued its steady motion underneath him, at its constant, indifferent speed. There were several small boats close by on the river, one ferrying passengers, another to the left and further downstream carrying a load of tightly bound cotton. A small boat came out from under the bridge just under Wayland. A young woman was poling the flat-bottomed craft, and she had a considerable cargo of fresh fish in the aft of the boat. She hummed gently as she piloted her way downriver, and Wayland recognized the melody; it was a song that one of the women at the mission had often sung.

"Hi there," Wayland called out, and the woman turned and

looked up at him. She smiled and waved, and then turned back to steering her boat, still humming her tune. Wayland watched as the current carried her on down the river. He thought of his father. "There are no 'ordinary' people," his father had said. "That's what Christ has taught us: each person you meet is unique, an immortal soul, made in the image of God."

Sometimes it was hard to believe, to comprehend the world and other people in that way, Wayland thought. Still, at a fundamental level, it did ring true. He watched as the woman and her boat floated further down the river and shrank into the distance.

He came off the bridge on the east side of the river, and turned down a street on the right to continue south, to the British concessions. A bell jingled behind him, and Wayland turned and stepped out of the way as a rickshaw driver pulled his cart past; the driver was carrying a well-to-do Chinese couple who were dressed in Western clothes. Wayland stopped walking for a moment and looked around. There was almost as much damage from the battles on this side of the river, with half-demolished houses and rubble a common sight. To his left, an older Chinese man was hammering up boards on what was presumably his dry-goods store, and his wife was sweeping out in front.

"Hello," Wayland said politely as he walked by, and the man nodded.

To Wayland's right, there was a tea-house restaurant that had a big sign up that said "open for business," even though a tarp had been hung over a large hole on the second story. Wayland saw several people going inside. They had a few customers, at least. As Wayland walked past the building, he got the distinct aroma of fried pork, scallions and ginger, and it made his mouth water. Maybe he'd stop there on the way back.

He had planned on sticking close to the riverbank, as he

had to cross over again to get to the British concessions back on the west side (given the layout of the Peiho river, it was a more direct route to cross it twice where it looped rather than follow along its west bank.) He wasn't always confident about his sense of direction, but the road was unusually broad and went right along the side of the river — it would be hard to lose his way.

Wayland wiped his brow; it was a crisp, cool day, but the sun was shining, and he was starting to sweat a bit. Up ahead there was some significant activity going on. A crew of eight or nine men was working with carts and wheelbarrows, loading rubble from a large stone building, almost entirely destroyed by shelling. A Western man was directing the Chinese workers, and as Wayland got closer, he heard the Westerner more clearly; his Chinese wasn't very good, and he had a distinctly American accent. He was tall, thin and bald, with a thick beard, and a focused demeanor. The appeal of talking to a fellow American was too much for Wayland to resist.

Wayland thought he'd have a little fun with the man first, though. "What are you up to?" Wayland said in Chinese.

"Busy," the American said back in Chinese. He waved his hand in the air, dismissing Wayland.

"You sure you know what you're doing?" Wayland said loudly, in English.

The man turned to Wayland with a frown, and he stared for a moment, perplexed.

Wayland took his hat off and ran his hand through his hair, and he smiled. "American."

"Well... what are you doing dressed like a Chinaman? You a missionary or something?" the man said. His expression was still gruff, but his tone was friendly. He held out his hand.

"Something like that," Wayland said, and he shook the man's hand. "It's a long story."

"Bill Edmonds,' the man said.

"Wayland Cooper. So what are you doing here?" Wayland asked.

"Just trying to rebuild the city, put people to work, that sort of thing," Edmonds said. "This is a work crew. We're getting them together all over the city. The TPG is organizing it. Job creation, get people working, pay 'em some wages, and distribute food."

"What's the 'TPG'? Wayland asked.

"Tientsin Provisional Government," Edmonds said. "Where have you been? Did you just get into China?"

"No, I've been in the country a while, but not that long in Tientsin," Wayland said, scratching the back of his neck. "Just out of touch, I guess."

"After we put down the Boxers a couple of months ago, the Eight Nations got together to administer the city. Lots of things to do. Food and water shortages, disgruntled people. We want to bring some order here. We don't want people starving and begging. The Chinese don't like to beg, you know. They got as much pride as anyone, if not more. That's why we get 'em working like this. That's why the TPG confiscated all the private food stores."

"Don't the Chinese have their own organizations, to look after the poor and distribute food and things?" Wayland asked.

"Sure they do. And I know you missionaries do stuff like that too. But the problem is—and no offense intended—they all play favorites. Even you religious folks. Food makes its way to the people they want it to, and it don't get to the people they don't want it to. That leaves a lot of hungry, angry people, and that's a recipe for more fightin', son. We try to deliver it pretty fair-like, if I do say so. Makes things run a lot smoother in the big picture."

Wayland nodded, as he looked over the crew loading stones onto a big horse-drawn cart. "Sounds good," he said. He wasn't sure he bought Edmonds' line of reasoning, but he wasn't in a mood to argue and didn't feel that he understood the situation enough to engage in much debate.

"Say, where are you from in the States?" Edmonds asked.

"Boston area," Wayland said.

Edmonds shook his head. "Never been East. I'm from Montana, way out in the mountains. Never thought I'd end up in China. But I got a cousin in San Francisco. He told me Uncle Sam was looking for some construction engineers to go to China, and they offered a good price. What the hell, I said to myself. It'll be an adventure. Been here about two months. I like the place. I like the people. I would'a made fun of Chinamen before I got over here, but when you spend some time as a stranger in their country, and you see everythin' they built and what kind of folks they are, it kinda changes your perspective a bit, you know? Takes some gettin' used to, though, that's for sure. Where you headin'?"

"Going to send a telegram to people back home," Wayland said. "I think I'm going to the British concession... or is there an American one? I can never get a straight answer on that."

"There's *kind* of an American one. It's on the map, and there's a few buildings that ol' Uncle Sam uses, for the troops and such. But for the most part, it's just a section of the British area. Yeah, that's the place to go. Germans and French are okay, but I can't understand a goddamn word they're saying."

Wayland grinned and nodded. "Well, I've got to get going. Best of luck to you."

"You too, son. I hope you find what you're looking for."

16

WAYLAND CONTINUED south through the narrow, bustling streets of Tientsin for another half mile or so, until he again met the Peiho river and came to another bridge. The steam horn of a locomotive sounded to his left and he realized he was close to the train tracks that led from the ports to further inland. The size of Tientsin again struck him. It was a very big city.

The bridge was a bit old and dilapidated, but the traffic on it was steady. Rickshaws and pedestrians, merchants with mule-drawn carts, men on horseback, and the odd camel and driver were all making their way over the bridge. Wayland stuck to the right-hand side as he made his way across, and he occasionally glanced down at the gray-green water flowing slowly but steadily underneath. Junks and smaller boats made their way under the bridge, all going about their various business. As Wayland got to the other side, he saw a large white sign with black lettering written in several languages, including English: "Entering French Concession."

He immediately noticed the difference in architecture. Interspersed with the more traditional Chinese buildings were grand Western structures that wouldn't have looked out of place in any European or American city. His French was a little rusty, but as he walked through the concession, he could make out the signs for "hospital," "police," and "school."

The French concession had been in place since 1860, and

within its boundaries, French law applied, not Chinese. Order was kept by a garrison of French marines, as well as local Chinese militiamen under French authority. French courts decided guilt or innocence in any criminal cases involving foreigners; if the parties to a case were all Chinese, though, the French usually left it to the Chinese courts.

Wayland continued. Although he didn't see a sign announcing that he had passed into the British concession area, he figured that must be the case as the street signs were now all in English. He came to an intersection, and he could see that the next street over, parallel to the one he was on, was much wider; it had to be the main street of the British concession. As he crossed over to it, he saw a street sign that said "Victoria Road," and it was indeed the main thoroughfare.

Wayland had never visited England, but as he walked down the tree-lined Victoria Road, it wasn't hard to imagine that he was strolling down a street in London. Classic British architecture was everywhere, from the Tientsin Anglo-Chinese School building and the London Missionary Society to the banks and trading companies, several stores, a rather modern-looking hospital, and numerous stately private mansions. The buildings on his left had the waters of the Peiho thirty yards behind them, as Victoria Road ran parallel to the river. Just on the other side of the river was the Russian concession area.

Wayland looked up to see a formation of some twenty mounted troops approaching on the right side of the road. He stepped further over to the left, far out of their way. As they approached, he saw that the riders were rather dark-skinned and with full beards. They wore beige uniforms and red and white striped turbans, and each had a cartridge belt slung diagonally over his shoulder and chest. In their right hands, each held vertically a long spear which was adorned with a small, triangular red and white flag near the point. These were some of the famed Bengal Lancers of the British army that Wayland had heard about. He stood and watched as they trotted by. Each had a saber in a scabbard around their waist, as well as a rifle in a holster attached to their saddle. They were undoubtedly a formidable force. None of them seemed even to notice Wayland as they went past.

Soon he came to the Astor House hotel on his left, a rather impressive building; it was a three-story structure with a veranda and the main tower facing to the west. There was probably a telegraph station in there, Wayland thought, but to his right, just across the street was an even more stately structure; this must be Gordon Hall, Wayland thought. Gordon Hall was the seat of the British government in Tientsin, and its size was indeed awe-inspiring. It looked to Wayland like nothing so much as a medieval English or Scottish castle transported to present-day China. A striking Union Jack flag flew proudly from the parapets of each of the two turrets that book-ended the massive stone structure.

He came to the main entrance, where a British guard stood watch. Wayland wasn't clear on how tight the security was for Gordon Hall, but he did notice that numerous Chinese and foreigners were walking around the grounds. Wayland decided to approach the guard.

"Excuse me, sir," Wayland said in English. "Is there a telegraph station inside?"

The guard responded in a formal tone. "There is indeed, sir," he said in a cockney accent. "Inside and to your right."

"Thank you," Wayland said, and the man nodded.

He walked into Gordon Hall and was struck by the bustle of activity going on under the high ceilings of the lobby. There were well-dressed English civilians, uniformed military officers, and Chinese locals moving about. He saw two British Indian soldiers engaged in a heated debate with each other, a couple of Japanese officers making their way to the exit, and two civilian men in expensive suits passed by him speaking Italian. Wayland continued over to the right, and he saw the sign that read "Telegraph Station."

He walked up to the window of the office and saw the clerk looking down with frustration, tapping his pen and focusing on the figures he was adding up. The man glanced up briefly as he noticed Wayland, and then looked back down at his paper. "Can I help you?" he said.

"Yes. I'd like to send a telegram to America, to Boston, in particular. Is that something you could do?"

"Certainly, sir," the man said. "Who is the recipient, and what is the message?"

Wayland dictated the telegram to his grandparents in Boston, letting them know that he was alive and well, expressing his sorrow over his parents' death, and explaining that he would be remaining in China for some time and that they shouldn't worry. He also requested that they convey to the rest of the family his situation and that he would be in touch with them in the near future.

"Very good, sir," the clerk said. He read the text back to Wayland. "How is that?"

"Yes, that sounds fine," Wayland said, nodding.

"I'm very sorry for your loss, Mr Cooper," the clerk said.

Wayland nodded. "Thank you."

"My name is Waithbraite. Tom, actually. So, you weren't in Tientsin during the troubles over the summer?"

"I was recovering from my injuries. But no, I wasn't aware of everything that went on."

"Whew," the clerk said. His tone was much more casual. "It

was nip and tuck there for a while, I can tell you that. Quite a battle against the Boxers. We didn't know if any of us were going to make it out alive. Gordon Hall here, this was our last stand. We had over 300 women and children here, holed up. You can still see some of the damage in the hall here from the fighting."

Wayland looked around. Everything seemed so normal and businesslike, and it was hard to picture the building on the verge of being overrun.

"Yes sir, it was a close run thing. Right around the 20th of June. I remember the date because it was the one-year anniversary of my first day on the job here. Well sir, we thought we were done for. When the Chinese government troops joined the Boxers and started firing on us, it wasn't looking good. Why, there was hardly a building in the concession that wasn't hit by fire. We had barricades up around all the streets to keep them from advancing. Your American Marines played a great role in defending us, I must say. Our Captain Bailey led them and some of our own troops in a bayonet charge, and they drove the Chinese back. Saved every foreigner in Gordon Hall. At one point, I even picked up a rifle myself, and I barely know which end to point at the enemy. Lucky I didn't have to use it though. Probably would have shot my foot off if I had!"

"Well, I guess I'm glad I missed it," Wayland said.

"It was awful, just awful," the clerk said. "So many lives lost... such a terrible waste."

Wayland paid the man. "Thank you again," he said.

"Best of luck," the man said. "I'll get that telegram out shortly."

Wayland walked back towards the exit. On a bench by the door, he saw a newspaper. It was a British paper, *The Daily Telegraph*, not a paper published in Tientsin. Wayland picked it up, and one article stuck out:

The Looting of Tientsin. Spoils to the Victors. Some Big Hauls.
The conduct of the "foreign devils" is not likely to impress John Chinaman with the virtues of European civilization. Laffan's correspondent's account of the looting of Tientsin sounds more like the proceedings of Drake's privateers in the Spanish Main than the operations of organized troops of great nations at the end of this century of light and learning...

The article described in great detail the looting that had taken place in the city during the unrest. From priceless artwork and antiques to jewels, furs, and cash, nothing was off-limits. The looters were from all the major powers in China: Russians, Japanese, British, Americans, French, Germans and Austrians. Common soldiers grabbed what they could find and hold, and in some cases the higher ranking officers even drew up plans and procedures to regulate the wanton theft and pillaging.

Wayland sighed and looked up from the paper. Hard to believe that that kind of chaos and lawlessness had been going on right around here just a few months ago. You can expect individual people to steal and rob out of selfish motives. But for the looting to be organized, and on such a massive scale; it wasn't hard to see why anti-foreigner groups like the Boxers had their appeal among the Chinese.

Wayland tucked the paper under his arm and made his way out of Gordon Hall and back to Victoria Street to head home. Overall, his day had been a success. He felt a sense of accomplishment, some satisfaction for having done his duty and informing his family that he was still alive. He tried to put himself in the shoes of his grandparents and other relatives. They had the same tragic loss that he did, but they were half a world away; also, they didn't have much of a frame of reference for his parents' life in China. The news of his survival would surely be a bright spot for them in these dark times. He had got on quite well with both sets of grandparents, and he knew that they not only loved him but that now he was a living link to his parents, the beloved children that they had lost. He was at least happy to be able to bring some good news to someone out of the terrible events of the last six months.

He paused as he looked over at a building on the other side of the street: Watson's Pharmacy. There was a British woman, probably in her thirties, standing just under the stone archway entrance. She wore glasses and had the book-smart appearance of some kind of civil servant. She had a dog on a leash, a small terrier of some sort. Wayland smiled as the woman squatted down to pet the dog, who put his front paws on the woman's knees and began licking her face. With the woman, the dog, and the storefront, for a moment Wayland could imagine that he was back in America, Boston or San Francisco, maybe. As he watched the woman, a Chinese laborer walked past her. The man wore a blue cotton shirt and pants, almost identical to what Wayland was wearing. The woman was focused on her dog and didn't look up as the man walked by her. The man and the woman were from two different worlds, and after all that had transpired, Wayland didn't really feel that he belonged to either.

17

W AYLAND WAS BACK at the East Gate of the walled city a little after five. Although there was still another half-hour before sunset, the sky had become overcast and the daylight was fading. He took some comfort in his recognition of the main avenue that he had come down this morning. His sense of direction wasn't the strongest, and it was always a bit of relief for him when he was finally sure of his location and route. One or two of the restaurants he passed had already lit their lamps, and they added a warm glow to the bustling street. Other shopkeepers were closing up their stores and stables for the day and preparing to head back home for the evening meal.

Master Gao didn't pay him much for his work other than room and board, but he did pay some. Since Wayland rarely left the compound, he didn't have much chance to spend anything and his funds had been starting to add up. It would be nice if he brought back a little something that everyone could enjoy. He remembered his friend Lihao had once brought them an aged vinegar as a gift, one that he said was the pride of Shensi cuisine, the best in China. Wayland and his family had found the flavor a bit strange at first but soon loved it. It became his mother's favorite vinegar to dress greens with. The vinegars that they had at Master Gao's were fine, but they didn't quite have that unique flavor. What was the brand name? Wayland tried to think. *Donghu.* That was it. He'd bring back a couple of bottles of that.

Up on the right was a weathered wooden sign hanging over a small doorway, and in bright red script was written "Wine and Dry Goods." Wayland pushed open the heavy oak door and stepped inside. He was immediately hit with the strange yet fairly pleasant aroma of various herbs, spices, alcohol, and vegetables. It was a small establishment, but every square inch was packed with neatly arranged bottles, tins, and boxes of all kinds of goods. Many things Wayland recognized, and quite a few that he didn't. To the right was a row of shallow wooden trays with various dried ingredients. He saw knobs of ginger root, dried lily buds, black mushrooms, wood-ear fungus, and radishes. There were jars of tiny salted shrimp, fermented black beans, and several types of dried produce that Wayland couldn't identify.

"Something you're looking for, sir?" the owner asked. She was in her late fifties, pretty, and dressed neatly.

"Yes," Wayland said. "I'm looking for some vinegar that I used to get in Fenchow. It was called Donghu, I think."

"I believe we have that," she said, and she walked over to the section of bottles in the back left corner of the room. She silently read the labels as she scanned them with her index finger. "Yes, Donghu. How many would you like?"

"Two, please," Wayland said.

She picked up a bottle in each hand. "Are you from Shensi? Your accent sounds a little strange."

"No, I'm originally from a bit further away," Wayland said.

She looked closer and saw that he was a foreigner, but she didn't look surprised. "Your Chinese isn't bad at all," she said. "British?"

"American," Wayland said. It was hard to judge what she thought of foreigners just from her reaction. Back in Fenchow, Wayland had just always assumed the best about people, about the Chinese. Now, he was less trusting.

"I have a cousin who's gone to America," she said. "He says things are pretty good. He's making money and sending it back. He says it's hard to get good food, though."

"It can be difficult to live in a strange country," Wayland said.

The woman nodded. "I'm sure you know about that. But still, Chinese just go to America to work. Why do foreigners come here to take over everything? I was no supporter of the Boxers, but do you understand why we Chinese would get angry at foreigners?"

"I do," Wayland said. He was a little annoyed that the conversation would escalate so rapidly into a political debate, but that was often how things went in China. "All I can say is that some of us came here with good intentions."

"I know, some did," she said. "But many didn't. Aiya, I still think most people everywhere just want to live simple lives. I only want to run my shop, be happy with my husband, raise my children. Isn't that what most people in America want, too?"

"I think it is," Wayland said. He paid her the money.

"Are you traveling? Would you like these wrapped up?"

"No, I'm staying in town," he said, and he put the two bottles in his satchel.

"Here," she said, handing him a small square of heavy cotton. "Wrap this around one, so they won't break."

Wayland did so and thanked her. "Goodbye," he said, putting his hat back on. "Nice talking to you."

"Good luck, sir," she said.

He came out into the street. The clouds had broken, and it was still mostly light. A donkey and cart passed by him going the same direction he was going, and he followed a ways behind. *Wait a minute. You're probably less than a quarter mile from home. Instead of taking the safe route, why don't you go back a different way and learn some of the smaller streets?*

Wayland turned off the main thoroughfare and took a side street to his left. A few more lanterns and lamps were lit on the buildings as he now as he made his way down the narrow road. He passed one building, and he heard someone call out to him from a second floor. He looked up to see a pretty young woman; her face was thick with makeup.

"Hey sir, don't you want to come up here? You're so handsome, and you look so lonely!"

"Thanks, but no," Wayland said, shaking his head. It instantly dawned on him: so that was a brothel. He felt himself blushing, but there was a side of him that was intrigued and stimulated, as well. *No, that's not what you really want.*

He hurried on his way, and then took a right onto another small street. This one must be running parallel with the main avenue, he thought. He'd follow this most of the way and then cut back over. That should have him coming out on one of those side streets right by Master Gao's house.

Wayland figured he had gone just about far enough to have reached the compound, so he decided to take the next right to cut over to the main avenue. There was a shop of some sort on the next corner, and five or six rough-looking young men were standing outside. They were talking and laughing. One shorter, stocky man was looking Wayland up and down as he came closer. He had an acne-scarred face, and his disposition didn't seem much nicer. Wayland instinctively sensed that this group was trouble. He picked up his pace as he passed by them.

"Hey, you in a hurry? Where are you going? You live around here or something?" The short man said. His tone was sarcastic and angry.

Wayland didn't respond or even look up as he walked by. One of the other men yelled something, presumably at him, but

Wayland couldn't make it out clearly. *Just get by them and down this street, and you'll be back home in a few minutes.*

Wayland turned down the cross street and walked a few yards, and then he saw something ahead of him that made his heart sink: a wall. This was a dead end. He would have to walk back past the group of young toughs. He inhaled deeply, and then breathed out. *Just keep your head down, and go quickly, and you'll be by them in no time.* But the men were well aware that the alley was a dead end, and as Wayland came back, they were standing abreast, blocking his way.

"What's the matter? Couldn't get through?" the short man said. He was standing confidently with his arms folded.

Wayland kept his head down, his hat covering his face as he walked closer to them. There were five of them, Wayland saw, and they were spread out enough to block his way entirely.

"Hey, there's a toll for going down that alley, you know," one of the others said. He was a heavy-set young man, his face round and stupid.

"I don't want any trouble," Wayland said. He paused about a yard in front of the short man. "I'm just trying to get home."

"That's fine, but as my friend said, it's going to cost you. You can't just walk down our road for free."

Wayland could smell both alcohol and opium on the men, and his heart was racing. He couldn't see any way out, but he made one last effort. He tried to walk past the short man, but the man took two steps to the side to block Wayland's way.

"I said you're not getting by us until you pay. Are you deaf?" The man brought his hand up quickly and it caught under the brim of Wayland's wide straw hat, knocking it off.

"Oh, look at this!" The man said. His mouth turned up in a cruel smile, and he turned to his friends, his tone almost triumphant. "He's not even Chinese. Just wearing our clothes.

What happened, foreigner? Get lost?"

"I'm not looking for a fight," Wayland said.

"No, I don't imagine you are," the man said. He walked around Wayland, eyeing him up and down. "You foreigners aren't so big on your own, are you? No soldiers here to protect you, no rifle or pistol. You think the Chinese are just shit, is that it? You think we're the "sick men" of Asia? Everything in the West is better, huh?"

"No, that's not what I think," Wayland said. The man slapped Wayland hard across the face. Wayland dropped the bag containing the vinegar, and the bottles smashed. A trickle of blood began dripping from his nose.

"See my friend here?" the man said. He nodded his head towards one of the other young men to his right. That man was taller and had a stocky, athletic build, and he walked closer to Wayland. The man's face was cold and expressionless.

The short man continued. Wayland wasn't entirely sure if he was the leader, but he was certainly the voice of the bunch. "His father had a shop here. He was a tailor. Just minding his own business. Foreign troops came through here, came into his shop. He tried to stop them, and they shot him."

"My father died in the street like a dog," the taller man said, walking towards Wayland. His face was cold. "He didn't deserve that."

"I'm sorry," Wayland said. He stepped back with his left foot and started to bring his hands up. "I've lost people too; I know what..."

The man swung at Wayland's jaw, and Wayland was just able to back out of the way at the last moment. But the young man came in again, and this time his punch connected with Wayland's upper chest. The blow was powerful, and Wayland staggered back from the impact. The man came in again with a savage punch, but Wayland was able to partially block that. He swung back at the man, but his swing was wild, and he barely grazed the man's forehead. Still, it was enough to send a bit of fear into his opponent, and the man backed up. Wayland tried to remember the fighting skills he had learned, but the memories of his boxing days in Boston and the rudimentary Chinese martial arts that he had learned from Lihao mixed in a confused jumble, and all Wayland was able to do was respond with a half-hearted straight punch to the man's face. It didn't connect, and Wayland was left off-balance; he didn't even see the palm strike coming from the taller man to his right. It hit him on his right temple, and the impact was like an explosion.

He had heard the expression "seeing stars" before, but he had always thought it was just a metaphor; it wasn't. An array of tiny lights winked and flickered around the periphery of his vision, and Wayland felt his legs giving way. He fell to the ground, although he was still conscious. He was able to get up to one knee before the first kick came in. He held his hand up, partly in physical defense and partly to implore his opponents to stop their assault, but to no avail. The man's heel caught him square in the face, and almost simultaneously Wayland's eyes filled with tears and blood began pouring from his nose. He snorted, and the copper-sweet taste of blood came down the back of his throat. He fell on all fours, and then there was a sharp kick to his ribs. Another, and another. Something popped, and Wayland was pretty sure it was the same rib that had been cracked months ago.

"Get him up, we're not done," the shorter man said.

Wayland felt hands on each of his arms, and he was pulled up to his feet, held up by two of the young men. The shorter man paced slowly back and forth in front of Wayland, never taking his eyes off the bloodied, semi-conscious foreigner.

He stopped in front of Wayland, grabbed a handful of hair and lifted Wayland's head until the two were staring at each other eye to eye. "What do you think now? Glad you came to our country, to tell us how we should live so that we could be just like you? Did you ever think that maybe we don't want to be like you? Did that ever even cross your mind?"

Wayland's eyes were mostly glazed over, and blood was still flowing steadily from his nose. It had coated most of his chin in dark red crimson. He moved his lips slowly, trying to speak, but the only sound that came out was a hoarse whisper.

"I didn't say you could talk," the young man said. He drew back and smashed his fist into Wayland's stomach, doubling him over. His legs gave way again, but the two men at his side propped him back up.

A voice came from the street. "You there? What are you doing to that young man?"

All turned to see an elderly man staring down the alley at the altercation. The voice sounded familiar to Wayland, and he looked up. It was Old Wu.

"Mind your own business, old man, or you'll get the same," the short man said. "Get out of here."

Old Wu shook his head as if confused. He walked closer a couple of steps. "You'll have to speak up, boy. My hearing isn't as good as it used to be."

Old Wu glanced at Wayland, and even in the dim light, he saw that Old Wu recognized him. *Great. Now Old Wu will get beaten too, and for an old man like him, it might be fatal. And once again, it will be my fault.*

"Leave me alone, Old Wu," Wayland said, sputtering blood. "Just get out of here!"

"Why, it's my friend Wei-lin!" Old Wu said, in mock surprise. "You young men will have to do me a favor. This foreigner is staying at our residence, and it would bring great shame to my master if anything were to happen to him. Please release him to me, and I'll get him out of your way."

"I said to get out of here, old man. I don't care if you know him or not, it's none of your business."

"Ah, that won't do, that won't do at all," Old Wu said, as he kept advancing.

One of the other young toughs stepped forward and tried to grab Old Wu by the shoulders. "Just go away, old man. We don't want to hurt you."

Old Wu, with an almost imperceptible turn of his waist, directed the young man's push to the left, and then he placed his left palm over his right wrist and struck out with such a burst of power that it bounced the young man a good two yards back. The man fell awkwardly onto the street, and his head bounced off the cobblestones. He groaned and tried to get up, but he couldn't. The others all turned and looked at Old Wu in amazement.

"I had hoped that we could come to some agreement without the need for violence," Old Wu said. "It's really not fair for you youngsters to gang up on an old man like myself."

The two holding Wayland released their grip, and Wayland fell to one knee. The big one smiled as he confidently walked towards Old Wu, and he stepped in to deliver a powerful palm strike to Old Wu's chest. Old Wu gently brushed the man's attack aside, and as the man's considerable weight propelled him forward, Old Wu flicked his hand out, striking the man just under the ear. The big man's eyes widened as he stopped in his tracks. He tried to speak but no words came, and he slumped to the ground, unconscious.

The short man grabbed Old Wu's left wrist, and he instantly realized his error. Old Wu clapped his right hand down on the young man's wrist and turned his waist; almost instantaneously the young man fell to his knees, his wrist locked and twisted almost to the point of breaking by Old Wu.

"I'm an old man, and while I enjoy playing with you youngsters, I really must be going." Old Wu turned his waist minutely, and just the tiny change of angle sent a fresh burst of pain through the young man; he knew his wrist was on the verge of snapping.

"You don't mind if I take my friend and leave now, do you?" Old Wu said.

"No," the short man said between gasps, shaking his head back and forth, and pleading for mercy with his eyes.

"Good, that's good," Old Wu said, as he released his grip on the young man. "Why don't you see to your friends here, I think they may be injured."

The young man nodded, his face contorted in pain, confusion, and humiliation. He helped his tall friend to his feet, and the lot of them scurried away.

Old Wu walked over to Wayland, who was just able to stand. "You don't seem to be having a very good day," Old Wu said.

"What are you doing here? How did you know where I was?"

"I didn't know. I was playing mahjong and having a few drinks with an old friend that lives on this street. I just happened to be walking by when I saw the commotion. Very lucky for you, I'd say."

Wayland smiled weakly. "Thank you, Old Wu. I... I don't know how you did that."

Old Wu grunted. "It's just like practice, that's all. Nothing to get too excited about. Should one be proud of being more skilled than people with no skill at all?"

Wayland managed a small grin. He sniffed and wiped the blood from his nose, and he tried to compose himself. "And I... was worried that you were going to get hurt."

18

WAYLAND WALKED across the courtyard and into his room and shut the door. He pulled his mattress and blankets out onto the *k'ang*, and lay down on his back. He could feel his left eye beginning to swell shut, and he thought he might have a broken rib, as his right side was extremely tender. That pain was bearable, though. He'd been through enough in the last few months to be keenly aware that physical pain was something that could be endured. But this was not just physical pain. *What was he even doing in this country, in this strange land? Why did his parents drag him halfway around the world? What did they get out of it besides struggle, hardship, and violence?* Not too much. He didn't fit in here, and he wasn't wanted. He'd go back to America. His grandparents in Boston would take him in; he knew that for a fact. He could finish up his education; maybe even become a professor of history in some American university as he had once supposed. He had quite a bit of first-hand experience with history; more than he wanted to, actually. He felt his swollen cheek and bruised eye and winced.

Leaving because things got tough? Is that what his parents raised him to do? His parents' killers hadn't even been brought to justice. Could he go back to his own life in America, when the killers were still out there? And they were most likely still nearby.

There was a knock at his door, and Wayland sat up. "Come in," he said. The door opened, and it was Suyin. She was carrying a steaming pot of hot water and a small satchel.

"No thanks, Suyin. I appreciate it, but I'm all right," Wayland said.

Suyin ignored him. "Take off your shirt," she said matter-of-factly as she set the pot down and opened up the satchel. Wayland did as she asked. There was a sizable reddish bruise on his right rib cage. Suyin dipped a cloth in the hot water and gently pressed it against Wayland's swollen eye, and then she wiped off the dried trickles of blood from his nose and the side of his mouth. Wayland was expressionless.

Master Gao appeared at the door. "Old Wu told us you had some trouble," he said.

Wayland didn't respond. He was usually polite to Master Gao — to everyone, really — but that was all wearing thin. He had had enough.

"Yeah, I'm fine," Wayland finally said.

Master Gao walked in and leaned over Wayland. He put one hand under Wayland's chin and examined the black eye. "Eye is just bruised," Master Gao said. He brought his hand down to Wayland's injured rib area and pressed gently. Wayland winced but didn't make a sound. Master Gao felt around with practiced skill.

"Rib is cracked, but not broken," Master Gao said. "Treat it with bruise liniment for a couple of weeks, and you should be fine. Suyin will show you how much to put on." He looked over at Suyin, and she nodded and reached to her satchel for the jar of liniment.

Master Gao got up to leave, but as he reached the doorway, he turned around and saw Suyin gently applying the liniment to the bare-chested Wayland. Wayland's eyes were closed, and he leaned back on his elbow on the mattress as Suyin attended to him. Master Gao paused for a second, and Suyin looked up at him, quite innocently.

"Better leave this open while you're here," Master Gao said to her. She nodded, and he pushed the door open wide and exited to the courtyard.

Suyin looked up at Wayland, and Wayland smiled meekly. She met his gaze and then looked down, and Wayland could feel himself blushing.

"Thank you, Suyin," he said. "You've been very kind to me."

Suyin dipped a cloth in the liniment and began gently applying it to Wayland's side. Wayland gazed at Suyin as she continued her ministrations. She was so beautiful, and so kind. *What do I have to lose? Life is short, and things can't get much worse.* He cautiously touched her forearm. She paused for a moment without looking up and then proceeded. When she didn't pull away, Wayland felt his heart beat faster. He gently ran his fingers slowly over her bare arm between her wrist and elbow. Wayland thought he had never felt skin so warm and feather-soft in his life. Suyin kept applying the liniment as if nothing was out of the ordinary, and Wayland kept up his gentle stroking of her arm. Her breathing became heavier. After a few moments she finished and then she put the cloth back in her satchel. She didn't make eye contact with him.

"You saw how much I put on?" Suyin asked. "Do that once in the morning, and once in the evening before bed. Leave your shirt off for fifteen minutes or so, until it dries. As Master Gao said, you should be fine in a couple of weeks. I'll leave the jar here."

"Thank you," Wayland said. He wanted to say more, to find just the right words that would navigate a path to her deeper emotions. He knew those emotions *had* to be under there somewhere. But the words didn't come.

"Why don't you ask Master Gao to teach you martial arts?" she said. "Don't you want to be able to defend yourself?" She gently brushed her fingers over his bruised eye.

"I don't think more violence is going to help anything," he said, but he felt more like he was reading from a script his father wrote than speaking his true feelings.

Suyin shrugged and stood up. "Suit yourself. Do you remember what I said about the liniment?"

"Yes, morning and night, I know," Wayland said.

Suyin opened the door to leave, but paused and then turned back to Wayland. "And when you ask Master Gao to teach you, you must get down on your knees. It's expected." She turned and left.

****

Wayland woke up early the next morning. He quickly washed and dressed, and instead of heading down to the inn, he walked across the courtyard over to Master Gao's quarters. He knocked on the door.

"Yes?" Old Wu said as he opened the door.

"I'm here to see Master Gao," Wayland said.

"He's out in the back practicing," Old Wu said. "Can you come back later?"

"It's important that I see him now," Wayland said. His rib was still extremely painful, and he knew his face looked terrible. It was all he could do to stand normally, but he didn't care about those things at the moment.

Old Wu looked at Wayland and slowly nodded. "Come in, but be respectful."

Wayland nodded, and he walked into Master Gao's quarters. Old Wu led him to the private courtyard, and Wayland saw Master Gao practicing his straight sword routine.

Old Wu put his finger to his lips. "Be quiet, and wait until he's done." He motioned to a wooden bench by the wall to the left, and Wayland sat down. Old Wu smiled to himself and left the courtyard.

Wayland watched intently as Master Gao went through the postures and techniques of the sword form. His movements were smooth and fluid, but with bursts of power interspersed throughout. The sword seemed to be a living extension of Master Gao's body, wielded with the same dexterity and precision that a painter turns his brush, and with the force that a blacksmith pounds his hammer. Power and subtlety seemed to be in equal measure, and Master Gao displayed a confidence in even the most minor techniques he was executing. His balance never wavered, and his footwork was steady and measured. After several minutes, he finished his last technique and then slowly brought himself back to his original posture, spinning his sword as he transferred it from his right hand to his left. He exhaled and slowly relaxed his body. Then, as if he had returned to the world, he turned and saw Wayland standing there.

"What is it, Wei-lin?"

"Master Gao, I... " Wayland started, but then he remembered what Suyin had said. He dropped to his knees. "Master Gao, I would ask that you take me on as your student, so that I can learn martial arts."

Master Gao looked at Wayland without expression. "And why do you want to learn martial arts?"

Wayland's face was still bruised from his beating. "I want to be able to defend myself."

"Is that all?" Master Gao said. "Your parents were Christian, is that not so?"

"Yes, and so am I," Wayland said.

Master Gao nodded. "I know very little about your religion, only what Old Wu has told me. But I understand that a Christian is forbidden from seeking revenge. Is that so?"

Wayland nodded. "That's true."

"The Lord Buddha also forbade vengeance. That is a value we share. Can you assure me that you are not motivated by vengeance and hatred?"

"I... I'm not. But justice and vengeance aren't the same," Wayland said.

"No, they are not," Master Gao said, nodding thoughtfully. "You are foreign and don't know all of our ways. A teacher does not take on a student lightly, because he will forever be responsible for that student's actions. And that student must know his duty to honor not only his teacher but the whole lineage. Do you understand that? Can you uphold my teachings, even if they go against your desires and natural inclinations?"

Wayland looked up, and his eyes were bright. "I think I can."

"And once you start the training, you will not quit?"

"I won't quit."

Master Gao paused for a moment. He rubbed his chin and nodded. "I will accept you. Show up in the training courtyard tomorrow morning."

Wayland felt a surge of gratitude and relief, and more than a little excitement. "Thank you, Master Gao. I will be there."

The training courtyard was adjacent to Master Gao's residence. Wayland had been vaguely aware that Master Gao and his students occasionally practiced there, but he had never paid it much attention. Nobody had told him exactly when the class started, but from what he had observed over the last few months, this was his best guess. Wayland tentatively knocked on the gate. After a moment, it opened.

"Come in, Wei-lin," Old Wu said, smiling.

Wayland nodded and looked around the courtyard. He met Suyin's eyes, and she flashed a hint of a smile but quickly turned away. There were four others there—Lunghui, two other young men and a young woman. They were all practicing their various drills and exercises. They briefly eyed Wayland but were mostly talking among themselves. Wayland felt a bit out of place. He went over to one side of the courtyard by himself and did a few toe-touches and stretches to loosen himself up.

After a minute or so, Master Gao arrived. He smiled and bid his greetings to his students. He looked at Wayland and nodded, and then he raised his hand. The other students stopped talking and formed an uneven line, facing Master Gao. Wayland wasn't sure what he should be doing, so he just walked over and stood behind the other students.

"Everyone," Master Gao said, "I want you to welcome your new classmate, Wei-lin."

The other students turned and smiled at Wayland.

"I'm Lunghui," the first young man said, extending his hand. They already knew each other, so apparently this was supposed to be some formal introduction. Wayland shook his hand and bowed.

Next was a slightly older woman, late twenties. She was short and stout. "Welcome, Wei-lin," she said, shaking his hand. "I'm Shih Hua." Unlike Lunghui, she was smiling and seemed quite jolly. Her grip was strong.

"My name is Shen Fai," said the next young man.

"I'm Wayland. Nice to meet you."

"Welcome to our small gang," Shen Fai said. He was about twenty, small and thin. He wore glasses, and he seemed to be perpetually smiling. "American, are you?"

"I am," Wayland said.

"I am Chinese. My name is Shen Fai. How do you do?" Shen Fai said in reasonably good English. This brought a smile to Wayland's face.

"Hey, that's pretty good," Wayland responded in Chinese. "I

think your English is better than my Chinese."

The remaining student made his introduction. "Well, I don't speak any English, but my name is Wu Chen." He took Wayland's hand and shook it. He was the oldest of the bunch, probably about thirty, and there were no two ways about it: he was big. He was several inches taller than Wayland, and a good fifty pounds heavier. He was actually a bit fat, but he was also just barrel-chested and big-boned. "If anyone gives you any trouble, you just come to me," he said. He was smiling, but from the look on his face, Wayland was quite sure the man meant every word.

"Thank you, Wu Chen. I appreciate it," Wayland said.

Suyin approached next. She acted as if it was her first time meeting Wayland. "I'm Suyin. Welcome."

"Thank you," Wayland said. He took Suyin's lead and refrained from expressing any familiarity.

"All of you please remember, Wei-lin is not Chinese, and many of the things that you understand without even thinking about may not be so clear to him. When you interact with him, put yourself in his position, and imagine that you are in a strange country with people that do things differently. And remember that I have judged him worthy to be my pupil, as I have so judged each of you."

"Yes, Master Gao," the other students responded in unison.

"And Wei-lin, you must understand this as well: all of these students are to be considered your seniors. You will obey them, you will accept their corrections, and you will not argue with them. Is that understood?"

"Yes, Master Gao, I understand," Wayland said.

"Good. Now, the class will begin," Master Gao said. "Take your positions for warm-up."

The others spread out a bit around the courtyard to give themselves room, and Wayland did likewise.

"No, Wei-lin," Master Gao said. "Please stand to the side. You will just be observing the class today. You may sit down if you wish."

Wayland bowed and walked over next to the wall. Standing, he faced the class.

"Now, everyone be seated," Master Gao said. The other students sat down cross-legged, and Wayland followed suit. Master Gao paced slowly in front of his students, with his hands clasped behind his back. "We've talked several times about the nature of *T'ai Chi Fist*. The opening posture of the *T'ai Chi* form is called *Wu Chi*. What is *Wu Chi*?"

Lunghui raised his hand, and Master Gao pointed to him. "*Wu Chi* means formless, no extremities, no boundaries. Infinite," Lunghui said.

Master Gao nodded. "That is correct. It may be said that *Wu Chi* means without shape, without definition. And what is *T'ai Chi*?"

Wayland raised his hand, and without waiting for Master Gao, he spoke. "*T'ai Chi* is yin and yang," he said.

"You are just observing this class, Wei-lin," Master Gao said. "You are not a participant."

Wayland nodded. He felt the sting of embarrassment, but he said nothing.

"Is that correct? Is *T'ai Chi* yin and yang?" Master Gao asked.

Suyin raised her hand. "No, that's incorrect. *T'ai Chi* is the *mother* of yin and yang; *T'ai Chi* is what causes *Wu Chi* to separate into yin and yang."

"That's correct, Suyin," Master Gao said. "And when we're talking about the martial art of *T'ai Chi Fist*, what is *T'ai Chi*?"

"*T'ai Chi* is the mind," Lunghui said. "It's the mind which initiates our movements of both yin and yang."

"Correct. From *T'ai Chi*, yin and yang can separate in a

thousand ways. With this martial art, the true power is in your mind, your knowledge, your creativity, your experience," Master Gao said.

Wayland thought about this and then scolded himself. Lihao had explained *T'ai Chi* to him, and he had remembered it wrong.

Master Gao continued the lecture for a while and then had them all stand to begin warm-ups.

Wayland stood, trying to follow what the others were doing, but he felt a hand on his shoulder. He turned. It was Old Wu.

"No, you've been instructed to observe today. That means you don't do anything but watch. You might as well take a seat," Old Wu said.

"I'll stand," Wayland said to Old Wu. Old Wu shrugged, and Wayland folded his arms in front of his chest and watched the class.

Over the next two hours, Wayland watched. He watched the class go through the stretching and warm-ups, he watched them go through the first ten moves of the empty-hand *T'ai Chi Fist* sequence. He watched Master Gao and Old Wu walk among the students, correcting their techniques and postures. He watched the paired practice of the students, and he watched them work on full speed, two-person offensive and defensive drills. Wayland knew he was more athletic than several of the students; he knew he could impress Master Gao if he was only given a chance. He was full of energy and full of potential. But he was just watching.

Finally, Master Gao said that class was over. He told them to practice on their own and to show up for the next class the day after tomorrow. Master Gao said something to Old Wu, and then left. The students talked and laughed; they had the demeanor that everyone has after an enjoyable athletic activity: physically tired but smiling and satisfied, enjoying the camaraderie of others with a shared interest.

Wayland was neither tired nor satisfied. He saw Old Wu approaching.

"Did you enjoy the class?" Old Wu asked.

Wayland frowned. "I would have enjoyed it more if I was doing something."

Old Wu raised his eyebrows. "Still, much can be gained from observing."

Wayland sighed. "Yeah, I guess so." He tried to be optimistic. "So the next class is the day after tomorrow?"

"Not for you," Old Wu said. "This was your introduction. Master Gao will inform you of the next class you are to attend."

Wayland nodded, and Old Wu smiled and walked away.

This was ridiculous. How was he supposed to learn anything like this?

Wayland was pretty sure that he could already beat most of Master Gao's students in a fight right now.

They think they're superior just because they're Master Gao's students, but they have no idea of my potential. Even Master Gao is going to be impressed when he can see my ability. I'm sure they mean well, but they're going to learn what I can do.

19

WAYLAND WAS frustrated. He had been to three of Master Gao's classes already, but he was still only allowed to observe, not participate. And on top of that, Master Gao had been asking him to do a lot more chores around the compound. He didn't like the way that this arrangement was going.

He brought the ax down on the last piece of wood, splitting the chunk of log cleanly in half. It was a chilly late-autumn evening, and the sun was almost gone. Wayland looked over at the pile of wood he had cut with some satisfaction. He had been at the Gao's compound long enough to have a good idea of how much wood they went through, and this pile would last them a few weeks. He held the ax out in front of him, and then stretched his neck and shoulder muscles. He felt good. The best he had felt since he had been here. Still, was he staying here just to learn how to chop wood?

"Thank you, Wei-lin," came a voice from behind him. It was Master Gao. "That will last us a while. We'll be getting another delivery of wood two weeks from now, and that should take us through the winter."

"Can I speak to you for a moment, Master Gao?" Wayland asked.

Master Gao stopped and nodded. "What is it?"

"Master Gao," Wayland said. "You know that I appreciate everything you've done for me."

Master Gao smiled politely, waiting for Wayland to continue.

"I can't thank you enough. I know that you saved my life. Literally."

"What did you want to say to me, Wei-lin?"

"I'm not sure I'm following everything. I thought that when you accepted me as a student that I would be learning martial arts."

Master Gao rubbed his chin. "That is so. You don't feel that I've lived up to my end of the bargain? Is that it?"

"I'm not complaining about the work. I expect to earn my stay. I can chop wood, I can do laundry. But I thought I'd be learning more than that. I know your other students learn how to fight. Is it just because I'm a foreigner?"

Master Gao smiled. "Oh, perhaps I've misunderstood. You want to learn how to *fight*, is that it?"

"I do," Wayland said. "I've studied Western boxing back in America, and I've learned some Chinese martial arts already. I think I know quite a bit, but I want to learn more."

"Hmm," Master Gao said. He scratched the back of his neck. He paused for a moment, and then looked Wayland in the eye. "Perhaps I've misjudged you. I didn't realize that you already had some martial arts training."

"I'd like to learn some more advanced techniques, if you'd be willing to teach me," Wayland said.

"I'll tell you what," Master Gao said. "I think that you may very well be ready for some higher-level training. Come over to the courtyard tomorrow morning at nine."

Wayland was elated. "Thank you, Master Gao!" Wayland bowed, and Master Gao smiled.

"Have a good evening, and get to bed early. You'll want to be rested for tomorrow," Master Gao said. He turned and walked back towards his own room in the compound.

The next morning Wayland got up early. He dressed and ate a quick breakfast of some tea and fried millet and then went out to the pile of wood that he had chopped the night before, and he stacked it all in a neat row. He returned to his room and splashed some cold water on his face. His body was limber, his energy was high, and he felt good. He was really going to join the class and learn martial arts! He was a bit nervous but very excited.

Master Gao had told him to be at the training courtyard by nine, and Wayland arrived at half-past eight. Suyin was already there, and she was doing some stretching and *ch'i kung* exercises. Lunghui was there as well. He cast a disparaging glance at Wayland, and then continued in his repetitions of the "brush knee, step forward" technique of *T'ai Chi Fist*. Wayland loosened up. He did some jumping-jacks, he jogged in place, and stretched his arms and legs out. He practiced a couple of the *chigong* exercises that Old Wu had shown him, and he tried to maintain a veneer of confidence in front of Suyin and Lunghui. He did a bit of Western shadow boxing, remembering his left hook and front jab and his bouncing footwork. He knew that this was something that neither Suyin nor Lunghui had seen before.

After another ten minutes, Shen Fai, Wu Chen, and Shih Hua came into the courtyard. Suyin walked over to Shih Hua, and they talked. She must have said something funny, because both she and Suyin looked over at Wayland and smiled, and then Suyin playfully shoved Shih Hua away, still laughing. She cast a quick glance to Wayland, but he pretended not to notice.

Master Gao and Old Wu came into the courtyard.

"All right," Master Gao said. "Let's get to our training." He began gently bouncing up and down, his arms loosely jiggling at his sides as he relaxed his shoulder muscles. All the students mirrored him, and Wayland did the same.

"Relax all your muscles," Master Gao said, as he continued bouncing, shifting his weight back and forth between his feet. "Let everything be loose and soft. Natural. Release all the tension. Let your *chi* flow." He stopped bouncing and began swinging both arms out from right to left and back again, turning his waist. The other students all mirrored Master Gao's movements, and Wayland did the same. They all followed the pattern of stretching their arms up in the air, turning to the side as far as possible, bending to the side, and then squatting down onto their heels.

After another few minutes of warm-up, Master Gao spoke. "We are going to have a demonstration this morning. Wei-lin, would you step forward, please?" Wayland was taken a bit off guard, but he did as he was asked and walked forward.

Master Gao continued. "It seems that our friend Wei-lin has had experience in martial arts, and has acquired some skill at fighting. I've learned that he is adept at Western boxing and that he has also studied our Chinese arts. This may be a valuable opportunity for us to benefit from his knowledge and skill."

Wayland smiled politely and shook his head. "I'm not really that good," Wayland said.

"There's no need to be modest, Wei-lin," Master Gao said. "I think we would all appreciate the opportunity to learn from you. Lunghui, please step forward."

A subtle smile flashed across Lunghui's face, and he walked forward and stood opposite Wayland, facing him.

"We're going to have a sparring match," Master Gao said.

Wayland shook his head. This wasn't a situation he was comfortable with. "Um... I don't claim any great skill. I'm not sure you'd learn much from me."

"Well, let's just see," Master Gao said. "You have been very honest with me about your training, so I don't see where this is a problem."

Wayland sensed he was being set up, but there didn't seem to be any way out at this point. Still, he needed to understand what he was facing. "Master Gao, I'm not familiar with the rules here. Could you tell me what is allowed?"

"Oh, most certainly," Master Gao said. "No strikes to the head, throat or groin, and no deliberate breaking of bones or joints. Everything else is permissible."

Wayland tried to process the rules in his mind as Lunghui stared at him intently. *Breaking bones or joints — it had to be explained that that wasn't allowed?* This was more serious than any sparring that Wayland had been involved in before. The other students backed away and sat down on the courtyard cobblestones, forming somewhat of a circle around Wayland and Lunghui and setting the boundaries of their fighting ring. Master Gao looked at them both impassively; Old Wu chuckled to himself as he sat down next to Suyin.

"Are you both ready?" Master Gao said.

"Ready," Lunghui said. His eyes were calm, and his focus was clear.

Wayland nodded. "Ready."

The two faced each other and began slowly, deliberately stepping in a counter-clockwise circle, each matching the other's movement and jockeying for an advantage.

Wayland sized up Lunghui. He was tall, probably two inches taller than Wayland. He was thin, though and not very muscular. Still, Wayland saw that his opponent moved confidently, smoothly; Lunghui was naturally athletic and coordinated. Wayland began bouncing up and down, as he had been taught in his boxing lessons back in Boston. Lunghui, in contrast, maintained his rooted, measured stepping. Wayland held his fists up in the standard Western boxing guard. He kept a safe distance from Lunghui, but he was looking for an opening. Lunghui held his hands up, palms open and facing down as he calmly faced Wayland.

"Huh!" Wayland shouted as he stepped in and threw a right hand at Lunghui's chest. He was fast, and he knew that he had a strong punch. He held back some of his power, though; he wanted to show up Lunghui, but he didn't want to hurt him.

He needn't have worried. Lunghui brought up his left hand to intercept Wayland's punch, turned his waist to dissipate the power, and then returned a palm strike to Wayland's chest. It all seemed a blur of motion to Wayland, and by the time he saw what was happening, Lunghui's palm struck him squarely in his upper chest. The impact was powerful, and it knocked Wayland back a good yard, although he stayed on his feet. Wayland stepped forward, trying to show that the blow didn't affect him much, but he felt the pain of the impact radiate from his chest out to his arms and up his neck. He shook his head and brought his hands back up in the guard position. *Okay, if that's how it's going to be, then I won't hold back.*

Wayland began bouncing again, and he made his way closer to Lunghui. He could feel himself breathing heavily, he was already a little winded. Lunghui jerked powerfully with his right shoulder and Wayland brought his hands up to block the attack, but it was just a feint; Lunghui smiled as he drew back and settled into his ready stance. Wayland's anger started to rise. He didn't want to be made a fool of, especially in front of Master Gao and Suyin. Wayland feinted in with a left jab and then threw a thrust kick towards Lunghui's midsection. Lunghui softly but swiftly brought his arm down in the "brush knee" technique from *T'ai Chi Fist*, leading Wayland's kick harmlessly into space, and then he stepped in and delivered a percussive punch directly into Wayland's solar plexus. The air shot out of Wayland's lungs, and he fell to his knees. He held his hand up, and tried to speak, but no words would come out. He tried to breathe, but he simply couldn't inhale; his chest seemed paralyzed. He got up and staggered, as he desperately tried to catch just a breath of air. Lunghui calmly stepped back, with a look of subtle satisfaction on his face. Master Gao looked on without expression.

Suyin stood up and hurried to Wayland's side, putting her arm on his shoulder. Wayland raised his hand and nodded that he was not seriously injured; still, he couldn't inhale, and he couldn't speak. He went back down to one knee. Suyin kneeled next to him, unsure as to what she should do. She cast an angry glance over at Lunghui. Lunghui shrugged indifferently.

"He'll be okay," Old Wu said, chuckling, as he got up and walked over to Wayland. He helped Wayland up to his feet. "He just got the wind knocked out of him. It's quite a shock the first time that happens to you."

"I'm... okay," Wayland said, gasping. He was now able to take small breaths.

"Sparring is done for today," Master Gao said to the other students. "Work on your forms by yourself for the next hour. After that, Lunghui will lead you in standing post training." The students shuffled off to their respective practice areas.

"What about this one?" Old Wu said, nodding towards Wayland.

Master Gao sighed and looked at Wayland. He then turned to Old Wu. "Please correct the other students on their forms, if you would, Old Wu." Old Wu bowed slightly, turned and withdrew.

"Let us talk," Master Gao said to Wayland. He gestured politely with his open hand, motioning Wayland to the side of the compound, under one of the bigger trees. Wayland nodded sheepishly and began walking. His breathing had returned to normal, more or less. Master Gao walked next to him.

"What did you learn today?"

"I learned that Lunghui doesn't like me very much. And that he's better than me," Wayland said.

"Those are two separate issues," Master Gao said. "Don't confuse them. Now, why did Lunghui defeat you?"

"I guess he was faster than me," Wayland said. "And he hit harder. He's stronger than me, and has a longer reach."

Master Gao grunted and shook his head. "You have some of it right, and most of it wrong. He has a longer reach, and he hits harder than you. That is true enough. But fast? You're naturally faster, more athletic than he is. You're also stronger."

Wayland felt a small bit of pride, being praised for his strengths by Master Gao. That was short-lived, however.

"So you had some natural advantages over Lunghui, and he still beat you easily. And believe me, he was holding back quite a bit, taking it easy on you. You said that you knew Western boxing, and some Chinese martial arts as well?"

"I... thought I did," Wayland said.

"It didn't look to me like you knew much of anything."

Wayland sighed and shook his head. "No sir, I guess not."

They reached the side of the compound, and there was a stack of several small old wooden benches stacked there. Master Gao pulled one bench down, turned it over, and sat down on it. He motioned for Wayland to do the same, and Wayland did so.

"Let me ask you, do you know how Lunghui got to be as good as he is?" Master Gao said.

"I guess he worked hard and practiced a lot," Wayland said.

"He has trained very diligently, that's true. But before he learned to fight, he also chopped wood. And he did laundry. And he cooked. He did that because that's what I told him to do, as I've told you. He didn't understand why he had to do it, either. And he didn't like it much more than you did. He was impatient to learn how to fight. Still, he followed my instructions, and the result is that he obtained a level of skill, a level sufficient to easily defeat you. Do you understand?"

Wayland rubbed his chin. "I think so."

"Your father taught philosophy and religion, didn't he?"

Wayland nodded.

"When you were learning from him, did you understand everything immediately?"

Wayland shook his head. "No, I didn't. In fact, some of it is still really difficult for me."

"Yet you accepted it from your father. Why was that?"

"Well, " Wayland said. "He was my father. I trusted him. I trusted his judgment, and that he knew what he was talking about and that he wanted the best for me." Wayland paused for a moment, and then looked Master Gao in the eyes. He was starting to understand.

"Of course you did," Master Gao said. "To learn anything worth learning, you must first humble yourself and admit the authority of the teacher. If you can't do that, you won't get very far. But certainly, you must be very careful in your choice of teacher. Your trust must be well-placed, or you will go down the wrong path. That is the way of master and student in Chinese martial arts. I don't know if you have relationships like this with your teachers in America. I'm not your father, but there must be a similar level of trust between teacher and student if one is to learn martial arts properly. This subject is not like mathematics or calligraphy. You are learning to fight, even to kill. These are powerful abilities that can affect your life, and the lives of others. And just as you should be careful in choosing a teacher, a teacher must be careful with who he takes as a student. Because he is responsible for his students, for their actions, for their behavior out in the world after they have learned their skills."

"I guess I didn't understand that," Wayland said.

"You've seen all my students. A motley group, and not a large one. They are all different, perhaps a little strange, and maybe they're not all the most skilled. But each of them is honorable. I trust them with my teachings. Maybe you thought that all you had to do was to kneel and ask, and that's why I accepted you as a student. That was not the case. I observed you while you stayed with us. Your temperament, your values, your character. I have little experience with foreigners. Some of your ways are strange to me. But I judged you as a worthy student, and I accepted you." A subtle smile came over Master Gao's face. "And I should add that Old Wu put in a good word for you, and I've always trusted his judgment."

"I appreciate that, Master Gao," Wayland said. "I can't tell you how much I do. My life has just been so confusing to me over this last year. I'm still trying to get my bearings. I want to learn from you."

"And if I ask you to go back to chopping wood and doing laundry?"

"Then I'll go back to chopping wood and doing laundry," Wayland said.

Master Gao stood up. "Then I think the matter is settled. You are my student. Continue with your daily work until you're told differently."

"Thank you, Master Gao," Wayland said. He bowed slightly and took leave of his teacher. As he walked back to his room, he felt the spot where Lunghui had struck him so forcefully. It still hurt a bit, but not nearly so much as it did before.

***

Wayland went back to his old chores with a newfound appreciation. When he chopped wood, he imagined he was cutting downwards with a big saber. When he did the laundry and wrung out the water from the clothes, he envisioned that he was grabbing and twisting an opponents wrist or arm. When he hauled heavy baskets or bags of flour, he saw himself lifting and tossing his opponents around left and right. And he felt himself getting stronger. His wounds and injuries were almost completely gone. He felt like his old self again. Perhaps even better than his old self, if the truth be told.

Wait a minute. He thought back to his days of boxing in Boston, and he remembered what the boxers often did to develop their conditioning: they jumped rope. His body was stronger now, and it could take stronger training. Jumping rope was certainly something he could do in the compound without much trouble at all. He remembered an old storage closet just off to the back of the main hall, and he seemed to recall that he had seen some coils of old rope there. He walked over there and looked inside, and sure enough, next to a few old brooms and some baskets, there were several dusty coils of rope hanging on a peg on the wall. He took one, held one end and tossed the coil, and as it unrolled Wayland saw that the whole length was about fifteen feet. Wayland felt someone behind him, and he saw Old Wu walking by.

"Excuse me, Old Wu," Wayland said, and the elderly man turned to him. "Is this rope any good? Do you think Master Gao would mind if I used it?

Old Wu walked over and took the rope in his hand, examining it. "This is so old; I don't think it would be good for much. I would say you can do what you want with it." Old Wu peered into the closet. "This has to be cleaned out sometime. Most of this old junk can just be thrown away."

"Thanks," Wayland said, as he coiled the rope back up.

Wayland went back to his room and measured out the length he'd need for a jump rope, about four feet. He cut the rope and tied knots on both ends, and then stepped out into the courtyard. He looked around quickly. Neither Old Wu nor anyone else seemed to be around. He swung the rope and jumped over it a couple of times, and then it hit his legs. It was a bit tricky to coordinate, but after a few attempts, he had the rhythm down. He decided to go to a hundred and see how he felt. His heart rate picked up as he kept jumping, but it felt pretty good. He got to a hundred and stopped. He was breathing a little heavily and starting to sweat. He remembered how quickly he had started to feel winded in his match with Lunghui, and it began to dawn on him why Western boxers spent so much time on conditioning. Granted, in Chinese martial arts, the fights were more serious and probably wouldn't last as long as most Western boxing matches, but still, good conditioning would always be an advantage. And unlike some of the more difficult martial techniques and tactics he might learn, conditioning was simple and something that he could accomplish without any help if he just worked on it.

I'll try for five hundred. He started up again and found a pace that challenged him but was not beyond his ability. He counted out the number of every ten jumps. It was a cool autumn day, and even though the air was dry, Wayland could feel the sweat beginning to come off his forehead. He was at about three hundred when he saw Old Wu and Master Gao approaching. He kept jumping. Master Gao stopped to watch Wayland for a few moments and studied his student's rope-jumping without expression. He turned to Old Wu, who just shrugged. Wayland kept jumping and counting off his repetitions.

Master Gao and Old Wu walked on until they were out of earshot from Wayland.

"Have you seen that before, jumping over the rope?" Master Gao asked.

"I saw a Western boxing exhibition once a few years ago, and one of the men did that before his fight."

"Interesting," Master Gao said. "He's pondering, thinking on his own about how to improve, beyond what I've shown him."

"Not every student does that," Old Wu said.

"Indeed," Master Gao said. They walked on in silence for a few moments before Master Gao finished his thought. "He may have some potential."

20

WAYLAND CONTINUED to work at his chores. Suyin had shown him how they usually cleaned everything, but when it came to washing dishes, Wayland put more trust in the lessons he had learned from his mother, and he largely adopted the system they had used in Fenchow. He first brought a big kettle of water to a boil, and then he filled two wooden tubs, one for cleaning the dishes and the other for rinsing. He would always start by dumping all the dirty chopsticks into the hot water, and then washing them with his scrub cloth. He picked up each one individually and ran the cloth over it, then rinsed it in the clean water and tossed it into the pile to be dried. He was getting pretty quick with them, and he could do a dozen in less than a minute. After the chopsticks, he did the rice bowls, and he washed them with similar enthusiasm. He liked to work fast, while the water in the tubs was still almost scalding hot. Next were the plates and after that the wine bowls. Wayland got his routine down pat, and he found he could finish all his chores much faster than before. That gave him more time during the day, and he took to both reading and practicing martial arts more.

One afternoon, Wayland got caught up in the most recent book that Old Wu had brought back to him from town, an English translation of the Chinese classic Journey to the West. The hours slipped away as he immersed himself in the fantastical adventures of the Monkey King, Pigsy and the Monk, and before he knew it, it was time for dinner. During the meal, Master Gao asked him if he had finished the laundry for the day, and he had to admit to Master Gao that he hadn't. Master Gao nodded and didn't say anything, but Wayland felt the sting of embarrassment.

As soon as the meal was done, Wayland excused himself and went to work on the laundry. He could have just gone to bed and done it tomorrow, but he felt too guilty and decided to finish it that night. He went over to the kitchen area and put the big kettle of water on to boil. When that was hot, he filled the washtub, threw in a bit of soap and got out the washboard. It was an overcast evening, and not much light from the moon or stars was coming down, so Wayland lit his oil lamp and hung it from a peg that was on the courtyard wall. He sat down on the bench and began working the clothes on the washboard. It was a cool evening, and to be honest, Wayland liked working by himself like this. There was something comforting about sitting outside under the warm glow of his little lamp, with a simple task ahead of him, and knowing that most people in town had finished their day and were preparing to settle in for the night. Wayland's mind began to drift as he rhythmically ran the garments over the washboard until they were clean, and then rinsed and wrung them out as dry as he could before tossing them into the empty washtub. He got into his routine, and his mind began drifting back to autumn days back in America, with his family…

Wayland snapped out of his reverie and stopped washing for a moment. He did hear something. There was some activity that seemed to be coming from the other courtyard, the small one next to Master Gao's room. Wayland cocked his head, and he could distinctly hear the sounds of "hah!" and "hen!", and it seemed to be coming from a couple of different people. Wayland wrung out the last shirt into the washtub and then tossed it in with the other clean clothes. He stood up and looked over in the direction of the sounds, and he could make out a faint light. His curiosity was piqued. He looked around, but the rest of the compound seemed to be empty and dark. Wayland thought about taking his lantern, but then he decided against it; he didn't want to be drawing any attention to himself. He slowly and silently made his way across the compound to the gate that led to Master Gao's room, and his private courtyard. The sounds of physical activity were louder now; they were definitely coming from that courtyard, just on the other side of the wall.

The wall was about ten feet high, and the surface was smooth; there was no way for Wayland to climb up the side. He looked around and saw what he needed: an old wooden bench that was next to the far wall of the main hall. Wayland silently scooted over and retrieved it. He placed it up against the wall and stood on it. He reached as high as he could, but his outstretched hands were still about a foot from the top. If he jumped, he thought, he could probably grab the top of the wall and then pull himself up. If he couldn't grab on, however, he would probably come crashing down on the bench, and make enough noise to draw attention. He jumped, and was indeed able to grab on to the edge of the wall. He pulled himself up, and then slowly brought his eyes up to the top and peered over. There were a couple of lanterns hanging up on poles, and although they didn't give off a great deal of light, Wayland could see who was there. Only Master Gao, Suyin, and Lunghui. Master Gao was pacing slowly under the lamplight, and although his voice was more hushed than usual, his words were audible.

"Breathing is the key to projecting physical power, and breathing must be coordinated with the *dantian*," Master Gao said.

"Does that come naturally, or is it always a special technique?" Lunghui asked.

Master Gao nodded. "It is natural, but it must also be trained. Both of you, put your right hand on your lower *dantian*, about two inches below your navel. Now, relax all the muscles in your upper body, shoulders, arms, neck, torso." Lunghui and Suyin did so. "Good," Master Gao said. "Now, take a deep, deep breath... now hold it... now exhale. What did you feel with your *dantian*?"

Suyin spoke. "When I inhaled, my *dantian* expanded, and when I exhaled it contracted." Lunghui nodded in agreement.

"Exactly," Master Gao said. "That is called 'natural breathing,' and it's how our bodies work most of the day. Now both of you go up and face the wall."

Wayland panicked for a moment and planned to let himself drop to the ground, but then he saw that Lunghui and Suyin were going to one of the side walls, not the one he was on. Wayland's arms were getting tired, and he didn't think he could hold on much longer. As quietly as he could, he swung his right leg up onto the wall. It was a little awkward, but it took some of the pressure off his hands, and he could hang like this for a while without too much discomfort. It was such an overcast night that Wayland was quite sure his silhouette was not visible to those inside the courtyard.

Lunghui and Suyin stood facing the wall.

"Now," Master Gao said. "I want you to keep your right hand on your *dantian*, and use your left hand to push against the wall as hard as you can, as if you're going to push the wall down. First, take a deep breath... now push!"

Lunghui and Suyin both did so. Suyin looked down at her right hand on her *dantian*, and then looked over to Master Gao. "It's different."

"This time, when I took the breath, my *dantian* contracted, and when I pushed against the wall, it expanded," Lunghui said.

Master Gao smiled and nodded. "That is what is called 'reverse breathing.' This is one of the most important things to understand in martial arts. When the human body is in a stressful situation, either physically or emotionally, it automatically changes to reverse breathing. In fighting, when one is attacking, one exhales forcefully when performing aggressive techniques. As we have been training, this is expressed by the sound 'hah!'. When one is withdrawing, defending or absorbing an opponent's attack, then one inhales sharply, with the sound 'hen!'. In these situations, the *dantian* expands with the exhale, and contracts with the inhale. The *dantian* controls the flow of the body's *chi*; when exhaling, the *chi* flows outward and combines with muscular strength to power the strike. With defensive techniques, the *chi* is withdrawn and absorbed."

"But *T'ai Chi Fist* is always supposed to be natural," Lunghui said. "Is that really natural?"

"It is indeed," Master Gao said. "Go ahead, try to push against the wall while inhaling. Imagine that you're trying to push the wall over."

Lunghui did so and then shook his head. "I don't feel like I'm pushing with all my strength. It doesn't work."

"No, it doesn't," Master Gao continued. "And it's not just with fighting or physical effort. It's also with our emotions. Both of you put your right hand on your *dantian* again."

Lunghui and Suyin did so.

"Now," Master Gao said. "Laugh. Go ahead, laugh. 'Ha ha ha ha!' Laughing is yang, and you will notice that you similarly use reverse breathing. And also that your exhalations are long and your inhalations are short. You feel your *dantian* expand with each ' ha'; you are expelling positive energy. Crying, on the other hand, is yin. Go ahead and mimic crying: 'hen hen hen!' (he inhaled dramatically) 'hen hen hen!' This is also reverse breathing, but your inhalations are much longer than your exhalations. This is the body trying to reclaim energy rather than expel it. This is yin. Do you understand?"

"Yes," Suyin said, and she and Lunghui looked at each other and nodded.

Although it was difficult for Wayland to keep his tenuous grip on the wall, he was still able to put his right hand on his *dantian*. He silently pretended he was laughing, and he indeed felt his *dantian* expand with each laugh. He then went back to 'normal breathing,' and he conversely felt his *dantian* expand when he inhaled. Why hadn't he noticed this before? It was how his body worked every single day, and it was so natural.

"Now," Master Gao said. "In *T'ai Chi Fist*, we can perform our techniques and our *ch'i kung* with either normal or reverse breathing. Neither is wrong, and both are natural. It just depends on what our goals are. If we are striving for health, we may want to use natural breathing, which is less strenuous for the body. If we are practicing for fighting, then we want to use reverse breathing. Both have their place in the complete art, and both should be studied. Now, let's practice 'four gates' breathing again."

Lunghui and Suyin both followed Master Gao's posture, and stood straight with their feet shoulder-width apart, and their hands at their waist, with their palms out and facing the ground.

"Practice this with reverse breathing. When you exhale, expand your *dantian*, and envision your bodies energy flowing down through the palms of your hand and the soles of your feet."

Wayland couldn't hold on any longer. He swung his foot down from the wall and lowered himself down with his hands. He dropped the last foot or so silently down onto the bench and slunk back across the central courtyard to his laundry area. He quickly hung up the wet clothes on the drying rack, and then went back to his room.

"Reverse breathing," he said to himself in a whisper. He stood upright and adopted the "four gates" breathing posture that he had just seen Master Gao and the others practicing in the courtyard. He began to use the reverse breathing technique, drawing his *dantian* in when he inhaled and pushing it out when he exhaled. He had also noticed Master Gao and the others rising slightly as they inhaled and sinking a bit as they exhaled. And keep the mind focused, and the body, especially the upper body, as relaxed as possible. That was a constant principle in *T'ai Chi Fist*.

Wayland breathed deeply and slowly, in and out, as he tried to keep all these principles in mind. After a few minutes, he began to feel the strangest sensation. His palms and the soles of his feet were starting to feel warm. As he almost imperceptibly sank his weight down with each exhalation, he began to feel a warmth course through his whole body, almost like waves of energy traveling from his center to his extremities. It was similar to the feeling he had when Old Wu first showed him the soft exercises, only now it was much stronger. Was this the feeling of *chi*, or was it just a trick of his mind? He certainly wasn't imagining the heat coursing to his hands and feet—that was real enough. Wayland practiced this breathing for another half hour before going to bed. That night he slept as soundly as he had since he had arrived at Master Gao's.

Over the next week, Wayland continued to practice the Four Gates training. He found that it became easier to switch back and forth between reverse breathing and normal breathing. He extended his practice time a few minutes each evening. He also remembered what Master Gao had said about reverse breathing, that it was what you naturally used when you tried to push something heavy. Wayland began putting that into practice. Now and then, either when he was at the inn or back home at the compound, he would look carefully to make sure no one was around, and then go up to the nearest wall and push against it. The reverse breathing came naturally and his *dantian* expanded, although Wayland realized that when he was pushing the wall, his exhalation slowed to match the duration of his push. If, however, he tried to give the wall a quick, hard push, his exhalation also became shorter, sharper. With one swift push, he instinctively gave out a "hah!" sound. He stopped. That was precisely the sound he had heard from Master Gao and the students. He put his hand on his *dantian* and quietly repeated it. Hah! He could feel the power of his *dantian* pushing out. Master Gao had said that this was how the body issued power, and Wayland was starting to understand.

The next day was Thursday, exactly one week since Wayland had first spied on Master Gao's specialized training. That evening Wayland ate dinner with Master Gao, Old Wu, and Suyin, and after some pleasant conversation he excused himself and went to his room a little after nine, as usual. After reading for a half hour or so, he turned out his lamp and pretended to go to bed. He lay on his bed for a while and then cocked his head to see if he could hear anything. He couldn't. Maybe last week was just a one-time training session. And besides, the others didn't say anything at dinner about training tonight. Although, Wayland thought, they didn't say anything about it last week, either.

Wayland hadn't undressed for bed anyway, so he just got up and slipped on his cotton shoes. He slowly opened the door to his room and peered out. Nobody was in sight. He crept out into the courtyard. The night was clear, and a cool breeze was gently blowing through the courtyard as he looked up at the bright star field above. He snuck across the compound to the far courtyard where he had seen them training last week. As he got closer, he could hear voices. They were there again!

Wayland got up on the bench, exactly as he had last week, and lifted himself to peer over the wall. Once again, it was only Master Gao with Lunghui and Suyin. This time, however, they were doing more than just working on breathing. Both of them were in a balanced stance, with their legs about shoulder-width apart and with their left foot forward. Lunghui and Suyin were both executing the same technique over and over: a simple punch with their right hand. Master Gao observed as the two punched steadily again and again. With each punch, they sounded "hah!" Wayland softly made the sound himself in unison with their punches, and he was conscious of his *dantian* expanding forcefully with each of his exhalations.

"Not quite right," Master Gao said, as he put his hand on Suyin's right shoulder. He lifted her arm, and Lunghui also stopped punching and turned to him. "Weak. Your hand is weak, your forearm is weak, and your shoulder is weak. They will always be weak. Don't hit with them."

Master Gao walked over to a small basket on the ground and came up holding an egg. He held the egg in his right palm and showed it to Lunghui and Suyin. He nodded to Lunghui, and Lunghui sunk into a stable stance. Master Gao readied himself, closed his fingers over the egg to form a fist, and then he delivered a controlled punch to Lunghui's chest. The force of the punch bounced Lunghui back a couple of feet, but he was ready for it and was able to maintain his balance.

"You see?" Master Gao said. He opened his hand, and the egg was unbroken. Lunghui and Suyin looked at each other in surprise, and Wayland was similarly impressed.

"There's no secret to it," Master Gao said. "The power of my punch doesn't come from the muscles of my hand, or arm, or shoulders." Master Gao tapped himself on his rear end. "This is where it comes from. The big muscles of the legs and thighs. You walk around on them all day. They're much stronger than your arms. That is what you want to hit your opponent with. The upper body only needs to be relaxed and properly aligned, and the power of the legs and the *chi* will flow through to your opponent. The egg didn't break because my hand, wrist, arm, and shoulder were relaxed and properly aligned. That is why *T'ai Chi Fist* places so much emphasis on relaxation, and that is what makes it different from other styles of martial arts. Don't ever forget this, it is the essence of the art."

That was it. Wayland knew that he had heard something essential, and he lowered himself down and then dropped the last couple of feet onto the bench. He didn't think he made too much noise, but he didn't want to take any chances. He crouched down against the wall, knowing that in the dark if anyone came out from the small compound, they wouldn't be able to see him. He breathed quietly for a few moments, but then he could hear Master Gao and the others speaking softly on the other side of the wall. They hadn't heard him. Wayland snuck back across the main compound to his room.

He walked in and closed the door behind him, then leaned his back up against it. His mind was racing with what he had just overheard. It was starting to make sense. Wayland thought back to the rudimentary martial arts lessons he had received from his friend Lihao. Lihao had been an intellectual, and he could explain the theories of Chinese martial arts quite well. But he was no fighter. Master Gao could actually express the theories physically, and with a level of skill that Wayland was just beginning to appreciate.

He didn't want to turn the lamp on, as the others might see the light. So he stood there in the dark. He got into the same stance that Suyin and Lunghui had stood in, and then he punched with his right hand. He felt the muscles in his forearm, and then his fist tense up as he punched. *No, that's exactly what Master Gao said you shouldn't do. The power doesn't come from the arm and shoulder. It comes from the legs, and from the turning of the waist.*

Wayland punched slowly, making a conscious effort not to tense the muscles of his arm. It felt awkward at first, weak and ineffective. How can you hit with your arm relaxed? It didn't make sense. *The egg.* He remembered what Master Gao had done with the egg. Wayland tried to think if he had anything in his room the size of an egg, but nothing came to mind. It didn't matter; he imagined the egg in his right hand, and he retook the stance. He punched, slowly at first. Yes, if he kept his knuckles, wrist, and forearm all aligned, it might work. He punched harder and faster. He realized his arm wasn't moving much at all. His hips were driving his fist forward, just as Master Gao had said. It felt right, but he wasn't wholly sure—he had to punch something.

He put his hand up against the wall of his room, and in the dark, he felt along the wall until he came to his heavy cotton coat hanging on a peg. He put his knuckles against it; it wasn't too thick, but it would do. He punched against it, and his fist impacted the brick behind the coat. *Nope. Still tensing your arm and fist. Remember the egg.* He relaxed his arm and punched again just as hard. Upon impact, his wrist twisted violently, and Wayland could tell that he came close to breaking it. *Alignment.* He steadied himself, imagined the egg in his palm, and punched the coat, at half-speed this time. Better, but the alignment was still off. He put his knuckles right up against the coat and leaned in. He relaxed the muscles in his arms as much as possible and leaned in further. He lifted his front foot off the ground so that his fist against the wall was supporting almost all of his weight.

He felt the alignment and adjusted his wrist and arm slightly, and it worked. It worked! He could keep his arm and shoulder relaxed with his fist up against the target, and he could lean in and comfortably support his whole body.

He drew back his fist and put his front leg back down. Maintaining the alignment, he began to punch slowly. He drove off his rear foot, turned his waist and hit the unforgiving wall through the coat. He increased his speed, punching the wall again and again, faster and faster. He was conscious of some pain in his knuckles, but he was even more aware of the power he was generating. It was strange and exhilarating. He was relaxed, yet it felt like he was hitting the wall with the power of his whole body. He stopped and stepped back from the wall and exhaled slowly. He unclenched his fist and opened up his fingers several times. He rubbed his right knuckles with his left hand, and he felt a warm wetness; he brought his hand to his nose and smelled the faint scent of blood. He felt his way over to the water basin in the corner and washed off his hand.

He smiled to himself as he took off his shirt and lay down on his bedding. As he lay there on his back, he punched up into the air slowly, once, twice, and a third time, remembering what he had just learned. He put his arm down, satisfied and weary, and in no time at all, he fell into a deep, dreamless sleep.

21

WAYLAND WOKE the next day at his usual time, washed up, and walked to the kitchen to round up some breakfast. Suyin was already there, and the steam rose from the fresh pot of tea she had just made. He picked up a bowl from the cabinet and sat down at the table. There was already a basin of warm millet congee there, and Wayland spooned some of that into his bowl. He closed his eyes and mouthed a silent grace, and then began eating.

"Tea?" She asked as she brought the teapot to the table.

"Thank you," Wayland said. Suyin filled his cup, and then her own. She sat down and served herself some of the congee. Wayland took a sip of tea, and Suyin saw his hand.

"What happened?" She asked.

"Huh?" Wayland said.

"Your hand is bruised," Suyin said.

"Oh... yeah. I scraped it on the wall when I was walking by."

"Should you wrap it?" Suyin asked.

"No, it's not that bad." He flexed his hand and fingers.

"That was quite a scrape", she said. "It's all of your knuckles."

"Yeah, I was clumsy," Wayland said. He finished his congee and tea and brought the dishes over to the table by the wash basin. He started to wash them, but Suyin spoke.

"I'll take care of those," Suyin said.

"Thanks," Wayland said. "I'm going to head out."

"Bye," Suyin said as Wayland left. She thought he was being a little evasive, but she couldn't quite put her finger on it.

After dinner that evening, Wayland went straight back to his room, He told the others that he was going to read, but as soon as he closed the door, he began practicing what he had learned. His right knuckles were still a little sore, so he switched over to his left hand, and continued punching the coat hanging against the wall. This was a little more challenging because he wasn't left-handed. Getting the alignment right didn't come as easily, and he couldn't punch as hard. After several hundred punches over twenty minutes, though, it started to feel more natural. He experimented and compared the difference between a vertical fist and a horizontal one. He struck low, and he hit high. After a while, he switched hands and threw several punches with his right, but it was still a bit too sore to strike as hard as he had the previous night. But he had the structure, the feeling of the technique down pat. He turned away from the wall and continued the method as shadow boxing. He punched over and over again into the air, and his arm and shoulder were almost completely relaxed. The techniques were starting to feel natural, almost second nature.

Wayland threw one potent punch, and he unconsciously made the sound "hah!" *That's right!* He put his left hand on his dantian, and punched with his right hand, voicing "hah!" He felt his *dantian* expand powerfully in coordination with the sound and the punch. He did this again several times, feeling the difference in power when he made the slight vocalization. He brought his scraped knuckles up and smiled as he looked at them.

Over the next week, Wayland continued his practice, combining the breathing with the relaxed, focused punching, and he could feel his steady improvement. When nobody was looking, he would utilize what he had learned in everyday situations. When he opened a door, he would gently hold out his perfectly aligned, relaxed arm, and push the door open with a step, a turn of the waist, and a quiet "hah." When he had to chop wood, he would use the weight of the ax and the force of his whole body rather than just the strength of his arms. When he had to move heavy chairs or tables across the floor to sweep at the inn, he would keep his upper body as relaxed as possible and push with his legs. Wayland's newfound method of expressing power started to feel slightly curious to him; it was as if he was relaxed and looser, but at the same time more heavy and rooted. It felt natural and powerful, and he liked it.

Wayland felt slightly guilty about spying on Master Gao and the others during their late-night lessons, but he was picking up so much that when Thursday evening came around again, he couldn't resist having another look.

"That's good," Wayland said, as he slowly peeked out his door. It was an overcast night with no moonlight or stars visible. He came out of his room and peered out into the central courtyard from behind his wall. Nobody in sight. As he had done the previous two weeks, he tip-toed his way across the main compound to Master Gao's private area. As he got within a couple of yards, he could hear the familiar voices of Master Gao and Lunghui. They were all training again. The old wooden bench was still in the same place, and it was now a familiar business for Wayland. He stepped up on it and in one motion jumped and grabbed onto the top of the wall. He quickly pulled himself up and found the same foothold on the stone wall to support himself. He slowly lifted his head just enough to see over the wall.

It was only Master Gao and Lunghui this evening. No sign of Suyin. They seemed to be working on some two-person drill.

Master Gao had Lunghui punch at his head, and Master Gao was deflecting the blow with his right hand in a gentle yet fast sweeping motion.

"Don't hold back when you're doing drills like this with a partner," Master Gao said, correcting Lunghui. "If you don't attack them seriously, they won't be learning to defend against a serious attack. And similarly, if I see that your punch isn't even going to hit me, why would I bother defending against it at all?"

Lunghui nodded. "Right."

"Now this is a cooperative drill, so I'm not saying to try to hit your partner as hard and fast as you possibly can. We are just training, and we're not attempting to injure one another. But make sure that if your partner fails to properly defend against your attack, he will be hit. Continue."

The two continued the drill, and Wayland watched with rapt attention.

"What are you doing?" A quiet but demanding voice came from behind him, and Wayland froze. It was Suyin.

"Get down from there!" she said, and although she sounded angry, she was still whispering.

Wayland lowered himself down and then dropped to the bench. He turned to face her as he sheepishly stepped down to the courtyard.

"You're *spying* on Master Gao?" Suyin said.

"I wasn't really spying," Wayland said, trying to think of a way to talk himself out of the predicament. "It was more like I was just *observing*. You know, learning."

Suyin walked up to him, angry. "Don't you want to keep training with Master Gao?"

"Sure I do," Wayland said. "That's why I'm doing this in the first place. I want to learn more."

"You're going to be learning, all right. You'll learn how

a teacher throws you out and disowns you. If you're caught spying by Master Gao," Suyin said, still whispering and looking around nervously, "that is probably what's going to happen. There are a lot of secrets in Chinese martial arts. Maybe you don't understand that, but that's how it is here. It's a grave offense to steal someone's teachings without their permission."

"But I'm really learning," Wayland said. "Watch this." He got into his stance and delivered a short, sharp punch with his right hand. The sleeve of his coat snapped audibly with the force of his strike.

Suyin's brow furrowed. "You learned that just from watching? How long have you been spying?"

"I've only seen a couple sessions," Wayland said.

"Well, that's the end of it, do you understand?" Suyin asked.

"All right."

"Look, maybe I can show you a few things. Here and there, to keep you on the right track. But you can't tell Master Gao. And you can't spy on him anymore. Agreed?"

"Agreed."

"Good. Now go back to your room," Suyin said.

Wayland grinned. "Okay. And what are you doing?"

"I'm going to train!" Suyin turned abruptly and went to join Master Gao and Lunghui.

***

Two days later, Wayland was up early practicing what he had learned. He wasn't sure who was around the house that day, so he just did his exercises in the privacy of his room. After an hour, he stepped out into the main courtyard to make his way to the kitchen for some breakfast. The day was overcast but dry, with a warm breeze blowing. As he walked by the wooden frame of the small pool in the main courtyard, something caught his eye. There was movement in the water, and as he looked down,

Wayland saw that it was a large goldfish. He watched it slowly swim the perimeter of the pool.

"What are you looking at?" Suyin said as she approached.

"Oh, I didn't know anyone else was here," Wayland said.

"Just me," Suyin said. "Master Gao and Old Wu have gone into town."

"I know you told me this pool is fed by a spring, and it doesn't fill fast enough to use for drinking water," Wayland said. "But why is there a goldfish in there?"

"It's very simple. I'm surprised you haven't figured it out, with your superior Western education," Suyin said.

"Okay, explain it to me," Wayland said, smiling.

"Standing water is a breeding ground for mosquitoes. A goldfish eats mosquito eggs. Put a goldfish in the water, and no more mosquitoes. Does that make sense, professor?"

"I guess it does," Wayland said.

Suyin raised her eyebrows and smiled confidently.

"Say, if we're by ourselves here," Wayland said. Suyin cast a sharp glance at him. "Weren't you going to help me with my training?"

Suyin rubbed her chin for a moment, and then her eyes lit up. "Stand in a 'bow' stance."

"I don't know what that is," Wayland said.

Suyin sighed and shook her head. "You should know, you watched us doing it enough from behind the wall."

"Oh, you mean like this?" Wayland asked. He stood with his shoulders square, facing forward and with his right leg out in front.

Suyin frowned slightly. "More or less," she said, shaking her head again. "Put your right arm out in front of your chest, your palm facing in, as if you've got a towel draped over your arm."

Wayland did so.

"Now," Suyin said. "I'm going to push on your arm, and you hold me back." Wayland nodded. Suyin put both of her hands on Wayland's arm, and she started pushing. Wayland was quite a bit stronger than Suyin, but she was using both hands and putting all of her weight into the push. The muscles in Wayland's arm tensed, and he was able to hold her back for a while, but then Suyin pushed hard, and Wayland's arm gave way, and Suyin pushed it into his chest.

"Well, I don't know what that proves," Wayland said. "If you use both hands and push with all your weight, you're stronger than my right arm. I could have told you that."

Suyin smiled. "Now you try." She settled into the same stance that Wayland had, and she held her right arm out in front.

Wayland shrugged his shoulders and smiled knowingly. "You really want to do this?"

"Just push. It should be easy for a strong man like you," Suyin said.

Wayland raised his eyebrows and cocked his head. *Okay, if that's how she wanted to play it.* He pushed against her with his right hand, expecting her arm to give way quickly. It didn't. Suyin looked straight ahead, a slightly bemused expression on her face.

"Okay, then," Wayland said. "I'm really going to push."

Suyin stood firm in her stance, not betraying any emotion. Wayland put both hands on Suyin's extended forearm and pushed. Nothing. He braced himself and drove from his back foot. Still nothing. He stood up straight and rolled up his sleeves. He inhaled, and again pushed with both hands. She was a good four inches shorter than him, and probably forty pounds lighter. Wayland pushed again, as hard as he could. This time, Suyin turned her waist ever so slightly to the right, and Wayland's momentum caused him to go crashing by Suyin and down to the ground.

Suyin relaxed and stood up straight, and she brushed her hands together as if she had just finished some mundane chore.

Wayland got to his feet. "Okay, some trick or something? How did you do that?"

"It's no trick," Suyin said. "It's just knowing how to use your body."

"Show me," Wayland said.

Suyin nodded. "Get in your stance."

Wayland settled down into the stance and put his right arm out in front.

"No, not like that," she said. She tapped his shoulder. "Relax. Everything is too tense, and the *chi* can't flow. Sink your shoulders, sink your weight. Pretend your root is going down below the soles of your feet, going down about six inches into the ground. Feel yourself becoming heavy, but relaxed."

Wayland relaxed his shoulders and arms. He let them drop to his side.

"No, relaxed does not mean limp," Suyin said. "Relaxed means ready, sensitive, alert, but not tensed."

Wayland tried his best to follow all of Suyin's instructions, even though some of them seemed contradictory. "Like this?'

Suyin nodded. "Right. Now your arm. You need to sink your chest. It shouldn't be puffed out, it should be drawn in, but relaxed. You want to form a circle with your arm and your chest, as if you're holding a big ball. Yes, that's it. Now, feel what happens when I push." Suyin put both hands on Wayland's extended forearm again, and she pushed. Wayland's structure held.

"That's good. Now I'm going to push hard, so be ready." She pushed with both hands, as hard as she could, and Wayland didn't budge.

"Hey, it works! I feel like I could hold back five men pushing against my arm."

"Look at the alignment," Suyin said. She traced a line in the air from Wayland's arm, waist, legs, and feet. "If everything is lined up correctly, when I push you I'm just pushing against the ground. You don't need to use much of your strength at all. Do you understand?"

Wayland looked down at his Arm and legs and nodded slowly. "I think I do."

"There is a saying in *T'ai Chi Fist* that 'four ounces can deflect a thousand pounds.' You get it?" Suyin asked. "When I push against your arm," she said, putting her hands back on Wayland's arm, "keep your structure, but just turn your waist a bit."

Wayland did so, and the force of Suyin's push went to his right, and even though she was expecting it, Suyin stumbled a bit before regaining her balance.

"Just like that," she said.

They both stood up straight, and Wayland looked down at his extended arm. "That's amazing. I didn't have to use any arm strength at all."

"That's your lesson for today, now let's get back to work."

"Sure," Wayland said, absentmindedly. He kept his arm extended, and turned his waist a few more times, replaying what he had been taught. He looked back up at Suyin. "Will you teach me more stuff?"

Suyin frowned and sighed. "Master Gao is your teacher, not me. He should be the one to decide what you're learning and when you learn it."

"But he always says you have to think, and practice, and ponder on your own if you're going to improve, doesn't he?" Wayland had a mischievous smile on his face. "And the students are supposed to help each other out, right?"

Suyin paused for a moment, looking at Wayland. "I'll answer your questions and offer some corrections if you ask. But I'm not your teacher, remember that."

"I will," Wayland said.

"And don't tell anyone about this. Not Master Gao, or Old Wu. You understand? I'll get in trouble."

"Sure," Wayland said. "Whatever you say. I appreciate anything you can show me."

Suyin's eyes met Wayland's, and the two gazed at each other for a moment without uttering a word. Suyin's hair was tied in the back, but a few strands fell in front of her face; Wayland felt an overwhelming urge to brush them away. His smile faded as he looked deeply into her eyes, and he took a step towards her. Suyin's lips slowly parted; her breathing slowed, but her heart began beating faster.

"Suyin, I... " Wayland wasn't exactly sure what he was trying to say.

Suyin averted her eyes and stepped back. "I have to go," she said, turning to walk away.

Wayland sighed deeply and stared, as if transfixed, at the empty space where Suyin had stood. He tried to gather his thoughts, but everything was a jumble. Whatever his future might hold, he now knew that separating himself from Suyin would not be easy.

22

Wayland settled into a regular schedule. He kept up with his chores and manual labor during the day, and in the evenings he practiced the *ch'i kung* breathing exercises that he had learned, as well as the stance and relaxation training. He had several more private lessons from Suyin, and he began to get the basics of the two-person pushing hands training of *T'ai Chi Fist*.

After lunch one day, Wayland was carrying two full water buckets balanced on a pole across his shoulders. He was half jogging across the courtyard with his heavy load when he heard Master Gao's voice.

"Wei-lin, can I see you for a moment?"

Wayland turned to see Master Gao approaching. He set down the water buckets and walked over to his teacher. "What is it, Master Gao? You need me to do something?"

Master Gao smiled and shook his head. "I don't need you to do anything. Wei-lin, over the last several weeks I've noticed that you seem to have taken well to your chores, and to life here in general."

Wayland shrugged. "I like it here. I like helping out at the inn, and here at your house. I feel like I'm... useful."

"I know both Old Wu and Suyin think very highly of you. I value their opinions and appreciate their judgment," Master Gao said.

"They've both been very kind to me," Wayland said.

Master Gao nodded. "Do you think you're ready to join the regular class?"

Wayland's face brightened. "I think I am, Master Gao."

"We'll see. Be there promptly tomorrow."

"Yes, I will. Thank you, Master Gao," Wayland said, bowing slightly.

"You can finish your chores now," Master Gao said.

Wayland went back to his water buckets and put the pole across his shoulders and stood up. The buckets didn't seem quite as heavy as they had been a few minutes ago.

Wu Chen and Shen Fai were over to one side of the courtyard practicing *chin-na* joint locking techniques, and Lunghui and Shih Hua were going through their saber form in synchronicity. Suyin was practicing her straight sword, working on individual cuts and deflections and the associated footwork. Wayland, however, as far as he could tell, was just standing there. He was in the posture he had been taught: spine straight, head upright, his whole body relaxed, his feet at shoulder width, and his two hands extended slightly in front of his body, with his palms open and facing down. He was told to stand like this and just breathe naturally; this was the "Four Gates Breathing."

Master Gao strolled among his students, observing.

"No, if you have the angle right, you don't have to force it," he said to Wu Chen who was unsuccessfully trying to lock the wrist of his partner in their cooperative training. Master Gao motioned for the student to move to the side and, he took his place. He nodded, and Shen Fai began the drill and grabbed in at Master Gao's wrist. As the student's hand made contact with his master's forearm, Master Gao turned his waist slightly and brought his other hand around, and with seemingly no effort he had wholly locked the student's wrist. He continued twisting ever so slightly, and the Shen Fai instantly dropped to one knee, grimacing in pain. Master Gao released his grip, and Shen Fai stood back up, smiling and wincing and rubbing his wrist. Master Gao raised his eyebrows to Wu Chen, who nodded. Master Gao clapped him on the back and had them continue with the drill.

Master Gao then walked over to Wayland.

"Keep your neck straight," he said to Wayland. "As if your head is a string of pearls being suspended from above."

Wayland nodded. "Master Gao, what exactly is this supposed to do?"

Master Gao looked slightly annoyed. "What do you feel?"

"My palms and the soles of my feet feel warm, and my legs burn a little," Wayland said.

"That's what you're supposed to feel. Your *chi* is flowing." Master Gao turned to walk away.

Wayland continued. "But I still don't really understand what *chi* is."

Master Gao stopped and turned.

"I know how it's like 'energy' or 'breath,' and I do feel something. But I don't quite see how it relates to fighting." Wayland asked.

Master Gao scratched his forehead and sighed heavily. "It's best for students to keep their mouths shut and their eyes and ears open."

Wayland bowed slightly. "I don't mean to be disrespectful, Master Gao. I want to learn but I just don't understand it. "

Master Gao stared at Wayland for a moment and then shook his head again. "Old Wu," Master Gao said, motioning the elderly man to come over.

"Yes?" Old Wu said as he approached.

"Wei-lin says Americans don't use *chi* to fight. Explain to him what *chi* is."

Old Wu smiled and nodded, and Master Gao turned and walked over to observe the sword practice of Suyin.

"What's to understand?" Old Wu said to Wayland. "Everyone has *chi*, if they're alive. How do you not know that?"

Wayland furrowed his brow.

"Aiya," Old Wu said, frowning and squinting as if he had just tasted something terrible. "Show me your punch," he said.

Wayland tried to remember everything he had been taught, and he delivered a hard, chest-level punch into the air.

"So how did you do that?" Old Wu said. He stroked his white beard.

"How did I do what?" Wayland asked. "Punch?"

"Describe the process of punching."

"I guess…I used my muscles and tendons and ligaments all together, all connected, and made a fist and punched," Wayland said.

"Muscles and tendons and ligaments, huh?" Old Wu said. He held out his own arm. "I have muscles and tendons and ligaments here, don't I? How come I'm not punching?"

Wayland looked confused. Old Wu leaned in and tapped him three times on the forehead.

"In here! That's where it starts. Your mind has to decide to punch before you can punch," Old Wu said. "That's why it's always said that 'the mind leads the *chi*, relax unnecessary muscles, and coordinate with breathing.' That's using *chi*," Old Wu said.

"So I'm pushing *chi* out when I punch?" Wayland asked.

"No, no," Old Wu said, shaking his head. He looked up for a moment and gathered his thoughts, and then smiled and looked back to Wayland. "*Chi* is like a bull with a ring in its nose. It can't be pushed, but it can be led."

Wayland focused, relaxed his arm, and he snapped out a

powerful punch He opened his fist and looked at his palm. "So that's what *chi* is?" he said. "I think I understand."

"No, you only understand the first page of the book. But that's good enough for now," Old Wu said, stroking his beard. He looked at Wayland a moment, and then turned and walked away.

That evening, Suyin prepared a simple dinner of steamed yu choy tips and hot noodles with a spicy ground pork sauce, which was one of Wayland's favorites. During the meal, Master Gao regaled them all with several funny stories of his own martial arts training as a youth.

When they had finished the meal and the old tales, Suyin got up to clear the dishes and Wayland helped her.

"I'm going to relax and enjoy my pipe out in the courtyard, I think," Master Gao said.

"I think I'll join you," Old Wu said. "If you want to stop by later to study, Wei-lin, I'll be up for a while."

"Thank you. I will," Wayland said.

Master Gao put his pipe in his mouth and pulled out his tobacco pouch. "Studying what?"

"The young man has an interest in Taoism, and I'm explaining the *Tao Te Ching* to him."

Master Gao raised his eyebrows, and he lit his pipe.

The days were getting shorter, and there were still some remains of light on the cool autumn evening as Wayland made his way across the compound to Old Wu's room. Wayland knocked.

"Yes, come in."

"Good evening, Old Wu," Wayland said.

"All right," Old Wu said. "Come out to my courtyard, I want

to show you a few things." He got up and opened the back door to the room, which opened to his small private courtyard.

"Aren't we going to work on the *Tao Te Ching*? I don't want to have lied to Master Gao," Wayland said.

Old Wu sighed and stroked his white beard. "All right. That's what we'll do, then. Too honest for your own good, that's your problem." He closed the door to the courtyard, went over to the bookshelf and pulled out his worn copy of the *Tao Te Ching*. "Sit down, sit down," he said, motioning Wayland over, with a hint of impatience.

"All right," Old Wu said. "We've studied philosophy for half an hour. You didn't lie to Master Gao. Now it's time to put the books away. He reached for the candle holder and stood up. He walked over and opened the door to the courtyard and motioned Wayland through. It was quite dark, and Old Wu lit the way with the candle as he walked over and lit each of the four lamps in the corners of the courtyard. Wayland was surprised at how well they brightened the area.

"Now, what happened when I helped you out of your situation with those ruffians?" Old Wu asked.

"I got the shit kicked out of me," Wayland said.

"You did indeed. I mean, what did *I* do?"

"Well, you knocked over two guys, and the others ran away." Wayland had been flat on his back, but he was pretty sure that's what had happened.

Old Wu shook his head impatiently. "No, no. That's not what I mean. Did you see what techniques I used?"

"I didn't see," Wayland said.

"Ah, you have to pay attention. Pay attention to what's going on around you. Real life is a better teacher than all the drills you can practice in a year."

Not that easy when you're bleeding and barely conscious, Wayland thought. Still, the old man knew what he was talking about. Wayland nodded.

"Now, the first man tried to grab me with both hands. He stepped at me with his left foot forward. I used Master Gao's *T'ai Chi Fist*, just as you've been taught. I used "Brush knee," with my left arm, and deflected his attack to my right. With his left leg forward, what does that mean?"

"Well... I guess... "

"It means he had an open door." He grabbed Wayland's arm and pulled him into the same position that the attacker had been in, with his left foot forward. "So as he came ahead, I slid to the left and then did the *T'ai Chi Fist* 'press' on his right shoulder."

Old Wu stepped and then pressed firmly on Wayland's right shoulder and pushed him diagonally backward to the left. With no means to support himself, Wayland fell hard. Wayland was amazed at the controlled power of the old man, and he could tell that Old Wu hadn't put much effort into it. The old man matter-of-factly reached down to pull Wayland up.

"Now you try," Old Wu said. "But don't push me down. I am an old man, after all."

Wayland wasn't too sure about that anymore, but he readied himself, and Old Wu came at him with both hands just like the attacker had done to him. Wayland used "brush knee" and then turned his waist to deflect the old man's attack. He then slid to his left to press the shoulder, when he felt a thunderclap on his chest and found himself on his rear end again. The pain radiated from his upper right chest down through his midsection, and out to his arms. He gasped for breath. Old Wu again helped him up. Wayland was still trying to get his breath.

"Oh, you're all right," Old Wu said. "You had the right idea, but you're thinking about what you have to do instead of just doing it. You gave me time to hit you. Your movement has to be natural, with no gaps."

Wayland nodded.

Old Wu looked at Wayland and stroked his beard. "You know what I hit you with just there?"

Wayland shook his head.

"It wasn't *T'ai Chi Fist*," Old Wu said.

"Shaolin?" Wayland asked.

"No," Old Wu said. "I trained with several masters before I studied with Master Gao's father. One of the styles I learned was called *Hsingyi Fist*. Have you heard of it?"

"I think so," Wayland said, furrowing his brow. "But just in passing. I don't know much about it."

Old Wu nodded. "It shares many of the principles of *T'ai Chi Fist*. It is closer to *T'ai Chi Fist* than Shaolin, in that it places a greater emphasis on the cultivation of *chi*, as opposed to muscular strength and speed. Still, it is not as subtle as *T'ai Chi Fist*. The movements are simple, sharp, linear. And it's easier to learn. When one strikes, one still generates power from the legs and keeps the body relaxed as in *T'ai Chi Fist*, but tenses up the muscles more at the moment of impact. While *T'ai Chi Fist* is a soft style, *Hsingyi Fist* may be called a soft-hard style. The technique I used against you is called the 'splitting fist,' and is the most basic technique. Let me teach you that."

Old Wu showed Wayland the basic preparatory stance, and how the hand movements of the strike coordinated with the stepping. Old Wu stepped forward with his right foot while striking with his right palm, and then alternated to his left foot, stepping in a straight line. Wayland stood next to Old Wu and studiously copied the older man's movements to the best of his ability. After a few strikes, Old Wu stopped but had Wayland continue.

"Good," Old Wu said. "When you hit with the palm, you should put all of your body weight behind the strike. Tense your palm only at the instant of impact. Your power should be exploding out. That's it. And above all, keep your mind focused. Not on the technique, but on the target. *Chi* must power your strike."

Wayland continued the stepping and the strikes until he came near to the wall.

"Now turn and reverse your direction," Old Wu said.

Wayland did so. He continued with the sequence of palm strikes, left, right and left again. His body felt relaxed and heavy at the same time. He moved easily, yet with focused power. With each strike, felt like he could put his palm through a stone wall. It felt good.

"Yes," Old Wu said. He smiled. "Now stop."

"What?" Wayland asked. He turned to Old Wu, slightly perplexed. "I thought I had it. It felt right."

"You do have it. And I want you to remember this feeling and this moment. To know that that the teaching you've received, your intellect, your body, and your spirit can all come together. These moments are rare when you're beginning your training, but it's important to recognize them. You will have many days in your life when all does not come together, and indeed, you will think it is impossible that they ever will. But it is not impossible. That is all for today. Remember what you've learned, and practice diligently what you've been taught."

"Thank you, Old Wu," Wayland said. "I greatly appreciate…"

Old Wu waved his hand dismissively at Wayland. "Yes, yes. Just practice."

He turned and walked away.

23

WAYLAND PRACTICED the techniques that Old Wu had taught him, along with the regular lessons that he was getting in the classes from Master Gao. Nothing that either of the men had told him contradicted what the other one had said, but Wayland saw that they each approached things from a different angle. Master Gao didn't like to explain things; he wanted to show them to you. If you didn't get it the first time, he'd show you again. But you had better pay attention because he didn't like to show things a third time. Old Wu was more relaxed, never getting angry, and always cracking jokes and bringing up obscure bits of philosophy and history whenever he was instructing. But if you didn't pay attention to his corrections, he'd just ignore you for the rest of the class and not offer you any insights again for a good while.

In addition to the regular lessons of Master Gao, Wayland greatly appreciated the occasional auxiliary training he was getting in secret from both Old Wu and Suyin. When he had a chance during the day between chores, Wayland would go to his room and study the notes he had written down. At night, after everyone else had gone to bed, Wayland would go out into the courtyard under the moonlight and practice the techniques again and again.

The next Thursday, a little before three in the afternoon, Wayland changed into his workout clothes and shoes. He stepped outside, and it was a little colder than he had expected. He quickly went back in and put on a light coat. As he walked across the courtyard, he looked up at the sky, grey and heavy with the threat of snow. He shivered a bit, but he knew he'd warm up once class started and he got moving.

The others were all there, except for Lunghui and Master Gao himself. Suyin was stretching, and Wu Chen and Shen Fai were engaged in pushing hands practice; they were of a similar skill level, and they pushed each other off balance at about an equal rate.

"Hello," Wayland said to everyone, and Suyin waved to him.

Old Wu nodded his greeting but then turned to the two pushing hands. "Aiya," he said frowning. "You're just shoving at each other. It's not a contest of strength, not a wrestling match. Softness, that is your goal." Old Wu motioned for Shen Fai to step aside, and then he stood to push with Wu Chen. "Now push," Old Wu said.

Wu Chen was trying to push but at the same time trying to keep Old Wu's advice, pushed gently at the older man.

"No good," Old Wu said, shaking his head. "Too weak. You're not going to push through a piece of paper like that. Push like you're trying to topple me over," Old Wu said.

"Good morning, everyone," Master Gao said as he walked into the compound, and Old Wu stood to one side.

"Good morning," all responded. Master Gao took his place up front, and everyone turned to face him. He bowed to his students and they to him, and then he began leading them all in a warm-up. He started by just gently bouncing up and down, relaxing his upper body and just letting his arms go where they might. Then he turned his waist from side to side, allowing his arms to follow, slapping on his shoulders as he turned back and forth.

"Now, follow," Master Gao said, as he began the familiar

"Four Gates" breathing exercise. They all stood straight and relaxed with their feet at shoulder width, with their arms held out at waist-level, with their palms facing down. With each inhalation, they would lift their bodies a bit, and then softly sink their weight as they exhaled.

For the next half hour, they worked on various applications found in the barehand form, focusing mostly on the "grasp sparrow's tail" technique. The first application of the method that they were learning was to bring the arm up and deflect an opponent's strike. Wayland was paired with Suyin, and she was taking the role of the attacker. She stepped in with a right palm strike to Wayland's chest, and Wayland brought his right hand up, his palm facing inward, and used his wrist and forearm to deflect Suyin's attack. They repeated this several times.

Master Gao was walking among the students, observing, and he stopped at Suyin and Wayland.

"Mmm," Master Gao grunted, with no expression. Wayland looked up at Master Gao for instruction. "Keep going," Master Gao said, and the two continued.

After another twenty minutes of practice, Master Gao motioned for all the students to come over to him.

"We're going to do some more sparring today. Everyone, please spread out. Lunghui and Wei-lin, please step to the center."

The two did so. Lunghui stared intently at Wayland, his face devoid of expression. Wayland stared back for a second and then broke eye contact, looking down. He flashed just a hint of a smile.

"You two are familiar with the rules," Master Gao said. "And remember the purpose of sparring. Defeating your opponent here is no victory if it is gained only through clumsy strength and natural ability."

Wayland and Lunghui both nodded.

"Begin," Master Gao said, and he stepped back.

Wayland and Lunghui began circling each other, pacing slowly, sizing each other up and looking for an opening. Suyin watched them both and felt herself tensing up. Old Wu put his hand on her shoulder, and Suyin looked back and smiled quickly at him.

Lunghui stepped in quickly with a low kick to Wayland's shin, but Wayland only shifted back, sensing that it was just a feint. But in a sharp movement, Lunghui hopped forward and with the same leg kicked higher, this time to Wayland's stomach. Wayland tried to bring his arm down to brush the kick away, but he was a little slow, and the kick grazed his ribs on his right side. It was a glancing blow, and Wayland wasn't fazed. Lunghui was slightly surprised that his kick didn't fully connect; Wayland seemed relaxed and steady. This was something new.

Lunghui continued circling, and Wayland kept distance, both fighters eyeing each other intently, their senses hyper-focused. Wayland stutter-stepped in and feinted a left jab at Lunghui's chest, and when Lunghui's hand went up to block it, Wayland stepped in with a palm strike to Lunghui's stomach. Lunghui was surprised, but he saw it in time and was able to turn his waist and lead Wayland's attack away. He grasped Wayland's wrist and tried to lock it, but Wayland twisted his hand free before Lunghui could complete the lock. The two were at close range, grappling distance, and Wayland knew that Lunghui's "sensing" and "listening" skills — the essence of *T'ai Chi Fist* — were much higher than his. Wayland pushed down on Lunghui's forearms, sealing them, and stepped back to get out of dangerous close range.

A look of frustration briefly appeared on Lunghui's face at the fact that Wayland was able to get away from him. He wasn't going to let that stand. He closed in on Wayland, but his anger had overtaken his better judgment. Instead of retreating as Lunghui expected, Wayland calmly stepped forward with a "splitting fist" palm strike of *Hsingyi Fist*, just as Old Wu had shown him. With no time to prepare for the impact, Lunghui's forward momentum was turned back against him, and combined with the power of the strike he was knocked back several feet and fell to the ground.

Master Gao raised one eyebrow slightly, and he glanced over at Old Wu. Old Wu stared straight ahead, making a concerted effort to avoid Master Gao's gaze. The match continued.

Lunghui quickly stood back up. His anger was gone, replaced by a razor-sharp intensity, and he squared up against Wayland again. The two circled for a moment before Lunghui came in with a back fist strike to Wayland's temple. Lunghui seemed more relaxed, more focused and quicker than Wayland had seen up to this point. Wayland brought his palm up and was just able to deflect that strike, but Lunghui swept his hand across and grasped Wayland's wrist. As he pulled Wayland's arm out, Lunghui brought his other arm under Wayland's armpit and, twisting, stepped in with the "diagonal flying" technique which lifted Wayland off his feet and sent him spiraling down onto the hard cobblestone of the compound.

"Oh!" Suyin exclaimed, louder than she meant to.

"That's enough for today," Master Gao said.

Lunghui took another step towards Wayland, but then he stopped and turned to Master Gao, and he bowed slightly to his teacher. Lunghui looked over to Wayland and saw that he was getting to his feet; he would be all right.

"I'm okay," Wayland said, as he saw the looks of concern from the others. He stood up and winced as he arched his back and rubbed the back of his neck.

"Wei-lin and Lunghui, good effort from both of you," Master Gao said. "Class is dismissed for today. Practice what you've learned, and we'll meet again in two days, at the same time."

Suyin walked towards Wayland, but Master Gao put his hand on her shoulder. "You attend to your chores. I want to talk to Wei-lin," he said.

"Yes, Master Gao," Suyin said. She cast another quick glance towards Wayland and then walked away.

"You're not injured?" Master Gao asked.

"I'll be all right," Wayland said, but his expression and body language were less convincing.

"You've improved. You've paid attention to what you've been taught, you've practiced, and pondered things on your own. That's the only secret to martial arts, you know."

"Thank you," Wayland said.

"And I suspect that you've had some other instruction on the side, in addition to the things that I've taught you... "

"Umm... well... " Wayland struggled with his desire to be honest with Master Gao while not betraying the confidence of either Old Wu or Suyin.

Master Gao sensed his dilemma and waved his hand dismissively. "At any rate, you've gotten better. Still, you're not better than Lunghui."

"I know," Wayland said.

"But you could be," Master Gao said.

Wayland tried to control his expression, but he was pretty sure that he was beaming.

"Put some liniment on your bruises and go to bed early tonight," Master Gao said. "And you'll have some time to recover before the next class. I've received word from Fenchow that my master is not well, and he has requested my presence. I will leave tomorrow morning, and I will be gone for several days, maybe longer."

The next morning was slightly overcast but mild. Old Wu and Lunghui had prepared the horse for Master Gao's journey, and Suyin had wrapped up a package of steamed pork buns and some pickled cabbage for him to take along the way. Master Gao was standing just outside the main gate of the compound, gently stroking his horse's mane.

"This should last you a while," Suyin said as she put the package into the saddlebag on Master Gao's horse. "Be careful out on the road. There is so much trouble these days," she said.

"I think I'll be all right, Suyin." Master Gao said. He was slightly amused at her concern.

Suyin smiled and nodded.

"Now as for you two," Master Gao said. His tone was stern as he pointed directly at Old Wu and Suyin. "Old Wu, I was a bit perplexed at Wei-lin's performance during the sparring yesterday."

"Yes," Old Wu said. He forced a smile that wasn't completely convincing. "He's quite a strange one, isn't he? Always coming up with his own techniques, and adding things to what you taught him. He's got a crazy way of doing things, that's for sure."

"He hit Lunghui with a strike that I didn't teach him," Master Gao said.

"Really?" Old Wu responded.

"Yes. It would be quite impressive if he invented that technique himself."

Old Wu looked up at the sun. "You should probably start off. We don't want to waste half the day standing here talking."

"... because what he hit Lunghui with was the splitting fist of *Hsingyi Fist*," Master Gao said.

"That *is* strange, now that you mention it, " Old Wu said, scratching the back of his neck. Suyin looked at Old Wu, and then at Master Gao, and then back to Old Wu. She smiled.

"And that's not all I noticed," Master Gao continued, turning his frown to Suyin. Her smile disappeared.

"Wei-lin seems to have been training the *yin-yang circle*. It's not a common technique," Master Gao said. "And I have only taught it to one student."

"Oh?" Suyin said, her gaze going to the ground. That was one of the lessons she had given to Wayland last week.

"Yes. To you," Master Gao said. Suyin didn't look up and traced a small pattern on the ground with the toe of her shoe.

"Listen to me, you two," Master Gao said. His tone was gentle but serious. Old Wu and Suyin looked at him respectfully. "There's only one teacher in charge here, and that's going to be me. You two don't know what I have planned for Wei-lin, you don't know my assessment of his abilities, his strengths, and his weaknesses. Isn't that correct?" Old Wu and Suyin nodded.

"So leave the teaching to me. Or at the very least, ask me first if you want to show him something. Learning things that he's not ready for, or that won't work for him, is not going to help him. Is that clear?"

"That's clear," Old Wu said. Suyin nodded as well.

"Good," Master Gao said. Suyin bowed and turned, and went back inside to attend to her chores. Old Wu went back to the horse, adjusting the saddle and bridle one last time.

Master Gao put his hand on Old Wu's back. "I have to say, you taught him the splitting fist pretty well," he said, speaking softly. "He looked like you from about forty years ago."

"Forty years ago?" Old Wu said. He didn't look up as he stroked the neck of the gelding. "My splitting fist is stronger now than it was then."

Master Gao smiled and gently patted Old Wu on the shoulder. That might very well be true. Old Wu had been full of surprises as long as he'd known him.

Master Gao swung up onto his horse and snapped the reins, and he trotted away.

24

IT WAS LATE in the morning, and Wayland lay in bed with his eyes open, just staring at the ceiling. Although he had been trying to put it out of his mind, it was one of those things that stuck there, just under the surface. It might go away for a little while, but it was never too far away. Today was December 2nd. His birthday. Nobody here would know that, of course. But his parents always knew, and never failed to plan something special for him.

A year ago at this time, Wayland remembered that his mother had him sit at the kitchen table after dinner. Neither his mother nor his father had mentioned anything about his birthday all day, and Wayland was sure they had just forgotten. It was understandable, with all the pressures and stresses of running the mission, worrying about the household and everything else.

"Close your eyes, and keep them closed,'" his mother had said, and he did so. He could sense some movement and hear some shuffling about, but he abided by his mother's wishes, and he didn't peek. Finally, his mother said, "All right, you can open your eyes."

Wayland did so, and he saw the smiling face of the cook, Tang Hu, and also the bemused grin of his father, and to his left the gentle, beaming face of his mother. Tang Hu was setting down a genuine American birthday cake, chocolate, two layers high with a buttercream frosting, and replete with several burning candles. His parents each had two brightly-wrapped gifts for him. They all joined in to sing "Happy Birthday," even Tang Hu. He didn't get the words exactly right, but he had a strong singing voice and a natural ear for the melody. It was a delightful day for Wayland, as much as he could have asked for.

But that was all gone. In the past. Wayland felt a deep wave of melancholy as he looked at the ceiling. But then he smiled as he remembered the words an old man had said to him, on the ship from San Francisco to Hawaii when he and his parents were first coming over to China. They were in the open ocean, several days out from San Francisco. Wayland was only thirteen at the time, and he was out on deck, looking over the railing into the vast blue of the Pacific. His father had come up to him to remind him that Sunday church service would begin shortly and that Wayland was expected to attend. Wayland responded with a frown and a nod, and his father raised his eyebrows, but said nothing and turned away. The old man had observed the exchange, and he approached Wayland.

"Young man," he said. The older gentleman was well-dressed but had an air of mischief in his eye. "Always appreciate your parents. They are the only two people who will ever truly give a shit about you your whole life. And they won't be around forever. Be glad you have them." The old man smiled and walked away, and Wayland never saw him again the whole rest of the voyage. Wayland didn't appreciate the old man's comments at the time, but now, some five years later, he did.

He got out of bed, washed his face in the basin, and got dressed. He made his way across the courtyard to the main hall, and had to pull up the collar of his padded jacket. It was a clear day, but cold, and the wind was blowing rather fiercely. Suyin was already cooking some millet mush, and hot tea was brewing in the pot.

"You're up late," she said.

"Did you eat?" Wayland asked.

"I had a steamed bun and some tea," Suyin said. She set down a bowl holding three more buns on the table in front of Wayland. "I have the pan hot. Do you want an egg or two?"

"One egg would be fine," Wayland said. "And the millet."

"I think I'll have one, too," Suyin said, and she broke and scrambled two eggs. She poured them into the smoking-hot oil in the carbon-steel pan, and the eggs hissed and puffed up instantly. She quickly removed them with her iron spatula, and then set the eggs and millet down in front of Wayland.

"Thank you," he said. Suyin nodded. Wayland took a bite of the egg with his chopsticks, and then pushed and stirred at his millet without much enthusiasm.

"You didn't like the egg?" Suyin asked. She took a bite with her chopsticks to make sure they tasted okay.

"Huh?" Wayland said. "Oh, no. It's fine. Your cooking is always excellent."

"Well?" Suyin said. She could sense that Wayland's spirit was subdued.

"Well, what?" Wayland asked. He tried to convey that nothing was amiss, but he knew he wasn't convincing, and Suyin was always perceptive. Suyin raised her eyebrows and looked him in the eyes.

Wayland sighed. "I'm just kind of down today. It's... my birthday."

"Oh," Suyin said.

"I know you don't really celebrate birthdays the way we do in the West," Wayland said.

"We sometimes do," Suyin said. "But it's more for a big one, and usually for older people. Like someone's fiftieth or sixtieth birthday. We show them respect, and it's a big celebration."

"For us," Wayland continued, "we celebrate it every year. It's kind of a special day for that person, where they're the center of attention. And they get a cake and candles. One candle for every year."

"Huh," Suyin said. "That must be a lot of candles for older people."

"We don't always do the full number of candles after people reach a certain age."

"So what else did you do?" Suyin asked. She had a mischievous expression on her face.

"Well, you would usually have a nice dinner, either at home, or you'd go out. And you'd get presents, and everyone would sing "Happy Birthday" to you."

"It sounds nice," Suyin said. She paused for a moment, and then looked at Wayland. "I know what it's like to not have a mother and father around."

"I know you do," Wayland said. He looked at Suyin. He wanted to say something else to her, but the words wouldn't come.

Suyin poured some water into the still hot pan and wiped it clean with a cloth. "We could do something like that today if you want," she said, without turning to Wayland.

"Like what?" Wayland was bemused. Suyin always said much less than she was thinking.

"We could go out, and get something to eat. It might not be like the ones you remember, but it could be your birthday lunch."

Wayland nodded slowly, but he wasn't going to let her off without a little teasing. "I guess that sounds okay. But to make it authentic, you'd have to sing to me."

"I don't know your foreign songs," Suyin said. "So I can't do that." She wasn't smiling, and Wayland wasn't quite sure if she was joking or not.

"That's okay. You can just sing me a Chinese song. But it has to be loud, and clearly directed at me so everyone around can hear it, and so they'll know it's my birthday."

Suyin scrubbed at the pan. "You wouldn't want to hear my singing voice," she said, without looking up.

Wayland smiled to himself. He couldn't imagine that he would find Suyin's voice unpleasant under any circumstances. "Well, okay then. I guess the birthday meal will have to do."

Suyin continued scrubbing the pan with her back to Wayland, but a smile crept across her face.

Wayland and Suyin left the compound at a little after eleven in the morning.

"So, where are we going?" Wayland asked as they stepped onto the street.

"You haven't been to the Chaoyin Temple?"

"No," Wayland said. He hadn't seen much of Tientsin since he had arrived at the Gao residence. He was always uncomfortable going out by himself, after his recent experience.

"We'll go there, then," Suyin said. Wayland nodded. "It's over five hundred years old," she said. "You can pay respects to your parents there."

They walked along the busy streets of Tientsin, and Wayland was again reminded of how much bigger this city was than Fenchow. The streets were bustling with all kinds of people — Chinese gentlemen, well-to-do ladies, street hawkers and performers, children, elderly people. Here was a patrol of Indian Sikh soldiers, there was a Japanese official with his kimono-clad wife. A couple of European men dressed in Western suits were coming the other way, and as they passed Wayland heard a few words spoken in German. It was a bit of sensory overload again for Wayland, who, except for his one outing to the British Concession, had spent so much of the last few months secluded behind the walls of the Gao compound.

"There it is," Suyin said. "The Chaoyin Temple."

The temple was comprised of a series of buildings: three main halls and four side halls, with two courtyards in the north and south. It was one of the few temples that faced east, and it looked out over the river. The buildings had the familiar Chinese upturned roof and were painted bright red and white. The grandeur of the layout struck Wayland; he hadn't seen temples like this in Fenchow.

They walked through the courtyards, and there were statues of Buddha all around, some small and some huge. All kinds of people were milling about, and there were several altars where people were burning sticks of incense.

"Is there some specific holiday going on, or is this just normal?"

"This is just a normal day," Suyin said. "People might pray for all sorts of things. Like those fishermen over there are praying for good fortune at sea. Most people come here to honor their ancestors by burning incense in their memory. I'm going to burn a stick in memory of my family. Would you like to do that as well?"

"I don't know," Wayland said. "I can't pray to Buddha."

"You can pray the way that you want. It's the secret we each hold in our heart, isn't it?"

"Okay, I'll light one," Wayland said.

Suyin got two sticks of incense and handed one to Wayland, and they lit them and placed them in the altar. Suyin bowed and said her prayers to Buddha, and Wayland kneeled and said his own prayer. He remembered happy times with his parents when all were in good health and good spirits, and the future teemed with wonderful possibilities for all of them. Wayland was surprised at how quickly tears came to his eyes. He finished with the Lord's Prayer and wiped his eyes with his sleeve. He stood up and was met with Suyin's kind-hearted and soulful gaze.

They toured the rest of the grounds, and Suyin told Wayland more about the history and customs of the temple. It was late afternoon when they left to go back home, and as it was near dinner time, they stopped at a small restaurant. They each had a bowl of spicy lamb and noodle soup, and Wayland also ordered a small jar of rice wine. The light of the day was just beginning to fade, and a waiter went around lighting the small lamps around the restaurant, which cast a warm glow over the dining area. The restaurant had filled up with patrons, and the conversations were lively and animated. The waiter brought over the wine, and he poured a cupful for both Suyin and Wayland.

"Cheers," Wayland said and held up his cup. "Thank you for today, Suyin."

Suyin lifted her cup with both hands and bowed slightly.

"Wait," Wayland said. Suyin looked perplexed.

"This is how we toast in the West," he said, and he gently clinked his cup against hers. She smiled, and they both drank their cupful. Wayland poured another round for Suyin and then for himself. They enjoyed their soup, and the conversation flowed easily. Suyin was very curious about Western ways, and Wayland enjoyed telling her of the ins and outs of daily life in America. Suyin laughed at some of it, and at other times shook her head in disbelief at the ways of foreigners.

"You've seen so much of the world, and I've hardly seen any of it," she said, but she was laughing. There was no envy or self-pity in her voice, merely an honest assessment.

"Maybe you'll see more of it in the future." Wayland smiled and looked into her eyes. He found her pretty, but that wasn't all of it, or even most of it. There was a depth of spirit, of kindness in her. She would stand by those she cared about, through thick or thin, of that Wayland was sure.

"Maybe," she said. She poured the last round of the wine to Wayland and then herself, and then she clinked her cup to Wayland's, and they both drank.

They paid their bill, and Wayland helped Suyin put on her coat as they made their way to the exit. He held the door open for her, and he gently put his hand on her shoulder as they walked out into the night. The air was cold, but Wayland hardly noticed it. His body and spirit felt warm, and it wasn't from the wine.

Light snow began falling as they made their way back through Tientsin to the Gao compound. They came in through the main entrance. There didn't seem to be anyone up and about.

Wayland's room was just to the right of the first courtyard, and they both stopped just outside his door.

"Good night," Suyin said.

"Hold on, I'm going to need a hug first," Wayland said, and he opened his arms.

Suyin looked around. "We... shouldn't be doing this."

"Doing what?" Wayland said. "It's just a friendly hug. In America, we hug all the time, family, friends, neighbors. It's just polite."

Suyin stepped in somewhat reluctantly, and the two embraced. "Thank you for a nice day, Suyin," Wayland said. When he suggested the hug his intentions were genuinely innocent, but, now as he held her close, and he felt the warmth of her cheek against his and smelled the sweet fragrance of her hair, his desire rose. *No. We've both had a bit to drink, this isn't the right time.*

Wayland relaxed his embrace, but to his surprise, Suyin did not.

"Is hugging... always just between family and friends in America?" she asked, her voice barely above a whisper. She held Wayland tightly.

"No... sometimes... it means more... " Wayland said. His heart was beating rapidly. He put his hands on Suyin's shoulders and took a step back; he held her at arm's length and looked deeply into her eyes. Then, trembling slightly, he pulled her close in again and brought his lips to hers. Suyin responded in kind, and the two kissed passionately under the gentle, silent snowfall. Wayland was lost in the moment, and his senses were reeling; he wanted this one kiss to last until morning at the least, but after a few seconds Suyin pulled away.

She flashed him a mischievous smile. "Good night, Wei-lin," she said and hurried off to her room.

Wayland watched her as she disappeared through the door into the next courtyard. He stood there for a moment, trying to process what had just happened. But no thoughts came. Something deep inside him told him that some moments are just meant to be felt, not understood. He ran his fingers over his mouth. *Did it really happen? Yes, it happened, and nobody can ever take that away from me.*

He took several steps towards his room when a sound behind him snapped him out of his reverie. He sensed that someone was there, and he turned around.

"I'm sorry, Wei-lin, I didn't mean to startle you." Old Wu stood there, smiling. "I was just getting a book I had left in the main hall when I heard some voices. I did not mean to eavesdrop on you."

"But..you saw... ?"

"I did see," Old Wu said.

"I'm sorry, Old Wu, it's just that... " Wayland said.

Old Wu waved his hand and frowned, shaking his head. "I saw two young people doing what the *Tao* has compelled young people to do. But you must take care. I know that many of the ways of your people are not the way of the Chinese. I must tell you that if you were to... take advantage of Suyin, Master Gao would not forgive you. It would be the gravest insult for you to do that under his roof, in his home that he has graciously allowed you to share."

Wayland nodded out of both shame and understanding. "Our ways aren't that different, Old Wu. My father would react exactly the same as Master Gao under those circumstances. But I really do care about Suyin, and I would never dishonor her. Never."

"I believe you, Wei-lin," Old Wu said. He stroked his white beard thoughtfully. "You're a good young man, and you were raised properly. Still, even good men can use some friendly advice and warnings of danger, isn't that so? In case their judgment gets clouded?"

"That's right," Wayland said. "Thank you, Old Wu, for everything. I think I'm going to go to bed now."

"As am I," Old Wu said. "It's cold out here. Good night."

"Good night," Wayland said, as he went up the steps and into his room, and closed the door.

A light covering of cotton-white snow had accumulated on the ground of the courtyard as Old Wu walked back to his room. He thought of the scene that he had just witnessed, and he stroked his beard as he smiled. "Oh, to be young again," he said out loud.

25

DURING THE WEEK leading up to Christmas, Master Gao still had not returned from Fenchow. Wayland tried not to think too much about the holiday. Old Wu had asked him about Christmas when they were all eating dinner together one evening, and Wayland had given a rote answer about it being both a religious and secular holiday. He told them about the traditions of putting up a Christmas tree, lighting candles, singing festive songs, and giving each other gifts. But Wayland consciously put a wall around his Christmas memories; they were too personal, too intimate, too precious. He knew that Suyin and Old Wu wouldn't really understand the depth of meaning the occasion had to him; to them, it was just a curious foreign custom. And that was to be expected. They were good people, and they meant well, but with some things, they were a world away from knowing what Wayland felt.

Christmas Eve of 1900 in Tientsin was a Sunday, and despite everything that had happened since last year, to Wayland, it still almost felt like Christmastime. The sky was clear, the air crisp and cold. He went out for a short walk, and he came through the main gate into the Gao compound a little after seven in the evening. He knew that Suyin would probably be preparing food in the kitchen, but he didn't feel like socializing, and he retired directly to his room. He lit his lamp, undressed and laid down on his bed, pulling his heavy padded cotton cover over him. He stared at the ceiling and thought of how far removed he was from Christmases past. He read for a while, but his eyes became heavy, and he dozed off and on for a few hours.

Wait a minute. Wayland reached over next to the lamp to check his clock. It was just a little after eleven. On his travels, he had gone past several churches in the British concession area; he distinctly remembered where both the Methodist and Anglican churches were, and he vaguely remembered passing a Baptist church, as well. Surely one would be having a Christmas Eve service. What was to prevent him from going? While he'd never stopped believing, he had felt his faith going a bit dry over the last year, with such drastic changes in his life. Receiving communion would be "good for his soul," as his mother was fond of saying. Wayland hopped out of bed, washed up, and put on his best clothes.

He stepped out of his door into the first courtyard. The stars above stood out against the inky blackness of the night sky. He had been almost ready to go to sleep ten minutes ago, but as he breathed in the dry, frigid winter air, he felt invigorated; he had a purpose tonight. He stepped through the gate into the inner courtyard for a peek. There was still a light on in Suyin's room, but Old Wu's room and Master Gao's were both dark. Wayland thought for a moment about letting Suyin know he was leaving but decided against it. This was something he had to do by himself. No need to bother her; he'd be back home in a couple of hours anyway. Nobody would even know he had been gone.

He closed the gate and walked back through the first courtyard and then out the main entrance to the street. The route was more familiar to him now, and the streets were mostly deserted at this time of night. He got to the main bridge over the Peiho and only passed a couple of rickshaw drivers along the way, both without passengers. There were lamps here and there from a few houses and buildings right on the river's edge, and they cast a gentle glow on the ever-constant flowing waters. Wayland took a deep breath of the cold air and exhaled slowly.

Before long he was walking down Victoria Road in the British concession. It was almost 11:45, and Wayland came up to the Methodist Episcopal church that he had remembered from his previous visit to the street. It was a nondescript building, but two lamps outside were lit, and people were milling about just outside the entrance.

"Excuse me," Wayland said to the white-bearded man standing at the entrance, certainly the minister. "Is there a midnight service her tonight?"

The man's expression was at first one of confusion as he looked at Wayland dressed in Chinese clothes, but then he smiled warmly and shook Wayland's hand. "There is indeed, young man. Would you like to join us?" The man had a strong Liverpudlian accent.

"I would," Wayland said.

"I'm Reverend Hartwell. American, are you?" the man said.

"I am."

"Well, that's all right. We even let Americans in on Christmas Eve! Welcome, my son." He grinned and clapped Wayland on the shoulder.

Wayland smiled and nodded respectfully, and he walked into the church. It was an old building, but well-maintained and tidy, with exposed wooden beams overhead. The pews were almost full already, and Wayland took his seat in the very back bench on the left, the only empty one.

The service began, and the Reverend read the nativity account from the book of Luke. Despite his different accent, the tone of the Reverend's voice sounded uncannily like Wayland's father, and Wayland thought back on the many Christmas Eve services that his father had presided over. It reminded him that he would never again hear his father deliver one of his sermons, that he would never hear his father's voice again. He swallowed as a lump came to his throat.

Still, there was something amiss here. Wayland looked around, and as far as he could see, there were no Chinese present. The attendees were all foreigners, and from the look of their dress, quite well-to-do.

When his father gave the sermon, the only foreigners present were his own family. That was why his father had come to China for in the first place, to spread the gospel to the people of this country. What was the point of building a church in a foreign land that had no natives among its parishioners?

As the service continued, Wayland saw that there was indeed one native person at the service. A little Chinese boy, probably nine or ten, was dressed in a white robe and he was assisting the Reverend. Soon it was time for communion, and the boy held the goblet of wine in both hands as he slowly and carefully made his way to the smiling minister. The boy was clearly focusing all of his attention on not dropping the goblet as he took one cautious step after and other, and it elicited some laughter from the congregation.

"Oh, isn't he adorable?" whispered a pretty young blonde woman in the pew in front of Wayland. Her accent was distinctly Scottish. She nudged her handsome male companion. "Wouldn't you just like to take him home? We could dress him up, and I'm sure he could be trained, too."

"Can you imagine the look on the face of your mother if you sent her a photo of that? The newest member of the family?" The man whispered back, and the woman giggled.

Wayland felt his anger rising. He was sorely tempted to give them a piece of his mind. Did they not know anything at all about this country? Did they have not the slightest respect for its people? Still, it was Christmas Eve, and it was a church; it was holy ground. He couldn't make a scene. Wayland rose from the pew and quietly made his way to the exit and out to the street.

He pulled his collar up against the cold wind as he cut across Victoria Road to a side street. The avenues were mostly empty at this time of night, and before long Wayland had made his way back through the foreign concessions to the East Gate of the old city. All was quiet, and nobody seemed to be out, and he cut across to a smaller street on the left to make his way back home. As he came around the corner, though, he saw two Chinese men and a woman standing outside a doorway in a building up ahead, next to a blacksmith's shop.

They were talking with each other but looking around somewhat furtively as Wayland approached. The younger man and woman turned away as Wayland approached, but the older man nodded politely.

Wayland raised his glance and bowed slightly to the man as he walked by.

"Happy Christmas," the man said without raising his voice.

Wayland stopped and turned. He walked back to the man. "Happy Christmas. You're Christian?"

"We are," the man said, nodding to his two companions. "I saw that you were a foreigner. Why are you dressed like that, and walking around here?"

"And how do you come to speak Chinese?" the young woman asked.

"It's a long story," Wayland said. "My parents were missionaries. I live here now, with a Chinese family."

"So you are a believer?" the younger man asked, his eyes hopeful.

Wayland paused for a moment to consider his response. "I

guess I am. I'm not sure of much of anything anymore."

"Please, won't you join us?" the older man said and held his open palm towards the entrance. "We're having a small Christmas Eve service now."

"Is it safe for you to meet here?" Wayland asked. "With everything that's been going on?"

The man had a glint in his eye, and it was the look of defiance in the face of mortal danger. "Was it safe for our Lord to tell the world the truth?"

Wayland was humbled, and he bowed as he entered their church, really just a small room with a few chairs and a table, and a makeshift pulpit. There were ten or twelve people in the room, men and women, all Chinese. Most were middle-aged, although two young girls seemed to be teenaged. There was also an elderly couple.

"Welcome, brother, and Happy Christmas," one of the women said to him. The lighting was dim from the oil lamps, and it wasn't until Wayland took off his hat that the others saw that he was a foreigner.

"Thank you," Wayland said in Chinese.

"You can speak the language?" One of the men said, surprised but smiling.

Wayland nodded.

"Husband, get him a seat," one of the women said, and the man bowed and hurried over to grab a small upturned bench that was leaning up against the wall. He set it down and brushed it off, and he motioned for Wayland to sit.

The three who were standing outside came in, and the man who had first talked to him was apparently the minister, as he made his way past the others up to the pulpit.

"Welcome, all of you, and thank you for coming. As you know, we have all suffered greatly these past weeks, and we have lost many of our brothers and sisters. Any day now, our fate may be the same as theirs. We know that we can expect no support from either the government or the Western powers. We are alone in the wilderness, and our enemies surround us. Still, we must be thankful for our blessings, that we few are able to gather here tonight, to celebrate the birth of our Lord. As He said, 'where two or three are gathered in my name, there I am with them.' Let us give thanks."

All bowed in prayer, and then the Reverend read the nativity story from the Book of Mathew.

This was a new experience for Wayland. This was not his father's sermon. His father, as good-hearted and strong a man as he was, was not Chinese, and he could only convey the Word from his perspective. Wayland had been speaking Chinese exclusively for several months now, and in some ways, it wasn't just speaking the same thoughts in different words, but rather it was seeing the world in a slightly different manner. From a Chinese viewpoint. This was something he didn't understand before. But the thought that struck him most was that holy words of the text were just as powerful when spoken in Chinese, and perhaps, given his circumstances, they seemed even more compelling. The message was shining and new and even more illuminating than he had ever remembered. It was as if he was now the native heathen, being preached the word of God for the first time.

Wayland still wasn't sure what denomination this Reverend and church were affiliated with, but he didn't really care. The warmth emanating from this small room was like nothing he had ever experienced before. It was soon time for communion, and Wayland took his place in the back of the line. When it was his turn, he took the morsel of bread and dipped it into the wine of the chalice that the Reverend held. He brought it to his mouth and swallowed. This was the Body and the Blood, and his sins would be forgiven.

The woman on his right handed Wayland a candle, and the Reverend cupped his hand over the wick of his candle as he struck a match and lit it. He passed on the flame to the younger woman closest to him, and she shared it with her neighbor, and the light was passed along. The Reverend began singing the familiar melody of Silent Night, and the rest joined in. It took Wayland a moment to realize what was different from what he had always known: all were singing the words in Chinese. Wayland joined in the gentle chorus of the hymn, and the glow from the candles made the shadows dance warmly on the walls. As the light finally made its way to him, he tipped his candle to receive the flame from the woman next to him. The melody and warmth of the timeless song reverberated in the small, simple room. The service ended, and all bid their sincere farewells.

Wayland made his way back through the quiet streets of Tientsin. He reached the Gao compound and came through the main gate. The night was still clear, and the stars were bright. In front of the door to his room, Wayland saw something. It was a package of some sort, wrapped in brown paper. He looked around, but everyone's room was dark. He picked it up, and went into his room, closing the door. He lit his lamp and looked more closely at the parcel. It was tied with string. Wayland took out his pocketknife and opened the package. Underneath the brown wrapping paper was a box and printed on the top were the words "Boulangerie Clemenceau." He lifted the flap and saw that the box contained a small cake of some sort, with white frosting. On top of the cake, in bright red letters, was written "Bon Anniversaire."

Suyin. Suyin must have gone to the foreign concessions, and she had bought him a birthday cake.

Wayland lay down on his k' ang and pulled the blankets up over himself. The room was cold, but he was not. He went to sleep that evening with a profound sense of gratitude.

26

The weather over the next few weeks was seasonable for Tientsin. It was a little cold, but dry and clear with little wind.

Wayland came into the central courtyard, and he saw Suyin practicing pushing hands with Lunghui. Lunghui pushed in at her with both hands, and she held her root and turned her waist to dissipate his power, and then she turned back and pushed against Lunghui's arms in return. Wayland watched the two go back and forth, each displaying the softness and "listening" skills that Master Gao had emphasized. As much as Wayland tried to focus solely on the martial techniques and practice of his classmates, it was all he could do refrain from staring at the lithe and sensual form of Suyin as she gently but confidently rocked back and forth, both receiving and issuing power through her practiced techniques.

"Wei-lin, let's practice," Shen Fai said. He came over and set himself in the standard pushing hands stance, with his right leg forward.

Wayland sighed, but not loud enough for anyone to hear. Shen Fai was a friendly young guy, and Wayland genuinely liked him. But as a prospect, Shen Fai didn't compare too favorably to Suyin. *Snap out of it. You're here to train martial arts.* "Sounds good," Wayland said with a smile, and he got into his position opposite Shen Fai.

"How are you this morning?" Shen Fai asked. He pushed

forward with one hand on Wayland's wrist. Wayland held his forearm out in front of him, his arm forming a half circle and his palm facing inward. As he sensed the push on his forearm, he turned his waist to the left and gently redirected the power of the push, and then Wayland pushed back, as the drill called for.

"Fine," Wayland said. "Although I did get called a "foreign devil" again the other day"

"Yes, foreigners are still a strange sight to a lot of the country people," Shen Fai said. "Don't take it too personally."

"I never do," Wayland said. "I remember once after we first came to China, and I heard someone call me that and I was pretty upset. My father said that in America, Chinese are sometimes called worse. It's just human nature, I guess. We're comfortable with people who look like us, but we don't trust strangers."

Shen Fai continued the drill and pushed back at Wayland. "I guess so," he said. "We're all human, and have the same bodies, but it's difficult when we look different, speak a different language, and see the world in our own way. I don't have much experience with foreign people. Take you, for instance. Are you a typical American? Are most Americans like you?

Wayland turned his waist and guided the force of Shen Fai's push to the side. "Well, most Americans don't go halfway around the world to live in China, learn the language, and study martial arts. So no, I guess most Americans aren't like me."

Shen Fai laughed. "Come on. You know what I mean. We hear so much about the "foreign devils," and some of the foreign soldiers are indeed vicious. They looted and raped and killed, not too long ago and right in this city. Yet at the same time, we hear of your peaceful Christian religion, your scientific advances, and your powerful medicines. It's all tough to understand. You've lived here a while, and you understand the Chinese people. How do foreigners compare to Chinese?"

"Well, I'm a Christian, and that shapes how I see everything, I guess. I was taught that all men in the world were made in the image of God, that God loves all, and that all life is a good thing. But at the same time, all men are flawed, foolish and weak, and gravitate towards sin. But to answer your question, I guess I would say that Westerners are not too different from Chinese."

"Really?" Shen Fai said. "Not different at all?"

"Not in the important things," Wayland said. "Men are the same everywhere. Some are smart, and some are stupid. Some are brave, and some are cowards. Some are kind and gentle, and some are violent and cruel. Some are honest and true, and some are deceitful and false."

Shen Fai thought for a moment and nodded. "I guess that's so. So if I meet a foreigner, I really don't know what to expect, then?"

Wayland shook his head. "That's right. You don't. I was taught to be as gentle as a dove and as wise as a serpent. That's the approach I take when I meet anyone from anywhere."

Shen Fai smiled. "Ha, I guess that makes sense."

"Less talk, and more focus on your training!" Lunghui yelled over to them.

Wayland looked over at Lunghui and bowed slightly. Not only was Lunghui his senior when it came to Master Gao's martial arts school, he was also right. Mental focus was the key to advancement in any endeavor. Wayland and Shen Fai continued the push hands practice. Wayland tried to remember all the principles of the style that Master Gao had told him to focus on. He maintained a loose waist. He kept his root firm and his *chi* sunken, he kept his body alert but relaxed, and he focused intently on sensing his opponent's energy. But on top of that, if you thought about everything too much, then nothing would flow naturally. And having things flow naturally was the ultimate goal of *T'ai Chi Fist*. Indeed, it was not easy to maintain all the principles at once.

There was a loud banging at the front gate to the Gao compound. This wasn't a polite knocking; it was loud and forceful. Wayland and Shen Fai stopped their drill, and as the pounding continued, Lunghui and Suyin also stopped.

"Go see who it is," Lunghui said to Wu Chen.

Wu Chen went over to the gate and opened it a crack. "Who's there?" he said, peering out.

The gate burst open, knocking Wu Chen back a couple of steps. Lunghui and Suyin turned to see who was entering, as did Wayland. As the figures came through the gate, Wayland's heart almost stopped.

"It's him!" he exclaimed, loud enough for everyone to hear. His heart began beating faster.

Lunghui had no idea what Wayland was talking about, but the four individuals coming through the gate were undoubtedly not ordinary. In the lead was a muscular man who brandished an iron ring in his right hand. He wore blue padded breeches and a coat of dark crimson. The ring was a little more than half a meter in diameter, and the man casually flipped and turned it with a practiced skill as he walked forward. He looked around the compound with a subtle expression of disdain. Behind him strode a young woman, dressed from head to toe in white. She walked with the same confidence as the first man, and she had an expression of barely-concealed cruelty; in her eyes shone a malevolent yet keen intelligence.

Suyin shot a quick glance at Lunghui. "Who are they?" she asked. Lunghui shook his head.

After the woman came a virtual giant of a man. He had to be well over six feet, Wayland thought. And he wasn't just tall; he was barrel-chested and muscular. He had a patch over one eye, and he had a fighting ax in each hand. In a steady cadence, he casually struck the blade of one ax at an angle against the other one, as if he was sharpening it. The "clang" of one piece of steel hitting the other, over and over again, reverberated through the compound like some unholy church bell. The man was smiling, but his grin was the expression of a dim-witted brute, the kind who enjoyed violence for its own sake. The three spread out slowly as they walked into the compound, never taking their eyes off of the students of Master Gao. The man with the eye patch kept hitting his axes together in the same rhythm, and the others stood still. Finally, the last man came into the compound. He was of medium build and older than the others, probably in his late fifties; his dark beard was flecked with gray. He was dressed in a full-length indigo blue *chongshan*, and his hair was tied back in the traditional queue. He held a spear in his right hand, point up, although the sharp spearhead was covered and tied with a leather sheath. He carried himself with purpose and power, and Wayland instantly recognized that this man was the leader of the group, and the others followers.

"Magic Spear," Lunghui said, loud enough for Wayland to hear. Suyin and Lunghui exchanged glances.

Wayland didn't know the leader, and he had never heard of anyone called "Magic Spear," but he did recognize the man with the iron ring. The man who had killed his parents.

27

"WHAT DO YOU want here?" Lunghui said. His back stiffened. "Why do you force your way in, like criminals?"

"Watch your tone!" the woman said, almost hissing. Magic Spear raised his left hand for her to be silent. She acceded to her master's command, but Wayland sensed that she was barely under his control.

"Where is your Master Gao?" Magic Spear said. "Have him come out. I have business with him." He spoke like someone who was used to being obeyed.

Wayland looked again at the man with the iron ring. *Was it really him, the man who killed his father, and probably his mother too, standing mere yards away?* The rage was rising in Wayland, and he could envision himself with his hands around the throat of that murderer. He looked over at the weapon rack and saw the array of swords, sabers, spears, knives and other implements of combat. Any one would do the trick. *No. Be patient. This isn't the time, and you're not ready. You'll just get yourself killed. Or worse, get your friends killed.*

"He's away on business," Lunghui said. "He won't be back for another day or two."

"Business where?" Magic Spear said.

"He went to Fenchow."

Magic Spear turned his head sharply and strode up to Lunghui. "Fenchow?" A humorless smile came over his face. "To see his old master, I suppose?"

"Whatever you have to tell him, you can tell me," Lunghui said. He didn't break eye contact with Magic Spear.

Magic Spear laughed. He looked over at the woman. "Did you hear that? He's permitted me to address him."

The woman sneered, and she kept her eyes focused on Suyin.

Magic Spear sighed and began walking around slowly, tapping the butt of his spear on the stone courtyard with each step.

"I'll tell you. I'll tell all of you why I'm here. First, some introductions are in order. I am known as Magic Spear, and these are my pupils."

He gestured towards the others.

"Iron Ring Wang, One-eye Chang, and Flying Faerie Yun Yan. And you can relay my message to your so-called 'master.' This school is to be shut down. After you leave here today, none of you will come back. You can find another teacher, or you can quit your studies. It makes no difference to me."

He walked up to Wu Chen and looked him up and down.

"From what I've seen, maybe most of you aren't suited for martial arts in the first place. You can find another pursuit. Perhaps farming, or music, or dancing."

Iron Ring Wang laughed out loud, and Wayland glared at him; he had never felt so much hatred for one individual in his life. He took a step forward, his fists clenched.

Magic Spear noticed Wayland for the first time and walked up to him. He shook his head, and he looked at Wayland as if he was looking at an animal.

"Even teaching our arts to foreign devils. I'm not sure how much lower one could get. To be a traitor to his Chinese heritage."

"Master Gao is no traitor," Wayland said. "He's a great man. Not a man who takes pleasure in violence and cruelty."

Magic Spear raised his eyebrows. "You speak the language? Yes. I suppose Gao Jinhai would be capable of teaching you that, at least. As far as martial arts, though… " He stepped forward and struck at Wayland's chest with his open left palm, and it was so fast and the movement so small that Wayland didn't have time to react. Wayland felt as if a sledgehammer had hit him, and he flew backward a good two yards, falling on his back and hitting the back of his head on the courtyard cobblestones.

Suyin ran over to him, but Wayland was already starting to get up; the adrenaline and rage were flowing through him. Suyin put her arm around his shoulders to help him, but Wayland tried to push her away and stand up. A searing pain emanated from his chest, and he fell back again; Suyin caught him this time, and she cradled his head as he sank back down.

"A pathetic bunch," Flying Faerie said. "Worse than dogs." She looked contemptuously at Suyin and Wayland.

"Why don't you just leave?" Suyin said as she stood up. "You've made your point!"

Shen Fai stepped forward towards Magic Spear, but Lunghui stopped him.

"Why should Master Gao stop teaching?" Lunghui said. He was trying to keep his emotions under control. He tried to think of how Master Gao would handle this situation. Logic, dialogue, a calm tone. "What right do you have to demand that?"

Magic Spear calmly walked back behind his pupils and then turned to Lunghui. "I say that he's not a legitimate teacher, that he has little understanding of martial arts, and that he's not qualified to represent his lineage. This is a well-established tradition in Chinese martial arts. If one wants to teach, one must accept challenges. And if he's too frightened to accept a challenge, then he must stop besmirching the legacy of our Chinese arts. Cowards have no business teaching." He looked over at Wayland with disdain.

"Master Gao is no coward!" Wu Chen shouted. He darted over to the weapons rack and grabbed a long-handled saber, a *pudao*. He turned, his face flushed with anger, and brandished the weapon at Magic Spear.

"No!" Lunghui yelled. This was not the time nor the place for a fight with Magic Spear and his pupils, and Lunghui understood the stakes. Wu Chen's heart had always been greater than his skills, and he was not a match for these fighters.

"Put down that blade, little man, before you hurt yourself," Magic Spear said, and Flying Faerie Yun Yan laughed heartily.

"Bastard!" Wu Chen shouted, and he rushed forward.

One-eye Chang swiftly stepped in, and he thrust out the ax in his right hand to block Wu Chen. Wu Chen abruptly stopped, and seeing his new opponent in front of him, he turned to face the giant.

"You can't come here and insult us like that! You think we're not men, that we'll just accept it?" Wu Chen said.

One-eye Chang smiled as if a child was threatening him. Still, Wu Chen was not unskilled with the blade he had chosen, and the *pudao* was a formidable weapon by any measure. Wu Chen thrust at Chang's upper body, and Chang easily deflected the attack with the ax in his left hand, the 'clang' of steel on steel reverberating through the courtyard. But Chang wasn't prepared for Wu Chen's next strike. As the blade of Wu Chen's *pudao* bounced off the heavy ax of Chang, Wu Chen reversed the motion and swept his weapon back in the opposite direction. Chang saw it at the last second and jerked his head back, but he was a second late, and the blade nicked his forehead. A small rivulet of blood began trickling down from the cut, and One-eye Chang stepped back, putting his index finger up to the wound, and then looking down at the blood on his finger. He slowly raised his head, and his gaze fixed on Wu Chen. There was no smile on his face as he stepped forward, and once again he began hitting the blade of his right ax at an angle against his left ax, in that same steady cadence.

"Get back!" Lunghui shouted. He knew that Wu Chen was no match for the giant.

Wu Chen, as if slowly sensing the gravity of his situation, stepped back steadily as his opponent advanced. One-eye Chang walked forward another step, and then his lips curled in rage as he attacked. He swung his right ax in towards Wu Chen and followed with a cut from the ax in his left. Wu Chen blocked both strikes, but then Chang came in with a third cut, much harder. Wu Chen put up the flat of his *pudao* blade to block it, but Chang's strike was so powerful that it knocked Wu Chen's weapon right out of his hand. Chang towered over the defenseless Wu Chen, and he spun his ax and thrust the blunt handle end into Wu Chen's stomach, causing his smaller foe to double over. He then hit Wu Chen on the head with the flat of his other ax, snapping Wu Chen's head back. In a daze, Wu Chen teetered. He looked up for a moment and coughed, spitting up blood on his white shirt. He gazed over at Lunghui plaintively, staggered forward a step, and then he collapsed onto the ground, motionless.

One-eye Chang walked over to the limp form of Wu Chen and touched the young man's ribs with the toe of his boot. Wu Chen groaned, barely conscious.

"I didn't hit him that hard,' Chang said, looking puzzled. Even though Chinese wasn't Wayland's first language, he could sense the limited intellect of Chang from his manner of speech.

"Doesn't seem like he was very well-trained," Iron Ring Wang said, chuckling. Flying Faerie smiled as well.

"There is no need for more violence," Magic Spear said, turning to Lunghui. "Your friend was foolish, and he paid the price. Don't make the same mistake. Convey what I said to your teacher, and leave this school. If you resist, I won't be held responsible."

But it was too late for talking now. Suyin, Wayland and Shen Fai were already at the weapons rack. Wayland grabbed a long, bladed polearm known as a *guandao*; it wasn't a weapon he had much experience with, but it was heavy and powerful, and deadly; that was the type of weapon he wanted. Shen Fai took a saber, and Suyin picked up the three-foot iron rod called a hard whip, and she tossed it over to Lunghui. He caught it effortlessly and turned to face Magic Spear. Flying Faerie, as if unleashed, rushed in towards Suyin. Suyin snatched a spear from the rack and turned to face her foe.

The spear wasn't her favorite, but Master Gao had always said the spear was the king of long weapons, and Suyin felt she needed any advantage she could get. She grasped the shaft firmly with both hands and turned to face her foe, but Flying Faerie wasn't where Suyin expected her. True to her name, the woman in white had leapt up and was turning in midair as she came down towards Suyin. Suyin stepped back quickly and adjusted her position, and thrust quickly towards the twisting shape of Flying Faerie Yun Yan. Suyin was almost sure that her thrust was true and centered, but at the last moment, Flying Faerie swung her right hand out with blinding speed. There was an audible "clang' as the spearhead struck Flying Faerie's wrist. Suyin caught a flash of metal wrapped around the woman's wrist. An iron bracelet?

Although her motion seemed almost inhuman, Flying Faerie twisted around enough to land squarely on her feet. The moment she touched the ground, she jerked her right hand out, and it seemed like a rope of metal exploded outwards. It wasn't an iron bracelet, but a chain whip that was wrapped around her wrist!

Suyin snapped her head back from pure instinct, and the deadly point of the chain whip narrowly missed her cheek.

Master Gao had told Suyin and the others about the chain whip, but this was a weapon that she had not personally experienced. Flexible weapons were incredibly dangerous, Master Gao had said, both for those facing them and even for those using them. The one Flying Faerie used appeared to be about eight feet in length, and she wielded it as naturally as she moved her arms and legs.

"Shih Hua, go to the yamen, get the authorities!" Lunghui shouted.

Shih Hua nodded, her face intense yet determined, and she sprinted towards the main gate.

"Stop her!" Magic spear shouted to Flying Faerie Yun Yan.

Flying Faerie turned her attention away from Suyin for just a moment, but that moment was all Suyin needed.

"No!" Suyin shouted, and she slashed down with her spearhead at Flying Faerie.

Flying Faerie had taken two steps towards Shih Hua, but out of the corner of her eye, she saw Suyin's spear coming at her in a downward arc. Rather than retreat, she tried to step in towards Suyin to avoid the spear point, but she was a fraction of a second too slow, and the shaft of Suyin's spear landed firmly on her shoulder, knocking her down to one knee. Suyin thrust again, but this time Flying Faerie was ready. As the spear came in, she ducked and grabbed the wooden shaft. With a practiced jerk of her body, she yanked the spear out of Suyin's hands and sent it flying behind. A spark flashed and a sharp "clang" reverberated as the steel spearhead impacted on the stone wall of the compound. Flying Faerie turned to Suyin and glared.

Shih Hua made it to the front gate and ran out.

"I told you to stop her!" Magic Spear yelled, his face contorted with anger. "You," he said as he turned to Lunghui. "You're going to pay for that."

"You think I'm just going to cower in fear before you?" Lunghui asked. He lifted his hard whip and brandished it confidently towards Magic Spear.

"If you had any sense, that's exactly what you'd do." Magic Spear said, sneering.

He stepped in at Lunghui with a mighty spear thrust to the young man's midsection. Lunghui deflected the spear point with his hard whip, but Magic Spear withdrew his weapon and came in again, twirling in mid-air as he swung his spear down at Lunghui. Lunghui was just able to twist his body out of the way, and the spearhead came down hard on the cobblestones of the compound. Lunghui swung his hard whip at the advancing Magic Spear, but his strike was intercepted by the spear shaft of his more experienced foe. With both hands Magic Spear held his spear horizontally and struck Lunghui squarely on his collarbone with the shaft; Lunghui grunted from the impact and flew backward.

"Lunghui!" Wayland shouted. His eyes darted back and forth between the fallen Lunghui and Iron Ring Wang, the man who had killed his parents. Shen Fai had his saber held at the ready, and he was circling Iron Ring Wang, pacing stealthily like a cat. Wang stood as still as a pillar, a half-grin on his face. Wayland desperately wanted to face Iron Ring Wang, but he looked back again at Magic Spear slowly approaching the fallen Lunghui. Wayland made his decision. "I'm coming, Lunghui!"

Flying Faerie swung her chain whip in a circle around her head as she approached Suyin. Suyin held her hands up defensively as she slowly but steadily retreated from her advancing foe.

"You weren't much of a foe when you had a weapon," Flying Faerie said to Suyin. "And now you're unarmed. I don't think your chances are good." She swung the chain whip at Suyin's head, and Suyin was just able to duck; Flying Faerie jerked the chain whip back and then relaunched the point. It was so fast that Suyin had no time to react, and in a brief instant, she realized that the steel point was heading straight for her head and she would not be able to stop it. Time seemed to slow down, and her eyes closed out of instinct. She was prepared for the deadly impact when she heard a "crack" echo through the air. She opened her eyes to see Old Wu in front of her, wielding his wooden staff. He had knocked away the deadly chain whip of Flying Faerie at the last instant.

"Old Bastard!" Flying Faerie yelled as she snapped her flexible weapon back into her hands. Her eyes shone with rage as she prepared herself to attack her new foe; there would be no mercy for this opponent just because of his age. But Old Wu wasn't static. With a deceptive speed that seemed uncanny for a man of his advanced years, he closed the gap and thrust his staff directly into the chest of Flying Faerie. She inhaled sharply, and a half-groan gurgled from her throat as she brought her hand to her chest and staggered backward several paces.

"Old Wu!" Suyin shouted, her face beaming with relief and pride as she ran to the old man's side.

"Wolves must be driven away!" Old Wu said. "Even the peaceful Lord Buddha said as much!"

"Wei-lin, no!" Suyin shouted as she turned to see Wayland squaring off against Magic Spear. "Get away from him! He'll kill you!"

Wayland heard her, but the time for running away was over. He faced Magic Spear, brandishing the *guandao*. The long weapon was heavy in his hands, and it didn't feel particularly comfortable; still, he held it with confidence. "You can't come here and do this. Master Gao has done nothing to deserve this.

None of us have."

"Master Gao?" Magic Spear said, laughing. "You call him that, but he's no master, boy. And he's done nothing to me? What would you know of that? What would a foreign devil like you know of anything? It's a disgrace that our Chinese arts should be taught to the likes of you. China had a grand civilization when your people were barbarians. And you dare to come to our country and look down upon us?"

"I don't look down on your country. Just you," Wayland said, gritting his teeth. He thought he saw an opening, and with all the strength and speed he could muster he thrust the blade of his *guandao* at Magic Spear. For a split second, Wayland was sure that his strike was true. His attack, however, found no purchase and instead cut through the empty space where Magic Spear had previously stood. Before Wayland's body could catch up with the perception of his mind, he saw a flash out of the corner of his eye. He felt the impact, and sudden sharp pain in the ribs on his right side as Magic Spear's palm struck him. The sky spun and then went dark, and for an instant, he thought he smelled the pleasant scent of peonies; he heard himself groan as he dropped to his knees and then fell to the ground, unconscious. His *guandao* fell with him and clattered onto the cobblestones.

"Another child playing with a toy," Magic Spear said. He ignored the fallen Wayland and picked up the *guandao*.

"What should I do with this one?" Iron Ring Wang asked his master. Wang spun his iron ring around his arm confidently, much more confidently than his nervous opponent, Shen Fai, who held his saber with a shaking hand as he faced the larger man.

"Don't kill him," Magic Spear said, with no emotion. "But do whatever else you like to teach him a lesson."

Given direction, it was as if Iron Ring Wang had been let loose from a leash. With one deft move, he slid his iron ring down his left arm and flipped it to his right hand. He stepped in and swung powerfully with the ring and with one blow knocked the saber out of Shen Fai's trembling hands. He then struck down, and Shen Fai was just able to get his arm up in defense. When the ring came down, the crack of Shen Fai's forearm breaking reverberated throughout the compound. Shen Fai didn't cry out, but he drew his broken arm in close, and he winced in pain. Iron Ring stood over him and raised his weapon for another strike.

"Stop! I'm no boy, but perhaps you have a lesson to teach me?" Old Wu said. Iron Ring Wang stopped his motion. He turned and looked at the old man blankly.

"Any of you?" Old Wu said, turning to Magic Spear. The old man's expression was calm but focused, and he held his wooden staff with relaxed strength, pointing the tip directly at Magic Spear.

"Don't let him talk to you that way, master," Flying Faerie said to Magic Spear, almost hissing. "Finish him." She had recovered her strength and stepped in front of Magic Spear.

"Know your place!" Magic Spear said. He grabbed her forearm and yanked her back behind him.

"Consider yourself lucky today, Old Wu. For the sake of our past, I will spare you," Magic Spear said.

"You will spare me?" Old Wu said. "Spare me from what? Every man dies, but it's you who's suffered a terrible fate, not me. It's you who's thrown everything away. You used to call me 'friend.' And what of Suyin? Would you kill her, too? Are those days so far in the past?"

Magic Spear sniffed, and his face was hard. He pointed his spear at Old Wu. "Yes, far in the past. Much is left there, things both joyful and tragic. It's not our fate as men to dwell on times gone by. We must move forward, and fight today for what is ours."

"Aiya!" Old Wu said. "So much good teaching has been wasted on you."

Magic Spear smiled and calmly drew his spear back. "Consider this visit a warning. I will leave you now. Nobody is dead, and your wounds will heal. Tell your 'Master' Gao that this is his last warning. He will retire from the martial world, and he will stop teaching. He's not fit to carry on the lineage of our style. I will be the sole inheritor of that line."

"He understood more of your master's teachings than you ever will," Old Wu said. "I pity you, I truly do."

"Convey my message to him, Old Wu. If I have to come here again, lives will be lost. That I promise you," Magic Spear said. He motioned with his hand, and One-eye Chang, Iron Ring Wang, and Flying Faerie came up to his side. Magic Spear stared grimly at Old Wu for another moment, and then he turned and walked away, followed by his students. They exited the compound through the main gate.

Wayland had regained consciousness, and with some difficulty, he rose to his feet. Suyin looked at Wayland for a moment, saw that he was mobile, and then turned her attention to the injured Shen Fai.

Wayland staggered over to the still unconscious Wu Chen. He bent down and put his ear to Wu Chen's chest. He was still breathing; he was alive.

The main gate opened, and Shih Hua darted in, nearly out of breath. She had brought one of the local constabularies with her.

"One policeman?" Wayland said, loud enough for Shih Hua to hear.

"That's all that they would send!" Shih Hua said, and it was clear that she was exhausted and nearly in tears from her efforts.

"What's going on here?" the policeman said. He was a thin

man in his late forties, and he had the look of someone displeased at being summoned.

"We've been attacked," Wayland said.

The policeman looked for a moment at Wayland, perplexed at a foreigner speaking Chinese.

"That's right," Old Wu said. "It was a criminal assault."

The policeman turned to Old Wu and addressed him formally but with little empathy. "This is Gao Jinhai's place, isn't it? Where is he?"

"Master Gao is away on business. I have been left in charge here," Old Wu said.

"Well, what happened?" the policeman demanded. His eyes darted around the compound, taking in the scene but paying scant attention to the injured around him. "Speak up, old man!"

"We were simply training as we always do, when Boxers attacked us," Old Wu said.

"The Boxers have all been disbanded. There are no Boxers," the policeman said curtly.

"It was Magic Spear and his students," Old Wu said. "It's the same thing."

"Are you doing martial arts training here?" The policeman asked as he looked around the compound again. He scratched the back of his neck and sighed.

"Yes, as we always do. Is that against the law now?" Old Wu said.

"You martial artists are always involved in some challenges, some grudges... probably some criminal activity, as well. You think the yamen doesn't have anything better to do than investigate your turf battles?"

"My friend was almost killed!" Wayland said, cradling Wu Chen's head in his hands. "Doesn't that mean anything to you?"

"There have been a lot of deaths around here recently," the

policeman said. "And it's not a foreigner's place to tell me my job! You keep going, and I'll take *you* into custody."

"Then you're not going to do anything?" Wayland said.

The policeman ignored Wayland and turned to Old Wu. "Listen, if you want to pursue it, go down to the yamen yourself tomorrow and file a formal complaint. I'll be honest with you, Old Man. Magic Spear has rank in Tientsin; he has friends in the government. The Boxers had their supporters here, and after all that the foreigners did, there's not much public sentiment for going after the likes of him. A lot of people see him as a hero, you know. Myself, I don't have any opinion on that, but if I were you, I'd just let this lie. Or take care of it yourself, if you're so inclined. That's all I can tell you."

"But..." Shih Hua started. Old Wu waved his hand for her to be silent.

"Thank you, Officer," Old Wu said. His tone was cold but polite. "We'll consider your words."

28

IT WAS A LITTLE after three in the afternoon on Wednesday, and the winter sun was already beginning to descend. This was the time of the week that Lunghui always practiced his standing post *ch'i kung* training, and despite the tragedy of the previous week, Wayland was reasonably sure that Lunghui would be in the training compound, as usual. He wasn't wrong. Wayland went around the wall and saw that Lunghui was alone in the middle of the courtyard; he was standing up, relaxed but straight, and his arms were held out in a semi-circle in front of him as if he was holding an invisible ball. His eyes were closed, and if he sensed Wayland approaching, he showed no sign.

"Lunghui," Wayland said.

"Yes?" He relaxed and turned to Wayland.

Wayland bowed slightly. "I'm sorry to bother you. I know we haven't been on the best of terms, but I just wanted to say that I appreciate the way you stood up for Master Gao and all of us. "

Lunghui looked Wayland in the eye for a moment before speaking. "You know, you're the first foreigner I have ever known, on a personal level, at least. You're not exactly what I expected. You fought bravely."

"Well, I didn't do too much," Wayland said, smiling sheepishly.

"No, you didn't," Lunghui said. "Your *kung fu* isn't very good, to be honest."

Wayland's shrugged.

"But you tried. You didn't run away. That's more than I expected from a foreigner," Lunghui said.

"Everything with you is about 'foreigners' and 'Chinese,'" Wayland said. "Did somebody make you the spokesman for everyone in China? And it's the same with me. I can tell you why my family came here, but if you want me to speak for every foreign government and group and businessman that's in your country, I just can't do it."

Lunghui paused for a moment, and then a rare hint of a smile came across his face. "I guess I can't expect that of you. Any more than you can ask me to justify the Boxers or the Manchu court." He stretched his arms up in the air and yawned. "I suppose it must be... a little difficult to travel halfway around the world, and live in a different country, among strange people."

"It's a complicated world," Wayland said. "But I'm not your enemy."

Lunghui looked at the ground for a moment, and then up at Wayland. "I know," he said. "After all, Master Gao's brother is the one who's really our foe."

"*What?*" Wayland asked, not sure that he heard what he thought he heard.

"... Magic Spear," Lunghui said, not understanding Wayland's confusion.

"Magic Spear is... Master Gao's *brother?*" Wayland was completely dumbfounded.

"You didn't know that?" Lunghui said. "Yes, they're siblings. And they studied under the same master years ago. They had a falling out. I just thought Old Wu or somebody had already explained that to you... "

"No," Wayland said, through gritted teeth. His face contorted. "Nobody explained that to me." *How could they be brothers? The man who had saved his life, and taken him into his home, was the brother of the man who was probably responsible for the death of his parents?*

"I'm sorry if I said something I shouldn't have…"

"No, you *should* have told me that," Wayland said. "Everyone else should have told me that when I first got here."

"I don't understand. What does it matter to you if Magic Spear is Master Gao's brother?"

"The man with the iron ring," Wayland said. "He killed my parents. Magic Spear is his master. It must have been under his orders."

"I didn't know that. But if Master Gao didn't tell you, he had his reasons," Lunghui said. "He's a good man, and it doesn't change anything."

"It changes everything," Wayland said, as he turned and walked away.

***

Wayland didn't sleep well that night, and he was up early the next day. He dressed, put on his hat and took his satchel. He stepped out into the courtyard and made his way directly to the front gate.

"Hey, where are you going? You want some breakfast?"

Wayland turned. It was Suyin. He didn't look towards her, and he didn't stop walking. "I'm not hungry. I'm going for a walk."

Suyin stood there, perplexed, and she watched Wayland go out and latch the gate behind him.

Wayland walked out onto the street. He walked quickly, but without purpose. He started on his familiar path towards the East Gate, but instead of continuing straight at the main intersection, he turned left. He was getting into the area where he had been cornered and beaten some weeks back, before Old Wu had saved him. He didn't care. Maybe it would be good to get another beating. Or perhaps this time he'd give one. *Why was he still in Tientsin, or for that matter, China? To bring justice to his parents' killers? How was he going to do that when Master Gao's brother was the culprit?* Maybe he still didn't fully understand China at this point, but he knew one thing: family ties came above most everything else in this country. In America, they say, "it's not what you know, it's who you know," and if anything that was even more true in China. *And I don't really know anyone here.*

Wayland walked for another half hour with no particular destination. It was a cold, sunny day with a clear blue sky, the kind that usually invigorated him, but he didn't notice the weather. The clouds and sky here were for the Chinese, not for him. The enticing aromas of steamed pork buns chili-and-leek pancakes wafted through the air from the various local stalls and restaurants, and they usually tempted him; now he had no appetite.

Another twenty yards up ahead on the crowded street, Wayland saw a commotion. Two men were having a heated argument, and one was a shopkeeper who was wielding a hammer in one hand. Wayland couldn't make out what the disagreement was about, but it seemed like both men had their groups of supporters, and the two sides were yelling back and forth at each other. Wayland envied them; even if one of them was in the wrong, he had friends and family to back him up, and he probably had a whole history in the city stretching back generations. He had roots. *I have nothing here. Even if I'm in the right, who would take my side in an argument?*

Wayland continued down to a road that ran by the river. There was the frame of an old pier there, but it was in disrepair and abandoned; the section that had once jutted out into the water was gone. Wayland walked over towards the water and leaned up against one of the old wooden posts, and he watched the flow of the river. Some boats drifted with the current, a few were making their way across, and about fifteen yards out a young man was making a great effort to pole his small boat back upstream. Wayland leaned against the post for a good while, not doing anything and not thinking about anything. Finally, he stood back up and adjusted his hat and satchel. *It's time for me to stop fighting the current.*

He came back to Master Gao's a little before lunchtime. As he latched the gate, he walked across the courtyard back towards his room. He met Old Wu.

"Wei-lin, are you ready for class tomorrow? I think Master Gao is going to have you spar with Lunghui again," Old Wu said with a chuckle.

"I won't be going to any more classes. I'm leaving," Wayland said. "For good."

"You're... ?" Old Wu said, stopping in his tracks as Wayland walked on by.

"I'm leaving," Wayland said, without turning back. He went to his room and closed the door.

Wayland took off his hat and threw his satchel in the corner. He looked around at the room. He had gotten rather fond of living here, but all things ended. He looked at the Bible on the small stand next to his bed, and he thought of his parents.

"You had some great plans for China, Dad," Wayland said out loud. "And you had some great plans for me too, I know. I guess neither of them worked out too well."

There was a knock at the door.

"Yeah?" Wayland said.

"It's me."

"I don't want to talk, Suyin," Wayland said.

"Please, there are some things you should know," Suyin said.

Wayland opened the door, and Suyin came in. She looked

down at the floor.

"Well?" Wayland asked.

Suyin hesitated for a moment, trying to find the right words. "Lunghui said he... told you about Magic Spear... "

"That he's Master Gao's brother? Yeah, he told me."

"Lunghui spoke out of turn. He shouldn't have told you in that way. We were trying to find the right time to explain things to you," Suyin said.

"The *right time?* The right time to tell me that I've joined the family that killed my parents?"

"That's not fair," Suyin said. "Master Gao had nothing to do with the Boxers. In fact, he saved your life, and he gave you a home. You can't say that he's done anything unkind to you."

Wayland exhaled deeply and shook his head. "I guess not. But that still doesn't change things. I can't stay here."

Suyin frowned and looked back down at the floor. "There is more to tell you."

Wayland looked at her. He wasn't sure what more there could be.

"Gao Jinghuo—that's Magic Spear's real name—is indeed the brother of Master Gao. It is a long story, but there was a tragedy, and the two had a falling out. They haven't spoken in years. Gao Jinghuo's young son died, and that destroyed his family. His wife passed away soon after."

"I know something about losing family," Wayland said. "But it didn't make me into a killer."

"Yes," Suyin said. "I'm not defending his actions."

"What, then?" Wayland asked.

Suyin paused for a moment, and then looked Wayland in the eye. "Gao Jinguo's son died, but he also had another child. A daughter, who was older."

"Okay," Wayland said.

"For... various reasons, he couldn't take care of her anymore. But a kind man did take her in, and raised her."

"So?" Wayland asked. He was getting impatient.

"That was the girl's uncle... whom you know as Master Gao." Suyin's eyes were tearing up.

"That's... it was *you*?" Wayland said, putting it all together.

Suyin bowed slightly to Wayland as she wiped her eyes.

"*You're the daughter of Magic Spear*?" Wayland asked.

"Yes. He is my father. I'm so very sorry for what happened to your parents, if my father had anything to do with it."

"Had anything to do with it? He had everything to do with it. Suyin, don't you think I deserved to know all this?"

"Maybe we should have told you. When Master Gao and Old Wu found you, they didn't know for sure who was responsible for the attack on your family. But when you told them about the man with the iron ring, we knew that Iron Ring Wang was a student of my father's, and that my father was one of the Boxer leaders. But what good would it have done you to tell you then?" Suyin said through her tears.

"It would have been good just to be honest and tell me the truth. I don't know, Suyin. If you came here to convince me to stay, you haven't done a very good job. I think you should leave." Wayland turned his back to her.

"I am sorry, Wei-lin... truly," Suyin said before turning and hurrying out the door.

Wayland sat down on his chair and put his head in his hands. Tears came to his eyes, and he sobbed.

29

For the next half hour, Wayland just lay on his bed, staring at the ceiling.

There was a knock.

"It's Suyin," came a voice.

Wayland opened the door and stared at her blankly. "Look, I've heard everything you had to say. It's time for me to go. That's all."

"Master Gao wants to see you. He's waiting," she said, and then turned and hurried away.

Wayland sighed and closed the door. *He snaps his fingers, and I'm supposed to come running. Yes, Master.*

He had everything mostly packed up and was ready to go, although "everything" didn't constitute too much. A change of clothes, some books and a few odds and ends. He would say his proper goodbyes to everyone, thank them, and then be off. He didn't have enough money for passage back to America, but he could afford to stay in the city for a couple of weeks, and he was sure someone from the American consulate could help him get back home. He could contact his grandparents in Boston, and they would certainly wire the money over for a ticket. And maybe it was all for the best. He picked up the Bible he had on his table, the one that Old Wu had bought for him shortly after arriving.

He opened the cover, and there was that small photograph

of his mother and father, the only picture that he had with him on that dreadful day, and now the only picture of them that he possessed. His mother had that enigmatic, confident half-smile, and his father displayed the dutiful solemnity that he always conveyed when having his picture taken.

Nobody here knew his parents, or would ever know them. At least back in Boston he could be around family again, and around people who knew his life and knew where he came from. No doubt it would be quite a change. He had barely spoken English at all in the last six months, and in truth he hadn't spent much time with his grandparents. But life was always about changes; he had certainly learned that lesson in the last year.

He left the picture where it was, and packed the Bible in his bag. Master Gao was waiting for him, he remembered. *He did save your life. Is it really too much for you to go and listen to what he has to say?*

Wayland knocked, and Master Gao opened the door.

"You wanted to see me?" Wayland asked.

Master Gao nodded. "Please, Wei-lin, come and have some tea."

He led Wayland to the small private cobblestone courtyard behind the main room. There was a small table with two chairs, and Master Gao bid Wayland to sit down. It was a beautiful, crisp winter day with a soft breeze blowing through the courtyard, and two crows were cawing and flitting about on the large tree just leaning over the wall of the Gao's compound.

"I hear that you're thinking of leaving us?" Master Gao said. He poured Wayland a cup of tea, and then one for himself.

"I've made my decision," Wayland said. "I appreciate everything you've done for me, Master Gao. It's time for me to leave."

Steam rose from Master Gao's hot cup of tea, and he brought it to his mouth and blew on it gently before taking a sip. "You don't owe us anything more, Wei-lin. You've done more than your share of work for us, and you've caused no trouble. I've come to have a great deal of respect for the boy—the man—that your parents raised. You can leave with my blessing, but I don't want anything left unsaid." Master Gao set his teacup down. "Do you have any questions for me?"

Wayland looked down and ran his finger around the rim of the teacup. "When the Boxers attacked last week, I recognized one of them."

"Oh?" Master Gao said.

"Yes," Wayland continued. "The man using the iron ring as a weapon. He was part of the group of Boxers that killed my parents. He killed my father, I believe. At least I saw him strike my father. That was the last thing I remember."

"Iron Ring Wang," Master Gao said. "I know of him."

"Yes, you know of him," Wayland said. His tone was accusatory. "He was one of Magic Spear's men. Suyin and Lunghui said that, that Magic Spear is your brother. Is that true?"

Master Gao leaned back in his chair and sighed. He paused for a moment and then looked Wayland in the eye. "Magic Spear Gao. Gao Jinguo. He is indeed my brother. By blood, and by school, as we studied martial arts under the same master."

Wayland's heart sank. He felt tears well up in his eyes, but they were not from sorrow.

"I lost everything, Master. My family, my world. You found me half-dead, you took me in, gave me a home, a real home. You saved me, and that meant everything to me. I came to trust you *with my life*. To find out that it was your brother who was responsible for my parents' death--and you knew that and didn't tell me? Do you understand what that does to me?"

"I am not my brother," Master Gao said.

"But you're from the same family, you learned martial arts from the same master, and I'm learning from you. What are the ethics of Chinese martial arts then, if they don't teach wrong from right?" Wayland asked.

Master Gao didn't show any expression. "When the foreign troops, including Americans, relieved the embassies here in Tientsin from the Boxer siege several months ago, they did not all behave honorably. There were killings of many innocent men who were not affiliated with the Boxers. There were rapes, there was looting. And it was not just the soldiers who acted that way. Even some of your missionaries took Chinese art and antiques to send back to their home countries. Does this disprove the ethics of Christianity? Does not your own religion say that all men are sinners, as you yourself told me?"

Wayland fumed. He shook his head, and stood up.

"I am truly sorry for your parents, Wei-lin," Master Gao said. "But if you will grant me a few moments, I will tell you the story of how my brother came to be as he is."

Wayland paused.

"Please," Master Gao said calmly. He motioned for Wayland to sit.

Despite everything, it was still difficult for Wayland to be rude to Master Gao. He sat back down. Master Gao brought out his pipe, packed it with tobacco, and lit it. He took a slow draw, and he sat back in his chair and blew out the smoke.

"My brother and I both had a love of martial arts from an early age. We saw the street performers; we heard the tales of the Water Margin, and of the swordswoman Hong Xian and Nie the Hermitess, and other heroes. I suppose all children are drawn to those types of stories. Master Han was a local martial arts master, whom our father knew. We begged Master Han to take us as students, and after a while, he did. I was about thirteen at the time, and my brother was fifteen. We left our parents and went to live with Master Han. Master Han knew Northern Shaolin and *T'ai Chi Fist*, one a hard style and the other a soft style, as you've learned. He was well-traveled, and a very brilliant man. A good man. He had studied with several different masters, and had made friends with numerous martial artists. He was easygoing and honest, and was well-liked among the martial arts community," Master Gao said.

Wayland took another sip of his tea, and sat back in his chair. Master Gao had never talked about his own training before, and Wayland was at least interested to hear the story.

Master Gao continued. "My brother was the best student that Master Han had ever had. He was a natural, and he also worked hard. I looked up to him, and aspired to reach his level of skill. I was not bad myself, but it seemed that no matter how hard I worked, I could not keep up with him. He mastered bare-hand fighting, saber, straight sword, and staff, but spear was his specialty. Master Han taught us that the spear was the king of all weapons, and my brother saw it as the pinnacle of martial arts skill. He worked on it tirelessly, and he eventually became much better than even Master Han. The problem, though, was that he had too much natural talent. He knew he was good, and he knew that nobody in the area could match his ability. He was polite to Master Han, and on the surface he projected humility, but his arrogance grew. He engaged in many challenge matches, and was never defeated. Master Han eventually told my brother that he was becoming a bully, and my brother accused Master Han of being jealous. This was an unforgivable insult to Master Han, and he expelled my brother from the school."

Wayland looked intently at Master Gao. Master Gao took a long draw from his pipe and slowly blew the smoke out, and it fell in billowy, white tendrils. He was silent for a moment as he watched the smoke dissipate.

"My brother left Master Han, and went out on his own to Tientsin," Master Gao continued. "He took a wife, and a year later they had a son. He started training his own students. He asked me to join him, but I would not leave Master Han. I loved my brother, but I knew that Master Han was right. Our parents felt the same, and they disowned my brother. He did not have the ethics of Master Han, but he was indeed able to train his students to a very high level. And yes, one of them was Iron Ring Wang, who was in the attack on your parents. Another of his students was Yun Yan, a young woman of exceptional ability. He taught her light body skills, among other things, and she reached such a level as to be known as Flying Faerie. I understand you encountered her in the attack last week." Master Gao sighed heavily, as if he didn't want to tell the next part of the tale.

"My brother… began to engage in criminal behavior, to put it bluntly. He began to use his skill to extort money from local shopkeepers, and he became quite rich and influential. Feared, actually. He became lax in his own training, as well. His skill had reached such a high level, he felt he did not need to continue training in the manner that he once had. He became fond of opium, and indeed came to spend most of his days under its influence. One day, his wife had gone to the market, and he was watching over his young son, Chanming, just three years old." Master Gao took another puff on his pipe. "My brother, as I have been told, was in an opium haze when his son, my nephew, darted out into the street. The boy was run over and killed by a horse and cart. The driver of the cart stopped and jumped down. He was distraught and, as I understand it, in tears. Upon hearing the commotion, my brother came out to the scene. When he learned what had transpired, he confronted the driver, and he struck the man and killed him right there," Master Gao said.

"I'm sorry." Wayland couldn't think of anything else to say. Master Gao nodded.

"My brother was a very powerful, influential man in the area. No charges were brought against him. But his wife could not withstand the grief. The next week she hanged herself. My brother changed. He became hard. He no longer enjoyed his leisure. He quit opium, and focused again on his martial training... he had nothing else. He blamed the foreigners for bringing opium to China, and he focused all of his hatred on them. When the Boxer movement arose he gravitated to them, and with his skills he quickly became one of their leaders. He was one of the few that had a high level of genuine martial skill. He trained many young Boxers, and taught them that the foreigners and foreign ways were the enemy of China."

Wayland nodded. "And that's when you took in Suyin?"

"Suyin was his other child, his eldest. She was just nine at the time, and my brother was in no condition to care for her. I offered to take her in, and he didn't object. She's been with me ever since. I love her as if she were my own daughter."

"I appreciate your situation, Master Gao," Wayland said, "But I don't know what else I can do. I apologize for the way I spoke to you. I understand that you aren't your brother. But I still think I have to go."

"You should do what you think is best, Wei-lin," Master Gao said. "But I should also tell you about the reason I was away."

Wayland frowned slightly and nodded, and he again sat back in the chair.

"My teacher, Master Han, passed away. I was at his funeral."

"Yes, you told us that before you left," Wayland said.

"There was more," Master Gao said. "When I was in Fenchow this past spring, on the trip when I came upon you and brought you back here, I was also visiting Master Han. He made me promise something. He made me promise to put an end to my brother's evil ways, to stop him from bringing further shame on our martial lineage. He told me I had to do it, one way or another."

Wayland stared blankly.

"And that is why my brother came here that day. He anticipated Master Han's wishes, and he wanted to face me at a time of his choosing. Both of us have known for quite some time that we would eventually meet in combat, and on that point I do agree with my brother. I now see that it cannot be put off any longer. You, Wei-lin, have firsthand experience of the evil that my brother has spread." Master Gao took his pipe out of his mouth and looked intently at Wayland. "Do you now understand why I must put a stop to him?

Wayland nodded slowly.

"Of course, if you want to leave, I will understand, and you will have my blessing," Master Gao added.

Wayland understood. He understood completely. Master Gao didn't say it, he didn't have to. *I'd be nothing but a coward if I left now, if I refused to help them stop Magic Spear, who was responsible for the death of my parents and many others besides.*

"I'll stay," Wayland said. Master Gao nodded and poured more tea for Wayland.

30

THE NEXT MORNING Wayland walked into the training courtyard. Suyin was already there, practicing her straight sword cuts. He approached her.

"Suyin," he said.

"Yes?" She brought her blade to her side and turned to him.

"I just want to apologize. I had no right to be angry with you. You've been very kind to me since I've been here. I can't hold you responsible for your father's actions."

Suyin bowed slightly. "I know it must have been a shock to you, and I'm sorry that you had to find out the way you did. There was just no easy way to tell you. It's difficult for all of us."

Wayland nodded. "I don't think anything more needs to be said. Let's train."

Suyin went back to her straight sword, and Wayland grabbed his saber from the weapon rack. He practiced the "wrapping" block and cut, trying to focus on keeping his center rooted and generating power from his legs and through his waist. He kept his grip on the saber relaxed yet firm. Master Gao was always emphasizing that one should have a "sense of enemy" when training alone, and Wayland visualized his opponent as he continued in the pattern. As his imaginary foe slashed downwards, Wayland brought his saber, its tip pointing to the ground, around to block. He then circled the blade around and riposted with a powerful horizontal cut at his phantom foe. Wayland continued, trying to balance speed, power, focus, and control. Too much speed and the focus was off. Too much aiming, and the power suffered. Too much power and the follow-through of his cut brought him off of his root and left him unbalanced.

He was getting frustrated trying to keep all the points in mind when he sensed Master Gao coming up behind him, observing. Wayland redoubled his focus, wanting to impress his teacher. Master Gao walked past Wayland and stopped. He turned and folded his hands behind his back as he watched his student go through his motions three, four and then five times.

"No," Master Gao said, shaking his head. "Deflect and strike are done together as one movement." He took the saber from Wayland's hand and performed the drill himself. "Not deflect," he stopped his motion abruptly, "…and then strike," he said as he finished his cut. "One motion. Seamless." He handed the saber back to Wayland. Wayland nodded and did the drill several more times, keeping everything he had been told in mind.

Master Gao watched him intently but showed little expression. "Better," he said. "Your basic cuts aren't bad, but cuts are not the same as fighting. Come and watch Suyin and me."

Master Gao called to Suyin, and she stopped her practice and walked over to Master Gao with her sword in hand.

Master Gao turned to Wayland. "This is called *San Cai Jian*." Three Power Sword. Heaven, man, Earth.

"This is one of the only straight sword routines that can be performed either as a solo form or as two-person practice. There are two parts to the routine. When one person is doing it alone, he will string together the two sections into one long sequence. When two are performing it together, one will perform the first section, and the other the second section at the same time. The patterns are designed so that every time one is attacking, and the other is defending against that actual attack. Do you understand?"

"I think so," Wayland said.

Master Gao turned to Suyin and nodded, and she took her position. The two stood to face each other, standing about five or six yards apart. Their posture was erect and alert, and as they looked at one another intently, their swords were each held in their left hands, with the blade vertical and the tip pointed up. At the same moment, they switched their swords to their right hands, and then both moved forward and engaged. Suyin thrust at Master Gao's head, and he subtly parried, and then instantaneously struck back with a slash towards Suyin. Their movements were smooth and fast, and Wayland marveled at their balance, coordination, and power. Suyin backed out of the way, Master Gao's blade tip missing her by inches, and then she shifted her footwork and came back in with a cut to Master Gao's knee. He lifted his leg out of the way, and came back and stabbed forcefully at Suyin's midsection.

This exchange continued for ten, fifteen, twenty-five moves with varying angles of cuts and thrusts, parries and evasions. Wayland thought that in some ways the coordination between the two was almost dance-like, yet at the same time he could see that the attacks were delivered with enough power and accuracy that if either of them had missed a parry, deflection or evasion, they would have indeed been struck with a severe, perhaps even fatal blow from the razor-sharp swords they both wielded with such precision. After the final exchange, they both stepped back several steps and smoothly transferred their swords back to their left hands and stood to face each other. They paused for a moment, and then formally bowed.

Suyin walked off to return to her solo practice, and Master Gao walked back to Wayland.

Wayland nodded appreciatively. "That was amazing. I can see how real fighting is quite a bit different than just practicing the individual moves."

"No," Master Gao said. "That wasn't real fighting. Real fighting is much faster, and not graceful at all. This is a crucial point to understand about martial arts. What you just saw with Suyin and me was simply the next step between individual techniques and real combat. These two-person patterns teach you how to move your whole body and coordinate your footwork while giving you an idea about attacking and defending. They teach you to gauge your distance and to perceive the force and timing needed to execute the techniques. Many beginning martial artists mistake skill in these drills as actual combat skill; they are not the same. Suyin and I were indeed delivering fast, powerful attacks, but still, we were not attempting to injure each other; these are cooperative drills. In combat, your opponent will try his best to wound and kill you. He will seize every opportunity; he will exploit the smallest weakness, he will take his advantage in any way possible."

He put his sword back in his sheath, and Wayland marveled at the deft, effortless control of the weapon that Master Gao displayed.

"In these drills, we know the pattern, we know what our next move will be, and we know what our partner's response will be. In combat, we do not know what will happen even after one or two moves; we must act reflexively and instantly. And fear." Master Gao paused for a moment, considering his words. "You have experienced fear for your life, that I know. Do you remember how your body felt?"

Wayland instantly flashed back to that terrible day and the jumble of half-remembered images and sounds that came forth seared him like hot iron. He winced almost imperceptibly and nodded. "I felt... my heart felt like it was pounding out of my chest. I almost think I could hear it. Everything got tight, too. All my muscles tensed up."

"In real combat, the terror of life and death can be all-consuming. It is said that if a man can remember even half of his training during a battle, he is doing well," Master Gao said.

"But how can I prepare for that?" Wayland asked.

"You cannot completely prepare for it. No training can exactly duplicate combat. But you can be aware of it, and be ready when the fear comes," Master Gao said. "And our time is short."

The morning was overcast, and the air was still and heavy; light snow was falling as Master Gao addressed Wayland, Suyin, and Lunghui.

"Thank you for being here," Master Gao said. "I have the greatest respect for each of you, but I must be very clear and leave nothing unsaid. None of you owe me anything. All debts that you feel you may have incurred, any formal allegiance that you have sincerely professed—I consider that each of you has more than fulfilled your obligation to me. I am deeply sorry that you were left alone to deal with the recent attack from my brother. Our feud is old and many-layered, and I did not intend for any of you to be involved. I purposely avoided challenging my brother's position regarding our martial arts training and the lineage of our teachings. There are many skilled martial arts teachers of numerous styles here in Tientsin, but I chose not to make martial arts my profession, and indeed I have only taught a handful of students over the years. I thought that would be enough to avoid the anger and resentment of my brother, but it was not. My family feud should have been none of your business, and I am ashamed that it has put you at risk and that it has resulted in injuries to some of my students. I have dismissed your classmates, and for the time being I have forbidden them to return. This conflict is not theirs. You three are different. I have either known you and trained you longer," he said, looking at Lunghui and Suyin, "or else your circumstance was unique." He glanced at Wayland and nodded slightly.

"Master, we're going to…" Lunghui started, but Master Gao raised his hand.

"Please hear me out, Lunghui. I want there to be no misunderstanding. My brother, the so-called Magic Spear, has sent me a formal challenge." Master Gao pulled out a folded piece of paper from inside his jacket and opened it so all could see its bright red calligraphy.

"On the last day of the third month, he will come here, and we will have our duel. For many reasons—some that you understand, and some that you don't—I must end his evil, once and for all. If I cannot do that, I will die in the effort. There are no other options. I expect that my brother will not come alone; I believe you are all familiar with his pupils. There is a real danger, and in truth, their skill level is quite high. As I have said, all of your obligations to me have been fulfilled. I will in no way think less of you should any decide that this is not your battle. You are free to leave with my blessing."

"You know my answer, Master," Wayland said.

"And mine," Suyin said.

Lunghui inhaled and sighed heavily, and then scratched the back of his neck as he looked down to the ground. "Well, you've put me in a position. How can I leave if a foreign devil and a young girl are brave enough to stay?"

Wayland gave Lunghui a playful shove and Suyin laughed, and a trace of a smile even crept over Master Gao's face.

"A teacher is fortunate to have one truly loyal student over the course of his life, and I have found three. But time is of the essence. We have barely two months to train. Lunghui and Suyin, you have a strong foundation, but Wei-lin—we're going to have to accelerate your training schedule greatly. For each of you, you must be focused all the time. This is no longer a hobby or an exercise. Your skill could mean the difference between life and death."

Wayland, Suyin, and Lunghui met Master Gao's stern gaze; their smiles faded, and their countenances began to reflect the deadly gravity of the situation they found themselves in.

The next day, their training began in earnest.

"As Sun Tzu has told us, 'if you know your enemies and know yourself, you will not be imperiled in a hundred battles; if you do not know your enemies but do know yourself, you will win one and lose one; if you do not know your enemies nor yourself, you will be imperiled in every single battle,'" Master Gao began. He paced slowly across the training area of the courtyard. "Over the next two months, I will make sure that you know your abilities and limitations, and, as far as possible, we will endeavor to know our opponents. I know my brother's style, as we shared the same training. I know most of what he has learned, and I know a good deal of what he has taught his pupils. Now tell me, who did you encounter during the attack, and what did you notice of them?"

"The big man had only one eye. He had a patch over the other one," Suyin said. "He was very powerful."

"He used double axes," Lunghui continued. "As Suyin said, he was like a bull. Maybe not as skilled as the others, but twice as strong as any of them."

Master Gao nodded. "The one they call One-eye Chang. He was a gangster here in Tientsin, and he got into trouble and fled to Shantung some years ago, where he met up with the Boxers. I don't know exactly what style he studied. I believe he's mostly a brawler, a street fighter. None of the martial arts community here in Tientsin had anything good to say about him. Some said that he would train at a school for several months, and then leave for another one. He was always causing trouble. I heard that he killed one of his old teachers in Shantung, but I don't know if that's true."

"If he doesn't have much training, that would give us an advantage, wouldn't it?" Wayland asked.

Master Gao shook his head. "Did he appear weak when you encountered him?"

Wayland shook his head.

"Don't let theories about martial arts take precedence over your real experiences. And don't underestimate the training one receives by actually engaging in fighting. That's a manner of learning in its own right, and perhaps the most profound. It's true that learning a martial art in depth will make you a better fighter, but natural abilities like speed, coordination and strength—and he surely has strength—are not to be taken lightly."

Master Gao turned to Lunghui. "But you will match up well with him, I think."

"I don't know," Lunghui said. He held up his thin but wiry arms. "I'm not going to match him in strength."

"Did I teach you to match strength with strength? Is that the theory of *T'ai Chi Fist*?" Master Gao asked.

"No," Lunghui said, as he thought about it. "You taught that four ounces can deflect a thousand pounds."

"Yang against yang, force against force—no good," Master Gao said. "His weapons are short, heavy and powerful. What should you challenge him with?"

Lunghui thought for a moment, and then it came to him. "I should match him with the spear."

Master Gao smiled. "Spear. Long, light, fast, and powerful.

That's right. You will use the spear against One-eye Chang."

Lunghui nodded. He liked the spear, and he had trained with it more than any other weapon. It made perfect sense.

"There was a woman, too," Suyin said. "She had light body skills."

Master Gao raised his index figure. Flying Faerie Yun Yan, he said. "She is perhaps the most dangerous of Magic Spear's pupils. Rumor has it that she was secretly in charge of several of the Red Lantern factions of the Boxer Movement before they were dissolved. She is reputed to have even killed one of her own students who was not progressing sufficiently.

"What are 'light body skills,' Master?" Wayland asked. "And as far as 'Flying Faerie,' she was pretty nimble, but... I mean, I heard lots of rumors about the Boxers and Red Lanterns, saying they can fly and cast spells." Wayland tried to keep his tone respectful. With his newfound understanding of Chinese martial arts, he had a greater appreciation for the incredible powers of skilled practitioners. But even so, there were still elements of myth that, as a Westerner, he was dubious of. "Those are just stories, superstitions. We don't really believe that, right?"

"No martial arts styles of China can teach one to fly, Wei-lin, that is correct," Master Gao said, holding back a smile. "It's a legend. But light body skills are not legend, they are fact. It is a manner of training which teaches one how to manipulate one's body weight, and to time one's steps and movements accordingly. When fully mastered, the skills are impressive and seem almost supernatural. One can leap to amazing heights, perform turns and twists in mid-air, run straight up walls, and even run several steps on top of water."

"She had a weapon, too," Lunghui said. "A chain whip."

Master Gao nodded. "Suyin," he said. "You have mastered pushing hands, you have practiced many hours of 'standing post' meditation to build your power. Your sword form is polished and stable. Where Flying Faerie leaps and bounds, you will maintain your firm root and sunken stance. While she dances in the air, you will have the Earth itself as your ally. Your nimble straight sword will match her flexible weapon."

Suyin drew her sword and looked at the shining blade. She nodded slowly.

"There was the man with the iron ring, as well," Wayland said with an air of resignation. He knew this would be his opponent, whether or not Master Gao agreed with him.

Master Gao turned to Wayland. "Your opponent will be very difficult, Wei-lin, and I am most concerned about you. You have trained with us for a relatively short time compared to Suyin and Lunghui. You have natural ability, and your skill level is already acceptable, but still... "

"I'm not afraid," Wayland said, and it was true. Any fear that he might have had for his own personal safety was overlaid by the image of that iron ring striking down his father on that fateful, terrible day.

"I don't doubt your courage, but there is more in play than that," Master Gao said. "Iron Ring Wang is his name. As you have experienced firsthand, his primary weapon is indeed that deadly iron ring. It is not a common weapon in China, but he has mastered it."

"But there has to be a counter to it," Lunghui said. "There's a counter for everything."

"I'm afraid there is more to consider than his iron ring," Master Gao said. "From what I have learned... he practices Golden Bell Cover."

Suyin and Lunghui exchanged nervous glances, but Wayland didn't understand.

"What's that?" Wayland asked. He was getting a little

perturbed at all of these strange terms and styles, and it was hard for him not to be just a bit skeptical of some of their supposed attributes.

"Golden Bell Cover is a method of training that makes one's body impervious to the effects of weapons," Master Gao intoned.

Wayland shook his head and smiled derisively. "That's what the Boxers claimed. But it never seems to work that well when they face the first shot from a Winchester or a Mauser. Suddenly, they're not all that invulnerable."

Master Gao raised his eyebrows. "Again, Wei-lin, don't dismiss these things so quickly. It's true that much of the Boxers' talk of magic spells and invulnerability was peasant superstition, exploited by the leaders of the Boxers to motivate and encourage the ignorant young men that they drew their ranks from. But Golden Bell Cover is very real. It involves years of physical conditioning of the skin, *ch'i kung* breathing exercises, and extreme mental focus. It will not make one impervious to bullets, that is a fact. And it will not stop a perfectly directed cut or thrust from a sword or spear. But one who has mastered this skill will indeed be mostly impervious to any barehand strikes, and also to any weak or poorly angled attacks from even sharp steel weapons."

"Okay... and how am I supposed to go against that?" Wayland asked.

"I'm not sure that you can defeat him by yourself," Master Gao said. "In fact, I'm quite sure that you can't. But I can teach you to defend yourself, and then with the help of one of us, perhaps Iron Ring Wang will be defeated."

"And what of Magic Spear?" Suyin asked. She paused for a moment, not wanting to be disrespectful. "He is the most powerful of all of them. How are we to defeat him?"

"That will be my concern," Master Gao said, and he sighed

heavily. "And it's something I must consider over the coming weeks. I will not deceive you: he was more skilled than I during our years training together. Still, he stopped his training for several years, which I never did. He also began training with a renewed ferocity after his son and wife died. To be honest, I don't know where I stand with him. We must all work together, and think together over the coming weeks."

"But if you both learned from the same master, and he was better, how can you match him?" Wayland asked.

Master Gao nodded. "That's something that I…"

"Time for some tea," Old Wu said, as he walked over holding a tray with a steaming teapot and five cups. He poured a cup for each as they all gathered around him.

There were many things for each of them to consider.

31

THE NEXT WEEK, Suyin and Old Wu were doing more cleaning than usual around the compound, and Wayland was wondering what it was all about. At around ten in the morning, he walked through the central courtyard and saw Suyin tacking up a bright red piece of paper, with the character *Fu* written on it. She had several in her hand, and was putting them up all around.

"What's this?" Wayland asked.

"Huh?" Suyin responded. "It says "good fortune. It's New Year tomorrow."

"Oh, right!" Wayland said. Chinese New Year, 1901. The year of the Ox. He had completely forgotten about the Western New Year, and now this was like a bonus holiday for him.

"We usually do a lot more, but with everything that's happening now... " Suyin said.

"Sure," Wayland said. "Is there anything I can do to help?"

"Tack this up on the main gate," Suyin said, handing Wayland a piece of red paper with the picture of a fierce-looking Chinese warrior on it. "This is a picture of Zhang Kui, one of the 'door gods.' He was a ghost fighter, and he will protect us from evil spirits. And after you do that, you can come in and help me make the dumplings."

It was nearly dark when the two had finished decorating. In the kitchen, Suyin showed Wayland how to roll out the dough for the dumplings, and while he was doing that she prepared the filling of ground pork, cabbage, scallions, garlic chives, ginger, soy sauce and sesame oil. She showed Wayland how to fill and shape the pleated dumplings, and they laid them out on the wooden cutting board.

"And that's pretty much all there is; they're quite simple," Suyin said.

"How are the dumplings coming?" Old Wu asked as he poked his head into the kitchen.

"Very well," Suyin said, smiling. "They're all made."

"How do we cook them?" Wayland asked.

"They're just boiled," Old Wu said. "Mmm... I can't wait. You always make the best dumplings, Suyin. Pay attention, Wei-lin. You will be doing well if you learn to make them half as well as she can."

Wayland nodded, and Old Wu cackled happily as he turned and exited the kitchen.

"Isn't it kind of late to have these for dinner now?" Wayland asked.

"They're served at midnight," Suyin said. "That's what we do on New Year's eve. We'll boil them just before that so they're nice and hot."

Master Gao and Old Wu were seated at the dining table in the main hall, and Suyin and Wayland brought out the plates of steaming hot dumplings just as midnight was met by the raucous cannonade of firecrackers throughout the city. It was a cold, clear night, and having skipped their ordinary dinner, everyone was famished. The aroma of the ginger and scallion-infused dumplings wafted enticingly through the winter air. Suyin made another trip to the kitchen to bring out two bowls of soy sauce and vinegar for dipping, and Master Gao opened a jar of wine and poured a round for all.

"To the New Year, with new friends and old family," Master Gao said, and raised his wine bowl. The others did the same and all downed their wine. Despite, or perhaps because of, the weight hanging over all of their shoulders, the merriment of a familiar tradition boosted all of their spirits. Old Wu told a joke that Suyin and Master Gao laughed heartily at. Wayland didn't quite get it, but he grinned as he and the others ate dumpling after dumpling; they were delicious.

"Oh, let's go out and see the fireworks," Suyin said. She was usually quite reserved with her emotions, but she had trouble holding back her glee.

The four of them walked out to the central courtyard to view the kaleidoscope of red, orange and blue fireworks and roman candles lighting up the ink-black sky over the old walled city. The sound of trumpets, tambourines, flutes and drums was also coming from the streets.

"Wow!" Wayland said, and he could see his breath in the cold air. He was warm from the alcohol and the dumplings, and he felt so alive in the bracing winter night.

"Do you know why we put up red paper and light fireworks and play music on New Years eve?" Old Wu asked.

Wayland shook his head.

"Many, many years ago, there was a terrible demon afoot in the land. The beast was called Nian. He terrorized the countryside, and he killed innocent people and devoured their children. An old man learned the secret of Nian: the beast couldn't be killed, but he could be kept at bay by the color red, by fireworks, and by the music of good-hearted people."

Wayland looked up at the dramatic, colorful explosions of light and color in the night sky, and he was thankful for the friends he had made here. Whether the story of Nian was true or not, Wayland didn't know. But there were indeed demons roaming this country, that he knew only too well.

They all knew the stakes, and the training intensified. The dynamic had changed, as well. No longer were they merely master and pupils, they were now something more — united, working together for one purpose.

Lunghui practiced his spear form relentlessly. He started at dawn with his stretching and *ch'i kung* breathing exercises, and then on to the actual spear techniques. He would go through the entire spear sequence several times, and as he performed each thrust, strike, and deflection, he envisioned his opponent; he trained with the 'sense of enemy.' His techniques were focused and crisp, and he delivered them with increasingly lethal power. His shirt was soaked with sweat as he deflected, stepped forward and thrust. The words of Master Gao echoed in his mind: 'fear not the man who has practiced many techniques once, but fear the man who has practiced one technique many times.' His muscles ached, and his arms and legs burned, but still he executed the same techniques, again and again.

Suyin began each day even earlier than Lunghui. She arose before dawn and started with the "standing post" *ch'i kung*. She stood upright, her whole body relaxed, and her knees slightly bent. She held both arms out in front of her in a circular shape, as if she was holding a giant ball. She focused on sinking her weight down to the Earth and relaxed every muscle as much as possible while still retaining a physically alert, lively posture. Her breathing became slow and deep, while at the same time her heart rate increased. She felt her *chi* flowing through her body, and root sinking into the ground. After a half hour or so, her legs shook, and her muscles burned, but she maintained the posture. After another half hour, the pain subsided, and she felt the detached warmth of her *chi*.When she finished, she raised her arms into the air and raised her heels off the ground, and then slowly lowered her arms, relaxed and exhaled as she sank back to her heels. The energy coursed through her body, and then it was time to pick up her sword for the next round of practice.

Over the following days, Master Gao focused most of his attention on Wayland, as he needed the most guidance. Master Gao had Wayland begin training with a wooden saber.

As Wayland practiced his cuts, Master Gao observed intently.

"Don't lose your root, that is the source of your power. Make sure to get your whole body into the strike. Send your *chi* through into the weapon. Muscles relaxed, and then in an instant, exploding body weight, all into the cut."

Wayland did his best to follow Master Gao's instructions. He kept his body relaxed and agile while at the same time keeping his *chi* sunken and rooted. His footwork was steady, and as he slashed with the wooden saber he generated power from his legs and *dantian*; the energy was directed by his waist and flowed through his relaxed upper body. He felt loose and dense at the same time, and he marveled at the power he was putting into the cuts. He hadn't realized that it was possible to generate so much force from a relaxed posture.

"Good," Master Gao said. "That is *T'ai Chi Fist*. It's not perfect, but you're on the correct path."

Master Gao had his saber in his hand, and he suddenly yelled: "Watch out!"

Wayland saw Master Gao's attack coming, a powerful downward slash to his head, and brought his wooden saber up and deflected the cut to his left. He immediately riposted with a thrust towards Master's Gao's chest. Master Gao parried Wayland's thrust and stepped back several paces. The two stood to face each other. Wayland's focus intensified. Where once he was completely intimidated by the idea of going up against

Master Gao in a sparring match, now he was engaged. He knew he wasn't better than his teacher, but you didn't have to be better than an opponent to give them a run for their money. *Relax your body. That's the key. Don't let emotions and fear cause your body to tense up.*

Master Gao was alert, and he held his weapon at the ready; he was preparing to attack again. Lunghui and Suyin stopped their practice in order to watch the duel between Master Gao and Wayland.

Wayland's heart was beating with excitement, but he kept his muscles relaxed. He observed Master Gao with a measured intensity; in the heightened atmosphere of the moment, he saw Master Gao not as a master, not as his teacher and not as an enemy, but just as a complex challenge, a problem to be solved. A problem composed of countless angles, varying speeds, numerous techniques, tactics and strategy, but still, just a task to be dealt with. At this moment, he thought that perhaps surprise could work best to his advantage.

"Watch out!" Wayland yelled as he stepped in quickly with a downward cut towards the left side of Master Gao's head.

The boldness and speed of Wayland's strike didn't wholly surprise Master Gao, but it delayed his reaction time a split second. Still, he turned his waist instinctively as he brought the flat of his saber up and slid Wayland's slash harmlessly to the side. Master Gao moved with a great economy of motion, not extending his center, his arms, or his weapon very far at all; then he saw his target. Wayland had put too much of his body's weight into the cut, and when it missed, the momentum threw him slightly off balance. Master Gao executed a simple "pi" cut with the wooden saber directly to the knuckles of Wayland's sword hand.

"Ungh!" Wayland uttered. The pain to his ring and middle

fingers was intense, and his saber dropped from his hand, clattering on the cobblestones of the courtyard. He shook his hand up and down as he hopped back, and he smiled at Master Gao's superior technique. He still had a lot to learn.

Master Gao wasn't smiling, however. He stepped in again and delivered a low, hard cut directly onto Wayland's shin, and then with his left hand, he hit Wayland squarely in the chest with a palm strike. Wayland fell on his back, and he put his arms up in front of his face as Master Gao raised his wooden saber as if to strike Wayland again.

Suyin and Lunghui looked at each other, unsure of what was happening.

"Get up," Master Gao said, and Wayland struggled to his feet. Wayland wasn't smiling anymore, and neither was Master Gao. "Pick up your weapon. That should *never* fall from your hand, for any reason!"

Wayland picked up his saber.

"What did you do wrong?" Master Gao asked.

Wayland stood at attention. He squeezed the handle of the saber, but his fingers were now mostly numb. Searing pain was coming from his leg. Master Gao's strike had hit him directly on the shin bone, and Wayland didn't know if he had ever felt anything more physically painful in his life. Still, he tried his best not to let it show.

"I lost my center, and I didn't protect my hand," he said.

"Your sword hand will typically be the closest part of your body to your opponent's weapon, the easiest target for him to strike. You must protect this at all costs. If I had been using a real sword or saber, I would have taken your fingers off," Master Gao said.

Wayland looked down at his hand and nodded sheepishly.

"And if I had taken your fingers off, then it would have been understandable for you to drop your weapon. But dropping it because your fingers hurt? Unacceptable. It could mean your life. Your opponent won't show you mercy as I did."

Master Gao looked to Suyin and Lunghui. This was a lesson for them as well.

"Get back to your practice," Master Gao said to them calmly. "We have another hour before lunch."

He calmly walked over and put his saber back in its place on the weapon rack, and then left the courtyard.

Wayland sighed heavily and reached down to rub his aching shin.

"How's the leg?" Lunghui yelled over to him, with a bit of a laugh. He was going through his same spear sequence. "I think they heard that wooden saber hit your shin on the other side of town."

"Yeah," Wayland said. "I think I'll be feeling that one for a while."

"Probably for a few weeks," Lunghui said. "That's how long it was for me. Although I think he was taking it easy on you."

"It's something we've all had to learn," Suyin said. "It's for your own good."

"I know," Wayland said. He understood the lesson, but that didn't lessen the pain. He looked again at his knuckles, and they were already red where he had been struck. He knew they would soon be black and blue. He closed and opened his fingers a couple of times, wincing.

"Fingers hurt, eh?" Old Wu said. Wayland turned around quickly to see the old man standing there, smiling. How he was always able to sneak up so quietly, Wayland could never understand. Old Wu seemed particularly gleeful about the lesson Wayland had just been taught.

"Oh, I knew it was going to be bad when you dropped your

saber," Old Wu said. "But then when you started smiling — aiya!" He slapped Wayland's shoulder and continued his cackling.

"Yes, I hope you enjoyed it," Wayland said. "That's what I'm here for, to provide you all with some entertainment."

"And you do a great job," Lunghui yelled over, and Suyin giggled.

"Lessons are hard to learn," Old Wu said. He stroked his beard for a moment and gathered his thoughts.

"Master Gao could have politely explained to you that you should protect your sword hand and that you should never drop your weapon, right? Do you think that explanation would have stayed with you longer than the lesson you learned today?"

"No, it wouldn't have," Wayland said.

"You learned something important, and you only paid with sore fingers and a bruise on your shin. Be grateful that Master Gao charged you so little. This world teaches many lessons that are much more expensive."

Wayland opened and closed the fingers on his right hand again. Some feeling was coming back to them.

Old Wu walked over to the weapon rack and picked up a saber. "Now, let's go over that sequence again. I'll play Master Gao's role, and you attack me as you did him."

Wayland nodded and gripped his wooden saber. He saw that Old Wu was ready, and he came at the older man with the same slash.

Old Wu deflected it and shook his head in frustration. "Come on. I'm not that old! Strike with some speed and power. If that's your best cut, I'm afraid there's not much hope for you."

Wayland sighed and smiled, shaking his head. *Okay, if Old Wu wanted a serious attack, he'd get one.* Wayland stepped in again with a downward slash at Old Wu's head, just as hard as he had cut at Master Gao.

Old Wu deflected as easily as Master Gao had, and he stepped in and gently touched his saber tip to the elbow of Wayland's sword arm.

"Remember, you must keep everything in control, whether you're striking fast or slow, whether your cut is powerful or delicate," Old Wu said. "And especially with the saber, most of your cuts will be based on power. Everything in a small circle. Try to remember that. For combat, keep your frame small, your range of movements small. Once you start to go too big, your swordplay becomes wild, and swinging too far one way will make you come back awkwardly, and you'll swing too far back the other way. You'll look like an old woman trying to shoo away flies with a broom. No good. Try again."

Wayland repeated the cut, and this time after Old Wu deflected, Wayland instantly drew his saber back into a defensive position and easily parried Old Wu's return thrust.

"Better," Old Wu said. "Now let's see how you do when you don't know what's coming. Again."

Old Wu worked with Wayland for the rest of the morning. By the time they were all ready to stop for lunch, Wayland had acquired several more bruises and aches on his body to go along with the sore fingers and throbbing shin, but he also knew that he was a slightly better swordsman than when he woke up that morning.

The next day was cold but bright and dry. Master Gao had the group assembled. Old Wu was setting up a wooden stand about three feet high, with a pointed wooden stake rising from its center. Old Wu then placed on the vertical stake a wet, tightly-rolled bamboo mat.

Wayland, Suyin, and Lunghui stood at attention as Master Gao addressed them.

"Learning the basic cuts, practicing two-person drills, and even free sparring does not fully teach one the breadth of swordplay. A blade is sharp so that it can cut, and one cannot truly learn the sword or saber without actually cutting. You have been taught the correct principles, and you've all worked diligently and learned your lessons well. But now you must put the principles into practice," Master Gao said. "Observe."

Old Wu held out Master Gao's sheathed straight sword, and Master Gao grasped the handle and drew his sword from the sheath. He walked over to the bamboo mat and held his sword at the ready. He paused, slowed his breathing, and raised his left hand, with the first two fingers held up. In one fluid motion he cut upward and to the left, and sliced off four inches of the bamboo mat; without any hesitation he then cut up to the right, taking off another three inches of the mat. The two severed sections of the mat flew into the air and landed on the cobblestones of the courtyard. Master Gao brought his sword back to a defensive position for a moment, and then smoothly rotated and transferred his sword back his left hand, handle down and the tip pointing up to the sky. He stepped back in two measured strides.

"Excellent," Wayland said. Master Gao's movements seemed almost effortless.

Master Gao bowed slightly and turned to Suyin. "Your turn."

Old Wu walked up and placed a fresh bamboo mat on the stand, and then he stepped back. Suyin drew her straight sword, inhaled deeply and then exhaled, relaxing her body. She stepped forward and slashed down at the mat, neatly slicing off the top three inches. She then cut again on the backstroke, but her sword only went halfway through the mat; the part that she had cut slowly turned over and drooped down, still attached to the rest of the wet bamboo mat. She withdrew her sword and cut again, severing the piece.

"Not bad," Master Gao said. "What happened with the second cut?"

"Angle was off," Suyin said.

"The angle was off," Master Gao repeated. "The sword and saber do not rely on strength to cut. Indeed, that is the whole reason why the sword has been the preeminent weapon for many centuries, in China, in Japan, in Europe. It is a great equalizer. It does not rely on brute strength for its effectiveness. Properly used, it will make a physically small and weak man, or woman, nearly as deadly as a large, strong man. But it must be wielded with precision. If the sword is well-made, tempered and balanced, it should not take crude strength to cut. Technique, timing and angles are all-important."

Master Gao walked over and put a fresh bamboo mat on the stake, and then he turned to Wayland and nodded.

"Right," Wayland said, nodding. He held his saber firmly in his right hand as he approached the target. He decided to employ a backhanded upward slash, from left to right. He faced the target with his right foot forward, and he inhaled deeply. *Keep the body relaxed, all joints linked together and working in unison, mental focus, let the energy flow naturally, coordinate breathing.* He pushed off with his back leg and stepped forward as he brought the blade up with a great deal of force. There was a loud "whap" as Wayland's blade hit the bamboo mat forcefully, and sent the intact mat flying off the stake, up into the air and several yards across the courtyard.

Old Wu shook his head, and Lunghui laughed.

Wayland turned back sheepishly and looked down at the saber in his hand. Why was he using this one? It was kind of old and beat-up, and it wasn't very sharp in the first place.

Master Gao didn't say anything, but walked over and put a fresh mat on the stake. He walked back over to Wayland.

"Let me have it," Master Gao said, and Wayland handed the saber to him. Master Gao calmly stepped forward and performed the same cut that Wayland had attempted. He seemed to use much less force, yet he cut cleanly through the mat once, then cut up again from the other side and sliced another piece of the target off. He cut once more and a final three-inch piece the mat was severed and fell to the ground.

"Nothing wrong with the blade," he said, handing the weapon back to Wayland. Wayland nodded. He felt fairly stupid and incompetent, but he was getting used to that feeling, and it didn't discourage him as it used to.

"You've got many mats there to cut, as well as some bamboo. Keep practicing," Master Gao said. "You two focus on cutting for the next couple days. Especially you, Wei-lin. You've got a ways to go before you even reach Suyin's level, and she's not that good." He turned and walked back to the other courtyard to observe Lunghui's spear training.

Over the next several days, Wayland and Suyin focused almost exclusively on cutting the mats and stalks of bamboo. After several hundred cuts, Wayland had eliminated a good deal of the error in his technique. The saber and sword were quite amazing weapons, he came to understand. When his timing, technique, and blade angle were perfect, his saber cut through the targets like a knife through butter. When his blade angle was a fraction of an inch off, though, or when he tried to muscle the technique using just his arm instead of the coordinated power of his whole body, the results were much less satisfactory. He still did damage to the target of course, either cutting partially through it or delivering a severe percussive blow. But that was not the goal of proper swordsmanship.

By lunchtime on the third day of their cutting practice,

Wayland and Suyin had cut over fifty mats, and at least that many bamboo stalks.

"You've picked up the saber very quickly," Suyin said.

"Thanks," Wayland said.

"All right, time for a break," Old Wu said, coming up behind them. He was holding a tray with a teapot and cups, and two steaming bowls of spicy noodles and greens in broth. He walked over and set the tray down on the small bench by the back wall of their courtyard. Wayland and Suyin leaned their weapons up against the cutting stand.

"I'm so hungry," Suyin said, taking her bowl.

"Be careful, it's hot," Old Wu said.

"Ow!" Suyin said, and set her bowl back down; it was indeed hot.

Old Wu poured three cups of tea, and Wayland and Suyin sat down on the bench. Old Wu remained standing. He looked at the massive pile of cut-up mats and bamboo and nodded.

"Seems like you two have had a productive morning," Old Wu said.

"I think we're getting better," Wayland said. He looked over at Suyin, and she nodded encouragingly.

"That's good," Old Wu said. He had that enigmatic half-smile that Wayland could never quite decipher.

"But I know it's still not the same as fighting," Wayland said. "It's like I'm learning the parts of real fighting, but I'm doing them all separately."

Old Wu raised his eyebrows and nodded. Steam was still coming off his tea in the fresh spring air, and he brought the cup to his mouth and took a sip. "No training method can completely duplicate real combat. But what do you think would make things more realistic?"

"I don't know," Wayland said. "Maybe if we did some

sparring and cutting in the same drill?"

"Is there a reason you haven't tried that?" Old Wu asked.

"Well... " Wayland said. He cast a glance over to Suyin. "Master Gao didn't tell us to do that."

"Chinese martial arts must always be creative. If you want to truly advance, you must contribute some of your own ideas to develop your skills; this will enhance what you've been taught. Now, your ideas may not always be correct, but you won't know that unless you try them. Master Gao will correct your errors of thought or practice. A master can only open the door for you. It's up to you to walk through it."

32

"Let's plan this out, and be careful—we're using live blades now," Suyin said.

"I know," Wayland said. He put a freshly rolled bamboo mat on the cutting stand, then gripped his saber and turned to Suyin.

"All right," Suyin said. "I'll go at about two-thirds speed."

Wayland nodded.

"And make sure you jump back out of the way after you thrust," Suyin added.

Suyin readied herself and then attacked with the downward slash, which Wayland deflected. She thrust at Wayland, and he turned his waist and with the base of his blade guided her thrust aside. He then whipped to the right to cut the mat, but he only knocked it off the stand. It fell to the ground intact.

"My angle was off again," Wayland said, as he put the mat back up on the stand. "It's hard to keep everything straight with the cut when I'm worried about your attacks."

"But that's what we'll face in combat," Suyin said.

"Right. Let's do it again," Wayland said.

They practiced the routine about twenty times, and the last five or six times, Wayland cut the mat cleanly. They then switched positions and arranged the drill so that Suyin would cut the mat as her final move. Suyin seemed to have much less difficulty than Wayland, and after only a couple of run-throughs, she was cutting the mat cleanly on the first cut, and then even coming back with another perfect cut, lopping off a three-inch section.

"Hey, you're pretty good," Wayland said, and Suyin flashed him a quick smile. "Let's switch back so that I'm cutting."

They changed sides, and as they began the drill, Master Gao approached. He held his hands clasped behind his back as he watched Suyin and Wayland exchanging techniques, and finally Wayland turning and cutting the mat. It was a perfect cut, and a slice of the target dropped cleanly to the ground. Wayland was surprised to see Master Gao standing there, but not as surprised as he was at what happened next. In a flash, Master Gao stepped in and delivered a palm strike to Wayland's chest. It wasn't hard, but it knocked Wayland back several steps.

"When you finish a cut, don't drop your guard," Master Gao said. "Always return immediately to an alert, defensive posture."

Wayland bowed slightly. "Yes, Master."

"And another thing, and this goes for both of you. Suyin, you should already know this. Don't ever deflect your opponent's strike with the edge of your blade." He held his hand out, and Suyin handed him her sword.

"Steel can have many characteristics, depending on how it is made, and for what purpose," Master Gao said. "It is easy to make steel that will hold a razor-sharp edge, but such a sword would be brittle and chip or shatter with the first contact of combat. Conversely, it is simple to make steel that is softer and less brittle, but that kind of steel doesn't hold an edge. Chinese swords are made of three layers. Rigid, sharp steel for the central core of the blade, and then two softer layers of steel surrounding the core. All hammered together. The central core forms the sharp edges, and the softer layers protect the central core. The result is a blade that is both sharp and durable."

Master Gao ran his finger lightly across the blade of Suyin's sword.

"The sharp edge is designed to cut your opponent, it is not designed to clash with the tempered steel of your opponent's weapon," he continued. "If the edge of your weapon is struck by tempered steel, it may very well chip and crack. In the best of circumstances this will leave your blade weakened, and at worst it may lead to your blade breaking, rendering your sword or saber useless. Then, you will find yourself unarmed against your opponent's weapon—not a desirable situation. So always deflect and parry with the flat of the blade, not the edge. And similarly, remember this when you attack. Try your best not to strike steel with your edge, whether your opponent is wielding a sword... or some other metal weapon, like a chain whip," Master Gao said, as he looked at Suyin. "Or an iron ring," he said, glancing to Wayland. "Protecting the edge of your blade may well mean protecting your life."

"Yes, Master," Wayland and Suyin said in unison.

Master Gao handed the sword back to Suyin. He turned to Old Wu. "Did you create this drill for them?"

Old Wu smiled and shook his head. "I had nothing to do with it. This is something they came up with on their own."

Master Gao nodded and looked to Wayland and Suyin. He fixed his gaze on them for a moment. "That's good. Very good. Keep practicing."

Master Gao beckoned for Old Wu to walk with him. "Let's go check on Lunghui," Master Gao said, as they left Wayland and Suyin to their drills.

When they were out of earshot, Old Wu tapped Master Gao on the arm. "What do you think? What's your honest opinion?"

The two watched as Lunghui practiced his spear. He had two man-sized cloth dummies propped up, as well as several small rings, just a few inches in diameter and covered in paper, hanging from the branches of one of the trees. Lunghui assumed his stance, stepped in smoothly with a powerful thrust to one of the dummies, then turned and expertly punctured the paper of first one, and then the second and third of the rings. He then went through one of his short spear forms. Every technique was executed with power and precision. He was calm, focused and intense. Master Gao nodded to Old Wu, and they turned to leave Lunghui to his practice.

"Lunghui is the best of the three," Master Gao said, once they were out of earshot of Lunghui. "He has great natural ability, he's intelligent and diligent, and he has spirit. I worry the least about him."

"I agree," Old Wu said. "He is a fine heir to your teachings. And the other two?"

"You tell me," Master Gao said.

Old Wu stroked his white beard as they strolled towards the far side of the courtyard. "Suyin, of course, doesn't have the strength of a man, and that is a disadvantage, objectively speaking. From my observation, however, that is her only area of deficiency. She is naturally athletic, her skill level is high, she's intelligent, adaptive and is in control of her emotions. She is calm, but can be fierce."

"And Wei-lin?" Master Gao said.

"Ah, Wei-lin," Old Wu said. He sighed and then paused for a moment. "Foreigners are strange in many ways, not always easy for us to judge, I would say. I believe he is honest and loyal, which is the most important thing."

"I agree," Master Gao said. "And his martial arts?"

"Surely you have your own opinion on that, a more informed opinion than my own?"

"If I didn't value your thoughts, old friend, I would not ask for them."

Old Wu nodded in silent appreciation. "Wei-lin is intelligent, and a quick learner. He is a fit, athletic young man with natural speed, strength, and coordination... "

"But?" Master Gao said, sensing that Old Wu was holding back.

"Well, he just hasn't been training very long. He has not put in as much time, and he does not have the foundation that the others possess."

"Agreed," Master Gao said. "Anything else?"

"I'm not sure about his mental and emotional focus. He has gone through great trauma this last year. The tragedy of his family, being left alone, staying in a strange country, with no contact with his own people. I see in his training that his mind often wanders, and he dreams of the past and the future. His emotions are unsettled, from anger and thoughts of revenge, to... "

"To... his feelings for Suyin? Do you see that as well?"

"I may be old, but I am not yet blind," Old Wu said.

Master Gao nodded. "The affairs of youth will be what they will be. That is an issue for Wei-lin and Suyin to resolve. However, I do worry about his thoughts of vengeance... of retribution."

"Yes," Old Wu said.

"Much cruelty and evil can result when those who have genuine grievances come to wield some power, as we have seen with the Boxers. And I am solely responsible for Wei-lin coming to some power. I have taught him to fight, to kill."

"No, Master," Old Wu said softly. "You have taught him *how* to fight and kill. Deciding when he should — well, that is up to him. Just as it was up to you and your brother, who learned from the same master."

The last few days of the second month were unseasonably warm, and after the bitter-cold winter, it was a welcome respite for everyone. Master Gao and Old Wu called everyone into the central courtyard and told them to bring their weapons. Lunghui, Suyin, and Wayland all stood at attention in a line, Lunghui holding his spear, Suyin with her sword, and Wayland with his saber. Old Wu was carrying a duffle bag of some sort, and he set it down next to the weapon rack. He reached into the bag and began pulling several objects out, although Wayland couldn't quite tell what they were.

"Lunghui, step forward," Master Gao said, and Lunghui did as he was asked. Master Gao stared intently at Lunghui and then held his right hand out. "Old Wu, the double axes, please."

"This is the weapon favored by One-eye Chang," Master Gao said, as Old Wu placed the pair of short axes in Master Gao's hand. Master Gao transferred one ax to his left hand and then held the pair out in front of him. "Double axes. Steel, sharp on both sides, powerful for both offense and defense. As with all double weapons, one can be used for attack and another for defense simultaneously. Lunghui, attack," he said calmly.

Lunghui nodded and lowered his spear point, pointing it directly at Master Gao. He stepped in and thrust at Master Gao's upper body, and Master Gao deflected the thrust away with the ax in his right hand. Lunghui withdrew his spear and in a flurry thrust several more times. With seemingly little effort, Master Gao's axes deflected each lightning-fast thrust to the side, with the occasional "clang" of steel against steel reverberating through the compound. Lunghui withdrew again and then went in low for a thrust at Master Gao's knees. Master Gao crossed both axes and pushed Lunghui's spear point to the ground. Lunghui tried to withdraw the spear, but Master Gao had the spearhead pressed tightly to the ground and locked with the axes. With a deft movement, Master Gao stepped forward to close the gap and eliminate the advantage in reach that Lunghui's spear gave him. As Master Gao released the spear, Lunghui withdrew it, but it was too late. Master Gao had made his way in past the dangerous spear point, and Lunghui couldn't retreat fast enough. Master Gao then cut down on the shaft of the spear with his left ax, knocking the weapon out of Lunghui's hand, and he then placed his right ax under the chin of his defeated student. Lunghui grimaced and bowed slightly.

"Spear is the most powerful weapon of all, but to take full advantage of its power, you must maintain the distance. Your opponent, if he is using short weapons, will always try to do what I just did, to get in close. Make sure you don't let him."

Master Gao walked back to Old Wu and set the double axes on the weapon rack.

"Suyin, step forward." She did and with a circular motion, deftly transferred her sword from her left hand to her right and adopted a ready stance. "Old Wu, the chain whip," Master Gao said, and Old Wu handed him the weapon. Master Gao stretched out the chain whip for all to see. "The chain whip. Nine linked sections of steel, with a pointed steel dart at the end. When folded together, less than a foot in length. When fully extended, eight feet long. Flexible weapons take great skill to wield, and are difficult to defend against." He looked at Suyin and nodded.

"Ready," Suyin said, her sword at the ready.

Master Gao gathered the chain whip into a compact bundle of steel and took several quick steps towards Suyin. He right hand thrust outwards, and with it, the steel dart end of the chain whip shot out in a straight line, directly at Suyin. She deflected the dart with the flat of her blade, and then stepped in quickly towards her teacher, cutting diagonally downwards towards his right shoulder. Although surprised by her aggressiveness, Master Gao pulled back on the chain whip and it wrapped once around his right wrist. He blocked Suyin's sword slash with the steel of the whip that was around his wrist, and in one motion he swung the length of the chain whip in a horizontal arc back at Suyin.

Suyin saw it coming and ducked down, and as she did, she slid forward towards Master Gao, and cut low at his left knee. Master Gao's chain whip continued its arc over Suyin's head and came back around, and he kept the whip circling and angled it down. As he stepped backward out of the way of Suyin's cut, the whip came around again and wrapped itself around the hand guard of Suyin's sword. Suyin tried to disentangle it, but Master Gao gave a sharp pull, and Suyin's sword flew out of her hand and through the air. It clanged on the cobblestones of the courtyard floor. Suyin frowned and glanced angrily at her sword. For a moment she thought of running over to pick it up and continue, but then she thought the better of it, and she bowed respectfully to her teacher.

"The chain whip is a deadly weapon, and even if you avoid the strike of the dart, your body or weapon can easily be entangled. Always be aware of two things when facing a flexible weapon: the maximum reach of the weapon, and the weighted end. Keep your focus on the end. If not, you will certainly be wrapped up and entangled," Master Gao said. He nodded, and Suyin went back the side.

Wayland didn't wait to be asked. He walked forward and took Suyin's place, and stood facing Master Gao with his saber held at the ready.

"The ring please, Old Wu," Master Gao said. Old Wu brought out an iron ring, roughly the same size as the one Wayland saw Iron Ring Wang use against his parents. "The iron ring—an uncommon weapon. It can deliver deadly percussive force when used for offense. When used for defense, its purpose is to bounce back the force against the opponent, and also to chip or damage the blade of any sharp weapon. Wei-lin, are you ready?"

Wayland nodded. "Ready, Master."

Wayland was anticipating a quick attack from his teacher, as Master Gao had done against Lunghui and Suyin. This time, however, Master Gao approached slowly. He took several calm, measured steps towards Wayland, and began to circle him.

Wayland felt his muscles instinctively start to tighten, and he consciously resisted. *The essence of T'ai Chi Fist is relaxation. Relaxed muscles allow the chi to flow, allow speed and power to be manifested.*

Wayland took a deep breath and centered his focus on his opponent. As Master Gao calmly circled him, Wayland remembered something he had read in Sun Tzu's *The Art of War*: "Appear weak when you are strong, and strong when you are weak." You intentionally leave yourself glaringly exposed so that your opponent will attack in precisely the manner you expect him to. Wayland rushed towards Master Gao with his saber held high, and his center left wide open and completely vulnerable. As Wayland expected, Master Gao stepped in to strike Wayland's chest with the iron ring. Adhering to the principles of *T'ai Chi Fist*, Wayland turned his waist and saber simultaneously to the left and deflected Master Gao's strike, and then he cut down towards Master Gao's head. At the last second, Master Gao understood what Wayland was attempting, and was barely able to block Wayland's slash with the iron ring. Wayland held back both speed and force, not wanting to injure his teacher, and both he and Master Gao instantly understood that if Wayland had not restrained his power, he would have cut Master Gao's head, perhaps fatally.

"I'm sorry, Master," Wayland said. He bowed respectfully as he stepped back.

A rare, broad smile appeared on Master Gao's face, and he

could hear Old Wu chuckling in the background.

"Very good, Wei-lin," Master Gao said. "Very good indeed."

Wayland nodded appreciatively. "Thank you, Master."

"Did you see what he did?" Master Gao said, turning to Lunghui and Suyin. "He feigned weakness and opened himself up to an attack that he was anticipating. This is often an effective technique. Deception and trickery are part of combat, and can prove extremely beneficial."

Master Gao turned slightly towards Wayland and raised his eyebrows.

"Never rely too heavily on such methods. They are not a substitute for genuine skill, but they should likewise not be discounted, either. As Sun Tzu said, 'All warfare is based on deception. Hence, when we can attack, we must seem unable; when using our forces, we must appear inactive; when we are near, we must make the enemy believe we are far away; when far away, we must make him believe we are near.'"

"Are you sure Wei-lin even meant to do that?" Lunghui said. "He could have just messed up what he was really trying to do and got lucky."

Old Wu chuckled, and Master Gao shot him a none-too-serious frown.

"Be serious, Lunghui," Master Gao said. Wayland stuck out his tongue at Lunghui and was just able to get it back inside his mouth as Master Gao turned around and, in turn, gave him a reproaching glance.

"One more lesson for you all. You've each reached a reasonable level of skill with your weapon, and you have an understanding of your opponents' weapons. But please remember that you are all on the same side, and must help each other whenever the situation arises. The strengths that you possess may be able to compensate for a deficiency in one of your classmates' skills."

Master Gao turned to Old Wu. "Hand me a saber, if you would."

Old Wu took a saber from the weapon rack and held the grip to Master Gao.

"Lunghui, thrust slowly towards me with your spear."

Lunghui did so, and Master Gao dodged the spearhead and then grabbed the shaft with his right hand and stepped in towards Lunghui. "Now, Lunghui is in trouble, because I've gotten past the point of his spear and he can't withdraw it quickly enough. Suyin, if you see this…"

"Yes," Suyin said, without being told. She stepped between Lunghui and Master Gao and slowly cut down towards her teacher's head.

Master Gao had to stop his advance towards Lunghui to defend against Suyin's cut.

"Exactly!" Master Gao said. He turned to engage Suyin, and with his superior technique, he was driving Suyin back without much trouble. "And Lunghui, if you see Suyin or Wei-lin in trouble…"

"Right!" Lunghui said. He stepped with his spear, thrusting several times at Master Gao to give Suyin some time to regroup.

Master Gao stepped back, and casually transferred his saber to his left hand, and dropped his guard. Lunghui and Suyin followed suit. "That's it," he said. "As you know your weapon and its capabilities, these are not difficult concepts for you. Very good."

"Hey, maybe these students aren't as dumb as they look after all," Old Wu said. He laughed to himself as he took Master Gao's saber and replaced it on the weapon rack.

Lunghui, Suyin, and Wayland smiled at each other, with more than a little sense of satisfaction.

"You're better than you were," Master Gao said, "and you've

made some progress. But I will leave you with one more saying from my teacher. 'When you train at martial arts, just put your head down and train. If you look around and see that others are better than you, you will be discouraged and want to quit. If you look around and see that you are better than others, you will become arrogant and lazy. So just put your head down and train."

"Eh, I've only heard that one a few hundred times," Old Wu said, partly under his breath. Suyin giggled, and Wayland and Lunghui smiled.

"And you'll probably hear it a few hundred times more before you're through," Master Gao said. His expression was serious, but his tone was light. "You can't hear words of wisdom enough times. And even then it doesn't stick with most people. Besides, Old Wu, isn't it about time you started making dinner?"

"All right, all right," Old Wu said. "Just trying to lighten things up a bit, that's all. Everyone so serious all the time... " he grumbled to himself as he walked across the courtyard towards the kitchen.

Master Gao turned to the three. "Our time is short before Magic Spear arrives for our duel. Over the next couple of days, I want you to continue your training as usual, but with a special focus on what we've done today. One of you should adopt the weapons of our opponents—the axes, the chain whip, the iron ring—and play that role. The other two will work on strategies and tactics to defeat that weapon. Remember, your creativity and cunning are skills every bit as crucial to develop as your cutting and thrusting, your speed and strength, your breathing and footwork. All must work together."

The three bowed politely and went back to their training as directed.

33

MOST NIGHTS Wayland went to bed sore. If it wasn't a black and blue mark or a cut somewhere, then it was pulled or aching muscles. Although they had different methods for teaching him, both Master Gao and Old Wu stressed one important concept that Wayland took to heart: it is far better to have high skill with a small number of techniques than to have middling knowledge of many.

Most of his training time was devoted to the saber. The reality of combat in Chinese martial arts, Master Gao had said, is that the use of weapons is of primary importance. Barehand fighting was useful to some degree, but in life-or-death situations, it was best left as a last resort. Perhaps when one had lost the primary weapon. Wayland was only taught the one form for the weapon, the basic Yang family saber routine.

It was a relatively short routine, with only thirteen offensive and defensive techniques, and its linear movements belied its origin as a military training form. In the beginning, Master Gao had instructed him to perform the routine very slowly, to ensure that his footing was firm, his movements smooth and steady, and his techniques balanced. But after he reached a level of proficiency in performing the routine slowly, Master Gao had him gradually increase the speed, until he was finally going through the entire form virtually at combat speed.

Practicing the test cutting against the bamboo mats had

significantly impacted Wayland's approach to the solo saber form. He now understood how important it was to generate enough power to cut through a target and also to have all of the angles properly aligned so that the power made its way through to the opponent. One broken link in the chain, whether it was an off-balance step, too much tension in his waist or arms, or his blade held at a slightly wrong angle, would seriously affect the impact of both his offensive and defensive techniques.

It was late in the afternoon on a Friday, and the day was overcast but pleasantly warm for the second month of the Chinese calendar. Wayland was by himself in the training courtyard, going through the saber routine again. He saw Master Gao and Suyin approaching, and Master Gao was holding a saber of his own. Wayland continued his sequence as if he didn't see his teacher, and indeed by this stage, he was past the stage of feeling any anxiety at Master Gao's observations. Wayland wasn't a master of the weapon, and he certainly knew that; he was, however, no longer a beginner. This was not arrogance, but rather an honest assessment of his abilities. False humility and unrealistic self-denigration could prove just as harmful and dangerous as over-confidence and conceit, as Master Gao had taught.

Master Gao walked up to Wayland, dispassionately observing his student's technique. As Wayland moved forward with a blocking technique from the form, Master Gao darted in with a hard downward cut with his saber. Wayland calmly deflected, and Master Gao's blade slid harmlessly to the side. Although Master Gao's practice saber wasn't razor sharp, it did have some edge; if Wayland's technique hadn't been perfect, he would have certainly received some cut on his shoulder blade. Wayland didn't miss a beat, however, and he followed the deflection with the next technique in the form, a diagonal upward cut to his left. Wayland saw that Master Gao was still in range of his weapon, but he continued with the full speed cut and didn't alter its trajectory. Master Gao was expecting as much, as he casually stepped back out of range to allow Wayland to finish the form.

"Good," Master Gao said, as Wayland drew back to his ready position, brought his saber to his side and exhaled.

At dinner, they all discussed their training of the day, as usual, and Master Gao told them a couple of stories of his own days of practice when he was their age. He then suggested that everyone retire early to get a good night's sleep. Wayland wasn't going to argue.

They each went to their rooms, and Wayland sighed heavily as he flopped down on his mattress in the dark. He lay there for a moment, but wasn't ready to go to sleep. He lit his oil lamp, and then opened up to the bookmark in his English copy of the Chinese classic *Outlaws of the Marshes*. He particularly enjoyed the story of Lin Chong, the righteous general falsely accused of treason. Lin Chong persevered through terrible trials, betrayals, and loss, but in the end his unscrupulous enemies got their just desserts. His eyes got heavy, and two hours later he awoke with the volume face down on his chest, where it had settled.

He looked over at his clock, and it was too early to retire for the night. Maybe he'd go for a walk. He put his shirt and shoes back on and stepped outside of his room out into the first courtyard. He looked up at the sky. It was a beautiful, clear night and the stars shone brightly. The fresh, bracing smell of the crisp spring air reminded him briefly of his days in Boston with his parents. It was strange how scents could stimulate such powerful, visceral memories. He walked through the gate to the second courtyard, where they did most of their training. The peaceful silence of Tientsin at night soothed his senses. It was a big world, and he was a small part of it. He shouldn't forget that.

He was not insignificant—he was made in the image of God, and he was put here for a purpose—but he was only one of the millions. He could only do what he was able to, nothing less, but nothing more, either.

As he came into the second courtyard, there was a figure standing off to the side, near the outer wall. Whoever it was, they were motionless. Wayland cautiously made his way closer, and as he got within several yards, he recognized the figure of Suyin. She was standing with her knees slightly bent, her arms held out in a half-circle in front of her. She was practicing her standing post *ch'i kung*. Suyin's eyes briefly met Wayland's as she noticed him, but other than that her body didn't move and she showed no reaction.

"That's a good idea," Wayland said softly. He took his position to the left of Suyin and adopted her same stance. His breathing slowed. He let his mind clear and his anxieties dissipate.

Wayland lost track of time. After a while, Suyin exhaled heavily, raised her heels and then lowered her arms.

"I think that's going to be all for me tonight," she said. She stretched her arms up into the air, and circled her waist slowly several times. Wayland followed suit and brought his own hands down and slowly opened his eyes.

"I didn't know it was you when I first came into the courtyard," Wayland said.

"Who did you think would be out here?' Suyin said, in her usual matter-of-fact manner.

They both started strolling back towards the gate to the first courtyard, and to their respective rooms.

"It's so clear tonight," Wayland said. "Look at all those stars."

Suyin looked up. "So many, you can't even count them."

"Those stars are all really suns, but millions of miles away. They might have planets around them, just like ours. Maybe some kind of people on them."

"I've heard about that," Suyin said. "Do you think it's true?"

Wayland shrugged. "Maybe it's true. I don't know."

"What will you do?" Suyin asked.

"Huh? What do you mean?"

"I mean, what are your plans? Are you going to go back to America?" Suyin asked. "When this is all settled?"

"I haven't thought much about that, to be honest. I don't even know if things will be settled... or what will happen... to any of us."

"You could still go," Suyin said. She put her hand on Wayland's arm. "You could go to the foreign concessions and tell them your story. They'd help you get back home. This is really our battle, not yours."

"You could leave too," Wayland said. "Take off before Magic Spear and his gang get here. You could be safe, and start a new life somewhere."

Suyin smiled and shook her head. "No, that's not the Chinese way. I could never leave Master Gao in a situation like this, not after all that he's done for me."

"But you expect less of me?" Wayland asked.

"It's... it's different for you."

"No, it's not," Wayland said. They walked in silence for a few moments.

"If everything is settled... if you bring justice for your parents... then what? Do you like this country enough to stay?" Suyin asked.

"The country?" Wayland said. "I do like it here. I've been away from America so long, I guess China is the closest thing I have to a home now."

"I understand," Suyin said. "It must be difficult to live in a strange..."

Wayland had held in his passions for so long, and he couldn't restrain himself any longer. He put his hands on Suyin's shoulders and turned her to face him. She didn't resist.

"Suyin... " Wayland said. He softly ran the tips of his fingers over her forehead and down her cheek. Suyin closed her eyes and parted her lips ever so slightly. Wayland leaned in and gently kissed her full lips, and then pulled back, unsure of Suyin's reaction.

"We have to wait," she said, and she leaned in and kissed him again. "But our time will come." She smiled warmly and gently stroked his cheek. "Good night."

Wayland stood there, watching her go. She didn't look back as she went to her room and latched the door behind her.

He sighed. Her breath had been sweet and her scent was still in his nostrils. It reminded him of the bloom of peonies that he remembered from his first springtime in Fenchow.

Still, what kind of plans were even possible? What did he have to offer her? He was little more than a common laborer here in China — and after the recent violence, he didn't know what the future held for foreigners living here. Would Suyin move to America for him? That was a lot to ask, and he had no idea if she would even consider that. And did he even want to go back to America?

Stop dreaming and fantasizing; you have more immediate concerns. You couldn't protect you parents when they most needed you, and you probably won't be able to safeguard Suyin, either. You'll be lucky to even defend yourself when the time comes.

And the time was coming.

Master Gao gave everyone the day off from training on the second-to-last day of the third month the day before Magic Spear was to arrive for their duel, but he did ask them to gather in the courtyard after dinner. It was a beautiful spring evening, with low humidity, pleasant temperature and a warm breeze blowing through the compound. Wayland and Suyin were waiting in the central courtyard just after sunset.

"What do you think he wants to see us about?" Wayland asked Suyin. "Do you think the duel has been called off?"

Suyin shook her head. "I don't think so. Maybe he wants to go over our strategy once more."

Wayland nodded, but he didn't think that was the case. That's why they had the day off in the first place. They had done as much preparing and training as possible. Whatever was going to happen was going to happen, at this point.

There was a knock at the main gate. "It's me," came the voice of Lunghui.

Suyin walked over and opened the gate, and Lunghui walked into the compound. Suyin bolted the gate behind him.

"Hello," Lunghui said to Wayland, and Wayland smiled. Neither was in the mood for their usual joking and teasing.

"It is a beautiful evening now, isn't it," Old Wu said. Wayland turned around abruptly. How did Old Wu always manage to sneak up unnoticed?

"It's a very nice night, Old Wu," Lunghui said, smiling gently, and he put his hand on the older man's shoulder.

There was the sound of a door unlatching and sliding open from the main hall, and they all turned to see Master Gao stepping out into the compound and walking towards them. They all bowed as their teacher approached, and Master Gao waved his hand in the air, politely acknowledging but dismissing their formality.

"Thank you all for coming tonight," he said. "And before anything else, I must first compliment you on your training over the last weeks and months. Each of you has shown great dedication, perseverance, loyalty, and diligence. I could not possibly ask for better students than the three of you, and I am sure that Old Wu would agree with me."

"I do," Old Wu said, nodding. His smile was warm and genuine.

"Suyin and Lunghui, you have been with me a long time, and I have come to know your character. I am truly honored to have you as my students. And Wei-lin," he said, turning to Wayland, "you have come to us by an act of fate, from far away. But good men can be found among all peoples, and you have surpassed all my expectations. I count you as equal with Lunghui and Suyin as my trusted students."

"Thank you, Master," Wayland said.

Master Gao continued. "I do not know what tomorrow will bring, but I feel I must explain to you again that any, or all of you may choose to stay away tomorrow if you wish. You are all young, and I know you have many dreams of what your life may yet bring. I am in a different stage of life, and my duties are more clear. The possibilities for danger tomorrow are very real, and I would never consider any of you disloyal for seeing things differently."

"Master," Wayland said.

"Yes, Wei-lin?"

"If you were our age, and your master needed your help, would you abandon him?" Wayland asked.

Master Gao looked at Wayland for a moment, and he almost smiled. "Are all foreigners so impertinent?"

Wayland grinned. "No, just me."

"Still, remember this," Master Gao continued. "There is still a good chance that the violence can be contained tomorrow, and may not involve you at all. By all rights, the duel should be a family matter, between my brother and me. I will do my best to hold him to that and not to involve his subordinates. And that is where I need your help. I have tried to prepare you as best I can for this encounter, but I did so considering the worst-case possibilities. Under no circumstances are you to instigate any conflict. You are only to act when all other means for your self-defense have been exhausted. Do I make myself perfectly clear?"

Wayland, Suyin, and Lunghui all responded in the affirmative.

"Good," Master Gao said. "Gather tomorrow morning at seven, but do not appear eager or even prepared for combat. Leave your weapons on the rack—out of your hands, but within easy reach if the need arises."

"I'm going to be carrying my staff," Old Wu said. "I don't care what you say. I can't be bothered to run over to the weapon rack if things turn violent."

"You can carry your staff, old friend," Master Gao said. His smile faded as he turned to the others. "Now, all of you try to get a good night's sleep, and we will see each other in the morning."

34

THE MORNING OF the last day of the third month had arrived, and it was sunny. Wayland had thought that perhaps a somber, black-clouded day, imbued with dark drama, might be more appropriate; nature, however, was indifferent to human affairs. It was nearly nine o'clock as Master Gao and his students gathered in the main courtyard. All were dressed in clean, pressed clothes, and Master Gao and Old Wu each wore a new cotton gown.

Master Gao bowed to his students, to his friends. "Thank you all for your support, old companions and new. Each of you has my utmost respect, more than I can express."

"Thank you, Master," each of the others responded, almost simultaneously.

"Now remember," Master Gao said, "None of you are to instigate any confrontations. Still," Master Gao continued, "I must face reality, and the reality is that my brother cannot be trusted. And as Buddha says, the toleration of evil is no virtue. I have been commanded by my teacher to put an end to my brother's evil, and that is what I shall strive to do. Should the situation escalate, however, I believe you are each well-prepared to handle yourselves. The only last advice I can give you is this: stay calm, remember your training, stay true to your principles, and support each other."

Lunghui, Suyin, and Wayland nodded and exchanged supportive glances with each other.

"Just relax," Old Wu said, as he came up behind Wayland and massaged his shoulders. "Fighting is no different than training. Keep the same mindset, and look at your opponents as training partners — no different than the ones you've faced before."

"Sure," Wayland said, smiling slightly. He wasn't sure he would be able to do that, but he understood what Old Wu was trying to communicate. Nerves and tension were as much of an enemy as Magic Spear. If he could relax, he could fight.

There was a knocking at the main gate. Suyin and Wayland flashed a glance to each other.

"Old Wu, if you would," Master Gao said, beckoning towards the main gate. Old Wu nodded and walked calmly to the entrance. He slid the bolt back and smoothly opened the front gate. Standing there was Magic Spear, with his acolytes behind him.

"Old Wu," Magic Spear said, bowing slightly. "How are you?" His tone was formal.

"Gao Jinguo," Old Wu said, without emotion. "Please come in."

Magic Spear nodded and stepped into the courtyard. He was dressed in a fine gold and red silk gown. Behind him followed his disciples.

One-eye Chang was wearing a sleeveless green shirt, highlighting his broad, barrel chest. He held both his short axes together in his right hand, and he had the same condescending smirk on his face he had the last time. Behind him walked Iron Ring Wang.

There he is. Wayland felt his heart beginning to beat faster.

Iron Ring Wang's green jacket and gray breeches were nondescript. They weren't particularly clean or particularly dirty. If he hadn't been carrying the iron ring, he would have looked like any local farmer.

Behind him strode Yun Yan, the Flying Faerie. She was dressed all in red this time, perhaps as an homage to the Red Lanterns. Her countenance bore nothing but contempt, and her hatred of Master Gao and his students was palpable. Magic Spear motioned them to stand back by the wall, and they did.

"This was to be a duel between you and me alone," Master Gao said. "Did you really need to bring them along? And with their weapons, no less?"

Magic Spear smiled. He waved his hand towards Lunghui, Suyin, and Wayland. "Seems that you're not here alone, either."

"Because I know what kind of a man you are. You, the so-called 'Magic Spear,'" Master Gao said.

"That's good. Never underestimate your opponent," Magic Spear said. "I guess you did learn something from the old man after all. And by the way, I heard that he's since passed. You have my condolences. We didn't see eye to eye, and I can't say he was the best teacher I ever had, but he had some skill, I'll give him that. You thought a lot of him, didn't you? Well, you never studied with anyone else, so you wouldn't know much about his limitations. Did the old man have any last words of wisdom for you? A wise man knows when to bow, or two rabbits run faster than a fox, or some other such nonsense?"

"He said that you were his greatest regret," Master Gao said. "And he said that if you had become evil and you couldn't be convinced to repent, then I should put a stop to you."

Magic Spear laughed loudly, but without humor. "Evil? We Boxers were trying to save our nation. Isn't that what the old man always taught? Love of one's country, and one's people? I thought those were the noblest values. To stand by and see China turned into a nation of beggars, whores, and lackeys to foreigners? To see the country flooded with opium? To have foreigners look down on our traditions? Do you want to know what evil is? It's to see that, and to do nothing!"

"China has its problems, but none that can be solved by hatred and murder," Master Gao said.

"It's a dirty business, and I don't deny it. And yes, if one does nothing, like you, one's hands don't get dirty."

"And just by coincidence, your selfless acts made you a very prominent, wealthy man, didn't they? Strange how things like that work out." Master Gao said.

"I've lost as much as anyone. More," Magic Spear said.

"And your own actions played no part in that?" Master Gao said.

Magic Spear untied the leather cover of his spearhead and tossed it to the side. The sharp steel of his spear point glistened in the sun. "We've talked enough."

Old Wu walked up to Master Gao carrying his sheathed sword. Master Gao drew out the blade, and Old Wu walked away with the sheath.

"Your sword against my spear? You sure you want to do that?"

Master Gao spun the sword deftly as he transferred it from his left hand to his right. He pressed his left fingers to his right wrist and pointed the tip of his sword directly at Magic Spear's eyes. It was true that in a one-on-one duel the spear had an advantage over the sword, but the sword was still Master Gao's preferred weapon, and he would not choose another for a fight of this significance.

"I wield the sword," Master Gao said. "And you, is the spear enough for you? Do you want me to wait while you say your magic spells or put a curse on me? Or perhaps call down some spirit to possess you, and make you invincible? No, I don't suppose you believe in that nonsense. Those are just the lies you told to exploit the simple peasants under your command. How many of them lost their lives simply because they believed your ridiculous stories, because they trusted you? Is that the martial arts that you were taught?"

"They died as heroes!" Magic Spear said. "They died for their country!"

"They died for a lie, and for your vanity," Master Gao responded.

Magic Spear swung his spear down to point towards Master Gao, and he did so with such force that the entire shaft vibrated as he held it firm. Without hesitation, he stepped in with a straight thrust towards Master Gao's midsection, but Master Gao deflected and stepped back to maintain the distance between them. At some point, he would have to close the gap to get into sword range with Magic Spear, but it would have to be at the proper moment. Getting past the deadly point of the spear was easier said than done.

Magic Spear thrust again, this time towards Master Gao's head. With a deftness that surprised Magic Spear, Master Gao ducked and came in low with a backhand sword cut to Magic Spear's left hand; that hand, being further down on the shaft, was the closest target. Magic Spear had no choice but to pull that hand off the spear, and there was a loud "chuck" as Master Gao's blade made contact with the spear shaft, sending splinters of wood flying. It was always possible for a swordsman to cut the wooden shaft of an opponent's spear, but it wasn't easy. It would usually take two or three hard cuts directly to the same spot on the shaft, and in the heat of combat, that was a difficult task.

Rather than press his advantage, Master Gao withdrew several steps, as did Magic Spear.

"Not bad," Magic Spear said. "You've improved since the last time we sparred."

Wayland looked over to Suyin, and she flashed him a nervous

smile. Master Gao was at least a match for Magic Spear.

This time Master Gao took to the attack. With the flat of his blade, he beat the spearhead of his opponent to one side and then stepped in to close the gap. He saw the exposed midsection of Magic Spear, but before he could strike, Magic Spear yanked back the spear point and then brought his right hand a couple of feet further up the shaft, shortening his grip dramatically. This instantly allowed him to match the short range of Master Gao's sword. The two exchanged a series of lightning-fast blows, the steel chiming and clanging, the sound reverberating off the stone walls of the compound.

Suyin gasped and stepped forward, but Old Wu grabbed her arm and pulled her back. On the other side, Flying Faerie Yun Yan was pacing back and forth anxiously as she watched the duel with a focused intensity. Wayland looked over at Iron Ring Wang, but the brute's face was expressionless as ever.

Master Gao turned his head to the side at the last split second to avoid a thrust from the razor-sharp spearhead, and as it went by his ear, he brought his hand underneath and pushed the shaft out of the way. He brought his sword up from behind to stab down into Magic Spear's shoulder blade, but before he could, Magic Spear delivered a powerful front kick that hit Master Gao in the chest. It connected with such intensity that it lifted Master Gao off his feet and sent him flying away, landing on his back on the cobblestone of the compound. Magic Spear knew the advantage was his, and he stepped forward and thrust directly into Master Gao's left shoulder, the spearhead slicing into tendon, muscle, and bone. Master Gao grimaced in pain, and his sword fell from his hand, clanging on the stone.

"Master!' Wayland shouted, rushing forward. Before he took more than three steps, however, he felt an iron-like grip on his shoulder, yanking him back, almost pulling him over. It was Old

Wu.

Magic Spear twisted the spearhead further into Master Gao's shoulder. With several whisper-quick steps, Old Wu stepped between the two, and as Magic Spear withdrew the point from Master Gao's shoulder to deliver the final blow, Old Wu grabbed the shaft. Magic Spear smiled. He jerked the spear back, but to his surprise, Old Wu's grip held firm.

One corner of Magic Spear's mouth turned down. He would not have thought it possible that the old man could still have such a powerful grip. "Get out of the way, Old Wu! This isn't your fight!"

"Let go of your spear and leave it. The battle is over, and you have won. There's no need for killing," Old Wu said calmly. He looked into Magic Spear's eyes without fear or anger. "You are brothers."

Magic Spear wasn't about to let an old man dictate to him. He snapped the spear back, expecting to wrench it from the elderly man's grip. To his amazement, he still couldn't pull it free. His fury rose, and he pulled back again. Old Wu was pulled forward, but he still held onto the spear.

"Let it go," Master Gao said to Old Wu. He struggled to get the words out. "This isn't your fight, old friend! Just let it…"

If he wasn't going to let the spear go, then the old man could have it, Magic Spear thought to himself. Old Wu pulled back on the spear, and Magic Spear accommodated. He relaxed his grip and stepped forward, and his forceful thrust blended with Old Wu's pulling. Magic spear jerked his waist and flicked his hands, and a wave of force rippled through the semi-flexible wax wood shaft of the spear. The power came through to the tip, and with Magic Spear's deft touch the flat of the spearhead cracked against Old Wu's temple. Old Wu's body instantly went limp, and he fell to the ground. He was still.

"Bastard!" Master Gao said, half shouting and half whispering.

The sound of the steel spearhead striking Old Wu's head was almost identical to that of the blow that had killed Wayland's father.

"Old Wu!" Wayland yelled. In a burst of emotion and instinct, he drew his saber from the rack and rushed at Magic Spear. One-eye Chang saw him, however, and moved with equal speed to intercept him. Before Wayland could get within three yards of Magic Spear, he found the blade of an ax thrust in front of him, blocking his way; he turned and saw the smiling, grim visage of One-eye Chang. Wayland stopped, and he glanced at Magic Spear, who was still looking at the motionless body of Old Wu.

"Wei-lin, get back!" Master Gao said.

Wayland turned quickly to his teacher and then snapped his attention back to One-eye Chang. With Chang's sinister eye patch and proud grin, Wayland felt his rage rising. He turned and swung his saber down at Chang's head. His emotions and adrenaline were flowing, and they both found their way into his wild strike. One-eye Chang easily dodged Wayland's slash, and then came in with a fierce backhand cut of his own with the ax in his left hand. Wayland was still off-balance from his own missed cut, and he was barely able to jerk his head out of the way of the ax. He wasn't able to regain his footing, however, and he fell to the ground, his saber clanking on the cobblestone of the courtyard. He scrambled on his knees to reach his saber. He grabbed it and stood up, stepping backward as One-eye Chang advanced on him.

That's terrible! Never drop your weapon! Relax! Breathe! Wayland focused all of his thoughts on what he had been taught. He inhaled deeply and slowly breathed out, then he raised his saber and readied himself against the advancing twin axes of One-eye Chang.

In a flash, the others had all fetched their weapons and joined in the melée, but not exactly as any of them had planned. Flying Faerie darted past Chang and Wayland towards Suyin, but before she could get there, Lunghui stepped in front of her. She sneered at him, her eyes ablaze with fury. Lunghui was calm and measured, and he thrust his spear towards her. Her nine-sectioned chain whip was wrapped around her right wrist, and it served as a kind of protective bracelet; she brought her arm up and deflected Lunghui's spear tip with a spark and a loud clang. Lunghui thrust again, and then once more, but the woman's reflexes were uncanny. Flying Faerie deflected each spear thrust with little effort, and after the last one, she went on the offensive. In a single deft motion, she thrust out her right arm, and the deadly steel whip uncoiled as the weighted, sharpened point flew directly at Lunghui's head. Lunghui was just able to spin the butt end of his spear shaft back and up to deflect the deadly missile.

Flying Faerie recovered quickly and snapped back the chain whip. In a seamless action, she swung the chain in an arc over her head and then back towards Lunghui; Lunghui ducked but at the same time slammed the butt of his spear down on the cobblestone, the spearhead pointing to the sky. The chain whip of Flying Faerie wrapped around the vertical spear, and Lunghui stood up, pulling his spear back. The chain whip was thoroughly entangled around the spear, and as Lunghui yanked, the woman was pulled forward. She regained her balance, and the two each pulled fiercely, struggling against each other to regain control of their respective weapons.

Flying Faerie's face contorted as she pulled, but Lunghui wouldn't relent. But as she pulled back sharply with all her might, Lunghui simultaneously loosened his grip and uncoiled his spear from her chain whip. Flying Faerie Yun Yan flew backward and landed hard on her side. She was able to lean up on one elbow, but the sky was spinning; she was dazed.

Suyin glanced over and saw that Master Gao was back on his feet with his sword in his hand, facing off against Magic Spear. He was bleeding heavily from the wound to his left shoulder, although his sword arm was still strong.

"You can just walk away, girl."

Suyin turned to see who was addressing her and saw Iron Ring Wang approaching. His face was blank, but Suyin couldn't quite tell whether it was from lack of intellect or an excess of it.

"This is my home," Suyin said. She circled her sword to her right hand and pointed the razor-sharp tip directly at her foe. "I'm not going anywhere."

Iron Ring Wang didn't respond, and he continued his advance. He held his iron ring in his right hand, and with practiced routine, he placed his left hand on his right forearm as he walked forward.

Suyin's heart was racing, but she willed herself to remember the principles of *T'ai Chi Fist*. She took a deep breath and exhaled slowly. She relaxed her muscles, sinking her shoulders and dropping her elbows.

She flicked the tip of her sword out at Wang to test him; both of them knew she was still slightly out of sword range, and as Suyin's blade passed in front of his face, Wang didn't flinch. Suyin backed up and slowly extended her sword, maintaining the distance as Wang advanced. Suddenly, Wang sprang forward, and his speed surprised Suyin. He thrust his iron ring at her, and Suyin was just able to draw in her chest to avoid the powerful strike. She riposted instinctively with her sword, delivering a backhand cut at Wang's head, but he brought his iron ring up to forcefully block her slash. Suyin cringed as she felt the impact of the tip of her sword hitting the iron ring; that was the surest way to chip or even shatter her blade, and that was undoubtedly Wang's thought as well.

She drew her sword back and retreated several steps. As she assumed a classic defensive stance, she slowly turned her waist and brought her sword back in front of her. She glanced down at the tip and simultaneously saw and felt that there was no damage to the blade. This gave her a sense of relief and a boost of confidence.

"Come on, boy, we're just getting started," One-eye Chang said. He hit one of his axes against the blade of the other one as he walked towards Wayland. "Let's see your foreign ways."

Wayland stepped back, keeping pace with the advancing giant who was confidently wielding his double weapons. He swallowed hard, but his mouth was dry. Both he and One-eye Chang knew that Wayland's skills were inferior.

Wayland's eyes became hard. Lack of skills couldn't be changed at this point, but he could still face his fate like a man. *Better to die on your feet than live on your knees.* He brought his saber up in a ready position, and he gritted his teeth as he prepared to face his foe. But before he could engage, a blurred shape rushed past him.

"Look out!" Lunghui shouted as he darted in front of Wayland to engage One-eye Chang. Lunghui's spear point punched at the big man's head, and Chang was just able to get his left ax in front of his face in time to deflect it. Still, he reeled; he was not prepared for Lunghui, and he was not prepared for Lunghui's level of skill. Lunghui's next thrust got past both axes and went through to Chang's right ribs. It wasn't a direct hit, but the spearhead cut through Chang's vest and drew blood. Chang grimaced, and he jumped back with remarkable agility for such a big man. Lunghui thrust again, and by this time Chang had adjusted himself both to the higher skill and longer weapon of his new opponent. He shook his head in anger, drew in a breath and exhaled forcefully as he sunk into a defensive stance, his two axes held at the ready to defend against Lunghui's deadly spear.

"Find your foe," Lunghui said to Wayland. "Quickly, as we trained!"

"Thanks!" Wayland said. Lunghui was squared off against his opponent, and now it was time for him and Suyin to do the same. Their whole plan hinged on it.

35

Flying Faerie Yun Yan recovered her footing, and she wasn't about to let Lunghui get away from her. She sprinted towards the wall, leaping and then running several steps straight up the face. Seemingly in defiance of gravity, she twisted and ran several steps horizontally across the surface of the wall, her body almost perpendicular to the ground. Suyin blinked twice to make sure she wasn't seeing things; the motions of Flying Faerie appeared nearly physically impossible. Flying Faerie darted above the ongoing battle between Master Gao and Magic Spear, and then came back down to the ground on the other side in pursuit of Lunghui. Lunghui was fully engaged with One-eye Chang, and he didn't see Flying Faerie approaching from his rear.

"No!" Suyin yelled. She threw one last wild cut at Iron Ring Wang as a distraction, and then darted over to block Flying Faerie from reaching Lunghui. Flying Faerie was surprised at this new obstacle in her path, and she pulled up quickly. Suyin crouched low and delivered a cut to Flying Faerie's forward leg, but the woman in red saw it clearly, and somersaulted backward to avoid the cut and landed effortlessly on her feet. She scowled at Suyin.

"Bitch, you'll regret that," Flying Faerie hissed. She smiled coldly at Suyin as she walked forward. "Your master is weak and useless. Look over at him. He's already badly wounded. You think he can stand up to Magic Spear? And you? Loyal to this bunch? The old fool is already dead, and your master will soon follow. All I can see is one good fighter in the bunch, and you. The foreigner has no skill at all. What's he even doing with you?"

Suyin's face contorted and in a lightning move, she thrust her sword at Flying Faerie. Faerie again had her chain whip wrapped around her right hand, and she brought it up to deflect Suyin's sword, but she was surprised by the speed of Suyin's attack; she was barely able to repel it. Still, she showed no concern as she stepped forward towards Suyin.

"Oh, I see now," Flying Faerie said, smiling coldly. "Why, you've got *feelings* for the foreign devil. Is that it? A traitor to your people with your deeds and even with your heart? You're worse than a dog."

Suyin understood that Flying Faerie was so driven by rage that she assumed others were as well, and that they could be goaded into rash actions. That wasn't Suyin's nature, and it wasn't what Master Gao had taught her, either. Suyin breathed deeply and calmed herself as she slowly stepped in a half-circle around Flying Faerie, keeping the tip of her sword pointed directly at her red-clad opponent.

Flying Faerie leaped in towards Suyin, using her chain-clad fist to beat away Suyin's sword and then to punch at her midsection. Suyin's sword was knocked off-center, but her empty-hand skills were up to the challenge. With a subtle turn of her waist, Suyin brought her left hand across her body and softly guided Flying Faerie's punch to the side. Flying Faerie tried to regain her balance and pull back her strike, but as she did so, Suyin stepped in with her forearm, the *peng* energy striking Flying Faerie in the chest and bouncing her off her feet and back nearly two yards.

Suyin was so focused on her foe that she hardly had time to assess her performance, but in the back of her mind, she knew she had delivered a nearly perfect "grasp sparrow's tail" technique from *T'ai Chi Fist*. She stepped forward with confidence but quickly saw that she was far from victory.

Any common foe, male or female, would have landed hard on their back after being on the receiving end of Suyin's strike. Flying Faerie Yun Yan was no common foe. With amazing agility she leaned backward and brought her hands to the ground and flipped back onto her feet, instantly facing Suyin again.

Without hesitation, she snapped her right hand out, and as she did so, the deadly steel tip of her flexible chain whip shot towards Suyin. Suyin saw the glint of metal coming towards her, and she brought her blade across to deflect it, but she was too late. She felt the impact of the pointed steel as it penetrated through her coat and into her left shoulder. She stepped back and looked down at the steel tip embedded in her, and she stared, perplexed, at the crimson stain rapidly spreading over the upper part of her coat. She knew it was a severe wound, but still, she felt no pain. She looked from her shoulder along the length of the attached chain, all the way back to the cruel countenance of Flying Faerie holding the other end of the steel whip.

"So sad. Your foreign lover will have his heart broken by your death," Flying Faerie said, in a tone as cold as ice. She advanced towards Suyin, a look of grim triumph on her face. "But don't worry, he'll join you soon."

With Lunghui and Suyin engaged with their foes and Master Gao battling his brother, Wayland turned and found himself facing Iron Ring Wang. The opponent that he had prepared for. The man who had brutally killed his parents, who had destroyed the kind, loving world that he had once known. Wayland was expecting, and perhaps even hoping, that Iron Ring Wang would have the sneering, malevolent countenance of the villain that he had pictured so often in his mind. Instead, the man's face was plain and nondescript; he had the expression of any common blacksmith or carpenter who was going about his day's work.

What was going on inside the man, Wayland had no idea. But he knew what was going on inside himself. He was a swirl of emotions — grief, rage, inadequacy — as images of his parents' murder flashed and darted through his subconscious, coalescing into almost clear pictures before they would fade and be replaced by others.

Physically, Wayland looked down and was surprised to see his sword hand shaking. He looked up to see if Iron Ring Wang had noticed it, but if he had, the man gave no hint of it. Wang walked closer, taking each step slowly, and Wayland backed up in time to try to maintain the distance. Wayland sized up his opponent. He was about Wayland's height, but heavier and broader. He was no doubt stronger than Wayland, but almost certainly slower.

I can do this. I just need to focus and relax. Wayland exhaled deeply, and as he did, he let his mind clear. This was only a man across from him, a man like himself. Nothing less, but nothing more, either. Wang brandished the ring in his right hand, slowly circling it in front of himself, and his open left palm faced out at Wayland.

In one motion Wayland extended the point of his saber and then jerked his body and lunged at Wang. But it was just a test; Wayland didn't lunge far enough quite to hit Wang.

Wang flinched and pulled his head back, and he brought his ring up to deflect Wayland's blade. Before any contact could be made, Wayland had already withdrawn his sword and recovered into his regular stance.

Wayland allowed himself a slight smile, and he made sure Wang saw it. Wang was taken aback by Wayland's speed. *Maybe Iron Ring wasn't so tough after all. Better stay on the offensive while he had the advantage.* Wayland intentionally left his head and shoulders exposed as he went in low for a backhand cut to Wang's knee. Wayland's cut was purposely short of the target, and then, as expected, Wang took the bait. He stepped in and brought his deadly ring down to strike the top of Wayland's head. Wayland reversed his cut and wrapped his saber around his body, point down, and the blunt base of his saber blade deflected the iron ring. Now Wang's head was exposed, and his ring was out of the way. Continuing the circular motion of his saber, Wayland stepped in and delivered a powerful forehand cut at Wang's exposed and defenseless head.

Wang flinched and snapped his head back, and Wayland's blade didn't make contact. With this opening, though, Wayland stepped forward, and with his empty left hand delivered the splitting fist strike from *Hsingyi Fist* that Old Wu had taught him. Wayland must have practiced the strike a thousand times, and he hit Iron Ring Wang with all of his force.

Iron Ring Wang exhaled sharply and was rocked back several steps. He brought his hand to his chest where Wayland had struck him and looked down. He slowly and powerfully inhaled and then exhaled. There was an expression on his face now, and it was one of malice.

He rushed in with his iron ring and knocked Wayland's saber away, and then he delivered almost the same strike to Wayland that Wayland had used against him. The impact reverberated through Wayland's whole body, and he flew backward. Wayland wasn't sure if he had lost consciousness or not, but the next thing he knew he was flat on his back. He opened his eyes and saw the slow drift of a single cotton-white cloud in the bright blue sky. He felt a cool breeze waft over him. *Am I dead?* Clarity came rushing back to him. No, he was still alive. The thought dimly occurred to him that had he been hit with Wang's iron ring, he might not be so lucky.

"Wei-lin!" Lunghui yelled as he saw Wang approaching the dazed Wayland.

"Worry about yourself, boy!" One-eye Chang said as he grinned as he spun his double axes with a flourish and advanced on Lunghui. "This is all going to be over shortly."

Lunghui shot a quick glance over at the others. Master Gao and Magic Spear were still engaged, exchanging blows at a furious pace, but Master Gao's wound was still bleeding; he didn't seem to be Magic Spear's match. Suyin was also wounded, and she was scrambling away from Flying Faerie, barely able to keep her footing.

Lunghui inhaled slowly and deeply, and he turned back to One-eye Chang. "It's going to be over for *you*, at least," Lunghui said.

One-eye Chang grinned and stepped forward eagerly, as if he genuinely enjoyed the conflict and had no doubt of its outcome. Lunghui didn't concur. His eyes narrowed to a steely focus, and he stepped in to engage Chang. Lunghui's first thrust clanged off one of Chang's axes, and in a fraction of a second, he came back with another thrust, then a third and fourth in rapid succession. Chang's grin faded as he whirled his axes, desperately trying to ward off Lunghui's relentless spear attacks. He was just able to deflect Lunghui's last head-level thrust, and the impact of the spearhead on the steel ax threw sparks.

"Bastard!" One-eye Chang said as he struggled to regain control.

Lunghui gritted his teeth and continued attacking. He thrust down at Chang's feet, and Chang jumped up out of the way, and then he came back with a high horizontal slash of his spearhead. Chang brought up both axes in unison to block the strike, and then he hooked the bottom of one ax blade under the spearhead and pulled it off to the side. Now was his chance to close the gap and destroy the advantage of Lunghui's longer weapon. Chang grunted and darted forward, and as he did he slid his left ax up along the spear shaft toward Lunghui's forward hand. With practiced skill, Lunghui simultaneously stepped backward and slid the shaft back through his hands until the lethal spearhead was again in front of the charging One-eye Chang.

One-eye Chang had a brief moment to realize the final gravity of his situation before he felt Lunghui's spearhead pierce him just below the rib cage. He groaned as the searing hot pain radiated from his wound and raced through his whole body. Lunghui stepped in off his back foot and pushed the spear in harder, lifting the bigger man almost off his feet and another yard backward before the spear went all the way through the giant's body.

Chang flashed his bloody teeth at Lunghui, and he dropped his right ax and grabbed the spear shaft that protruded from his chest. With a final, vengeful effort he pulled the spear further through him and stepped forward; he raised his left ax as he almost got within range of his opponent. Lunghui yanked the spear completely out of Chang's body, and he stepped back into a defensive stance. He stood motionless, his bloody spearhead pointed at his dying opponent.

Chang stumbled backward, looking blankly at Lunghui, and then he turned and spun, and fell face-first onto the cobblestone, his remaining ax clanging on the stone. He was dead.

36

Wayland's chest hurt, but he had managed to get back to his feet. He held his saber up, but the whole right side of his body was numb from Wang's palm strike. Wang darted in quickly with his ring and feigned an attack; Wayland waved his saber in front of him, but his motions were frantic, uncontrolled.

Wang advanced calmly towards Wayland. He cast a quick glance over towards the motionless, prostrate figure of One-eye Chang, and then turned back to Wayland. He brought one finger up and pressed against a nostril and blew his nose.

If I have to die, I'll go down fighting. Wayland clenched his jaw and stepped forward with a slash at Iron Ring's head. Wang brought his heavy ring up to block it, and Wayland felt precisely what he didn't want to feel: a dull, percussive crack as the sharp edge of his tempered steel blade impacted with full force onto the iron ring. The vibrations went down the blade and up Wayland's forearm, and out of the corner of his eye, he saw a glint of metal flying away. He brought his saber back and saw a sizable chip in the blade. Just what Old Wu had warned him about. Now the structural integrity of his weapon was compromised; another hit like that, and it might well break in two. With a sword in his hand, his chances weren't good against Iron Ring Wang. With no blade at all, he would be dead in moments.

So this is how it ends. No justice for my parents. Another failure. Wayland prepared for the end as Iron Ring Wang advanced steadily towards him. But then Wang stopped, and for once an expression came across his face. It was one of surprise.

Wayland felt someone coming up and then past him—it was Lunghui! With blinding speed Lunghui stepped in with several powerful spear thrusts. Wang was caught off guard and backed up rapidly as he brought his iron ring up again and again to deflect Lunghui's deadly spear attacks.

"I'll stay back, and you go in!" Lunghui said, and Wayland instinctively knew what he meant. With his spear, Lunghui could fight Wang from long range, and while Wang was occupied with that Wayland could get in closer with the saber.

Lunghui and Wayland kept up their two-pronged attack on Iron Ring Wang, driving him back towards the wall of the compound, but the killer wasn't showing signs of panic. If anything, he seemed to have raised the level of his fighting. Lunghui thrust towards Wang's head, and Wayland went low to cut at his knee. Wang deflected the spear with his ring and at the same time lifted his leg to avoid Wayland's cut; he threw the same leg forward and landed a powerful kick to Wayland's shoulder, sending him spinning back onto the cobblestone. Lunghui struck again at Wang with his spear, but this time Wang was able to dodge the point and grab the wooden shaft. Lunghui pulled back, but Wang's grip was as strong as the iron in his ring, and Lunghui couldn't withdraw his weapon.

Wayland got back to his feet and rushed in with his saber. Maybe Lunghui couldn't break Wang's grip by pulling, but Wayland had a better method. He brought the sharp blade of his saber down onto Wang's forearm that was gripping the spear. To Wayland's shock, his blade hit the bare forearm of Wang with a dull thud, and Wang held on to the spear. Wayland drew his saber back and slashed at Wang's neck; Wang brought the same arm up, and the result was the same. *Wang's bare arm had twice stopped a powerful strike from the edge of Wayland's saber, and he wasn't even cut.*

"Golden Bell Cover!" Lunghui yelled.

Wayland's sensed reeled. When Master Gao had told him that Chinese martial artists could train parts of their body to become impervious to edged weapons, Wayland was dubious. He was sure it was just Chinese superstition, about as ludicrous as the Boxer's claim that their magic spells could render them immune to Western bullets. But Wayland couldn't deny what he had just seen with his own eyes. And if it was true, how could he hope to defeat someone who was virtually invulnerable?

"He can't protect all of his vital points at the same time!" Lunghui yelled, as he ferociously attacked Wang again with his spear. Wang used his iron ring to deflect one of the thrusts, but the second one got through his defenses. Lunghui's razor-sharp spear point struck Wang in the shoulder, but it didn't penetrate; it was as if the point was hitting armor. Lunghui withdrew and thrust once more, but this time Wang was able to bring his iron ring back in time so that the spear point went directly through the ring. Wang then turned the ring against the shaft to trap the spear, and he pulled back. Lunghui and Wang were locked in a stalemate, each pulling against the other.

With their weapons locked, Iron Ring Wang stepped forward towards Lunghui. Lunghui threw a palm strike at Wang, but Wang blocked it and came back with a back fist of his own, striking Lunghui in the forehead. Lunghui was stunned, and staggered backward; his spear fell to the ground. With his weapon now free, Wang stepped in with his ring and delivered a punishing blow to Lunghui's midsection. Lunghui gasped and dropped to his knees. Wang stepped in and raised the iron ring to deliver the killing blow.

"Here!" Wayland yelled. With all of his focus, he relaxed the muscles of his upper body and made sure his saber, wrist, arm, spine, and legs were perfectly aligned. From his rooted rear foot, he pushed forward at his foe, focusing his mind on the target and letting his *chi* flow like a wave through his body and into his weapon. Every ounce of his body's energy coalesced into the point of his saber, and he thrust forward, striking Iron Ring Wang in the upper thigh. Wang's Golden Bell Cover training made him impervious to all but the most perfect of strikes from edged weapons; Wayland's attack was perfect. His saber pierced Wang's thigh, and the blood flowed profusely from the wound.

"You broke his Bell Cover!" Lunghui yelled as he scrambled to his feet. He grabbed his spear and stood in the classic *T'ai Chi Fist* forward bow stance, his spear point aimed at Wang.

Wayland stepped in and delivered a series of slashes; Wang's invincible armor might have been destroyed, but he still had his skill, and with his iron ring he deftly blocked Wayland's flurry of saber cuts. But two opponents proved too much for Wang. As he grabbed Wayland's wrist and wound up to strike with his deadly ring, Lunghui's spear found its mark. The spear penetrated Wang's left side, breaking several ribs.

Wang groaned, and it was the first sound he had made since the battle began.

Wayland turned the tables and grabbed Wang's wrist, keeping the iron ring in check, and then he smashed the pommel of his saber down on Wang's temple. Wang's head snapped back, and he crumpled, knocked unconscious before he even hit the ground. Wayland stared at the limp figure of his enemy sprawled on the ground, and he saw a steady trickle of blood beginning to flow from Wang's head. *This is the man that killed my parents in cold blood.* Wayland felt a strange sense of both satisfaction and disgust, and he almost swooned from his newfound sense of power; he could decide this man's fate. He smiled coldly. If anyone deserved death, it was this man. Wayland raised his saber.

"Suyin!" Lunghui yelled, and Wayland turned to see Lunghui darting away. Suyin was reeling from the onslaught of Flying Faerie. The woman's chain whip was whirling furiously, and Suyin staggered backward, bleeding from several wounds already inflicted by Flying Faerie.

Lunghui rushed in with his spear, but as he thrust at her, Flying Faerie twisted and pushed Lunghui's spear to the side. She strode forward and struck Lunghui in the chest with her forearm, sending Lunghui flying away. She then turned back to Suyin, smiling cruelly as she advanced.

Wayland looked back quickly at the semi-conscious form of Iron Ring Wang at his feet, and then back to Suyin. He made his choice.

"Get away from her!" Wayland yelled in English as he raised his saber and rushed towards the woman in white. He cut towards Flying Faerie's midsection, but she leaped and twisted over Wayland's blade. Wayland had put so much force into his strike that when it failed to hit its target, the momentum carried him off balance and he fell to the ground. He got to his feet and turned just in time to see a flash of metal flying towards him; it was the deadly steel point of Flying Faerie's chain whip. He jerked his head back, but the steel projectile glanced off his lower cheek. The sharp point didn't break the skin, but the weight of the metal impacted forcefully on his jaw.

The sky spun as Wayland fell to his knees, but before his body went to the ground, he felt a firm hand under his arm, supporting him. He turned and looked into the determined face of Suyin. She was bleeding slightly from her forehead and more from her shoulder, and she was nearly exhausted from the battle, but the look of concern and compassion on her face gave Wayland an almost immeasurable boost. The two looked into each other's eyes; their smiles were subtle, but their emotions surged.

"Are you all right?" Wayland asked.

"As well as you are," Suyin said, grinning weakly.

"Oh, the loving couple," Flying Faerie said. She strode confidently towards Wayland and Suyin, her chain whip wrapped around her wrist. "What a tragic twist of fate, for you to die in each other's arms. So young, without even the chance to taste love. I don't think you two have even…"

Before she could finish her sentence, the gleam of Lunghui's spear point flashed towards Flying Faerie's. She caught it out of the corner of her eye and was just able to bring her wrist up, deflecting the spear with her coiled steel whip. Lunghui thrust again, but Flying Faerie grabbed the spear just below the point and stepped in to close the gap. Much to her surprise, this was just what Lunghui had wanted. He stepped in with a shoulder strike; the whole weight of his body met Flying Faerie's forward movement, and the impact sent the woman to the ground.

"Ughh!" Flying Faerie groaned as she put her hand down to stabilize herself. She looked up at Lunghui, her face twisted with rage.

Lunghui snapped his spear down as he stood in a ready stance, facing Flying Faerie, and the sharp spear point vibrated with his internal energy.

"Look!" Wayland said, and he pointed over to the other side of the compound. Suyin turned and saw Master Gao locked in combat with Magic Spear. He appeared over-matched as he retreated rapidly from the advancing attacks of Magic Spear. Master Gao's gown was dark with blood over his left shoulder, and he was weak; he seemed barely able to defend himself with his sword.

"Master!" Wayland yelled, fearing the worst. Much to

his surprise, though, Master Gao deftly turned his waist and deflected Magic Spear's thrust to the side, and then with surprising speed he cut back at Magic Spear's arm. The sword found it's target, and Magic Spear groaned aloud as the blade cut through his gown and into his upper arm.

"Don't worry about me!" Master Gao yelled at Wayland, as he surged back on the offensive against Magic Spear.

Wayland turned to smile at Suyin, but a blurred shape flashed before his eyes; Flying Faerie appeared from out of nowhere and struck both Wayland and Suyin, sending them crashing to the ground. Lunghui rushed in, thrusting his spear at the woman, but Flying Faerie leaped back and threw her chain whip while she was still in mid-air; it wrapped around Lunghui's spear, and as she landed, Flying Faerie jerked her whip back, and Lunghui's spear was snapped out of his hands. It clattered to the ground. Lunghui brought his hands up to engage Flying Faerie without his weapon, but it was no good. She immediately launched the steel point of her whip back at Lunghui, and it struck him just under the rib cage.

Lunghui gasped in pain and tried to get his arms up to defend himself, but he was unable to.

"Hahh!" Flying Faerie grunted as she struck Lunghui in the chest with her steel-wrapped wrapped fist. Lunghui didn't fall, but as he lurched backward, trying to regain his footing, Flying Faerie stepped in again. This time she just attacked with just her index finger; she crouched and struck Lunghui's vital point under his left armpit. Lunghui immediately collapsed, and a strange expression came across his face as he struggled to maintain consciousness.

Wayland was able to get to his feet, but Flying Faerie wasn't about to allow him to get back into the fray. She stepped in with her open palm, striking Wayland in the jaw. Wayland fell, and the woman sneered in triumph.

Suyin came back to consciousness, but was unable to rise; she saw Flying Faerie approaching, and she retreated on her palms and heels.

"Now it's your turn, little flower," Flying Faerie said with a cold smile. Crimson smears of blood darkened her red jacket, and her expression was one of exhaustion, malevolence, and bitter triumph. She swung her chain whip in an arc above her head as she walked towards Suyin.

"Do what you will," Suyin said, with a tone of defiance. Her face displayed no fear, and she retreated more as a matter of practicality as she stared unblinkingly at her foe. Still, she knew her fate was sealed; she could no longer match Flying Faerie in combat.

"Let her be!" Magic Spear shouted to Flying Faerie, casting a quick glance at his pupil as he engaged the onslaught of sword attacks from Master Gao. Master Gao's sword strikes were powerful but desperate. He was still bleeding, and getting weaker. Magic Spear was increasingly confident of his victory. "This is almost done. The girl is of no consequence!"

Flying Faerie looked back dismissively at Magic Spear, and she continued advancing towards Suyin, swinging her chain whip. "Better to finish things here."

"Your own daughter," Master Gao said. Blood trickled from the corner of his mouth, and his stance was unsteady. But as he pointed his sword towards his brother, his eyes still shone. "She's of no consequence to you, and she never was. Our parents would be ashamed."

Magic Spear's face contorted and he swung his spear at Master Gao's head, but the attack was wild, and Master Gao easily leaned back out of the weapon's path.

"I did what was best for her!" Magic Spear shouted. "She is

in danger now only because of you!" He thrust again at Master Gao, and once more his attack missed.

"You did what was best for yourself, as you always did," Master Gao said.

"Suyin!" Wayland yelled. He tried to get to his feet, but it was too late. Flying Faerie's chain whip swung around, and the weighted steel point hit Suyin just above her cheek. Her head snapped back, and she fell onto her side.

"No!" Magic Spear shouted as he turned to see Suyin struck. "No more!"

Flying Faerie ignored him and rushed to the barely-moving figure of Suyin. Her chain whip was again wrapped around her wrist, and she bent down and grabbed Suyin by the hair, and raised her arm to strike.

Master Gao started towards her, but in one motion Magic Spear snapped the butt end of his spear into Master Gao's midsection, sending his brother to the ground. Magic Spear then turned and delivered a powerful strike to Flying Faerie with the flat of his spearhead. The woman reeled at the percussive blow that came from her master, and she was knocked back several steps.

"I told you to stop! You will..."

Flying Faerie shot her chain whip out at Magic Spear, who was just able to dodge the flexible steel weapon. "I've had enough of your orders!" she yelled. "We need men of steel. You're not one of them."

Magic Spear jabbed his weapon at Flying Faerie, but she twisted out of the way of its deadly point and closed the gap on her former master. She struck with her fingers and hit two pressure points on his abdomen, and then whipped her index finger towards his throat. Magic Spear caught her hand, but not the kick that Flying Faerie delivered to his midsection.

Magic Spear staggered back but found himself facing the renewed sword attack of Master Gao. He deflected his brother's first cut, but not the next thrust. Master Gao's straight sword pierced Magic Spear's chest, going all the way through. Magic Spear had an expression of both surprise and resignation; Master Gao pulled the sword back out, and a spurt of blood flew into the air as Magic Spear spun around once and then fell to the ground.

Master Gao turned to face Flying Faerie, and Lunghui and Wayland, having regained their footing, stood by his side, their weapons at the ready. The three were bruised, bloodied and exhausted, but undaunted.

Flying Faerie sneered and paused for a moment as she took in the situation. Then she laughed out loud, and darted away. She didn't slow down as she approached the main wall of the compound; in three steps she ran straight up the sheer face, some fifteen feet high. She landed on top of the wall, looked back for a moment on the carnage of the battlefield, and then dropped over the other side and was gone.

"Suyin," Magic Spear said weakly. His breathing was halting and uneven.

Suyin crawled over to Magic Spear. She put her hand on his cheek. "Father..."

Magic Spear Gao struggled to speak. "I... did love you, Suyin. Know that. I was not much of a father, but I loved you."

"I always knew," Suyin said. Tears came to her eyes, and her mouth was dry. "I knew that you did."

"I did what I thought was best... " Magic Spear said. He coughed again, and blood trickled out of the corner of his mouth.

"I know you did," Suyin said, now sobbing. "I always... " She tried to think of the proper words to say, but her father's eyes closed, and she felt him slipping away.

"Brother, I am... truly sorry," Master Gao said, fighting back the tears as he kneeled next to Magic Spear. He put his arm around Suyin's shoulder, and he pulled her close.

Wayland reached over to pick up his saber, and then he got to his feet. He walked over to Iron Ring Wang, who was still semiconscious from his wounds.

"You," Wayland said. He pointed the tip of his saber at Wang. "You killed my father. A man who never said an unkind word to anyone his whole life, who gave up everything and traveled halfway around the world for the sake of people like you. You killed my mother, who would have given you her coat and gone cold if you needed it, who would have gone hungry if it meant that you were fed."

Suyin turned to Wayland. "Wait!"

Wayland raised his saber as he approached Iron Ring Wang. Everything that had gone wrong in his life, every good thing that was taken from him, all of that was personified in the vile form of Iron Ring Wang. Every fiber of Wayland's being told him to swing his saber with all his might, to destroy this murderer, this defiler of life.

"Is that what your father would do?" Suyin shouted as she stumbled across the cobblestone towards Wayland. "Is that what your mother would want? Is that what they taught you, what they believed in, killing and vengeance? Is that the man you want to become?"

Wayland stood over Wang with his weapon held high, and Wang stared back without emotion, ready to accept his fate. The words of Suyin hit Wayland harder than any other blow he had received that day. He slowly lowered his saber as he stared at Wang.

Wang paused for a moment, looking at Wayland, and then got to his feet; he staggered to the front gate and ran out without looking back.

Wayland felt Suyin's hand on his shoulder, and he turned to her; for a brief moment, he could almost see his mother's eyes in Suyin.

"Why did you stop me?" Wayland said. "I could have ended it all."

"He was already defeated, helpless. If you had killed him, it would have been murder."

Wayland shook his head. "Not murder... it was a battle... it was war... "

"You said that you and your parents came here to save Chinese souls," Suyin said. Her face was dirty and bruised, and her shoulder was bloody. "Well... maybe I care about *your* soul, too."

Wayland looked deeply into Suyin's eyes. Both of them were so severely injured that they could barely stand. He gently brushed back the wisps of hair that had fallen in front of her face, and then he embraced her and held her tightly.

A weary groan came from the other side of the courtyard. "Doesn't anyone care about me? I am an old man, after all."

It was Old Wu!

Master Gao rushed over to him, followed closely by Suyin and Wayland.

"Old friend!" Master Gao said, as he kneeled down and cradled Old Wu's head in his arms.

"We thought you were dead," Wayland said, and he also kneeled down.

"From one little blow to the head?" Old Wu asked as he propped himself up on his elbow. "What do you take me for?"

Suyin laughed as she wiped tears from her eyes. She brushed Old Wu's cheek, and then ran to get a blanket and some bandages.

37

As BATTERED and bruised as he was, Wayland slept as deeply as he had ever slept that night. There were no fleeting thoughts or gnawing concerns, no vague impressions, and no dreams. There was only the complete submission to physical, mental, and emotional exhaustion. When he finally awoke, the sun was coming in through the courtyard, and from its position, he figured it must already be noon; he couldn't recall the last time he had slept that late. He lay still on his bed. The chirping of sparrows just outside his window brought him momentarily back to his childhood, and to pleasant times with his mother and father.

He turned over on his side, and the pain shot through his body. He brought his hands up to his face and examined them. They were both bloodied and bruised. He sat up in bed, and then felt the throbbing of his head, where he had taken more than one severe strike in the previous day's battle.

He groaned as he pulled himself out of bed, and gingerly slipped on his pants and shirt. He hobbled over to the water basin. It was almost easier to list the parts of his body that didn't hurt. He splashed water on his face and made a great effort to stretch his arms up in the air.

"I'm alive," he said out loud, and he smiled. Yesterday morning, that outcome was less than certain. He thought for a moment, and then slowly dropped to his knees.

"Thank you, God," he said. He tried to think of an appropriate formal prayer, but none came to mind. "I... I know I haven't been the kind of man you wanted me to be, and I've fallen short in many ways, but thank you for the outcome of yesterday. I know it's said that no one can come to salvation except through you, Jesus. Even though Master Gao, Lunghui and Suyin may not worship you with their words, I believe they are close to you in their hearts, and I pray that you will bless them and have mercy on their souls in this world and the next. Lord, you know how I feel about Suyin. Whatever may happen to me, please bless her with a long and happy life. I've never met anyone like her; I can see the power you have to create goodness in many shapes and forms, anywhere in this world. I know I'm not much of a Christian, and I've failed in almost every way, but thank you for your blessings."

Wayland finished with the Lord's Prayer, and then he slowly stood up and grimaced again at the pain. There was a knock at the door.

"Yes?" Wayland asked.

"It's me."

Wayland opened the door, and Suyin walked in. She looked as beaten up as he felt. Her shoulder was freshly bandaged, and her arm was in a sling.

"How are you?"

"Probably about the same as you. I'll live. Here," she said and handed Wayland a white envelope.

"What's this?" Wayland asked.

"It's an invitation to my father's funeral."

"Oh," Wayland said. Even after all that had transpired yesterday, Suyin was already taking care of her responsibilities. He nodded respectfully and opened the envelope.

"I know you only saw him as an enemy," Suyin said. "But I

hope you can appreciate that he was more than that to Master Gao, Old Wu, and myself."

Wayland tried to read the text, but he still wasn't able to read Chinese anywhere near as well as he could speak it. "It's difficult for me. What does it say?"

Suyin ran her finger along the text for him. "It just says that there will be a wake here for one day, and then there will be a service at the Buddhist temple down the street."

"I'll go," Wayland said. He still couldn't find it in his heart to feel any sympathy for Magic Spear, but it was Suyin asking. He wouldn't refuse her.

The wake was held the next day at the Gao compound. It was a cloudy day and almost hinted at snow. Magic Spear's closed casket was placed in the central courtyard, set on two stools. The main gate was left open for mourners to pay their respects.

Wayland was sitting on his bed in his room when he heard the knock on his door.

"Come," he said.

Suyin entered. She bowed slightly, and a gentle smile crossed her face. "Are you ready? We should be out there for the wake. People will arrive soon."

"What should I wear? A black gown?" Wayland asked.

Suyin shook her head. "No, black is only worn by the children of the deceased. I will wear black. For you, just don't wear bright colors."

Wayland nodded. He had a nice dark gray gown that Master Gao had given him, and he hadn't worn it at all yet. That would work well.

"Then come out, and we'll stand together by the coffin, with Master Gao and Old Wu," Suyin said. "There won't be too many people. Given the circumstances, this will be mostly a private ceremony."

Wayland changed into his gown and came out of his room and into the crisp air of the open courtyard. Master Gao, Old Wu, Suyin, and Lunghui were already standing by the coffin of Magic Spear. Master Gao and Lunghui didn't look to be in much better shape than he and Suyin, but their wounds were dressed and they were able to move about with some normalcy. Old Wu had a large dark blue bruise by his temple but otherwise was his old self.

The coffin sat about a foot off the ground, on two sturdy wooden stools. It was open, and Magic Spear was dressed in a white robe; his face was covered with a yellow cloth, and his body was draped with a light blue fabric. At the foot of the coffin was a pen-and-ink portrait, a remarkable likeness of Magic Spear from his younger days. To the right of the picture was a white lit candle and several sticks of burning incense. Next to the coffin was a table, upon which Suyin had placed a simple but beautiful arrangement of white and yellow chrysanthemums.

Wayland bowed politely to the others and took his place beside Suyin. He leaned over and whispered in Suyin's ear, "Just tell me if I'm doing anything wrong."

"Don't worry, you'll be fine," Suyin said.

Over the next several hours, Wayland smiled and bowed politely as the small procession of mourners came by. A few did a double-take and looked slightly confused when they saw that a foreigner was standing with the family, but out of either indifference or respect for the ceremony, no one made an issue of it. Several of the guests brought a wreath made of white irises, and all lit a stick of incense at the altar.

"Why are some burning paper over there?" Wayland asked when there was a pause between the mourners.

"That's joss money, or prayer money, that they're burning. It's done so that the deceased will have security and good things in the afterlife."

"But there's a box by the altar, and people are putting white envelopes in there, too," Wayland whispered, slightly confused. "What is that?"

"That's real money," Suyin said. "That's for Master Gao, to help with the funeral costs."

"Oh," Wayland said. "What's this coming?" Wayland said quietly to Suyin as he nudged her with his elbow.

Suyin heard the same noise Wayland did, and she turned to see an older man dressed in an orange robe entering the main gate. He was chanting, and two younger men followed him, similarly attired; one was rhythmically beating a drum, and the other was ringing a small bell.

"That's the Buddhist monk, reciting a funeral prayer," Suyin said quietly to Wayland.

The monk and his juniors made their way across the compound. The various groups of mourners would stop their conversations and bow respectfully as the trio passed them.

When they reached the coffin, the three stopped. The two juniors ceased playing their instruments, and the head monk read a section of Buddhist scripture. Wayland couldn't make out all of it, but he thought he heard these lines:

"The days and nights are flying past,
Life dwindles hurriedly away,
The life of mortals vanishes
Like water in a tiny stream."

The monk and his juniors lit incense sticks and placed them at the altar. Master Gao thanked them, and then the three made their way back across the compound, chanting and playing as they went out the main gate.

Suyin smiled and turned to Wayland. "Does this all seem very strange to you?"

Wayland shrugged. "Not so much, I guess. The monk says a prayer to help your father on his journey to the next world?" Suyin nodded.

"Then maybe not so different," he said.

"Do you think you can stay awake all night?" Suyin asked.

"Why do I need to stay awake all night?"

"The family members have to stand a vigil over the coffin overnight. So that we can show respect for the deceased so that he won't be left alone."

"All right," Wayland said, sighing slowly. "When in Rome... "

"What?" Suyin asked, looking puzzled.

"Never mind," Wayland said. He squinted and scratched the back of his neck. "It sounds better in English."

Wayland and the others all watched over the coffin that evening. Wayland caught himself dozing off several times, and once when he woke up, he saw that both Suyin and Lunghui had also fallen asleep. Wayland looked over at Old Wu, who was wide awake. Old Wu smiled warmly at him.

Shortly after dawn, several men came into the compound, carrying tools and some boards.

"Turn away," Suyin said to Wayland.

"Huh?" Wayland asked.

"They're going to nail the coffin shut before it is taken to the cemetery for the funeral. It's bad luck for family members to watch."

Wayland and the others turned away, and the men nailed the coffin shut. When they were done, Master Gao said something to the men that Wayland couldn't make out.

The coffin was loaded onto a horse and carriage in the street just outside the compound, and Master Gao, Old Wu, Suyin, Lunghui and Wayland, along with a few neighbors, friends and mourners, joined the funeral procession. With the musicians playing their flutes, drums, and cymbals leading the way, their total number was over thirty as they made their way through the streets of Tientsin.

The day was bright and cold, but with just a whisper of spring in the air. The pedestrians, shopkeepers, and other people on the street would nod or bow politely as the procession passed, and then return to their everyday activities. One man's life, Wayland mused. Decades of hopes and fears, laughter and love, treasured friends, bitter enemies, and simple pleasures. And for most of the world, even those nearby, its end warrants nothing more than a brief formal acknowledgment, and at most a fleeting, momentary hint of sadness.

As the procession neared the cemetery, the orange-robed monk offered one final prayer in his resonant baritone:

"Impermanent are all conditioned things.

Of a nature to arise and pass away.

Having arisen, they pass away.

Their calming and cessation is true bliss."

At the cemetery, the pallbearers lowered the coffin into the grave.

"Wei-lin," Suyin said, nudging him with her elbow. She and the others were bending down to pick up a handful of earth, and Wayland nodded and followed their lead. Master Gao threw the first handful of soil onto Magic Spear Gao Jinguo's coffin, and then the rest did the same.

The cemetery keeper offered one final prayer as the workers finished covering the coffin with earth, and the burial was over.

Suyin presented Wayland and the others with a red envelope, and upon taking it, Wayland felt something solid in the paper: a coin. He looked at her for an explanation.

"It's money, and you must spend it soon. For good fortune," Suyin said.

Wayland nodded.

He was silent on the walk back through the streets to the Gao compound. He had imagined that he would feel some sense of triumph at Magic Spear's death, but what was to him the death of an enemy was to Suyin the loss of her father. Wayland could take little satisfaction in anything that grieved Suyin.

She was walking beside him, and he turned to her, but she was gazing ahead blankly, lost in her thoughts. Wayland reflected on the funeral ceremony of Magic Spear, and his thoughts again turned to his own parents. They never had their proper service and burial. He vowed to himself that they would.

***

By the next month, most of their injuries had healed, and the routine of the Gao compound was more or less back to normal. Wayland was stacking wood when Suyin approached.

"Master Gao would like to see you," she said. She bowed somewhat formally and walked away. From her mannerisms, Wayland inferred this was a matter of some importance. He stood up and brushed off his shirt and walked across the compound to Master Gao's private courtyard. Master Gao was standing by the entrance.

"You wanted to see me, Master?" Wayland asked.

Master Gao nodded and motioned for Wayland to enter.

"Please, be seated," he said to Wayland, and he held his open palm towards the small table with two chairs. The two sat down facing each other.

"I wanted to talk to you about your plans for the future," Master Gao said. "Have you made any decisions?"

Wayland shook his head. "I haven't."

"You are a young man with great promise, and you have many options. Still, I gather that you like it here, in this country. Is that not so?"

"I do," Wayland said. "Even though I've lived in China for six years now, it's only since you've taken me in that I've really felt a part of the country. With all that's happened in the last year, both good and bad, I guess I see things from a different perspective now."

"Yes," Master Gao said. "I think that Old Wu, Suyin, and myself see you differently, as well. We also see you as a part of this country, as a member of our family."

Wayland smiled and bowed slightly.

"Do you know what a 'disciple' is in Chinese martial arts?" Master Gao asked.

Wayland's brow furrowed. "It's a top student, kind of like an assistant to the master?"

"It's much more than that," Master Gao said. "I'm not sure that you have anything like it in your country. When a student becomes a disciple to his master, in a sense, he becomes part of the family of the school. It is a lifetime commitment for both the master and the disciple. The master vows to teach the disciple the entire art and to hold back nothing. The master will forever look out for the well-being of the disciple. The disciple, in turn, must promise to endure all the training and learn the entire art, and he must pass it on to the next generation. He will also be responsible for upholding the morality and honor of the master and the school, as long as he lives."

Wayland paused for a moment and then looked into Master Gao's eyes. "Are you offering this to me?"

"It is not common for a master to offer discipleship to such a recent student--and a foreigner at that. However, given the extraordinary events of these last months, I feel that you are worthy. Are you willing?"

"I am," Wayland said. "Thank you, Master!" He felt a surge of excitement, and his doubts and confusion about his future faded away. It felt right. This was what he was supposed to be doing.

"Good," Master Gao said. "You may talk of this with Suyin, as she and Lunghui are my only other disciples. She can explain things in more detail. If you change your mind and feel you cannot meet this commitment, you may tell me tomorrow, and there will be no hard feelings. Otherwise, the disciple ceremony will be mid-morning the day after tomorrow."

"Thank you again, master," Wayland said. He bowed and left Master Gao's courtyard. He would talk to Suyin about what was expected of him at the ceremony, but he knew he would not change his mind.

It was a clear, warm day of the fifth month of the Chinese calendar, and at the appointed time for the ceremony, Wayland arrived at Master Gao's courtyard wearing his best blue *changshan*. Old Wu, Suyin, and Lunghui were already there, standing to the side. Master Gao was seated at the front of the courtyard in his wooden chair. He motioned for Wayland to approach.

Wayland kneeled, and he bowed three times before Master Gao, touching his head to the ground each time. Lunghui brought a cup of tea to Wayland, and Wayland drank it in one gulp. Lunghui then handed another cup of tea to Wayland, and with both hands, Wayland presented it to Master Gao. Master Gao took the cup, nodded at Wayland, and then drank. Wayland looked up, and for the briefest of moments, he thought that Master Gao almost smiled. The ceremony was over. Wayland was now and forever more a disciple of Master Gao.

***

They all gathered for dinner that evening, and the conversation flowed.

"China is going through a difficult period," Master Gao

said. "Times have changed, and the country is in transition and turmoil. The old ways, for better or worse, are on their way out. We Chinese have had a view of the world, and of ourselves, that hasn't changed for centuries. But we've been presented with a new reality. The world is different now; it's smaller and more connected. For my father and his father, and going back generations, they wouldn't have imagined that foreigners would have the power to influence our civilization so profoundly."

"That's not necessarily a bad thing," Suyin said. "Maybe some of our traditions are best left in the past."

Master Gao looked thoughtfully at Suyin. "That's certainly true. We may indeed have some things to learn from the West. On the other hand, all nations have their weaknesses, and we must be careful not to discard the treasures of the Chinese in favor of the flaws of foreigners. Our nation is in a time of transition." Master Gao looked intently at Wayland. "We can use the help of all Chinese patriots, and of anyone who wishes well for China."

Wayland appreciated Master Gao's sentiments.

Wayland stood up again. He took the wine jar and poured everyone another round. "I have something to say to all of you, and especially to you, Master Gao. If you and Old Wu had not come across me on that day, I would not be here. Many men would have passed on by and done nothing, but that's not what you did, and I thank God that it was you and Old Wu who found me. I've lost so much in this country, more than I thought I could even bear. But I've also gained something, gained a great deal. In fact," Wayland said, looking at the others and then pausing slightly on Suyin, "I think more of the people here in this room than I could possibly express. I thank you all for giving me...a home."

They all downed their wine, and Master Gao, Old Wu, Lunghui, and Suyin applauded. They continued talking and laughing for a good while into the evening.

***

It was a typical spring night in Tientsin, cool, but dry and clear. Lunghui had gone home, and Master Gao and Old Wu had retired to their quarters. Wayland was helping Suyin clean up after the dinner.

"Why don't you go to bed," Suyin said. "There's not much left here. I can finish up."

Wayland was going to refuse, but he looked Suyin in the eyes. He saw in her expression that matter-of-fact generosity that was so often there, and he accepted it. "Thank you," he said. "I'll see you tomorrow."

Wayland walked outside into the courtyard, and he gazed upwards. The moon and stars were bright in the dense, ink-black night, and the only sound was the chirping of the spring crickets. So many stars, Wayland thought. He stood there, just looking up at the night sky. His mind began to drift, thinking of everything, and after a few minutes, thinking of nothing. Was there a plan up there? Wayland was sure that God did have a plan for him. Was it a plan that he could understand and follow? He wasn't too sure of that. He heard someone slowly walking up behind him.

"What do you see?" Suyin said, as she put her hand on Wayland's shoulder and slowly rubbed it.

Wayland didn't turn to her, although her touch was more than welcome.

"I see a lot of things," he said, and he put his hand on Suyin's, caressing it gently. They both stood for a moment as they gazed up at the endless sea of stars in the cool night air. Suyin put her arm around Wayland's waist, and she leaned her head on his shoulder.

373

Acknowledgments

IN WRITING THIS novel, I am indebted to the journals of Eva Jane Price, published as *China Journal, 1889-1900*. Her heartfelt account of her family's daily life as missionaries in China during the turbulent time of the Boxer Rebellion provided invaluable details for the setting of this story, and it also gave me some insight into the emotional and spiritual life of Western missionaries who devoted themselves to a people and a nation that they hardly knew. They had little hope of any earthly reward for their efforts, and for some, like the Price family, their fate was ultimately tragic.

I studied under two masters of Chinese martial arts, Dr. Yang Jwing-Ming and Scott M. Rodell. Although I was only a casual student of both and barely scratched the surface of what they had to teach, I thank both of them for giving me a profound appreciation for the scope and depth of Chinese martial arts. I hope I accurately conveyed something of their teachings in my writing.

I sincerely appreciate the wonderful cover artwork of Robert P. "Kung Fu Bob" O'Brien. He and I share a lifelong love of martial arts films, and it was great to work with a fellow fan of the genre and to see his incredible talent utilized for the visual realization of my characters.

I would also like to express my gratitude to everyone at Earnshaw Books. In particular, I would like to thank Alice Poon for her encouragement for me to write this novel in the first place, and I'd especially like to thank Graham Earnshaw for having faith in my story and vision, and for his considerable and patient efforts in editing and helping me to see how my story could be strengthened and improved.

My father passed away while I was writing this story, and I can't possibly thank my parents enough for their lifelong love, support, and encouragement. I was blessed with a fairly idyllic childhood, and that has deeply influenced both my creativity and my worldview.

Finally, I'd like to thank my family, friends, and acquaintances for their continued support and positive feedback. Writing a novel is a long process with many ups and downs, and it's easy to get discouraged. Even small gestures of interest and goodwill can sometimes mean more than one would suspect. God bless all.

2019 Kyle Fiske

About the Author

Kyle Fiske grew up on a farm near the Canadian border in northern New York State. He studied history and English at St. Lawrence University and the University of Copenhagen, as well as museum studies at Tufts University. Kyle was a competitive fencer for several years and has been a practitioner of Chinese martial arts for more than two decades, with a special focus on Chinese swordsmanship. He is the author of the short story collection Even Closer Than the Sea, and he's also a long-time guitar player and songwriter. Kyle now makes his home on scenic and historic Cape Ann, Massachusetts.

www.ingramcontent.com/pod-product-compliance
Lightning Source LLC
Chambersburg PA
CBHW011845300726
48970CB00009B/2661